2003   3-4   Febr

the

CHARMER

the

SINNER

Also by Madeline Hunter

BY ARRANGEMENT
BY POSSESSION
BY DESIGN
THE PROTECTOR
LORD OF A THOUSAND NIGHTS
STEALING HEAVEN
THE SEDUCER
THE SAINT

the

CHARMER

the

SINNER

Madeline Hunter

BANTAM BOOKS

Bantam Dell
A Division of Random House, Inc.
New York, New York

Copyright © 2003 by Madeline Hunter

ISBN 0-7394-3943-X

Printed in the U.S.A.

CONTENTS

THE CHARMER   1

THE SINNER   231

the CHARMER

chapter I

~ May 1831

Adrian crossed the drawing room's threshold and found himself in the middle of an Arab harem.

Women swathed in colorful pantaloons and veils lounged beside men dressed in flowing robes. A fortune in silk billowed down from the high, frescoed ceiling, forming a massive tent. Two tiger skins stretched over the pastel tapestry rugs, and bejeweled pillows and throws buried settees and chairs. An exotic, heavy scent drifted under those of incense and perfume. Hashish. In the darkest corners some men kissed and fondled their ladies, but no outright orgy had ensued.

Yet.

A man on a mission, with no interest in this type of diversion, Adrian walked slowly through the costumed bodies, looking for a female who fit the description of the Duchess of Everdon.

He noticed a canopied corner that appeared to be the place of honor. He aimed for it, ignoring the women who looked his way and smiled invitingly.

The canopy draped a small dais holding a chaise longue. A woman rested on it in a man's arms. Her eyes were closed, and the man was plying her with wine. Adrian's card had fallen ignobly to the floor from her lax fingers.

"I am grateful that you have finally received me, Duchess," he said, announcing his presence. Actually, she had not agreed to receive him at all. He had threatened and bluffed his way past the butler.

Her lids slit and she peered down her body at him. She wore a garment that swaddled her from breasts to bare feet, but which left her neck and arms uncovered, revealing pale, glowing skin. In the low light he could not judge her face well, but her hair was a mass of dark curls tamed by a gold band circling her head.

She looked very sensual with the red silk wrapping her curves and her armlets and anklets gleaming in the candlelight. The blond, bare-chested man who held her thought so too. Adrian half-expected him to take a bite out of her while he watched.

The duchess gave Adrian a frank assessment and he returned one of his own. The only living child of the last Duke of Everdon had attained instant importance with her father's unexpected death. For the last two weeks everyone who was anyone in England had been speculating about Sophia Raughley, and wondering what she had been up to during her long absence from England.

Adrian did not relish reporting the answer to the men who had sent him here. From the looks of things, the new duchess had occupied herself lo these last eight years in Paris with becoming a shameless libertine.

She twisted out of her lover's hold and stretched to grope for the card, almost falling off the chaise longue. She appeared childishly clumsy suddenly, and a bit helpless, and Adrian experienced a pang of pity. He picked up the card and placed it in her fingers. She squinted, and gestured to her partner to bring a candle close.

"Mister Adrian Burchard," she read.

"At your service, Your Grace. If we could speak privately, please."

Gathering her drapery, she rose to her feet. With the breeding of centuries stiffening her posture, she faced him.

"I think that I know what service you offer, and you have wasted your journey. I am not going back with you."

Of course she was. "Again, I ask to speak with you privately."

"Come back tomorrow."

"I have come the last two days, and now tonight. It is time for you to hear what I have to say. It is time for you to face reality."

Anger flashed in her eyes. She advanced toward him. For a moment she appeared quite formidable. Then her foot caught in the flowing silk. She tripped and hurtled forward, right into his arms.

He grappled with the feminine onslaught, gripping her soft back and bottom. She wore no stays or petticoats under that red silk. No wonder her blond Arab gleamed with expectation.

She looked up in dazed shock, her green eyes glinting. Her smile of embarrassment broadened until he expected her ears to move out of the way.

She was drunk. Completely foxed.

Wonderful.

He set her upright and held her arm until she attained some balance.

"I do not much care for reality. If that is what you offer, go away." She sounded like a rebellious, petulant child, provoking the temptation in him to treat her like one. She waved around the drawing room. "This is real enough for me."

"Hardly real. Not even very accurate."

"My *seraglio* is most accurate. Stefan and I planned it for weeks. Delacroix himself designed the costumes."

"The costumes are correct, but you have created a European fantasy. A *seraglio* is nothing like this. In a true harem, except for the rare visitor, all the men are eunuchs."

She laughed and gave Stefan a playful poke. "Not so loud, Mister Burchard, or the men will run away. And the women? Did I get that right at least?"

"Not entirely. For one thing, an entire *seraglio* exists for the pleasure of one man, not many. For another . . ."

Stefan's expression distracted him. His smile revealed the conceit of a man who assumed that if only one sultan were to enjoy the pleasures of this particular harem, it went without dispute that it would be him.

Stefan was going to be a problem.

"For another, except for a few ornaments, the women in a harem are naked."

Suggestive laughter trickled to the dais from the onlookers. Bawdy shouts pierced the smoky shadows. As if his words had been a cue, a woman on the other side of the room rose up from her circle of admirers and unclasped a broach. Her diaphanous drape fluttered to the floor amidst shouts and clapping.

Another woman rose and stripped. The situation deteriorated rapidly. Garments flew through the air. The shadows filled with the swells of breasts and buttocks. Embraces became much more intimate.

The duchess's eyes widened. She appeared dismayed at the turn things had taken. Ridiculous, of course. She had just explained that she had planned it herself.

Stefan reached for her. "Come, Sophia, *moi skarb.*"

The duchess staggered back with his pull and fell onto his lap. Adrian watched, a forgotten presence. Stefan began caressing her arm while he held the goblet to her mouth.

Adrian turned to go. This promised to be a distasteful task. Still, it was essential for him to complete it. A lot was riding on this foolish, debauched woman. Quite possibly the future of England itself.

He glanced back to the chaise longue. Stefan had loosened her gown from one shoulder and now worked on the other. Her head lolled on his shoulder but her dull reaction did not deter Stefan in the least. She sat limply while the man undressed her.

Adrian stepped back onto the dais just as Stefan bared the duchess's pretty breasts.

"Perhaps in your amorous zeal you have not noticed, my friend, but the woman is no longer with you. She is out cold."

Stefan was pulling the canopy's drapes closed. "Mind your own affairs."

"Gentlemen rarely mind their own affairs when a lady is about to be raped. But then, you would not know how gentlemen react, would you?"

Stefan rose indignantly and the duchess slid away into a half-naked heap on the chaise longue. "How dare you insinuate that I am not a gentleman. I will have you know that I am a prince of the royal house of Poland."

"Are you? What are you doing in Paris? With your countrymen fighting to throw out the Russians, shouldn't a prince be leading an army somewhere? Or are you one of those princes who doesn't like war much?"

"Now you call me a coward!"

"Only if you are really a prince, which I will wager you are not. I suspect that, in truth, you clawed your way out of the Warsaw gutters and have been living off women since you left home."

Stefan's eyes bugged with fury. Adrian casually dragged red silk discreetly over the duchess's naked breasts. "Exactly how do you employ yourself, Stefan? When you aren't whoring for rich women, that is, and helping them plan orgies?"

"I am a poet," Stefan snarled.

"Ahhh. A *poet*. Well, that makes all the difference, doesn't it? Women do not *keep* you, they *patronize* you."

Adrian bent and slid his arms under the duchess. "I am taking the duchess to where she can recover. Interfere, and I will kill you."

Stefan sputtered with indignation, but his expression quickly turned taunting and mean. As Adrian lifted his burden, Stefan moved to block their way.

"I am serious, Stefan. Stand aside or I will call you out and kill you. Since you are a scoundrel, it will not even ruin my day."

Stefan was almost drunk enough to ignore the threat, but, to Adrian's disappointment, not quite. With a scowl he moved away.

Adrian carried the duchess off the dais. Movement caused the loose garment to shift so that a breast peeked out of the red silk. Noting once more that her breasts were quite lovely, he bore the duchess out of the *seraglio* with as much dignity as he could muster for the two of them.

The old butler lurked in the corridor. Adrian called for the man to accompany him.

"Your name."

"Charles, sir. She insists that we all use our Christian names here. The French influence, I'm afraid."

The evidence that the duchess harbored some frivolous egalitarian notions was not welcome news. "Are any of the other servants English besides you, Charles?"

"Her maid, Jenny, that is all. The rest are French, and there is an assortment of Poles and Austrians and Bohemians feeding at the trough, but they are here to serve their own masters, who in turn are permanent guests, as it were."

"How many permanent guests?"

"Four at the moment."

"All men?"

Charles flushed to the top of his balding pate and nodded. "Artist types. Writers and whatnot. They are known in the city as Miss Raughley's Ensemble. All of them full of the high sensibility. My lady is a great patroness of the new romantic style in the arts." He looked at his mistress's lolling head with affection, and delicately reached to ease some silk over her bare breast. "I would like to say that this is not like her. Since hearing of her father's death, she has not been herself."

"Grief-stricken?"

"Terrified's more like it. Not much love between her and the duke. It's why we are here, isn't it? But the news affected her badly. It is as if she knows that she cannot hide anymore."

They had reached the grand staircase. "Show me her chambers, Charles, and call for Jenny and two other women whom you trust. Then I will give you instructions for packing. The duchess will be leaving Paris. If you have any doubts regarding my authority to initiate these plans while she is indisposed, I should tell you that I have a letter from King William himself summoning her home."

"The King!" The news rendered Charles suitably impressed until they reached the second landing. "I do not think it will be possible to affect a departure so quickly."

"If closing the house proves complicated, you will stay behind and do it. The duchess comes with me at once."

"I do not think she will agree to that."

Adrian had no intention of letting Sophia Raughley's lack of agreement interfere with his mission. Charles pointed him down a corridor and they stopped at a large double door. "Why will she want to delay, Charles? If it is because of Stefan, I will deal with that."

"I was not thinking of the Polish poet. It is the animals. She would never leave without them."

"A small matter. We can take them. I have a good hand with dogs."

Charles turned the doors' handles. "As it happens, not just dogs."

Adrian entered and stopped in his tracks. Dozens of inhuman eyes peered at him from around the chamber.

He had escaped the harem only to find himself in a menagerie.

.   .   .

"There are more," Charles said.

Of course there were. Adrian strolled around the opulent sitting room. The bright plumed birds had ceased their noise, but the little monkey was still throwing a tantrum because his mistress's arrival had not meant freedom from the cage. There was an odd-looking reptile in a glass case, and two large snakes in another. An ocelot skin stretched under the window. Unlike the pelts in the drawing room, this one still had the animal inside it.

And, of course, there were indeed dogs. Three of them. Mean-faced mastiffs. They posed like soldiers in front of the hearth and tensely eyed Adrian's neck. The feminine shrieks coming from the dressing room had put them on edge.

"The big ones are at the country house," Charles explained. "Well, one can hardly house a giraffe and a lion and such here in the city, can one?"

"Indeed not. I tried that once with my giraffe and lion and they destroyed the library." Adrian threw himself into a chair right in the middle of the mastiffs and proceeded to stare them down.

More screams sounded from the dressing room where three servants were bathing the duchess. With luck, at least half of her wits would return so he could explain what was going to happen.

Hopefully she would not remember the first few moments of her reawakening. Jenny had turned out to be a little thing, and the two French servants were even smaller. They could not lift the duchess, so he had been forced to carry her in when the bath was ready.

In the interests of modesty he had lowered her into the water still clothed, but the wet silk adhered like a second skin and created an image much more erotic than mere nudity. The duchess had thoroughly quashed his sexual reactions by regaining consciousness upon submersion. She half came to, absorbed her situation, and then awoke with a roar.

At which point she had gotten sick.

Yes, this was turning out to be quite a night.

Two of the mastiffs assumed positions of submission at his feet, but the third refused to budge, bow, or blink. Adrian intensified the contest while his memory perused the last hour's events, pausing longer than it should on various images of Sophia Raughley soaked, in *dishabille,* or bare-breasted.

The duchess's angry voice could be heard, threatening the sack to one and all. Charles shot Adrian a beseeching glance.

"You may leave. You know what to do," Adrian said.

The last hound broke and lowered his tail. Adrian permitted some friendly sniffing, then gestured for the animal to lie. He poured some of the wine brought in for his refreshment, stretched out his legs, and waited.

Sophia cradled her spinning head in her hands. She had drunk a glass or two more wine than normal tonight, but nothing to deserve this misery.

"Is he still there?"

Jenny cracked open the door and stuck her nose to it. "Yes, sitting by the hearth like he has a right to be here."

Sophia gestured to the two women mopping up the water around the tub. "Leave now and go to bed. The rest can wait until morning."

Lisette and Linette bustled to the door. As they slipped out, Sophia caught a glimpse of the man sitting amidst her hounds.

Adrian Burchard. She knew of the Burchards. Randall Burchard, the Earl of Dincaster, had been a friend of her father.

The only thing that she knew about this particular Burchard, however, was what she had learned from Jenny. He was here on an errand from the King, no less, to bring her back to England.

"Send him away."

"I do not think that he will go. He said that he would wait until you were well enough disposed to speak with him."

Sophia pushed Jenny aside and stuck her own nose to the crack. Adrian Burchard drank her wine, gazed at her fire, and scratched Yuri's ear. It was a wonder he had not removed his shoes. He cut a stunning figure with his dark tousled hair, dark eyes, and black evening dress. Many women would not mind finding him ensconced in their chambers.

He possessed a compelling presence that affected her even in her pitiful condition. Still, he struck her as somehow fraudulent. The cut of his clothes and the manner in which he lounged, announced his Englishness. He exuded an English aristocratic breeding that could not be faked. But . . . his face, yes, that was it. There was something suspiciously un-English about his face.

He did not resemble the fair-haired Earl of Dincaster. This man had thick, wavy, black hair, and very dark eyes, deep-set and shaped the way they are in Mediterranean countries. The contrast with his fair skin created a slightly unnatural appearance. There was something foreign about his mouth, too, a hard definition that gave it a cruel aspect.

She could not shake the impression that if he changed his clothes, demeanor, and a few physical details, Adrian Burchard could pass for a Spanish prince much more successfully than that rapscallion Stefan passed for a Polish one. Which was peculiar because while Stefan might not be a prince, he most certainly was Polish.

The more she peered, the more familiar Burchard looked in ways that uncomfortably pricked at her recollections. She tried to brush aside the thick clouds that obscured the events of the night. It was extremely disconcerting to realize that several hours of your life had passed without your awareness of them.

Jenny held up some stays for her attention. "Will you be feeling well enough to dress now, my lady?"

"I have no intention of getting fully dressed again to greet him. Fetch my violet undressing gown, do something with my hair, and throw a shawl over my shoulders. If he is shocked, I do not care."

"Oh, I do not think you could shock him," Jenny mused while she pulled open doors of armoires. "After what he has already seen, it would be peculiar if he was scandalized by a perfectly respectable undressing gown, wouldn't it?"

Well, now, that depended upon what it was that he had already seen.

"What do you think of him, Jenny?"

Jenny glanced to the door. "He is very formidable. He does not frighten the way your father did, but there is something to him that makes one want to put things in his hands, because he is sure to make it come out as he intends. And he is every inch a gentleman. Charles said that while he carried you up here you were partly exposed, and not once did Mister Burchard look."

Sophia's unsettled stomach kicked in outrage. Through some bizarre misadventure, this stranger had seen her partly undressed.

"And he can be very gentle, my lady," Jenny continued while she tried to tame Sophia's curls with combs. "He carried you to the bath like a baby, and when you got sick he assisted and showed no dismay."

Sophia felt her face burn. Suddenly *that* memory broke through the mist. Sloshing water. Masculine hands holding her chin and forehead over a porcelain rim. Yards of ruined, soaked red silk.

Jenny pinned her curls back and encased them in a thin net. Sophia rose to don the violet satin sack gown.

Gathering the tattered shreds of her dignity around her, she made as grand an entrance into the next room as circumstances permitted.

The effect, if any, was wasted. Adrian was bent over Yuri's prostrate, panting form, giving a good scratch to the stomach slavishly begging for attention.

Sophia waited. He had heard her entrance but was pretending he had not. He planned to make this a contest. She really was not in the mood, even if his dark looks left her mouth dry.

He finally acknowledged her. Rising, he snapped his fingers and pointed Yuri back to his place by the hearth. Sophia did not miss the symbolism. *Your household is already mine to command,* the gesture said.

He gave her a sharp assessment with those wonderful eyes. His expression implied that he expected to find the next conquest quick work too.

He advanced and she presented her hand. He bowed over it. "Under the circumstances, perhaps we should start at the beginning and repeat the introduction, Duchess. I am Adrian Burchard. You are feeling better? I took the liberty to ask that some food be brought up. It will help if you eat something."

Tea and cakes waited atop a table. He guided her over, sat her down, poured her tea, and settled himself several feet away. Masterfully.

"Please eat something." It wasn't a request. Not really.

She reached for a cake in spite of herself. She nibbled and drank a bit of tea under his watchful approval. A silly, still-inebriated part of her wanted to glow with delight that he was pleased.

A different, sensible part, the part that had developed a gargantuan headache, knew what he was doing. He was taking her in hand, as if she was some dimwit.

"You are one of the Earl of Dincaster's sons, are you not? I met your parents, years ago." She was amazed that she got the words out. He was so handsome that she couldn't concentrate. She had to force herself not to stare at his face. Close like this, she found it astonishing in its severe beauty.

He possessed a square jaw and defined cheekbones and his eyes positively glowed in the candlelight. His black hair fell carelessly about his forehead and face and collar, but not in the carefully mussed styles seen in drawing rooms these days. Rather it seemed to really grow that way because nature decreed it be a little wild.

Tell me, Mister Burchard, as I have always wondered. What is it like to be so beautiful that hearts skip when you pass by?

"I am his third son, after my brothers Gavin and Colin."

Third son. After the "heir and a spare." Lady Dincaster had been as fair as her husband, Sophia recalled. She examined Adrian's dark, foreign appearance with new interest.

"You have a letter for me, I believe," she said, barely swallowing a tactless query regarding his legitimacy that wanted to blurt out.

He extricated a small missive from inside his frock coat. Sophia noted the royal seal.

"What does it say?"

"The King was surprised that you did not return to England upon your father's passing. He summons you at once. It would be his pleasure to welcome the newest peer to her position."

It appeared that they were going to talk about sad, complicated things. She found him a tad less attractive all of a sudden.

"My father was dead. Attending his funeral would not bridge the gulf that we found impossible to cross during his life. As to His Majesty, I expect that he wants his lords to enjoy the joke of a peeress in a country ruled by primogeniture. Let them find their amusement elsewhere."

"Your situation is unusual, but it is not a joke. Nor will you be alone. As you know, there are other women who have benefited from traditions of inheritance in their families as you have."

"Two hundred years ago an ancestor convinced a king to permit a daughter to inherit his title, and I am now forced to play the duchess." She leaned toward him. "I do not want this. I will not do it. A steward can manage the estate. I intend to stay here in Paris."

"You must return. Certainly you know what is occurring in England. The French journals describe it, and English visitors surely report it."

"I do not associate with English visitors much, but yes, I am aware of what is occurring."

"Then you know that Parliament has been dissolved and elections are being held. A movement to change the representation in the House of Commons has swept the country, pitting class against class. If an act of reform passes the next Parliament, it will change how England is governed as no war ever did."

"Perhaps it is time for some changes. I myself wouldn't know. I will let others decide."

His eyes flashed. Magnificently. Goodness, he was handsome.

"There are those who want revolution rather than reform. The power of Everdon cannot sit this out in France." He caught her gaze and held it with his compelling own. "I have come to bring you home, and if I have to carry you slung over my shoulder to the coast and across the channel, I will do so."

He maintained an utterly cool demeanor while he made his threat. No pomposity at which to laugh. No posturing to puncture. He laid out the facts in a quiet, firm voice. *This is how it is,* he said. *This is what will happen.*

"As a woman I cannot sit in Parliament. I inherited no political power along with the title and estate."

He examined her thoughtfully. "I cannot decide if you are truly as ignorant as you claim, or if you have adopted the pose in the vain hope that it will make a difference."

"You come very close to insult, Mister Burchard."

"Forgive me. Allow me to explain the situation in broad terms. As Duchess of Everdon you control twelve members of the Commons. They come from boroughs under your control in Devon and Cornwall."

"Rotten boroughs."

"Mostly. Your nomination is required to return them to the Commons in this election. Your direction on their votes, once elected, will also be needed. Every vote will matter. So, while you cannot participate directly, you still hold significant power."

It was accepted tradition that hundreds of seats in the Commons were "owned" by peers sitting in the upper house. She had no idea that Everdon controlled so many, however.

Very suddenly she experienced complete, horrible sobriety. It was going to be much worse than she had feared. Her situation promised to be terribly precarious.

"You were sent by the King. Who else?"

A spark of approval flickered in his dark eyes. "The Duke of Wellington, and other men of influence in the Tory party."

"We both know that these men have no intention of leaving the power that you describe in my hands. They need to find a way to dictate to me, and the surest way to do that with a woman is through her husband. So I ask you, who is the man who has been chosen for me?"

His hard mouth quirked with quiet amusement. He appeared extremely charming like that. "If I had to venture a guess, I would say Mister Gerald Stidolph."

Oh, Lord, not Gerald. *Anyone* but Gerald.

Fury and fear flashed like lightning through her aching head. It sought a destination and Adrian Burchard was the closest one available.

"Why were you chosen to bring me back? Why did they send you instead of someone else?"

"I knew your father. I am the M.P. from Stockton in Devon. It is one of your boroughs."

"Don't you fear alienating me with your interference in my life? Tell me, what would happen if I did not nominate you for this election?"

His lids lowered and he quirked another smile, less amused and friendly this time. "I expect that the party would find another seat for me to stand to. If not, I would be forced to pursue my other interests."

"So you are an important member of the party, and not just a back bencher."

"Not especially important, but useful."

"No wonder they sent you. You are not too beholden. You serve me, but only to the extent it suits your true masters. For this meeting to be complete, shouldn't you be giving me something. A ring or seal?"

She said it to goad him. The last thing she expected was for him to reach into his pocket and indeed withdraw a ring. She recognized it as her father's, with the crest of Everdon raised on its jewel.

He held his hand out for hers. She glared at that ring. A chill shuddered through her, trembling out of time and memory. He reached down and raised her hand from her lap.

His hand holding hers felt incredibly comforting, so much that she almost embarrassed them both by asking him not to let go right away. He slid the circle of heavy gold on her finger. It looked ridiculous on her.

His touch fell away and she was left to support the ring alone.

"Since it was not clear how long you would be indisposed, I took the liberty of giving Charles instructions for your journey." He looked at her impassively. She was a problem to be managed, a difficulty to be cleaned up.

"Regarding my indisposition, Mister Burchard, I would like to clarify something."

"Yes, I expect that you would," he said dryly.

He expected excuses. She had intended to give some, but she abruptly changed tack. "My maid tells me that you accompanied me into the dressing room. If I had been alert I would have forbidden it, and I expect you to show more respect for my modesty in the future."

"I did not accompany you, I carried you. I needed you conscious and your maids could not manage it alone. I suggest that you replace them. If you intend to continue on your course of living, you will need women far more substantial to assist you." He rose. "Now, I think that you should sleep. You will need to direct the packing of your private things tomorrow, but I will see to the household for you, with Charles's assistance."

She stood as well. "Perhaps I did not make myself clear. I am not going."

"Yes, Duchess, you are. The morning next we depart. Bring whatever you need for your comfort. Bring your menageries and your artists. Bring your Arab silks and your hashish. Bring your orgies, for all I care. But believe me when I say to you, finally and definitely, that you will accompany me back to England."

She watched him leave with her mouth agape. Hashish and orgies, indeed. To accuse her of such things was insulting. Why, it was—

With horrible abruptness, memories lurched out of the fog. Bits of images pressed on her.

Perfumes and silk and laughter. Her *seraglio* a success, but a few of society's leading lights departing too early . . . the fantasy growing too real and too dreamlike at the same time . . . colors becoming too vivid and sounds too far away.

More memories now, a flood of them . . . A hand on her body and a thick accent in her ear . . . Garments flying through the air . . .

"Jenny."

Her maid scurried out of the dressing room.

"Jenny, tell Charles that I must speak with him in the morning as soon as I wake."

Scandalous visions, observed through a haze . . . naked women and male flesh . . . bodies entwining . . .

"And Jenny, tell the footmen that they are to enter the drawing room and invite any remaining guests to leave. *At once.*"

chapter 3

Beginning at dawn, Adrian initiated preparations for Sophia Raughley's removal to her title's seat in Devon.

Long before noon he had arranged for the eventual transport of the menagerie, assigned caretaker duties to servants recommended by Charles, hired wagons to accompany them to the coast, and ordered the packing of valuables to be carted along. Things were well in hand by the time Miss Raughley's Ensemble came down from their chambers.

They all looked to be tousle-haired men of the world a few years out of university. That made them several years younger than the duchess herself, who was twenty-nine. Adrian, at thirty-four, thought they appeared unseasoned and untried and too contented by far.

He put aside the portfolio containing the letters of instructions that awaited the duchess's signature (or, if necessary, its forgery) and joined them at breakfast.

Charles had explained that membership in the Ensemble flowed and fluxed. Stefan was the most recent arrival, while a Greek had departed several months ago. The duchess had been maintaining guests for at least five years. She possessed a weakness for artists from countries torn by revolution and strife, but that was not a requirement for her patronage.

Adrian sat at the table while the artists looked him over.

"What are you doing here?" Stefan snarled.

"The duchess offered me her hospitality for a day or two," Adrian said. "At first I did not want to impose, but then I thought, What will one footloose man more or less matter?"

Everyone chuckled with self-deprecating humor.

Everyone except Stefan. "Who the hell are you? What are you?"

"Adrian Burchard. I am her countryman."

"A damned nuisance is what you are, and you don't look like one of her countrymen."

A dark, thickly built man with a heavy mustache at the other end of the table laughed heartily. "Ignore him, Mister Burchard. Stefan is always surly in the morning. I am Attila Toth, and you are welcome at our board."

"You are Attila Toth, the Hungarian composer?" Adrian asked, employing the information he had pumped out of Charles this morning regarding the permanent guests.

A smile of delight broke beneath the brush of mustache. "You know my music? I knew that my *Sonata Hongrois* was introduced in London at a small performance, but that you should have heard it and remembered my name overwhelms me."

He did look overwhelmed. So much that Adrian feared he might do something of embarrassingly high sensibility like cry or swoon. It had become fashionable for young men of creative dispositions to display their turbulent moods. The trend was the human counterpart to the strongly expressive dynamics in their music and art.

The composer retreated into his dreams of artistic grandeur, gazing out the window to the garden. Attila was a bit of a fool, but not a scoundrel like Stefan, Adrian decided. Possibly the Hungarian was the duchess's lover instead of the Pole. Hell, maybe they both were.

Actually, maybe they *all* were.

That notion raised an edgy irritation in him.

It went without saying that Stefan would not be coming to England, but he had been prepared to follow the duchess's wishes regarding the others. Now he abruptly decided that none of the Ensemble would make the trip back to Devon.

"Allow me to complete the introductions," the man closest to him said. "I am Jacques Delaroche, and this handsome rogue to my left is Dieter Wurzer."

Adrian dipped into Charles's coaching again. "It is my pleasure to meet such a talented poet, and also one of Prussia's leading young novelists."

Jacques, the French poet, was all sleek, fine-boned, dark elegance, the sort of man who would go hungry before he wore an unfashionable coat. Dieter, whose surname announced his humble origins, possessed a quiet blond nobility that Stefan, the would-be Polish Prince, would do well to emulate.

Two poets, a novelist, and a composer. Not an Englishman in the batch. Nor a painter, for that matter. This human menagerie was unbalanced and incomplete. Adrian considered that a mark in the duchess's favor. Spontaneous extravagance had the potential to be charming, while calculated self-indulgence promised no redemption whatsoever.

"Are you another artist?" Dieter asked.

"No."

The three of them eyed him more curiously. Attila still communed with nature.

"Would you happen to have anything to do with the sudden activity among the servants?" Jacques asked. "The confusion woke me."

"It looks as if they are turning the place out for a thorough cleaning," Dieter commented. "A footman intruded to remove the silver from my chamber."

"Not a thorough cleaning," Adrian explained. "A thorough move."

"To the countryside?" Attila asked with enthusiasm, his attention returning to the group.

"Yes."

Dieter cast Adrian a careful look. "How long before she leaves? For the country?"

"Tomorrow is the plan."

Adrian finished his breakfast and took his leave. It was time to make sure that the duchess was awake, aware, and packing. He strode to the staircase. Rapid footsteps alerted him to Jacques following.

"Dieter seems to think that Sophia will be traveling alone," he said, falling into step.

"I will accompany her."

"Dieter also thinks—he is very quiet but also most observant—he also thinks that all of this activity means that this house is being closed."

"That is Her Grace's pleasure."

"She said nothing to us. The last anyone saw her was when you carried her away last night. I feel bound to ask if you have the right to make these arrangements in her name, especially since they affect us."

"If any man does, I do." Which meant nothing, of course, since no man did.

Jacques' face fell. "She told me once . . . but I just assumed the arrangement was . . . my apologies for questioning you, but I am sure that you will understand that my concern was for So—, for the duchess, whose heart is too generous, and whom some try to take advantage of, like Stefan, who I am sure will rue the day he was born when he learns who you are, especially since you caught him last night attempting such liberties. . . ."

The smooth, urbane Jacques blurted his endless sentence in a manner that implied he had concluded Adrian was someone who actually mattered.

Not daring to respond, Adrian merely smiled. Jacques' relief bordered on a swoon. The French poet aimed down the corridor and back into the breakfast room.

Jenny admitted Adrian to Sophia's apartment only to inform him that her lady had taken the ocelot, Camilla, to the garden.

He surveyed the preparations that had turned the dressing room into a disaster. He had never imagined that one woman could accumulate so many clothes. Dozens of gowns, a field of bonnets, stacks of gloves and shoes . . . It appeared that one of the duchess's favorite diversions was shopping.

"Two portmanteaus only for tomorrow. The rest must be sent later," he reminded Jenny. He then made his way to the garden to inform the lady of his own progress on her behalf.

She rested on a bench beneath a pear tree budding with new flowers. Camilla paced on a long lead, cautious and slit-eyed. The duchess wore the latest fashion, a wide-skirted, gargantuan-sleeved rose gown that revealed little form except a sashed waist and no skin except pale hands and neck.

Adrian disliked the new fashions for women, and remembered the softer, classical styles of his youth with nostalgia. The duchess was just a bit on the plumply curved side, and not very tall, and the style did not become her. Neither did the gown's color, although it was very beautiful. He pictured her falling in love with the hue and not caring whether it complemented her skin and eyes. An extravagant woman, perhaps, but not an overly vain one.

He advanced through the fertile spring smells filling the garden. This was the first decent look he had gotten of her, since last night's candles obscured more than they revealed.

He noticed now that her dark hair was as lustrous and jubilant in its curls as it had appeared on the dais, and that the cruel gown did not completely hide the pleasant feminine softness that he had briefly held in his arms. Her creamy complexion possessed a luminous quality.

He could see the duke's blood in her firm little chin and full lower lip and the fine, gently crooked bone of her nose. She was attractive, and even striking when she focused those green eyes on something. At the moment she did so, and the something was him.

Unfortunately, the way she appraised him indicated that she had not yet surrendered.

Time to take matters in hand.

H e came to her through the low grass, bringing his aura of command and dark magnetism. She resented her tingling reaction to his slow smile.

Camilla paced over to block his path. Adrian had the good sense to halt. The ocelot was no larger than a medium-sized dog, but she could be dangerous.

"She has been with people since birth," the duchess reassured, calling Camilla aside. She noted Adrian's reaction. "You do not approve."

He shrugged. "The imprisonment of wild animals for educational purposes is one thing, but . . ."

"But the unnatural restriction of one to be a woman's plaything is another. I agree. Camilla belonged to a foreign diplomat who was marrying. His bride was afraid of Camilla, and he was going to have her shot. I took her instead." She scratched Camilla's ears and the big cat moved for more, just like a huge tabby.

He lounged with his shoulder against the tree, a disturbingly attractive presence intruding on her peace. He felt closer than he actually was.

"Did all of the animals come to you that way? As strays and homeless petitioners?"

"The big ones came with the country chateau. The former owner had collected them. As for the rest, it just happened. One bird amuses you so you accept another. You agree to take a dog, and his brothers ask to come too."

"Certainly. It would be cruel to refuse." He stretched his hand toward Camilla. She ignored him with disdain.

"Unlike my servants and my hounds, Camilla is suspicious of you."

"I am a stranger. She does not know my scent. And unlike your dogs, she is female. They are often more cautious, but with patience and the proper handling, they usually come around."

"Is that why you were sent, Mister Burchard? Because you know how to make women come around?"

"I was speaking of four-legged females, not the human variety."

No, you were not.

"What were you told about me?" she asked.

"Very little."

"I take it that you are shocked by what you have found."

"Your tastes in diversions are not my concern. Getting you quickly and safely back to England is."

"You have been hard at work preparing for that. Charles tells me that you have accomplished in one morning a feat of organization that should take at least a week. Do you have some experience as a man of affairs or a military officer?"

"I have experience as neither, although as a young man I served as an assistant to the Foreign Secretary, and on occasion accompanied ambassadors who could not have found the right ship on their own, much less the correct country."

"And now you are sent to fetch errant duchesses who don't want to go home."

A chill trembled through her. Perhaps it was because the sun had moved and shade now covered her head. More likely it was the thought of going home and confronting the memories waiting there.

He noticed. Without a word he slipped off his frock coat and placed it around her shoulders.

It was the sort of thing that any gentleman would do. It didn't really mean anything other than simple courtesy. However, the protective gesture touched her so profoundly that her soul quaked. The greedy way her heart grasped at its insinuation of friendship laid bare how lonely she had been in this foreign city, despite all the animals and diversions and guests.

The May weather in Paris still carried a northern bite, but he appeared comfortable enough in his shirtsleeves and dark neckcloth and gray silk waistcoat. And devastatingly dashing. She rather suspected that he *had* been chosen because of the way he could handle women.

A part of her wished that she had it in her to make him demonstrate his skill. She would know some closeness then, for a while at least. She could probably lie to herself that it meant something. She had a bit of experience in doing that.

His presence was making her foolish and nostalgic. She had avoided the English community in Paris. She had forgotten how very pleasant it was to talk with someone who shared a common history and language. It created a flow of essential familiarity even though they did not know each other at all.

"Mister Burchard, there are reasons why I have not lived in England and why I do not even visit."

He sat on the far end of the bench, where he could see Camilla's face. "I respect that you have had your reasons, but they are not important enough anymore."

"That is an unbearably arrogant thing to say. Are you the kind of man who assumes that a woman's concerns must be frivolous?"

"No. I am a man who believes that there are times when the greater good is more important than any individual's preference."

"We must find another way to do this. I will give you letters saying whatever needs to be written. I will give you my father's ring so others can speak in my name."

"You must be seen in the boroughs, and your nominations known as your choice. There is no other way." He engaged Camilla's attention, and held out his hand to her. The ocelot sniffed warily. "If there were, I would gladly spare you, whatever your reasons for rejecting your family and homeland."

She thought that she heard an invitation to confide. It would be delicious to do so. But what could she tell? She had no tales of great injuries or insults. Her story was the age-old one of a woman who had discovered that she had been born only to be used.

Now this man had come to take her back, to be used again.

In the next moment he elegantly vanquished Camilla. His hand turned, and one long finger lined up the cat's nose in a seductive scratch. With a rumble of pleasure, Camilla stretched for more. Up on her feet now, she rubbed against his leg, positioning her spine. With languid strokes, Adrian Burchard bound one female to him forever.

Sophia watched his hand move, mesmerized. Splaying through fur, rubbing along head, scratching near tail. For a moment that palm was on her, warming down her body in a confident, possessive caress. Her own visceral, silent purr joined Camilla's.

One more ally lost. He was good at this. By supper she would undoubtedly stand alone.

A small commotion near the house caught her attention.

Then again, maybe not totally alone.

Jacques, Dieter, Attila, and Stefan had entered the garden. They noticed her under the pear tree and headed her way.

"You told them," she said.

"Yes."

"I cannot just abandon them."

"You cannot step off the King's own ship with four acolytes in tow. Also, before they reach us I should warn you that Jacques has decided that I am someone of significance to you."

"Are you saying that you permitted Jacques to think that you are my lover?"

"He thinks that I am a man from your past. Whether I am supposed to be a lover from your past, I do not know."

Sophia examined the young men bearing down on her. Their serious expressions suddenly made sense. They were afraid.

She beamed her best smile of welcome. Her friendliness counted for nothing, as Adrian's dark gaze brought them up short. They stopped thirty feet away to discuss the situation.

Adrian observed with fascination. "It would help if I know who they think I am."

"It was convenient for me while I lived here to invent events in my past in order to protect myself," she explained. "On occasion I would attract the attention of a man whom I wished to discourage. I discovered that the best way to do that was to have a husband."

"Except you never married. Even in France that would be well known about a woman of your birth."

"He is a secret husband. Someone thoroughly unsuitable, and very dangerous. He possesses a terrible temper. He has dueled five times and killed four men. If he ever learned that someone had pressed unwanted attentions on me, who knows what he might do."

"How did you explain why he isn't living here with you?"

"He is a spy for the English government and has been active in Turkey and the Balkans for years now."

He gave her a very peculiar look. "What an outlandish tale."

"Isn't it? In addition to his spying, my father never knew of the marriage, so he could not live with me openly anyway."

The artists had worked themselves into something approaching bravery. Attila had been elected standard-bearer.

"With your father dead, however . . ."

"Jacques must have concluded that my secret husband could come to claim me now." She sighed. "I had completely forgotten that I had told Jacques that secret when we first met."

Attila stepped up and performed an elaborate bow. "Mister Burchard, the other gentlemen and I would have a word with you."

Sophia rolled her eyes. "Leave this to me, Mister Burchard. I need to speak with my friends anyway about something else. I will explain the mistake."

Adrian looked down his nose at her. "The gentlemen wish to speak with me, not you, my dear. Also we should drop the formalities. I have made it clear that I am not prepared to continue the secret any longer."

She stared at him. *My dear? Secret?*

Oh, good heavens. He was taking up the role.

He turned his attention to Attila. Attila swallowed so hard that it was audible.

"Mister Burchard, we feel some necessity to clarify the arrangement here," Attila said. "Soph—your wife has, on occasion, been generous enough to extend her hospitality to poor artists who arrive in this magnificent city ill-provided for its expenses. Her salons are attended by the leading lights in the arts, and of course such introductions are invaluable as well. Currently, we four are fortunate to have the patronage of this great lady. We would not want you to wonder, however, whether our affections for her have ever been other than of the purest nature."

Sophia felt her face getting redder and redder. "Attila, there has been a ridiculous misunder—"

"Actually, it had never occurred to me that any of you might have dishonored my wife, and through her me," Adrian interrupted. "Except for Prince Stefan, of course."

Three men exhaled in relief. Stefan struck a brave pose, but he appeared sickly.

"However, now that you mention it, I expect that I had better interrogate the lady herself and learn the truth."

Attila's eyes widened with horror. He dropped to his knee in front of Sophia. "Oh, *kedvesem,* we have made a bad business worse for you. We only sought to allay any suspicions that he might have because, you must admit, the situation here could be seen as a little peculiar by a husband not aware of your excess generosity."

"Except that he is not—"

" 'A little peculiar' puts it rather too finely. After I speak with the duchess, I'll be dealing with any man here who so much as suggested anything improper."

That was not good news. Stefan went pale, but all of them looked uncomfortable. At one time or another each had made a suggestion or two. It was to be expected. Part of being patronized was to make sure the patron was happy. When the largesse came from a woman, it behooved a young artist to explore just what sort of services were required.

Attila clutched her hand and pressed his lips to it. "*Istenem, istenem.* My sweet lady, if I had known. Jacques told us but this morning. That accepting your kindness might put you in danger like this fills me with guilt."

"Oh, for goodness sake, I keep trying to tell you that he is not—"

"She isn't in danger. You are," Adrian clarified. "Although, after all these years on her own, she forgets who is her master. I may have to discipline her, but nothing dangerous is in store."

Jacques had been holding back, but now he stepped forward boldly. "You speak like a rogue instead of a gentleman. It will be uncivilized if you touch her in anger. She confided that you were a cruel, vile man, but I never expected such harshness."

One dark eyebrow rose devilishly above one dark eye. "Is that what you called me to your lovers, my sweet? *A cruel, vile man?*"

She rose and forced Attila up as well. "Heaven's mercy, Burchard, look what you have done. Jacques, he isn't going to beat me. Nor is he going to hurt any of you." She slid his coat off her shoulders and threw it to him. "Are you enjoying yourself? Tell them that your wit got the better of you."

She faced her friends with her back to Adrian. "He is not my husband. I never saw him before last night. Stefan will tell you that I had to read his card to know his name."

"That was a standard ruse to hide our relationship," his voice countered from behind. "Repudiating me will do no good, my dear."

"He is lying and he has taken over this house without authority."

"If a husband does not have authority, who does, I ask you, gentlemen?"

"He thinks to force me to return to England. I have explained that I am not going, but it has occurred to me that a journey would be pleasant all the same. How would all of you like to join me? I have decided to make a long visit to Italy."

Like a *tableau vivant,* her Ensemble froze and looked at her in surprise.

After a stunned five count, Attila clasped his hands, happy again. "Italy?"

A voice, not happy at all, spoke right behind her head. *"Italy?"*

"Venice first, then we will make our way down the coast. Ravenna, then over to Rome and up to Florence. We will lease a villa in the Tuscan Hills. It will be grand. All you need to do—"

A masculine warmth along her back distracted her. Hands circled her waist possessively. "I must forbid this, my darling."

She tried in vain to squirm away. "All you need to do to make it happen, dear friends, is to get rid of this man who has intruded on my life against my will. Tie him up and put him on a slow boat back to England."

They considered it. She could see it in their eyes. Jacques wavered, with one foot already over the line.

"Italy," she cried brightly, reminding him of the prize.

"Death," Adrian said coolly, spelling out the cost.

Jacques threw up his arms in surrender, casting her a regretful smile and shrug. Her worthless Ensemble eased away.

"Not fair." She twisted around to face her adversary. "You are all bluff. You have no intention of hurting them."

"Would you prefer if I did? Now, smile at me sweetly or I will have to drive them out completely to make sure that they do not aid you in any foolish schemes you might have."

He still held her, his hands pressing her through sash and gown and stays, keeping her in place despite her squirming resistance. He glanced to the circle of men who had moved off into the garden.

"They are just four more strays, aren't they? Like the animals in your sitting room."

Those hands and his closeness were making her feel horribly flighty and foolish and female. He could probably tell, which was even worse.

"Do not presume to know what they are to me. Furthermore, there have been others. I have lived here eight years."

His fingers pressed more obviously, as if he checked the feel of her and tested the fit of his hands. She arched away but he did not release her.

"Then on the chance that one of them is your lover and willing to risk all for you, I should convince him that, with my return, *none* of his services are required now."

He eased her closer. She realized his intention. Shocked, she tilted away. "Don't you dare. I am a peeress of the realm. There is probably some law against taking liberties with me. This is—"

His mouth silenced her.

It probably was not a long kiss, even though it seemed to last forever. He did not even embrace her, just controlled her with his hands on her waist. It began discreetly, like a kiss of farewell or welcome between friends. Hardly a passionate exchange. A mild liberty, that was all, to discourage Jacques and the others.

But its tenderness stunned her. The taste of sweet connection pierced her heart with nostalgia and yearning, and she could not fight him as she had planned. She submitted, limp and dazed, her skirt crushed against his legs. Maybe she even softened in a way that might be construed as kissing him back.

He lingered. One hand rose to caress her face and hold it to a brief, warm exploration of the boundaries of discretion. Emotions long ignored and denied stirred within her, a frightening rumble that almost made her gasp.

He stopped but he still held her, with that warm palm against her cheek. His touch was so gentle that she could not feel indignant like she wanted to. She sensed that he saw everything during the few moments his dark gaze looked into her eyes. All of it. That kiss was dangerously seductive in ways that had nothing to do with sex.

He moved away and looked to the Ensemble. She blushed when she saw Attila's grin and Jacques' roguish expression.

"Make what arrangements you will for them. Let them follow in a month or so, if you insist. But not Stefan."

"No, not Stefan."

"You remember, then? That he drugged you last night?"

"Drugged me!"

"Your memory loss suggests it, as does your rapid fall into unconsciousness. Your Polish prince intended to have you without bothering to plead for your consent. To what end, I cannot imagine. Blackmail?"

"I confess that I have regained some memories that made me wonder what occurred with him. If it was as you say, I owe you my gratitude. I had planned to request his departure, and will be sure to do so now."

"There is no need, really, since *you* depart in the morning."

He seemed very confident of that. He spoke with a quiet authority that said further resistance was futile. That piqued her annoyance. He probably thought that kiss had thoroughly established his dominance.

He took a few steps toward the house. "Have you eaten? Come and have something now. I do not want to risk your getting sick on the crossing."

"I will come later. I want to speak with them."

"I must insist that you do so in my presence. Also, I will stay in your house tonight, to ensure that all is ready at dawn. If you give me your word that you will not try to sneak away for Italy or elsewhere, I could find a room and not lie across the threshold to your chambers."

Camilla cried for release. Sophia untied the lead from the tree branch. The ocelot trotted to Adrian's side, where she made delicate pivots in order to rub his legs with her head.

Adrian waited. Sophia joined him and Camilla and they all strolled toward the house.

She would let him think he had won. Tomorrow morning, however, she would not be leaving for England with him.

chapter 5

S ophia gazed down at the activity in the street below. Servants tucked items into a wagon laden with portmanteaus, boxes, and cages. Her coach stood at the ready.

Adrian Burchard strolled past it all, calmly surveying the results of his high-handed interference in her life. He appeared contented and confident. The relaxed ease of his gait irritated her.

She welcomed the vexation. Anger was soothing compared to the nauseous hollow in her stomach that had plagued her since rising.

"Are you ready, my lady?" Jenny asked.

Sophia turned. Trunks filled the wardrobe, waiting their turn to make the voyage to England. Gowns and dresses and slippers and trinkets nestled inside them.

"Mister Burchard is amazing," Jenny said, with what Sophia considered traitorous admiration. "All of this so quickly arranged."

"Yes. He managed to pack up my whole life in two days. Since the substance of that life consists of little more than the objects I purchase, however, it was not such a difficult feat."

"That is not true. Your life is full and wonderful. You will be much missed. Paris will mourn your departure."

She doubted that Paris would give much notice. This city had lost better than her and survived the gap with ease.

"I do not want to do this," Sophia said. "He has no right to force it on me."

Jenny beamed an encouraging smile. "It will not be so bad, you will see. You are the duchess now. Your father is gone. It will not be as it was before."

Sophia wanted to believe that. The emptiness inside her knew differently, however. For one thing, her father was not really gone. He lived on in the estate and the title and the duties. Worse, he survived in the way he shadowed her soul.

Jenny tried again. "Shall we go down now?"

Without responding, Sophia walked past her. Going down was the easy part. It was what came after that sickened her.

She marched forward, forcing herself not to look at the familiar furniture and appointments of the house. She was determined not to get weepy and nostalgic. She was not a child. Besides, it was not what she left that grieved her, but what she returned to.

Sadness and fear, that was what she carried down the grand staircase. The sadness and fear of a desperate young woman running away from a life she could no longer live.

The girl she had been in England had resurrected during the night as she lay in bed, trying to find a way to thwart Burchard. With the growing realization that she could not abort his plans, that he would indeed drag her back to England, all the old, unhappy emotions had started to drown her.

They flooded again as she stood on the bottom step and looked out the open door. Its lines framed Burchard as he stood with his back to her, supervising the last of the packing.

It wasn't his fault that she fought a losing war against all the bad memories. He knew nothing about her life and was only obeying his masters.

Admitting that did not help. What was left of her spirit began a simmering rebellion against this man who was making her return to a world that she hated.

Jenny looked around. "Where are your artists? I expected them to be here."

"Mister Burchard made sure I was alone this morning. He bought off my guests by saying they could stay in the house until it was closed if they remained in their chambers this morning. We said our farewells last night. Perhaps it was just as well, since Attila cried so much."

"Well, I never cared for long leave-takings anyway." Jenny walked forward a few paces and looked back at her expectantly. "Shall we go?"

Adrian heard. He turned, then stepped aside two paces to indicate all was ready and they could leave the house.

Sophia gazed past him to the waiting coach. It would take her to the coast and to a ship that would carry her to England where another coach would transport her to Marleigh, the country seat of her family and title.

Adrian Burchard thought he was taking her home.

Not a normal home. Not a place that one longed to see and remembered with fondness. Ghosts waited for her there. So did her own weakness and humiliation.

The little rebellion grew. She grabbed it as a raft of support amidst the chaos swimming in her head and heart.

Early this morning she had resigned herself to this journey as inevitable. She had decided to wear a sophisticated mask to hide her panic and melancholy.

Now, facing that coach, she knew that stepping out the door would destroy what little contentment she had built in her life.

She ignored Jenny's expression of encouragement.

She did not move.

Adrian stepped back to his old place and faced her over the threshold. "We are prepared to depart, Your Grace."

"Then all who are prepared should indeed depart, Mister Burchard. I regret that I cannot be counted among you."

If a body could sigh, his did.

He walked into the house.

A few servants lingered at the top of the stairs to the lower level. With the subtlest of gestures, he told them to leave. They scurried down.

Sophia resented the docility he could command from everyone. She narrowed her eyes on the cool, dark figure of Adrian Burchard.

"Jenny, wait in the coach. The duchess will join you shortly," he said.

Jenny hesitated, looking at Sophia helplessly. With an expression of apology and surrender, she left the house.

Sophia and Adrian faced each other. He did not say anything for a while. During that brief span, the lights in his eyes changed. His expression grew less stern and annoyed and even a little sympathetic.

"There is no choice," he said.

Did he mean for her, or for him? "Only because you do not give me one."

"Since there is none, let us do this with the dignity that befits your position."

"That is the odd fate of women, isn't it? Being a dignified adult means submission and surrender. Resistance to the whims of men makes one an obstinate child. You must forgive me, but I think the world has that backwards."

"You may be correct. Today, however, there is still no choice."

She hated the confident way he announced his control of her life.

He held out his hand, beckoning her forward. "It is time to go, Duchess."

A vivid memory came to her, of entering port after her flight from home. She had taken a deep breath when her foot landed on French soil. In that instant she had experienced a profound sense of deliverance and safety.

The relief had been so physical that she might have just survived a drowning or strangulation. She felt as if she had not been able to breathe for years and suddenly she could.

Entering the coach meant gasping for air again.

She would not embrace that fate willingly.

She ignored his offer of an escort. Instead she sank down and sat on the bottom step of the grand staircase and stared straight ahead.

He did not speak. He did not move. She refused to acknowledge him. She knew she was acting childish and spoiled, but she did not care. Every speck of her screamed against taking another step.

Suddenly he was standing right in front of her and she gazed only at his hips. That embarrassed her enough that she looked up.

She expected to see exasperation. Instead he looked down with a warmth that surprised her. He was not angry at all, only resigned.

In that instant she knew that he understood. Some of it, at least.

"As I said yesterday, I would spare you if I could," he said.

But he could not, so he would not.

"I said that I would carry you if I have to, and I will."

She looked away, swallowing hot tears. She would not accept this, but it was going to happen anyway.

"My sincere apologies, Duchess."

He reached down and lifted her to her feet. When she did not stand on her own, he dipped, grasped, and rose.

She found herself facing his back, slung over his shoulder, with his arms wrapped around her legs.

Carrying her like a carpet, he forced her to begin the journey back to England.

She stood at the railing of the ship and let the wind do its worst. It dismantled the careful style in which Jenny had fixed her hair. Its spray wet the mantle that she clutched to her body. She faced the gray expanse, and imagined the coast that would come into view soon.

A presence warmed her side and she glanced over. Adrian Burchard had joined her.

"You keep hovering nearby," she said. "Do you fear I will jump over? I assure you that I lack both the despair and the courage. I almost drowned once when I was a girl, and I would never ask for such terror again."

"I am more concerned that the damp will make you ill."

"I am dry beneath my mantle."

If he had inclinations to order her away from the railing, he did not speak them. Instead he leaned his forearms against the railing himself and looked to the sea with her.

"Where will we put in?" she asked.

"Portsmouth. Is that the port that you used when you left England?"

"Yes."

The sea appeared endless. Only it was not. She kept watching the horizon for evidence of land. Watching too hard.

"I rode there, on my horse. I carried only a bunch of jewels in my reticule. No clothing, nothing else at all."

"It sounds very bold and daring."

"I was not the least bit bold. I was terrified, but other emotions were stronger than fear and so I did it, much to my own amazement."

She did not know why she told him. He was the enemy. Something about him, however, offered a peculiar solace and a vague friendship. His eyes still contained that soft comprehension that she had been in the house. She wished they did not. She could hate him if not for that glimmer of understanding.

"My father was in London, but I knew the Parliament would end soon," she said. "I was not happy at Marleigh, but I could tolerate it when he was not there. When the letter came, announcing his imminent return, I knew that I could not bear his presence every day. So I ran." She laughed at the memory of her astonishing recklessness. "I had no idea what I was doing. I even had to ask other travelers for the way to Portsmouth. I kept worrying that he would catch me at an inn if I rested the horse, so I did so in the fields and woods. It was all very dramatic."

"Since he did not catch you, perhaps your caution was wise."

"It was unnecessary. He did not follow. I learned later that he made no attempt to catch me. He wrote to me in Paris and explained that the Duke of Everdon does not tear after a headstrong daughter who is determined to court scandal and ruin. The story would be too undignified."

"He simply washed his hands of you?"

"I was not that fortunate. I was his heir. If his young wife had borne him a son, I would have been free of him, but she did not."

Her steady gaze locked on a shadow in the distance. The smallest ridge had appeared on the horizon. She squinted, hoping it was just the distant mist, but her heart fell because she knew it was not.

Adrian must have seen it too. "We will stay in Portsmouth for the night, and then begin our journey to Marleigh in the morning."

"How long will I have before I must go to Court and meet with the King?"

"He will be traveling to Marleigh to see you there."

She turned her gaze from the horizon to him. She no longer needed to look to the distance. The landfall would grow in her head without her watching it. Her soul would tick off the time until this ship pulled into port.

"You did not tell me that my trials would begin so quickly, Mister Burchard. I assumed that I would have some time to accommodate myself before the worst of this ordeal started."

"I did not make the arrangements. Others did."

And those others had not worried whether their arrangements were considerate of her. She really did not matter. It was the power of Everdon that they waited for. It was only the bad luck of fate that made her the vessel in which that power now rested.

Heartsickness and agitation began sneaking into her again. She instinctively let go of her mantle and crossed her arms over her stomach.

The wind caught the edge of her wrap and whipped it back until it flew behind her.

Adrian caught it and gently tucked it around her again. His polite protection touched her battered spirit.

She looked in his eyes. She guessed that this man could be very hard if he needed to be, but he was not now. He gazed back with a familiarity not at all appropriate, but undeniably compelling. Once more she had the sensation that he examined her heart and soul until he knew her better than she knew herself.

Oddly enough, she saw no criticism in his eyes. They reflected none of the harsh judgments that she expected, considering what he had learned of her during their brief association. The depths of those dark pools contained determination and confidence, but not of a type to threaten her.

And maybe, just possibly, she saw lights of genuine concern.

Her spirit calmed. It seemed as if the wind did, too, until they were standing in a tiny spot of serenity. His quiet strength provoked a latent courage in her. It was almost as if he willed a transference of fortitude as he looked at her.

The ship clearly turned, commanding her attention. With a start she saw that the land loomed far closer than she expected.

That confused her. How long had they been connected by that naked gaze? The ship's progress suggested it had been much longer than she thought.

"England," she said, narrowing her eyes on the buildings and ships growing with each moment.

"Home," he said softly.

"That home was my prison, Mister Burchard. Do not expect me to meekly surrender to its chains again."

chapter 6

H e created a mild disturbance wherever he walked. Like a pebble skimming the surface of a placid lake, his stroll around the periphery of the guests caused ripples of attention.

Even men glanced his way, but the women actually repositioned themselves to get a better view. Several trailed behind him at a distance, as if hooked on invisible lines that he had cast their way.

Sophia watched from the highest terrace at Marleigh, Everdon's country estate. Below her two more landings stepped down to where the garden spread out in its spring splendor. Officially the guests were not here for entertainment. That would be unthinkable with the recent demise of the duke, not to mention the month left in the year of mourning for the last king. All the same, despite their somber colors, the throng of notables drinking punch bore a remarkable resemblance to a garden party.

They had called *en masse* to welcome her return and to express their sympathies. Their collective descent on Marleigh had been arranged by Celine, her father's second wife and widow. A house cramped with curious aristocrats was the last thing that Sophia wanted to endure. She suspected that Celine had planned it specifically to discomfort her.

This should have occurred four days after her return, but demonstrating mobs had necessitated a circuitous route from Portsmouth, so she had only arrived last night. Despite such hazards of travel, it looked as if half of the House of Lords and their ladies had made the trek to Devon. They probably thought the danger and inconvenience well worth it. After all, the King had come, Sophia promised to be grist for the rumor mill, and this was the closest thing to a decent assembly to occur in almost a year.

She knew that the real point of the day was not to welcome her home. The lords' interest and the royal favor had a purpose. Time was of the essence. It was imperative to cajole the sacrificial lamb to the altar.

Recognizing one's fate does not mean that one must run to it with open arms. Sophia had slept late, dawdled in dressing, and delayed making her entrance. Upon finally emerging from her chambers, dressed in a black gown that was ten years old, she had looked for the one man who was not a stranger. It had not been difficult to locate him in the crowd.

He did not seem to realize how women reacted. Secretly watching him, Sophia marveled at how oblivious he appeared to most of it, and how indifferent he was to what he did see.

"He is a bit too dramatic-looking, don't you think?" a voice asked. Celine stepped up close and tilted her black parasol at an angle over her blonde curls, providing a bit of shade for Sophia too. Anyone watching would think they were old friends seeking solace in their grief, which was hardly the case. Although Celine was actually a year younger than Sophia and might indeed have become a friend, the two had never liked each other.

"Of whom do you speak?"

"As if you do not know. The stallion down there, creating so much heat in the herd, of course. Your escort, Burchard."

"Is he dramatic-looking? I had not noticed." She actually said it with a straight face.

Celine gave a sardonic smirk, as opposed to one of her other ones. She had perfected a whole repertoire of them. One of the great beauties of society since she had left the schoolroom, she assumed that her reactions should be of interest to everyone. Her face left men stammering in ways no one had ever reacted to Sophia, and Sophia admitted that her dislike of Celine contained a big dose of jealousy. Right now she thought it highly unfair that even black crepe flattered the young dowager duchess.

Celine's eyes narrowed as she examined the strolling Adrian. "What do you think? Italian? I have a friend who says Persian. He is a mongrel bastard, of course. It is so embarrassingly obvious, and to his credit that he does not try to grasp for full acceptance. You would think that if the Countess of Dincaster was going to bolt the corral, that she would at least have picked up with one of her own."

Perhaps it was exhaustion from the trip, but this critique of Adrian incited a vivid flash of anger. "Is that how it is done, Celine? Discretion now means choosing a man with the same nationality and coloring as your husband? Perhaps Lady Dincaster's heart did not understand the rules governing infidelity as well as you do."

Celine's lids lowered. "I can see that you have not changed much, Sophia."

Actually I have changed a lot. So much that I do not belong here anymore. So much that sometimes I do not even know who I am.

Her presence on the terrace had unfortunately been noticed. A footman wearing royal livery began the long climb up the stone stairs toward her.

Celine watched resentfully. The royal welcome waiting inside would change her life as surely as Sophia's. "You are glad that he is dead, aren't you? You have been waiting for it."

"I am not glad, Celine. He was my father. Nor do I want what his death brings me."

"Liar. It is all yours, despite your willfulness and disobedience. It sickened him to know that it would all go to you, after everything you had done."

"I do not know why you speak as though I am to blame. You were the one who was supposed to guarantee that this day never came to pass."

Celine flushed. "The least you can do is finally respect his wishes."

"I was counting on your solving the problem for us all by providing him with another son to replace my brother Brandon. Now the only wishes that I intend to respect are my own."

The footman had reached their level. Sophia listened to the formal request for her presence by King William. She stared Celine down until the dowager duchess retreated. Then she stepped closer to the footman and gave him new instructions.

Adrian strolled through the copse of trees bordering the water garden, wondering how the duchess was managing. Their delayed arrival meant she had not had much time to rest before this ordeal. The ride from Portsmouth had been slow and tiring, with him sitting with pistols at the ready atop the carriage. The extreme tension in England rarely exploded into deadly violence, but it only took one radical or one displaced farmer to hurt a woman.

She had grown quiet upon their landing. Her withdrawal had troubled him. She did not castigate or accuse, she barely seemed to notice him at all, but by the time he had deposited her here at Marleigh last night, he had begun to feel guilty for crimes unnamed.

A crunch on the path behind him broke through his thoughts. A delicate cough demanded his attention. He pretended he had not heard either announcement. The Dowager Duchess of Everdon had been stalking him all day. In a manner of speaking, she had been stalking him for years.

As an unmarried ingenue named Miss Celine Lacey, the duchess had not given serious consideration to the Earl of Dincaster's third son. The vain mind inside her pretty head did not seem to grasp that she had insulted him later by offering her favors in adultery. Nor had it ever concerned her that he was beholden to her husband in ways that would make an affair especially dishonorable.

Still, some men might have ruthlessly accepted the opportunity. He had strongly suspected, however, that no matter what his motivations in bedding the willing Celine, he would have ended up feeling like an exotic animal permitted into the lady's boudoir, to be petted and admired as a trophy.

A bit like the animals in Sophia Raughley's menagerie, come to think of it.

Speaking of Sophia Raughley . . . He glanced through the trees to the terraces rising up against the beautiful classical palace. Things must be underway now.

The crunches sounded closer and faster. Adrian quickened his pace and cut toward the garden. His brother Colin and his Aunt Dorothy rounded the pond and hailed him just as he exited the copse.

"There you are. Everyone is singing your praises in getting the duchess back so quickly," Colin said.

Adrian greeted his brother and kissed Dorothy Burchard, the earl's maiden sister. With his mother dead, she and Colin were the only two people whom he really considered family. "Good to see you, Dot. It has been some weeks."

Colin glanced slyly to his left, where Celine had retreated to study some new buds on a bush. "Thought you looked on the run and could use a rescue, although why you would ignore her I'll never know. The duke won't mind now."

Dorothy swatted Colin with her fan. "Disgraceful, that's what it is. The man is barely cold and she is casting enough lines to empty the Thames of fish."

"Dowager duchesses are not for me, Colin, any more than the Celine Laceys were," Adrian said.

"This dowager does not want to marry you, Adrian," Colin said, only to get swatted by Dorothy's fan again.

Precisely.

Colin kicked up gravel with his casual gait. "Is Gavin in with Father?"

"Yes, Gavin is with the earl and the King. So is half of the House of Lords."

"Not very sporting of them," Dorothy said. "She is only one woman."

"I was just thinking the same thing. One would assume that Wellington could defeat her with only the King and one or two earls to help."

"What is she like? There have been rumors about her life in Paris. Did you find the den of decadence that some whisper about?"

"Is that what is said, Dot? I wish you had told me. I would have girded myself with more moral outrage in preparation."

They had circled the small pond. Celine had not and now awaited his approach.

He had kissed her once over ten years ago during her first season. It had been a long embrace on a dark terrace the night before she became engaged to the Duke of Everdon. There had been others like her, girls who stuck one toe into the lake of audacity by permitting him small liberties.

Later the liberties became less small and the females less innocent, but the game remained the same. Eventually he had refused to play the role of the safely English foreigner whom every sophisticated girl should try at least once.

He acknowledged Celine as blandly as possible, but it looked as though he would not escape. Dorothy separated from their group, bore down on Celine with outstretched arms, and engaged the widow in effusive expressions of sorrow. Spared by the generous diversion, Adrian and Colin continued toward the great house.

"So, what is the duchess like?" Colin prodded.

"Trouble."

"Is she? What fun."

"I know that you have no interest in politics, but this is no laughing matter."

Colin frowned. "She isn't going to boot you out of your Commons seat, is she?"

"She may withhold the nomination just to get back at me. She truly did not want to return to England."

"Any problems there?"

"When it came down to it she refused to budge and I had to make good on an earlier threat and carry her out of her house, slung over my shoulder."

Colin cocked an eyebrow and half a smile. "You jest."

"Damned if I do. She wears at least ten petticoats, and all I could think was that if a strong wind should whip under her skirt, we might both take to flight like one of those big air balloons."

Colin laughed. "With all the revolutions on the Continent, who knows where you might have been shot down. Then to find all of that trouble on the road from Portsmouth."

"I have exaggerated that somewhat. Part of our delay came when we landed in Portsmouth itself. The monkey climbed to the top of the ship's main mast and it took half a day to get him down. I am sure that she deliberately let Prinny out of his cage."

"Prinny? She named a monkey after the late king?"

"He was alive when she named her monkey after him. It gets worse. She and I had an interesting conversation during the crossing. We discussed last summer's *petite revolution* in France, and the deposition of King Charles in favor of Louis Philippe. The duchess thought it a splendid drama. Her exact words, and I quote, were 'helping the citizens of Paris man the ramparts last July was the most exciting and worthwhile thing I have ever done in my life.' "

"Now, that *is* trouble. Have you told Wellington about this?"

"Do I look like a man who wants to die?"

They had reached the second terrace. Their reflections sparkled sharply in the new plate glass that had recently been installed in the windows and French doors. All over England the great houses were embracing the new, costly, large planes, and all over England mobs were smashing them. Even Wellington's Apsley House in London had seen all of its new glass destroyed a month earlier by a rampaging mob after dissolution of the last Parliament had killed the first Reform Bill.

The glass produced an eerie effect that was very different from deliberately gazing in a mirror. It caught casual vignettes and poses and showed one in the world as others saw one. Now it displayed the contradictory appearance of Adrian and his brother. Colin was all fair and blond, with an angelic face of perfect features. Adrian looked like night to his day, Satan to his saint.

He did not resemble the earl or Gavin, either, but the contrast was greatest with Colin. Colin never seemed to have noticed, or at least acted as if he had not, except during those fights at school when he had stood by Adrian's shoulder to defend the honor of their mother. Gavin always seemed to be away on the playing field whenever that happened.

A footman approached them and informed Adrian that the duchess requested his attendance in her sitting room.

"It sounds as though it is over," Adrian said after the footman left.

"What do you suppose she wants?"

"Perhaps she thinks that her new position permits her to order my execution."

He entered the drawing room, walked through the immense house, found Charles serving as underbutler, and followed his balding head up to Sophia's chambers.

The doors stood open. She paced the sitting room with Yuri and the other two mastiffs on short leads and Camilla following behind. Prinny the Monkey climbed up and down a chair.

Black did not become the duchess. With her dark curls and pale skin and strained expression, she looked like death itself. Annoyance and worry formed faint lines that framed her mouth. Her hair was pulled into an unattractive style that caused curls to spring out from under a silly little bonnet. Her old-fashioned bombazine dress covered fewer petticoats and showed less fullness than current styles, but she could not have looked less attractive if she had tried.

Which probably meant that she *had* tried. Adrian wondered how Gerald Stidolph had reacted upon seeing his intended after eight years.

"I trust that the King and lords are satisfied now," he said after her greeting. "Confess, it was not nearly as bad as you anticipated."

"I wouldn't know. I haven't met with them yet."

"Are you saying that you have kept the King waiting over two hours?"

"I was indisposed. However, he has summoned me again, so it cannot be avoided any longer."

"You left it to His Majesty to summon you *twice* to greet him in your own house? King William may be generous about this, but I assure you that Wellington will not find it amusing."

She yanked the dogs to a halt. "Let me guess. He is your hero. You have regretted all your life that you were too young to fight at Waterloo. As a schoolboy you idolized the general and dreamed of sharing his glory."

"He has the King's ear and is a force to be reckoned with. You do not want him as an enemy. I advise that you present yourself to the King at once."

She gathered the leads tighter, pulling the hounds closer. They circled her, their heads rising to her elbows. Camilla took up position by her side. Prinny happily climbed onto her shoulder and clutched the little black bonnet.

She presented a positively bizarre picture.

Which, God help him, he actually found endearing in addition to exasperating.

"I intend to go down now. You will escort me," she announced. "I am ready."

"Don't you want to drape the snakes around your bosom? If the point is to convince them that you are a madwoman, why not tuck the iguana under your arm?" He walked over, grabbed a squealing Prinny, dumped him in his cage, and slammed the door. "Camilla stays here too."

"I will not go unguarded."

"A passion for dogs is a respectably English eccentricity. They may accompany you, but you need no guards at the audience."

"I suppose not, since you are coming."

"I was not called. I cannot go in."

She pierced him with an accusing glare. "You forced me to come back here. Dragged me out of my home, abducted me for all intents and purposes, and subjected me to unknown dangers and possible death."

"At no time was your life in danger."

"You cut me off from my dearest friends and dumped me here, where I know almost no one and do not much like the ones whom I know. There is an army waiting for me in the study, Mister Burchard, led by the great Wellington himself. You are no ally of mine, and one of them, but I will be damned if I will enter their camp totally alone. Either you come with me or I do not go."

He considered refusing. It would cause an ungodly stir. And he could not help her. What was going to happen was inevitable.

The glint of obstinacy in her eyes gave way to one of distress. It flickered and burned, deepening their color. She did not look at him, but at Yuri and his brothers. "Please accompany me." The words came low, as if making the request strangled her. "It will be my *faux pas,* not yours."

He had glimpsed her vulnerability several times since meeting her, and it always twisted something inside him. It was probably why her bouts of resistance about coming back had made him more concerned than angry. His role in this had made him responsible for her, in a way.

He stepped to her side and offered his arm. "I promised to deliver you, and if I take my words too literally no one can blame me for it, I suppose."

chapter 7

Steeling her strength, Sophia accepted his escort down to where the meeting would be held. The hounds behaved magnificently since Adrian's commanding eye watched.

"You will not bring them in," Adrian insisted at the study's door, prying the leads from her fingers and handing them to a footman.

As it turned out, the whole army did not await her. Most of the lords had arrayed themselves in the library and corridors. Only ten men sat in the study itself.

They rose upon her entry, forming a masculine wall. The breadth of nobility was as daunting as their number. Besides the King she counted two dukes, two earls, a marquess, and an assortment of minor titles. Adrian's father, the Earl of Dincaster, sat by the window with his eldest son Gavin.

She made her bow to the elderly, rotund King. At his royal gesture she sat in a chair facing him, smack in the middle of the room like a curiosity on display.

"Well, now, my dear, it is good to see you again," hailed King William after all the introductions had been made. His gray head inclined her way and he favored her with an avuncular smile.

"And I you, Your Majesty. Your presence honors us."

"My pleasure. Came to settle things. Delightful house. Near the sea too. Old navy man myself. Glad to come. We need to settle this, don't we? Ill winds blowing and all that. Need to settle things."

A man with gray hair and bright eyes and a hooked nose caught her attention and smiled. "What His Majesty is trying to say, is that we need to settle things."

She knew this man. His presence did not bode well for her, even if he invited her to join him in a speck of disrespectful wit. She might be able to outsmart the new King known as "Silly Billy," but not the famous Duke of Wellington.

Having made his official welcome, the old King grew distracted. From the far wall Gerald Stidolph caught her eye and smiled with warm recognition. She hadn't expected him to be here. Even more than the phalanx of lords, even more than the dominating presence of Wellington, she resented the assumptions that had invited Gerald to participate.

Adrian had retreated against the wall closest to her. His magnetism created an intensification of gravity where he stood. Sophia half-expected the lords seated by the window to slide across the floor, right into the hearth.

Did no one else notice but her?

At least one other person did. The Earl of Dincaster's pink-tinted skin flushed a deeper hue. "My youngest son's errand ended with your arrival, Duchess."

"Mister Adrian Burchard is present at my request."

"This is a matter for the upper House, and not—"

"If the duchess wants him to stay, he stays," Wellington snapped.

King William jolted alert at the sharp military tone. "Quite. Let us move along." He pressed his hands on his thick knees. "Now, my dear, here you finally are. Should have come home on your own as soon as you heard. Odd choice not to, but we are not here to talk of that. There's work to be done, and quickly. Ill winds blowing and we need every man on deck. The problem is, you're not a man, are you?"

"It would appear not, Your Majesty."

"Only one thing for it, of course. If the captain can't take the helm, his first officer is sent instead."

"What His Majesty is saying," Wellington clarified, "is that, while at another time your inheritance might not cause problems, at this particular moment it does. Revolution threatens. These elections are crucial to the future of the nation."

The King slapped his hand on his knee. "Duty. Duty. That is what it is about for the likes of us. Marriage, Duchess. That is what it must be. Nothing else for it. Your father favored your cousin Stidolph over there, didn't he? Good man. Only right to make the match now."

She summoned every speck of courage that she could. "I could not possibly consider marriage while I mourn my father. Perhaps next summer."

"Normally such restraint would be expected, of course," Wellington said, his gaze sharpening on her in a way that said he immediately saw her game. "You honor your father more, however, by doing his will, and the situation in the country cannot permit such delay."

"It is more than my grief. My cousin and I have become strangers to each other. It may be that we do not suit each other. I will not take such an important step so impetuously." She got it all out, but her voice sounded awfully small.

Wellington rose. He instantly dominated the King, the study, and her. He looked down his hooked nose at her much as he must have examined the lowest of his soldiers.

"Gentlemen, if you would."

His brittle tone left no room for argument. The lords bobbed toward the door in obedient formation.

"I must insist that Mister Burchard remain," she said.

"Of course," Wellington agreed unctuously. He gave Adrian a glance that said, *Why not? After all, he is my man.*

Seeing that Adrian had not budged, Dincaster kept his seat too. Wellington stared at him until the earl's face was red with outrage, but still the father would not move if the third son stayed. Finally only Adrian, the Earl of Dincaster, the King, and Wellington remained.

Except that the King had fallen asleep, so he wasn't with them in truth.

"Now, Duchess, let us speak frankly," the Iron Duke said, pinning her in place with an eagle's stare. "I am aware that you are a woman of the world, so I will be plain. If marriage to your cousin does not appeal to you, that is unfortunate but hardly a major problem. Produce an heir and then do as you will."

"I am not such a woman of the world that my views are as practical as yours."

"This is not about you. It is about Britain. It is about responsibility. Furthermore, there are other matters at work. We did not want to frighten you, but you should marry for your own sake too. There is some possibility that you are in danger, and a husband would be protection."

In some danger. The words sucked the wind out of her gathering storm of indignation. A seed of raw fear and sickening guilt that had been planted upon hearing of her father's death suddenly shot out stems and roots.

"What do you mean, *danger?* What sort of danger?" Adrian asked.

The Iron Duke looked at her as if requesting permission to speak of it. The branching fear made her nauseous and she suddenly did not care what was said or done.

"As a girl the duchess had a friendship with a young radical who operated in this area and the midlands. He called himself Captain Brutus. Her father learned of it, laid a trap for the man, and got him transported. That was almost nine years ago, but it appears that Captain Brutus is back. Broadsides have been found with calls to action over his name." The duke paused. "Under the circumstances, the Duke of Everdon's death while hunting is somewhat suspicious. Those of us who know about the tie between Captain Brutus and this family think that caution is in order."

"If what you say is true, wouldn't the duchess have been safer in France?"

Adrian's icy tone made her twist and look up. He stood closely now, next to her shoulder.

"If she is in danger, it was just a matter of time before the man learned she was there. Better the war be fought on ground she knows, where there are those who want to protect her."

"We are speaking of one woman's safety, damn it, not the deployment of an army."

"See here, Adrian . . ." the forgotten earl began severely.

"That is where you are wrong, Burchard," Wellington countered. He turned back to her. "I am sure that you see the rightness of the solution. It is in everyone's interest, including yours, for this marriage to happen. Gerald Stidolph was in the army, and will both see to your protection and to the proper exercise of Everdon's considerable political influence."

Wellington's formidable presence, his very size and demeanor, demanded submission.

She raised her chin until she looked the most famous man in England squarely in the face. There was only one thing to do if she did not want to be browbeaten into agreement.

"I am sorry. I will not marry," she said. "I cannot. You see, I already have a husband."

Somehow Adrian got the duchess out of that study and away from the shock that greeted her announcement and story.

With perfect poise she allowed him to collect the dogs and make a retreating processional past all those lords, and up to the third level where her apartment sprawled. Once there he banished Jenny and closed the doors of the sitting room.

He pried the gripping hand that revealed her true emotions off his arm and stepped back. "I cannot believe that you told the King that bald lie."

Her bland expression broke, but she did not appear dismayed. She looked pleased with herself.

"I did not tell the King any lies. He was snoring. I fibbed a bit with Wellington, but since he was trying to force me to marry Gerald, I don't feel guilty."

"*Fibbed a bit?* You told him the whole ridiculous tale. He probably thinks that you married Captain Brutus and that Everdon is now at the mercy of a man who encourages insurrection."

She propped herself on a chair. "I made it very clear that it is not Captain Brutus because, God forbid he really has come back, I certainly do not want to be stuck proving that he *isn't* my husband. Nor did I tell the whole tale.

I never mentioned about my husband being a spy for the government, for example . . ."

And thank God for that.

". . . because Wellington would probably know all the spies and would be able to figure out who it was, or rather who it wasn't, which is all of them. I decided that I had to keep it mysterious. Using that excuse was brilliant, if I do say so myself. He doesn't believe me, but he cannot prove that I am lying."

She appeared happier than she had since he met her. "I have you to thank. When you faced the duke down like that, I realized that he was just another man. The way you were not intimidated gave me strength. I could never have stood my ground without your help."

He supposed that it was incumbent upon him to give the plan one last try, not that he had much stomach left for it.

"The news about Captain Brutus appeared to frighten you. If there is the chance that he is a danger, it really may be best if—"

"The man I knew would not be a danger to me."

"Men change, especially if they are embittered."

"Possibly. I knew his seven years were up, of course. I have wondered if he would come back, and if he would blame me. If he has, perhaps I deserve it."

"You must take care, just in case."

She quirked a trembling grin at him. "I will keep the dogs nearby." He could see her force her mind to other business. "Please bring Wellington a message from me. Tell him that I will accept his advice in exercising Everdon's power. Tell him that I am prepared to nominate the men recommended to me, and will send his selections to the new Parliament."

Adrian had no trouble recognizing what she offered, and what she withheld. The elections were imminent, and she would submit to the Tory leadership for them, but she made no other promises. Those twelve seats would remain twelve question marks when anyone tried to anticipate voting.

Her green eyes met his in frank acknowledgment that she had survived a crucial battle and found the victory exhilarating.

When he had told Colin that she was trouble, he had not known just how much.

He went in search of Wellington, thankful that his part was done and that he was out of it.

"You have to stay on."

Wellington gave the order upon receiving Sophia's message. "Offer to help her settle her father's affairs. She probably has no head for that herself and will be glad to have advice. I doubt that she trusts the old duke's lawyers and stewards, since she trusts no one in England, from what I can tell. Except you, a bit." He stood beside the study window, enjoying a cigar. The King and the earl had departed and Adrian and Wellington were alone.

"Find someone else."

"Who? She will refuse. She is not sure of you, either, but you at least are the devil she knows."

"Tell Stidolph to take care of it."

"I am sure he will try, but having met her, I don't have much faith in Stidolph anymore. I think that he exaggerates their affection for each other, and her claim of being married closes that door until she recants. Even if he should win her, I doubt that he can control her."

"Then you do it."

"My good man, I am the enemy. You are only the ambassador."

"No, I am the man who forced her to return here even though doing so places her in danger." He had been finding their use of her increasingly distasteful. The realization that they had been using him, too, was thoroughly unpalatable. "Damn it, I should have been told."

"From your reaction, I am glad that you were not. She had to come back. As to Captain Brutus, I meant what I said. She is no safer in France if the man is determined. If you are feeling responsible, all the more reason to stay close to her."

First duty, now guilt. First for England, now for his conscience. The Iron Duke was very good at this, but then he would have to be, wouldn't he? You couldn't get thousands to die at your command unless you were.

"Stay and keep an eye on her," Wellington continued. "While you do, reason with her. With some influence and persuasion, she'll see what needs to be done. She just wants it to be her decision. Should have expected that. Willful blood in the family. Do you believe that story about a husband?"

"It is a fiction she invented in Paris and told to selected men."

"Clever woman. Damned shrewd. You are hard-pressed to prove someone *isn't* married if they want to claim they are. I convinced Dincaster to keep quiet about it. If word got out, she might be tangled in her own lie. Anyway, I leave her to you. Get her to the boroughs for the nominations and get her in line for the Commons vote. Shouldn't be hard. You've managed Serbs and Turks, one woman should be easy."

Not so easy, and not at all the same. This mission had a face and a name and a troubled sadness.

He would do what the Iron Duke wanted. He would take her to the boroughs and he would even reason with her. But his priority in staying nearby would be to make sure that she came to no harm because he had forced her to leave Paris.

"Take care of it, Burchard. Hell, seduce her if that is what it takes. Just make sure that she delivers those damn votes."

Marleigh's chambers were apportioned out according to precedence that night, which meant that Adrian slept at a nearby inn. The next morning he returned and went looking for the duchess.

He found her in the duke's study. She sat on the floor in a black riding habit behind the huge desk, immersed in a mountain of paper. She had caused a mess that would take several days for someone to reorganize.

"I can't find it," she muttered when she saw him. "The will. I can't find it."

"He probably kept it in a safer place than his desk. Besides, his solicitor has a copy. Why do you want it now?"

"I was hoping he added a codicil and found some way to keep me from inheriting *this*." She raised her arms in reference to the house and the rest. Papers flew.

"It was not in his power to prevent your inheriting most of it, and you know it." He waded in and lifted her up.

"Oh, dear, I have made a shambles of it." Her black-covered backside curved up to him while she bent to gather documents into a useless stack. He experienced contradictory urges to both swat that bottom and caress it.

The events in Paris had breached some fundamental formalities between them, so he did not contemplate his action much before circling her waist with one arm and carrying her, derriere first, away from the documents before she did anymore damage.

She squirmed until he released her. "You go too far, Mister Burchard."

"Your secretary will need salts when he sees this."

"I have no secretary. I released my father's last evening. I think that I will change solicitors too. Papa's caused me a lot of trouble when I wanted to have my income from Mother's portion sent to me in Paris."

Adrian gestured to the mountain of documents. "May I suggest that you wait on either change until that is dealt with?"

"I am sure that you will take care of it neatly. Didn't you come here this morning to offer your help in such things? I just assumed that Wellington would want someone spying on me and would realize that you are his best chance."

She did not look at all sly, but Adrian suspected that the duchess had just revealed a depth of perception that would make everything about this business more difficult.

"The Duke of Wellington does not set spies on British citizens."

She looked at the Mont Blanc of parchment. "Oh, dear. Then I did that for nothing. I wanted to see how quickly you could fix it all."

"Wellington did, however, express concerns for your safety, and thought that you might accept my continued presence on that count."

She settled herself on a chair and lounged with a pose more relaxed than was proper. It was probably one more example of the inappropriate behavior that she had adopted in Paris. That behavior, and just how inappropriate it might have been, had been on his mind quite a bit. The musings had been part of very male speculations regarding the duchess, Parisian freedom, and provocative memories of soft curves and soaked red silk.

"I do not expect to be in danger, and I have a dozen strapping footmen if I should be, so a position as a guard is overdoing it. However, if you are going to be underfoot, we have to find something for you to do."

She made a display of contemplating hard. Her attitude provoked the devil in him.

"I don't suppose you play the pianoforte or violin?" she asked.

"Not well enough to be your entertainment."

"Hmmm. Do you write poetry?"

"Sorry."

"Then I am afraid that we are back to the documents."

"Actually, Wellington suggested a different role for me. He thought it would be convenient if I became your lover." He said it to retrieve the upper hand, but he waited for her reaction with interest.

"Considering your proven efficiency, you should make quick work of it," she said, gesturing to the mess, simply ignoring his last comment.

"Not too quick. I'm sure we both want it done right."

"A few days should get it all suitably arranged, I would think." She spoke blandly, but a blush betrayed that she recognized the double meaning of the exchange.

"Only if you cooperate."

Redder now, she persevered. "I will leave it to you, Burchard. I have no competence with such matters."

He really shouldn't . . . "Women always say that, and then often prove amazingly adept at the business. It is really just a matter of proceeding with care and attention until one is satisfied."

Her eyes widened. He gestured innocently to the mound of papers. "We will work at it together and I will teach you. We will get right to it after you nominate your candidates."

The abrupt change in subject confused her. "Candidates?"

"The election. You must visit the boroughs at once. We will leave tomorrow. Jenny is already packing."

"Oh, no, you don't. Not again. *I* will make the arrangements for this circuit and I will complete the journey alone. You just write down where I need to go."

"The locations of the boroughs are often obscure. I will map out the general route for your planning purposes, but you will never find them without a guide."

Her brow puckered peevishly. "Very well. If I need a guide, it may as well be you. You can come, but only for that purpose. You are not to give a single order, least of all to me." She rose and headed for the door. "Now, please excuse me. I need to leave this house. It oppresses me even more than I thought it would."

He followed her into the marble corridor, and gestured to her habit. "You are going riding?"

"Since my guests will not come down for at least an hour, I decided to take the opportunity."

"May I join you?"

"I do not need a guardian angel. I am in no danger on Everdon's lands."

She had not really refused his company, so he followed her to the stables and called for his horse. Her confidence in her safety was misplaced. The duke had died on Everdon lands.

However, as he watched the duchess settle on her saddle, he admitted that the idea of a long, private ride with this errant daughter of the nobility appealed to him for other reasons besides protecting her.

They walked their horses through the formal gardens and park behind the house. She stopped atop a rise and looked down its hill to where the family graveyard hugged one side of a little chapel. A freshly built small marble building dominated the sculpted memorials.

"My apologies," he said. "I should have guessed that you might want to visit there."

"I did not come out today to say prayers at my father's grave."

She kept looking at the sepulcher. Adrian backed his horse away. She may not be saying prayers, but whatever worked through her mind absorbed her just as completely.

He watched her serious expression from his short distance, wondering what she tried to reconcile. He noticed that, as with her other mourning ensembles, her riding habit was old-fashioned and girlish for her age. They must all be costumes made when her brother Brandon died.

He remembered the accumulation of clothing tumbled around her dressing room in Paris. That extravagance spoke of a woman who would never be seen in dated fashions, no matter what the situation. He would have expected her to have modistes stay up all night sewing and altering to make sure she was turned out appropriately.

She didn't really care about it, he realized. Shopping was just a diversion, like her salons and parties. All of her behavior in Paris had been a means of distracting herself from something. What had Charles said that first night, about her reaction to the duke's death? *It is as if she knows that she cannot hide anymore.*

A complex woman. An interesting one, with a compelling combination of strength and vulnerability. Pain hid behind the studied gaiety. A mask of frivolity deliberately obscured intriguing layers.

She turned her horse abruptly and broke into a gallop. Adrian pursued.

She rode away from the house as if devils drove her from its shadow. When they entered a wooded section of park that hid the palace from view, she finally reined in beside a large rock and used it to dismount. Adrian swung off his horse and they strolled together along the sun-dappled path. Rich, earthy odors of spring filled the air around them.

Slowly, her self-absorption lifted. "You think me heartless not to visit his grave."

"You were estranged from him. Death does not always resolve that."

"Especially because he is not dead. His body lies in that stone monument, but I am under his thumb more surely now than I was a year ago." She smiled ruefully. "I was counting on his fathering another son. I never gave up hope for that. Nor did he. However, it appears that he let others know about his plans for Gerald and me, just in case."

"It is typical for fathers to try and influence their children's matches, especially if the child will become a duchess."

"I doubt that Gerald sees me as a duchess. To him I will always be Alistair's difficult little girl."

"You, difficult? I can't imagine that."

She laughed, in frank admission that she had been little else since they met.

"How long have you known Stidolph?" he asked.

"Ever since his mother married my late uncle, my father's brother. It was her second marriage. I was ten then. Gerald was at Oxford. He entered the army for a few years after and I never saw him much, but once he sold out his commission, he always seemed to be around. Papa favored him. He became like another son to him. Rather like Wellington and you."

"Wellington hardly thinks of me as a son. I am useful to him, that is all. Did you go to Paris to avoid the match?"

"That is one of the reasons I went."

"Why didn't you just marry someone else?"

"There was no one else. Papa could be very discouraging. I was isolated too. I was presented, but I never came out. My mother died when I was seventeen, so we were in mourning the season I should have done it, and other circumstances interfered later. I think that Papa was glad. He did not approve of marriages based on *tendres* with men met at London balls. The choice should be his, as with every other detail in my life."

"I knew your father only through politics, but I suppose I can see how his sense of order might have appeared harsh to his family."

"My father was an autocratic, cold man, too aware of his power. He treated my mother with little warmth. My brother and I were opportunities to be exploited and responsibilities to be managed. He forced Brandon into his own mold, and then harped when bits and pieces of my brother's nature bulged out of the container. He could be unbelievably cruel."

She blurted it out with piercing bitterness. Her whole body tensed, as if she braced an invisible shield against the memory of the man. Even her hands tightened on the reins that led her horse.

"Men are what they are, Duchess. Their basic natures rarely change, even if they wish they might. Your father probably thought that he was doing what was best for his family."

"He thought that he was doing what was best for Everdon. But then, I would expect you to defend him. You were his man."

"I was his M.P., a position negotiated by Wellington."

"I am well aware of where your first loyalty lies, Mister Burchard. As to my father, his family should have had more than a peer of the realm in their midst. There should have been some consideration of our dreams, and some love along with the lectures and criticism."

Her resentful words speared his heart. He understood her bitterness more than he wanted to admit. Understood it at the visceral level that only a shared experience can evoke. He had long ago come to terms with that childhood misery, but that did not mean that her unhappiness moved him any less.

In spitting out her memories about Alistair, she also gave voice to his own about Dincaster. His attempt to soothe her had been an articulation of the boyhood excuses that he had used to assuage his own pain.

"Should there have been some love? I expect so," he said.

She paused in her stroll and those green eyes turned on him with naked perception. He suddenly felt exposed, so complete was the comprehension in her expression. She knew that he understood, and she knew why.

An emotional bridge instantly formed between them. The empathy made something long-buried within him suddenly real again, and raw.

The silent, mutual acknowledgment that they had both lived with that void touched him profoundly. The urge to pull her into his arms flashed through him. He would carry her off to a private meadow and show her how embracing the present could free one from the past.

"Do you plan to live your whole life getting back at him? Will you let that consume your heart and rule your nature? If so, it will be a terrible waste, and his greatest victory."

She glanced about desperately, as if he had cornered her.

"I cannot imagine why it should matter to you."

He reached over and brushed at an errant curl, grazing her temple with his touch. Her eyes widened in surprise. The intimacy born of her revelations pulsed harder between them. "It matters to me, and you do know why."

He may never have made his interest explicit, or at least not so soon. He might have continued expressing it through light flirtation unless she encouraged something more. But the mood of the moment not only permitted this, it demanded it, and also much, much more.

He laid his palm against her cheek and kissed her without deciding to. It was an impulse born of the urge to soothe her distress and acknowledge their little bond. He also wanted to taste again the trembling lips he had kissed in her Parisian garden, and feel once more her pliant surrender.

She responded. He could feel it in her rapidly fading shock and hear it on her quick breaths.

He began to embrace her so he could lead her to the exploration waiting.

When his hands touched her body, she jumped back and turned her face away. She appeared frightened and tragically vulnerable. "I suppose that I do know why it matters to you. If revenge against my father drives me, it will make me more predictable. Easier to manage."

He smiled at her attempt to pretend that she did not comprehend what had just happened. "Just as long as you understand my intentions, Duchess."

Her blush revealed that she indeed understood them. She gathered her reins clumsily and pulled her horse closer. "I think that I will go visit some of the farms."

He helped her to mount, more charmed than disappointed by how flustered she had become. Surely she had learned in Paris that ignoring a bridge was not the same as burning it. This one would remain there, connecting their two islands, whether they ever acknowledged it again or not.

He would have to cross over now. He was curious about what lay on the other side.

She did not hate all of her inheritance. She loved the land and the distant sound of the sea. The parks and farms and hills had been her refuge as a girl. If she could be rid of the ghosts and memories, she would welcome this part of the legacy. She could probably even reconcile herself to the duties and restrictions if her heart could find peace with the past.

She aimed toward the closest village, too aware of the exciting man riding beside her. He always made her jumpy and alert. She wondered if she would ever learn to ignore his presence. After what had just occurred, probably not.

That worried her. She knew how to handle flirtatious wit and flippant innuendoes. That was a game with certain rules. This kiss had been different, and much more dangerous.

It had disarmed her, coming as it had during that spell of deep empathy. She still struggled to control her reactions. The appeal of what he might be offering shook her soul. A reflexive yearning gushed, frightening her with its force. It had been foolish to get drawn into that discussion of Alistair. She had revealed much more than she ever had to anyone before.

His quiet strength had encouraged that. It still beckoned, as surely as a hand reaching toward her, offering to make everything better.

They turned onto a dirt road and a little village appeared on the horizon. Its low, small buildings clustered picturesquely in the distance. A cart lumbered toward them, pulled by a woman and a youth. Three children walked alongside it.

She recognized the woman. Her name was Sarah, and she was the wife of Henry Johnson, a farmer. Both Sarah's and Henry's families had lived for generations on the estate as tenants.

The boy paused as she approached, more from fatigue than deference. He and his mother set down the cart's arms. Sophia noticed the cloth sacks that each of the children carried, and the pack sashed to Sarah's back.

"Your Grace," Sarah said, bobbing her head. Eight years had aged her tremendously. Sophia remembered a bright-eyed young mother, not this pale, tired matron.

"Sarah, it is good to meet a familiar face. I see that your brood has increased since I left. And your husband, Henry, how does he fare?"

The boy gestured to the cart with his head. "See for yourself."

She paced her horse around. Henry lay barely conscious inside the cart, wedged among pans and household goods. His pallor and labored breathing marked him as a very sick man.

"Mister Burchard, will you help me down, please."

He was with her at once, lowering her from the sidesaddle. Together they considered Henry's condition.

"He is dying," Adrian muttered.

"Sarah, what is ailing him?"

"Don't know, Your Grace. He's been poorly for months, just getting worse."

"What did the physician say?" Adrian asked.

"No money for a physician. Old woman Cooper gave us some potion, but it didn't help much."

Sophia surveyed the family, noticing again the cloth sacks. "Where are you going?"

Her son glared insolently. "Crops didn't get planted, did they? Steward knows no rent will be paid, so we are out."

"But your father . . ."

"Out of his head now. Won't know where he dies." He turned away, dismissing her interest. He bent to lift the cart's arms again, placing his young body where a donkey or ox should be.

"Turn the cart around, young man," she ordered. "Mister Burchard, will you help Sarah onto my horse? It is a long way back to the village, and she is exhausted."

Sarah looked confused and frightened. "Your Grace, the steward, he will—"

"You can remain in your home, Sarah. Marleigh is mine now. If I say that you can stay, that is how it will be."

Adrian lifted an astonished Sarah onto his horse, instead, and then settled two of the children on Sophia's. "I will help the boy," he said, taking the cart's other arm.

As they drew closer to the village, its details became clearer. The picturesque vignette turned into one of creeping decay. Adrian and the boy pulled the cart down a lane of graying wood and rotting plaster until they stopped in front of a sad little cottage. Adrian set down the cart's arm, carried Henry into the cottage, and then returned to lift the children and Sarah from the horses.

Sarah clasped Sophia's hand. "Your Grace, this is so generous. It will ease his passing so. We will be on our way afterwards, I promise you."

"Nonsense. I will have a physician sent, and perhaps Henry can be helped. If not, you will stay anyway, Sarah. Your son will be strong enough in a few years to manage the fields, and your other boy will be old enough to help him. I will see to your keep until then. Now, go and make Henry comfortable."

The family disappeared into the cottage. Adrian helped her onto her horse, his firm hands grasping her waist and his strong arms slowly lifting her. His closeness made her heady.

She surveyed the village as they rode out. "I do not remember it looking so poor."

"The cottages show little recent improvement."

"I cannot believe my father let things get to this state. He most likely never saw it. Tenants were just a source of income to him. It was my mother who knew their names and visited the sick. She probably badgered my father to make improvements. When she died, I suppose his conscience did too."

"It is your own conscience that will matter now. Such decisions are yours."

They were, weren't they? One word from her and this tired village could look once more as it did when she and Brandon would ride over to play with the tenants' children.

"I suppose that I can plan some improvements and establish some new policies before I leave."

He reached over and grabbed her horse's bridle, stopping her. "Leave?"

"Of course. I will nominate the candidates as agreed, but then I am returning to France."

"I do not think so. If you leave, I will probably be sent to drag you home again."

She jerked her horse from his grasp, and kept moving. "If I decide to go back, you cannot stop me."

"Try it and see whether I can or not," he said. "You have duties here. You just accepted that in helping that family. You cannot set policies and then leave the realm. Your stewards and managers will do things in the old ways if you are not here to oversee them."

"If I stay, those duties will form a yoke around my neck. They will control my life, and Alistair's ghost will be the teamster with the whip, driving me for the rest of my days."

His expression softened. "It will not go away. You cannot pretend it hasn't happened. And you have been given the power to do good too."

"Helping one family and improving a few cottages is easy. Managing all of it, that is different."

"Do you doubt that you can do it? I don't."

It was a simple statement, and not spoken in flattery. Just there, in his quiet, firm way.

Her heart lurched at the calm affirmation. It provoked that sense of empathy again. For a moment she tasted once more an intimacy such as she had not experienced in many years.

He assumed that she was better and stronger than she could ever be. She was going to disappoint him if he got to know her better.

She wanted badly to explain why she could not stay. Some things burned too deeply for her to confide, however, so she only broached the reason easiest to understand.

"If I accept the duties, the most important will be to preserve Everdon by giving birth to the next duke. When I marry, my own competence will no longer matter. I will be reduced to a figurehead. At least if I direct a steward from Paris, I will own him and not him own me. I cannot bear the notion of being chained to Gerald that way."

"It need not be Gerald."

"If I accept that part of it, it will not make any difference who the man is. It will be Everdon he marries, not Sophia Raughley."

"Until that day, it is yours as surely as if you were a man. You can use your position until you hand the reins to a husband. Why not take them up yourself for a while? Why not see whether being the Duchess of Everdon is in you?"

She almost laughed. She had made it a point never to discover what was in her.

His challenge prodded at her on the ride back to the house. It was strange to have someone who hardly knew her express belief in her abilities. Her own father had seen nothing but deficiencies.

The royal coach was waiting by the house when they arrived. The King would be leaving soon. She would have to run and change so that she could see him off.

She dismounted and faced Adrian under the eaves of the stable. "I think that you may be right. While I am in England, I should take up those reins."

"Your tenants will be glad for it."

"I do not think I should just attend to the lands. That is only one rein. If I am going to use this power for a while, I should try and do it right. My members of Parliament, for example."

His lids lowered. "What about them?"

"If I am expected to direct their votes after the election, I think that I should start learning all that I can about the issues."

From the expression on his face as she turned away, Sophia suspected that Adrian had not fully considered the implications before he encouraged her to take Everdon's power in hand.

She suffered the slow departure of guests, mentally urging them on. She had no history with these people. Since she had never come out, she had never enjoyed a London season. Everyone knew everyone else, but she knew almost no one at all.

The ghosts of Marleigh watched. She could feel their presence in the chambers and corridors. Her father and mother. Brandon, and the sister who had died as a baby. Even old servants from her childhood seemed to have left some of their essence in the building. The whole time she talked and sat and moved, she saw them in filmy pageants as memories distracted her. It only took an object or a smell to call them forth.

Finally only one guest remained. Gerald Stidolph had disappeared every-time a group departed, adroitly ducking below the current whenever the flow threatened to carry him out.

She found him in the drawing room after seeing off the last carriage. He stood near the terrace doors, gazing out to the garden, the image of a man determined to have his say.

She did not dislike Gerald exactly. He was very decent. He possessed no bad habits that she knew of. He stood tall and strong, his early years in the army still stiffening his posture. His face was composed of pleasant features and a strong jaw, and his sedate dress and short brown hair spoke of the temperance of his habits and tastes.

There wasn't anything specifically wrong with him. He was a little dull and a little too formal and a bit too enamored of power and wealth, but many women would consider him an appealing match.

So why had the very notion of marriage to Gerald always turned her blood cold? She contemplated him from the threshold and an eerie familiarity nudged at her. Suddenly she knew the answer. Marrying Gerald would be like marrying her father.

He stood like him. He walked like him. Now that she thought about it, he had adopted the duke's manner of speaking. The thoughtful pauses. The judgmental sarcasm that could shred even while it amused. Of all the people with whom Gerald had labored to ingratiate himself, the duke had been the primary target.

He had succeeded magnificently. In some ways, Gerald had become more the duke's offspring than even Brandon, and definitely more so than herself. Gerald had methodically modeled himself after the duke until, when the duke looked at him, he saw a younger version of himself. Small wonder her father had favored him, and had wanted him to have Everdon's power through her. It would be a form of life after death.

She walked toward him and he turned on the sound of her step. He hesitated, as if deciding how to deal with her. Would he have the good sense to play the petitioning admirer, and not the reincarnation of Alistair Raughley?

"I have overlooked much, Sophia, but your refusal to speak privately with me until now piques my annoyance."

"I had guests to attend to, Gerald."

"You managed to ignore them often enough when it suited you."

"True, but ignoring them in order to have an argument with you did not suit me."

"As willful as ever, I see. No doubt your time in Paris only reinforced those inclinations. It does you no credit."

"Circumstances mean that it is a duchess's will that I exert now. I am rather enjoying that."

"You made that abundantly clear yesterday with His Majesty. Your stubbornness was an embarrassment."

"Gerald, in the last half-minute you have criticized me three times. Is it any wonder that I grew obstinate at the King's suggestion that we marry?"

His censorious expression softened. "Forgive me. My surprise at your attitude has made me forget myself."

"No, it has interfered with your hiding yourself, and I am glad for it. I cannot imagine why my attitude should surprise you. I resented how Father tried to browbeat me into marriage when he was alive. Do not expect me to tolerate such handling from you and Wellington now that he is dead."

He held out his hands beseechingly and smiled. "I have blundered it badly, haven't I? This has gotten off to a bad start."

"I think it has gotten off to a splendid start. I had feared we might spend hours pretending first."

He evidently decided that petitioning admirer would be the better tack after all. He gestured to a settee. "Please sit with me, Sophia. I wish to learn how you have been."

She considered refusing to be diverted from the confrontation that needed to be finished. Years of training in civility won out, however, and she perched herself on the settee's edge.

Gerald eased beside her. His sharp brown eyes had grown hard with the years, but his expression of appeasement dulled their harshness a little.

"You are looking very lovely. Maturity suits you," he offered.

She looked terrible and she knew it. In fact, she had worked at it, and just for him too. He had never found her very lovely, not even when youth had given her some claim to it. She had overheard him once, when she was sixteen, frankly discussing her lack of beauty with a friend.

"By maturity you mean age. You think that I make an attractive spinster?"

He feigned a fluster. "I am heartened and grateful that you never married."

She considered telling him the lie about the secret husband. It would make mercifully quick work of this for the time being. Her pride resisted it. She had not needed the story of a violent husband to fend off Gerald when she was young and vulnerable. She certainly would not rely on a hoax to do so now.

"While in Paris I learned the sweet life available to a single woman of wealth. In comparison, marriage has little to recommend it."

"I have been told that you were a leading light in the arts circles there. It must have been fascinating."

"Yes, fascinating. And educational. And exciting. And sometimes, deliciously naughty. Paris was always freer than England, of course, but among the artistic community a whole separate code of behavior reigns."

She saw a scold begin forming, but he restrained himself. "Well, you are back home now at last. What is in the past is done with."

"Goodness, Gerald, do I hear absolution? You will forgive and ignore any indiscretions?"

"Of course, my dear."

"We wipe the slate clean? Any excesses are forgotten?"

"Certainly."

"And my young artists, Gerald, are you prepared to ignore them too? Father knew all about Paris. Certainly he told you."

This time the fluster was not feigned. "He did warn that you might come to our marriage with more experience than one might prefer."

"How nicely put. When did you plan to raise the problem with me, and conduct your interrogation?"

He flushed to his receding hairline. "I assumed that we would never speak of it. It is indelicate to do so."

"But you contemplate marriage. Would you never wonder? Never be jealous? For the rest of our lives, you intend to never ask about Paris, or throw your suspicions in my face? My father would never have restrained himself thus, nor, I think, would you. I suspect that there are men who could, but you are not one of them."

"I can understand that you might fear my anger about it. Is that the reason for your refusal yesterday? I promise you now, Sophia, that I will never ask about your lovers, or upbraid you for past liaisons."

"Yes, with a life interest in Everdon's wealth and a seat in the House of Lords as my dowry, I expect that you could forgive me just about anything."

"You insult me. My wish to marry you is not grounded in avarice and ambition."

"In what, then? Affection?"

"Of course."

"Please, let us at least keep this honest. Whatever you have convinced yourself, this is all about ambition. It always was. I do not begrudge you that. After Brandon died, I knew that no man could ever look at me again without seeing the map of this estate engraved on my face. Nor was it my concern about your reactions to my past that gave me reason for refusing you yesterday. I will not marry you, because I do not want to. You are too much like him, Gerald. Too much like Alistair. I went to Paris to escape him. I will hardly bind myself to him for life now."

"You speak nonsense. I am not Alistair."

"You imitated him for so long that you even look a bit like him now."

Signs of annoyance quivered through his face. What a battle it must be for him not to let loose the biting sarcasm that would establish his dominance.

"It was wrong of me to force this today. You are still tired from your journey. We will discuss this in a few days when you have reaccustomed yourself to where you are and who you are."

"I do not think so. For one thing, you will be back home by then."

"You are inviting me to leave?"

"I am accepting with regret your desire to depart in the morning."

He rose and paced away, as if composure were impossible if he remained beside her. "You need someone to take care of you, Sophia."

"I did well enough on my own in France. I am not a girl anymore, as you so ungenerously noted."

"It is not only that. I do not know if anyone has told you, but you may be in some danger."

"I know all about Captain Brutus, and the suspicions regarding my father's death. Even so, there is no point in your staying now. As it happens, I must leave at once to nominate my candidates."

This explanation for his dismissal relieved him. "Yes, of course. That must be done at once. I will arrange it, and accompany you."

"That is not necessary. I already have assistance. In fact, I already have a guardian for my safety. Wellington saw to everything."

He started, as if someone had poked him in the ribs. "I do not understand. Surely the duke would have consulted me. Who is this guardian who assists you?"

"Adrian Burchard."

"He will accompany you? It will not be proper."

"No less proper than if you did, since I share as much blood with him as I do you. Besides, I think it is safe to say that if Mister Burchard seeks a liaison with some woman, he can do better than me."

He had the good sense not to concur outright, but his expression cleared in agreement. That hurt more than she wanted to admit. For an instant she truly hated Gerald.

"I don't know why Wellington patronizes Burchard so much," he muttered.

"Maybe he sees something of himself in Mister Burchard. Older men often favor the young who possess similar traits. But then, you would know about that better than I."

"He more than favors him. Wellington has promoted Burchard in the party. He intends for him to get a position in the Treasury in the next government, with an income in the thousands. A rather large prize, no matter what services Burchard has performed or what talent he possesses. Even Dincaster thinks it excessive."

A thick fullness suddenly pressed inside her chest, choking her breath. So, Adrian had personal reasons for wanting this election to go a certain way. His bright political future, as mapped out by the great Wellington, depended upon it.

No wonder he was displaying such tenacity about staying with her. She had rather hoped . . . what had she hoped? Maybe that he really was motivated by concern for her safety. Maybe that something like friendship drove him.

It had been a mistake to agree he could accompany her to the boroughs. He was not doing it to protect her, but to manage her. As to what had happened this morning—well, a man who looked like Adrian Burchard probably knew all kinds of ways to make women come around.

Humiliation at her reaction to that kiss seeped through her, making her feel like a fool. She knew that he was Wellington's man, but she had not understood how ruthlessly he would exploit every opportunity to achieve his master's goals. But then, he had warned her, hadn't he? *Wellington thinks it would be convenient if I became your lover.*

An astonishing disappointment throbbed beneath her embarrassment. For an instant Gerald became Alistair, cruelly forcing her to face unpleasant realities. *He only uses you, Sophia. You are nothing but a means to an end for him.*

Not if she had anything to say about it. She had no intention of being used by any of them, least of all Adrian Burchard. She would make that very clear to him. She would sever the connections that had been stringing between them since that first night in Paris.

Foolish connections. Tempting and delicious too. Disillusionment stabbed sharply, penetrating her heart with wistful regret.

She pushed to her feet, suddenly exhausted to the bone. "Please forgive me, but I must rest now. I will leave early in the morning."

He took her hand between his two, making a little stack. How icy his skin felt, compared to Adrian's warmth. A false warmth. At least with Gerald, one knew what one had.

"I will come and see you when you return."

"Come when you will. This house has been more your home than mine for years. However, I will not change my mind about the marriage, Gerald. I will never get so reaccustomed to being home that I agree to that."

chapter 10

T he sun peeked over the park's horizon at Marleigh. It illuminated a confusion of activity in front of the house.

Obscured by the deep shadows in the woods that flanked the drive, a man watched the preparations for the duchess's journey. Servants ran out of the house with baggage that others stacked into a large wagon and tied to the huge coach that displayed Everdon's crest. A tall, somewhat foreign-looking gentleman lounged serenely against an open carriage as the chaos rained down around him.

The watcher narrowed his eyes on the waiting gentleman and a vicious annoyance spiked through his mind. He had not expected the duchess to arrange that kind of special protection. His own plans would have to change now.

He calmed himself by considering how this might be a blessing in disguise. Someone charged with protecting the duchess would recognize danger in ways the duchess might not herself, and help her to see her vulnerability. She was not strong, and would be more pliable if she was afraid. The sooner she felt helpless, the better. That had been the whole point of announcing with those broadsides that Captain Brutus was back, after all.

A groom exited the house with three large dogs on leads, accompanied by stable boys bearing cages. The servants who had just tied down everything in the wagon took one look at the new arrivals, made pantomimes of exasperation, and began untying the whole lot again.

A small figure dressed in black strode out of the house, waving her hand, calling for attention. A few feminine orders drifted on the breeze to the woods. A footman tried to speak to the duchess, but she marched to her coach.

From his dark spot in the trees, he watched the imperious display. It was not the first time he had seen little Sophia play the duchess since her return. He had witnessed it, from his hidden shadows, at the dock in Portsmouth and on the road as she traveled to Marleigh and even the day all those lords had descended. Yes, Sophia could appear quite formidable if she tried.

It would not matter. He knew her very well, in ways no one else did. He would have his way with her. She would do what he wanted.

He had known she would come back once her father died. Come back to him, to aid his quest. How convenient that her brother was gone too. Now she would help him achieve what was necessary, whether she wanted to or not. He would have justice and an accounting, and she would pay the old debt she owed.

The coach rolled. The open carriage, now filled with servants, followed. The wagon took up the rear. With an entourage like that, the duchess would make slow progress and be easy to find.

He walked through the woods to where he had left his horse. It was time for Sophia to learn exactly what coming home really meant.

"I need to tell them where I stand. I'll like as get lynched if I don't." Frustration tinged James Hawkins' emphatic statement.

He echoed the concerns of the three other Cornwall M.P.'s whom Sophia had nominated this day.

The duchess gave Hawkins a sympathetic smile. Adrian noted that it had been one of the few to crack her face all day. She had been in a prickly mood ever since leaving Marleigh.

The departure itself had been a confused affair. Adrian knew that she did not travel light, but the parade of grand coach, servants' carriage, and wagons loaded with animal cages and portmanteaus proved she had little experience with logistics. By the time she had finally emerged from the house and abruptly ordered them all off, he was very sure she had lost track of what and whom had been packed. Since she had insisted that he not interfere, he had not felt obliged to mention several glaring omissions.

It had been afternoon before it all rolled into Lyburgh. Determined to hold to her schedule, the duchess had left the servants and wagons in the town and continued immediately on to the nearby boroughs.

Now, instead of retiring to rest for tomorrow's journey, she had invited Hawkins to join her for an evening supper at the inn in Lyburgh, where her entourage had been left earlier. She had not even visited her chamber first, so she did not know about the surprise that awaited her there.

The youthful, blond, handsome M.P. had been awed and delighted that his patroness had honored him. He now picked at his lamb and bubbled with earnestness. For twenty minutes he had been regaling the duchess with breathless stories regarding the tense mood of the population.

She sat across the table from Hawkins in the private room where they all ate, giving the callow young man her attention.

All of it.

Adrian bristled. Her attitude toward him had been cool and distant all day. Their hours in the coach had been very silent. They might have never taken that ride and built that bridge.

Hawkins himself further pricked Adrian's annoyance. The young man was about the same age as Ensemble members present and past. At best, a year or two out of university, he was the son of a local gentry family and no doubt expected to be Prime Minister one day.

"You will have to explain that you are assessing the various positions on reform and will exercise judgment in due time," Sophia said with a sweet smile.

"Not sure that will work, Your Grace."

"It will have to. It is the truth, isn't it?"

Hawkins looked confused by the question, as well he might. His own judgment had nothing to do with it.

"What *is* your view on all of this so far, Mister Hawkins?" she asked. "I value it, since you have been in the thick of things while I have been abroad. No, do not look to Mister Burchard for permission to speak your mind. I am sincerely interested in what you have to say, and it will not be held against you."

Hawkins flushed and debated his answer.

Adrian waited for him to choose the wrong one, which of course he did.

"Well, Your Grace, I'm not sure it can be avoided. Reapportionment, that is. I've actually got an opponent in the election. He has come out solidly for reform and he may win."

"Nonsense," Adrian interrupted. "There are only thirty voters in your borough, and twenty of those men farm lands on lease from Everdon. Your seat is secure."

"That is how it is supposed to work, but there's been lots of talk here in town, and broadsides flying." Hawkins fished in his pocket and withdrew a stack of folded papers. "They have a way of inflaming people."

Sophia unfolded the three pages and perused them with a puckered brow. She halted over the second one. Adrian noticed its signatory name. Captain Brutus.

He plucked it up along with the others, from under her suddenly frozen expression. "More nonsense," he said, stuffing them in his coat. "Your borough will vote you in. Unless you plan to exercise unseemly independence once seated, your position will remain secure. As to any consideration which you may have given to such a move, I remind you that during the last Parliament your seat was one of those slated for abolishment."

The young M.P. actually had the brass to work up some indignation. "To be sure, Burchard. Still, a man has a brain and a soul, no matter what his debts. There are times when the greater good—"

"Let others with more experience judge the greater good."

"Enough, gentlemen," Sophia said. "Straddle the fence for now, Mister Hawkins. I must still educate myself on this issue and have not yet decided how my M.P.'s should vote."

She turned a melting smile on Hawkins. "Let us be done with politics. Tell me about yourself. Have you any special interests besides government?" She reached over and patted his arm.

Hawkins' gaze slid to the informal gesture. Suddenly he looked very much a man and not at all a lad. Possibilities instantly loomed behind his clear blue eyes.

"I have a great passion for the literary arts, Your Grace."

"A scholarly interest?"

"I confess that I dabble myself. Poetry."

Sophia's face lit with admiration. Hawkins drank it in. Adrian could practically hear the young man calculating that the duchess was an attractive, worldly woman with whom an affair would be appealing and advantageous.

"You must let me read some of your poetry. When we go up to London for the sessions, I expect you to visit and bring them," she said. "What form do you prefer? Sonnets? Epics?"

They embarked on a spirited dialogue of poets and poetry, of rhymes and meter. Adrian drank his wine, watching like an intruding chaperon. Sophia forgot Adrian existed, but Hawkins did not. He glanced over on occasion. *Time to remove yourself, old man,* those darting looks said. *You know how it goes.*

Yes, he did. He read Hawkins like an open book, and could see Sophia's familiarity turning vague speculation into bold decision. The belief that he might become the lover of the Duchess of Everdon before morning glimmered in the sparkling looks Hawkins gave her.

The hell you will, boy.

The three mastiffs dozed by the hearth. Adrian dropped his arm and quietly snapped his fingers. Suddenly awake, they rose in formation. They began circling the table, eyeing its scraps.

The canine entourage interrupted a lengthy discussion about Coleridge. Sophia scolded the dogs to no avail.

"It appears they want to go out," Adrian said. At the last word they pranced over to her with excitement. "They have been away from you all day and are acting jealous. I would take them, but I don't think it will pacify them."

Her frown broke as her demanding children drooled delight at her attention. With a mother's sigh she rose. "Mister Burchard is right, you must excuse me, Mister Hawkins. I always give them a brief walk in the evening. There is still a bit of light, so I had best do it now." She fetched their leads from a bench near the hearth. "Only down the street and back, Yuri. Feel free to smoke, gentlemen."

With hounds straining for freedom, she tripped out of the chamber.

He knew which chamber was hers. While her entourage had unpacked and settled into the inn, he had joined them, one more anonymous body moving about in the confusion, with hat pulled low and boots scuffed with dirt. The inn servants had assumed he was with the duchess, and the duchess's servants thought him with the inn, and no one had given him more than a passing glance.

He stood beneath the side eaves of the stable, waiting in the gathering dusk. Through a lower window he could see her face at the table, and the profiles of two men. She should retire soon.

His boot tapped the sack on the ground. Time for Sophia to learn that the man with first claims on her heart and soul was very close by.

A movement caught his eye. Sophia had risen and left the table. He waited for her companions to do the same.

The inn's door opened, and Sophia stepped out into the twilight. She was not alone. Three huge dogs lunged ahead, straining on their leads, pulling her into the lane.

The temptation to follow entered his head. She would be alone and vulnerable.

His better sense rejected the idea. So did the presence of those dogs. No, he would wait, and take this in the small steps he had planned. The unseen watcher was more unnerving than the assailant. Fear would give him more power than any attack ever could, and his ultimate goal was not really about her at all. He had to remember to keep those things separate.

He settled against the stable wall to wait, but the impulse to follow did not die. He pictured her tripping down the silent lanes, and saw himself following and dragging her into an alley and releasing all the fury against her that had built in him over the long years.

The possibilities titillated him, tempting him to give in to the cold anger in his blood. Bitterness beckoned him to forget the bigger game in favor of some personal satisfaction.

Hawkins lit a cigar and assumed the demeanor of a contented man biding his time.

"I expect the duchess will be gone longer than she thinks. The dogs will expect a good walk," Adrian advised.

"There is a moon if I need to ride back after dark falls."

Adrian poured them both some port. "I admire your self-confidence. At your age I would have been less at ease with the notion."

Hawkins drew on his cigar in a cocky manner. "Well, I have had a lot of experience."

"I envy your precocity. I was a few years older than you before I even had my first affair with a Frenchwoman, let alone sufficient experience that would let me face the next few hours with the *savoir faire* that you are showing."

"Frenchwoman? The duchess is not French."

"Officially not, but she has lived in Paris for eight years."

The smallest frown marred Hawkins' perfect brow.

Adrian stretched out his legs and gestured with his cigar through their cloud of smoke. "The first time was a shock for me. Claudette, her name was. An angel in the drawing room. Who would have thought she could be such a taskmaster in bed? But then, you know all about that, eh? I say that their French lovers have spoiled them, don't you agree?"

"Um, well . . ."

"Nothing but demands. I didn't even know what she was after half the time. The really discomfiting part was being compared. One always suspects that with a woman of experience, but at least English ladies are discreet and don't *tsk* and sigh about it."

Hawkins fidgeted.

"Of course, Claudette really was French and her imperfect English might have had something to do with her bluntness. Presumably a woman who was fluent in our language would be able to express her disappointment with more tact."

Hawkins smiled weakly. "No doubt."

"Yes, I admire your aplomb, especially since you will be dealing with the duchess long-term. I remember untold relief when Claudette's family was called back to France. I am thoroughly impressed, Hawkins. I had no idea you were such a man of the world." He fished in his pocket and withdrew the broadsides. "Now, tell me about this sheet here. The one signed Captain Brutus."

Hawkins blinked away whatever worries distracted him while he perused the paper.

"A new name. I doubt it is a local," he said, handing it back. "More virulent than the others. The last line caused a lot of talk. *If the aristocrats will not share the power, it must be seized from them.* Damned revolutionary sounding, isn't it? I hear that up north there are a lot of such calls, but not in Cornwall."

"True, but then Cornwall has more than its share of boroughs. What kind of talk did it raise?"

"More agreement than one would like. Emotions are running high here. The whole country is a tinderbox."

"When did this appear?"

"Some boys were posting it around the town today. They said a man called them into an alley and offered them three pence each."

"*Today?*"

Captain Brutus had been in this town this very day.

Cursing himself, Adrian leapt out of his chair.

He was halfway to the door when it opened. Sophia stumbled in, dragged by Yuri and his jubilant brothers.

Slowly, very slowly, Adrian's heart returned to a normal beat.

"I fear that took longer than I expected," she said, pulling the dogs in line. "I should bring them upstairs to my chamber where the cages are. Finish your cigar, Mister Hawkins. We can continue momentarily." She disappeared again.

Adrian gritted his teeth. She had actually invited Hawkins to stay. Right in front of him.

"If you will excuse me, I will retire," he said.

"Don't! . . . that is, don't you think it would be improper? If she is returning . . ."

He was damned if he would watch this unfold. "I leave you a clear field. However, if you take uninvited liberties, I will make you wish you had never been born."

The warning came out a tad too pointedly.

Hawkins flushed. "I should take my leave. Not all that much moon tonight, and what with those broadsides, there could be trouble on the road later."

Seeing that his sabre had found its mark, Adrian could not resist twisting it. "They have no argument with you. Besides, if all unfolds as you expect, you will be busy until dawn."

"*Dawn?* Oh, yes, all the same, I wouldn't want to wear out my welcome."

"No fear of that. The duchess invited you to stay." He clamped a firm grasp on Hawkins' shoulder. "Do England proud, my man."

Hawkins edged toward the door. "She should rest, what with the other boroughs to be visited. You will give her my farewell, won't you?"

He hurried out of the room.

Adrian awaited Sophia's return. No matter what her intentions with Hawkins, she would be back. For one thing, right about now she was discovering the surprise up in her chamber.

In short order the quiet inn sounded with stomping feminine feet descending the stairs. The door flew open and a furious column of black crepe trembled in the threshold. She looked absolutely stunning when her green eyes flashed like that.

She nailed him with an accusing glare. "Where is Jenny?"

"Where you left her, I expect."

"I left her here this afternoon with the other carriage and the wagon. But she is not in my chamber, and nothing has been prepared. Camilla's cage is empty, too, but if she had taken her out I would have seen them when I walked the dogs."

"You indeed left her, but not here. She is back at Marleigh."

"Do not be absurd. She was with the footmen in the other carriage when we departed."

"I am sure she was not. She had gone up to fetch Camilla and you ordered your entourage off before she returned."

Her brow puckered while she searched her memory. She strode over and stuck her face up at him. "You *knew*. Why didn't you say something?"

"You made it explicitly clear that I was not to interfere. When one of your footmen tried to explain and you wouldn't listen, I assumed you had decided at the last moment not to take Jenny and Camilla." His pique about Hawkins got the better of him. "After all, you could hardly initiate a liaison with a man if Jenny slept in your chamber."

"You dared to manipulate it so that I would not have my maid with me?"

She had misunderstood. She thought that he referred to a liaison with himself, not Hawkins.

On the other hand, she had misunderstood nothing. He had considered the provocative possibilities presented by this journey.

The evidence that she also had recognized them raised a sensual edge in his annoyance with her. She had never intended to take Hawkins as a lover. She had only been using the young M.P., much as she had used her brittle mood all day, to create a shield.

He held her wary gaze with his own, letting her see that he understood, enjoying her growing discomfort more than was fair. This special vulnerability hardly incited the protective response that he often felt for her. Very different inclinations took over, and he did nothing to suppress them.

They had just crossed a line, and he would not pretend they had not.

She knew as soon as she blurted it out that she had made a mistake. His gaze sharpened with a heart-stopping expression that made it very clear that he was a man and that she was a woman who thought he wanted to sleep with her. It had been a huge error to make that explicit. She had stupidly kicked open a door and he did not look inclined to let her shut it again.

His eyes burned with a frank warmth. "When I spoke of a liaison, I referred to our junior M.P., not myself."

She walked away with a scalding face. It felt as if her body were iron that she had to yank from a magnet. "No matter whom you meant, it was extremely presumptuous of you to let me travel without my maid."

"Since presumptuous was the earl's favorite rebuke in my youth, I dislike the word intensely. Do not use it with me again unless you want to see just how presumptuous I can be."

The subtle threat sent a dismaying streak of excitement down her core. "You have been overbold from the start, and much more so this evening. It must be the port."

"Having just watched you with Hawkins, I have concluded that I have been far too timid."

She whirled around at him. "Your insinuation is insulting. I was holding a simple conversation."

"He pursued more than a conversation, and you know it."

"Why shouldn't I enjoy his attention? Do you think he forced himself to flatter me merely out of his own self-interest?" *Like you.*

"Every man's pursuit of a woman contains an essential self-interest, and I do not think that Hawkins had to force himself at all. I have thought from the first that making love to you would be very pleasant. I daresay he reached the same conclusion. With your encouragement."

The announcement of his thoughts was cast out straightforwardly. From the start he had always spoken to her with a disconcerting man-to-woman tenor, but tonight the casual wit had been dropped.

"Where is he?" She felt a need for the protection of another person. Anyone would do.

"He felt obliged to leave."

"What did you say to him?"

"Nothing to hasten his departure. Rather the opposite."

"What did you say?"

"I reminded him that you had asked him to stay. Oh, yes, I recall that I also admonished him to do England proud."

"To do England proud?"

"Considering the international flavor of your diversions in Paris, we wouldn't want you disappointed in your own countryman."

He strolled toward her. She almost jumped out of her skin.

"What is this fascination that you have with boys barely out of school, Duchess? Do they seem safe to you? Controllable? You can dole out only what you choose to bestow and they are too callow to comprehend what you withhold?"

The room moved. No, she did. She instinctively backed away. She bumped into a stool and almost fell. He reached to help her but she righted herself and scurried far out of the way.

He reacted to her clumsy distress with a devastating smile. She pulled herself into some semblance of dignity while she edged away from his meandering approach. "My fascinations are my own business. Or do you intend to manage my love life now too?"

"That is exactly what I intend."

Now, that was blunt. Her flirtation with Hawkins had probably forced his hand.

She dug in her heels and stood her ground. He advanced until only an inch separated them and she could smell the soap that he used. Stubbornness stiffened her straight.

"Now you truly are being presumptuous."

"Despite my warning, you provoke me again with that accusation, when my behavior thus far has been anything but presumptuous."

"You can say that with a straight face? Since the moment that you stepped into my house in Paris you have engulfed me in a wave of high-handed, tyrannical, *presumptuous* interference."

"I have been a citadel of restraint in the things that matter."

"You don't think that where I live matters? You don't think that being carried out of my home like a carpet matters?"

"I think that we are really speaking about other things. For example, true presumption would be taking you in my arms right now and kissing you again."

Her eyes narrowed. "Don't you dare." The words came out one by one in flat enunciation.

"After a challenge like that, I think that I must."

She could have gotten away. He hesitated just long enough for her to stop it, but she decided that the only way to end his dishonorable game was to let him kiss her again and show absolutely no reaction.

That was the plan, at least.

Strength and warmth encompassed her. Fingers stretched into her hair, to position her head. The decisive pressure of his lips and the command of his embrace took control.

This was not the kiss in the garden, or even the one in the park. Masterfully, deliberately, he drew passion from wherever it hid in her. With a greed that stunned her, the void of loneliness accepted the offer of intimacy, heedless of the cost. Her soul groaned with relief, as if a long thirst was being quenched. Her secure understanding of his motivations quickly dimmed, eclipsed by the marvelous glow of pleasure sparkling in brilliant rays.

Within instants she possessed no control over any of it. She neither encouraged nor denied, but she definitely reacted. When the kiss deepened and he demanded more, her limp will acquiesced. She permitted the startling, invasive joining that meant she could never lie about this kiss in the future.

If it could have gone on just like that, she might have welcomed the connection forever. To surrender to such innocent happiness, to breathe in another's essence and bask in another's light, created a bliss that blotted out all unpleasant memories and realities. To be wanted at all, for whatever reason, soothed the oldest hungers in ways that overwhelmed her.

He broke the kiss but pulled her closer. With palm on her cheek and thumb caressing her lips, he looked down with a breath-stopping warmth. If he kissed her again, she would have no strength to stop him.

"An even greater presumption would be for me to escort you to your chamber and not leave you at the door as I had intended."

The warning was really an oblique request. In demanding that she choose, he threw a lifeline into the turbulent river of her emotions. Gratefully, regretfully, she grabbed it. "A good thing that you are not a presumptuous man, then."

His lips brushed hers gently. "That was not the answer I hoped for."

"It is the one that I have to give."

"Pity. I had hoped to discover what was underneath all those layers."

"Just an average body. You have undoubtedly known better."

"I did not refer to layers of petticoats. I have already seen what is under them." He released her. "If you are determined to thwart my great conquest, we had better get you some sleep. Tomorrow will be a long day."

For a man who had just been rejected, he was taking it awfully well. Better than she was.

He held out his hand in that commanding way of his. She forced her body not to tremble while she let him lead her from the chamber and hand her up the stairs of the silent, sleeping inn.

They stopped in front of her door. She almost crumbled with relief when he made no move to enter. At least she told herself that the emotion that sagged down to her toes was relief, even if it felt a bit like disappointment too. She nervously jimmied the key in the lock.

"It seems that with Jenny's absence we have finally found a role for me in your entourage."

She froze with renewed caution. "It is bad form for you to pursue this. We will not be lovers. Wellington will have to be disappointed."

"I meant the role of lady's maid."

"I will find an inn servant to help."

"They have all gone to bed."

"I can manage on my own."

"If so, you are the only woman who can." He firmly turned her to face the door. Nimble fingers found the closure of her gown, and the black fabric loosened.

"I said that I can manage," she repeated desperately, twisting to escape. He pressed her back in place until she hugged the door's oak planks.

Level by level, with excruciating slowness, he unlaced her stays. The warmth of his hands permeated the thin chemise underneath. She tried to give voice to indignation, but vibrating sensations full of forbidden desires and anticipation trapped her voice in her throat.

Finally the gown and stays gaped loosely down her back to her hips. She reached behind and tried to clutch them closed.

"So now you see what is beneath the layers," she said nervously, fumbling at the door key with her other hand.

A sly caress snaked up her spine. "I never forgot the soft pale skin, or the pleasant curves in my arms."

She trembled so badly it seemed as if the corridor had shaken. The damn key was sticking. "You have the advantage on me again, since I was unconscious."

"You aren't unconscious now."

That was an understatement. She was awkwardly, embarrassingly, unnaturally alert. Her back felt him as if he pressed against her even though space separated them.

He stepped closer and the space became very tiny. He slid her gown down her shoulder and bent to kiss the exposed flesh. The heat of his lips seared right into her blood. Only his commanding hold on her arms kept her upright.

He turned his mouth to her neck. Mesmerizing pleasure shot through her in hot little streaks. His magnetic aura lured her, waiting an inch away. The temptation to sink back into his confident strength almost defeated her.

She closed her eyes and savored the glory for a moment, then gritted her teeth and bent away, twisting and turning so that she faced him. "Unconscious or not, you still have the advantage and it is not fair to press it. What if someone comes out of another chamber and sees me like this?"

"Then open your door and go inside."

"The key is stuck."

He took it from her and poked the lock. Of course it turned at once. He pushed the door open.

"You will not come in," she said. "I do not want you to." A lie, that. A pitiful lie.

"I have never had much patience with the games that accompany these things. For whatever reason, you will not let me make love to you tonight. But you do want me to, maybe almost as much as I want to."

"Your self-confidence is extremely presumptuous."

"At least I am a presumptuous man and not a presumptuous boy. We will have to find a way to overcome your fear of that."

He stepped aside. Forcing her heart down out of her throat, she backed in, clutching her gaping gown and stays to her back.

Humiliation suffused her as soon as the door closed. So much for the sophisticated woman of the world. Instead of putting him in his place, she had fumbled and stumbled and melted like a schoolgirl.

But, heaven help her, she had not known that he would be so bold. Or so merciless. Nor that her attraction to him would make her so weak.

This was not like her flirtations in Paris. This man created cravings that she had never expected to know. The excitement obscured reality and reason. The pleasure even submerged her resentments of why he pursued her.

Nothing but disillusionment waited if he succeeded. She could not let this happen again, that much was certain.

There was only one way to make sure it would not.

They made love on white sand at the edge of the surf. Red silk formed the sea, lapping lightly against them, as if air created its swells. A turquoise tent of sky stretched above, framing Sophia's face. Clouds of gold drifted overhead.

Pleasure moistened her eyes, and joy softened her mouth. She eased forward so he could lick the tips of her breasts. Her sighs of anxious desire came in a rapid rhythm that matched the speed of his thrusts. He caressed up the thighs straddling his hips. Grabbing her waist he pressed her body close and careened toward the end. Her scream pierced the bliss, and shattered the world. . . .

Adrian's eyes snapped open. An aggressive chorus of dog barks assaulted his disoriented senses.

The scream had been real. A scream of shock, not ecstasy.

He shot out of bed and dragged on trousers and shirt and boots. He threw open the door and instantly faced the backs of two footmen dressed in Everdon's livery. The hounds' vicious snarls behind Sophia's door discouraged any investigation.

"We heard glass break and her scream," one explained. "Someone should go in, don't you think?" He stepped aside, making clear who he thought the someone should not be.

One of the inn's maids fretted near the stairs. "She came for me to fix her gown, then sent me to wake the coachman and footmen," she said. "I didn't see no one about, sir."

Adrian shoved open the door and strode into Sophia's chamber. The mastiffs were halfway to his throat before they caught his scent. They quieted immediately and crowded his legs, demanding orders to kill someone.

An open portmanteau stood beneath a broken window whose remaining shards hung like teeth. Splintered glass littered the floor. Sophia sat on the bed in last night's black gown, holding a wad of cloth to her arm. She turned wide, terrified eyes on him.

He went over and moved her hand away. With a firm rip he tore her sleeve apart. Blood oozed freely from a cut near her shoulder. He wiped it away with the cloth, and then pressed against the wound.

"You are understandably frightened, but you are safe now. For all the blood, it is not a bad cut. Tell me what happened."

She gestured toward the corner of the chamber. A good-sized rock rested there. "Someone hurled it through the window. It missed me. I was cut by a piece of flying glass."

A mixture of anger and worry clapped through him. "You could have been seriously injured. Had you been leaning over that portmanteau, the glass would have showered you. If you had been in bed as you should be at this hour, you wouldn't have been hurt at all."

"Well, I wasn't in bed."

"No, you were up and packing at three o'clock in the morning. Your footmen are dressed for travel, as are you."

"I could not sleep. Since there is a moon, I decided to make good use of the time."

"So you roused your whole retinue. Except me."

"Weren't you told? Goodness, that was a terrible oversight."

"The oversight was deliberate, and we both know it."

She glared at him, pushed his hand away, and took the cloth from him. She blanched when she saw how much blood it had absorbed.

"It looks worse than it is," he reassured again. He let her tend to herself for the time being, and walked over to the rock.

There was a folded paper tied to it. A letter. He scanned down to the signature. Captain Brutus.

The note carried a familiar tone. Its writer urged the duchess to see the light, and cajoled her to support not just Parliamentary reform but also universal suffrage. He scolded her for hesitating to use her new power for the greater good. He addressed her as "Sweet Sophia," closed with unseemly affection, and claimed to presume the communication because of their "old friendship."

Nowhere did it contain any threats, but Captain Brutus was letting the duchess know that he was back, that he was watching, and that hurting her would be easy.

He gave her the letter. "I doubt that your attacker is still about, but I will go and check to be sure."

He made an inspection of the streets nearby, but Lyburgh slept silently. No evidence of Captain Brutus could be found.

He returned to the inn's carriage yard. Everdon's grand coach stood ready, with its horses in rein. The coachman lounged at its open door.

"Where is the other carriage? And the wagon?" Adrian asked.

The coachman groaned. "Will she be wanting them, too, now? If so, it will delay us. Just so's she knows that."

"Actually, she will not be wanting any of them. The duchess has changed her mind and will wait until morning."

Shaking his head at the inconstancy of women, the coachman lumbered to the lead horses and began undoing all of his labor.

Inside the inn, Adrian found the two footmen cooling their heels in the public room.

"You will be relieved to know that Her Grace was not badly hurt," he said. "Where are the others?"

"We were all the inn maid came and got. Just to be us, she made that very clear. Tom and Harry are still asleep, unless the noise woke them," one explained.

One carriage and only two footmen. Free of the slower vehicles, that coach could make good speed. He doubted she had planned to aim for the next borough.

"I expect that her change in plans surprised you."

"Not for us to question, is it? If the duchess wants to leave at night instead of morning, if she wants to go to Portsmouth instead of Devon, we do it."

"The plans have changed again. Her Grace has thought better of this night journey."

Adrian headed for the bedchambers. The maid still huddled on the top stair. He sent her for some warm water and salves, then returned to Sophia.

The letter had fallen to the floor by her feet. Blood smears on the paper said she had read it.

He took over with the cloth again. "I had hoped the suspicions about Captain Brutus were wrong, but that letter says not. I apologize for prying, but now I need you to tell me about him. What is his real name?"

"I do not know. He was sentenced to New South Wales as John Brutus."

"Would you recognize him?"

"He was an educated young man. Golden-haired. Of middle height and stature. Eyes ablaze with purpose. I do not know if I would recognize him. Seven years of servitude probably wrought some changes."

Her expression had softened with a wistful sadness. A pulse of jealousy beat quietly in Adrian's head.

"How did you know him?"

"I chanced upon him one day by accident. I rode deep into the woods that edge the estate. Suddenly I entered a clearing and there he was with five other young men, like a Robin Hood. They were preparing to go on one of their raids that night, to burn threshing machines. The whole county had been in an uproar about him for weeks. I was not alone in finding his grow-ing legend very exciting and romantic."

"You are lucky that you left that clearing alive."

"He only asked for my oath of silence. Two days later a note came for me, unsigned, asking me to come to the woods' edge that afternoon. I knew it was from him. Mother had died recently and my life was terribly vacant. I went. Five times over the next month we spent the afternoon together."

"Your father found out?"

She nodded. "He never confronted me. He never asked me to betray him, but he arranged for the betrayal anyway. He let me learn that a trap was be-ing set one night. Of course I ran to tell Captain Brutus. But I was the trap. Papa and some others followed me. I never forgave my father for using me like that. He in turn produced evidence that Brutus had been learning the movements of the landowners from me, so that he could plan his raids. My Robin Hood had a reason for listening to my girlish social gossip. I guess I never forgave my father for laying that out so brutally either. The lesson of the episode was not lost on me."

He did not doubt that. Two men who claimed to care for her had used her to their own ends most ignobly.

"When he went before the Assize court, my father demanded that I bring witness. I refused. Papa tried to break me the way you might a horse. He browbeat me endlessly." She shrugged. "When that did not work, he beat me literally."

Adrian bit back a curse, but a breath of it sounded anyway.

He pictured Alistair Raughley, self-righteous in his sense of civic duty, taking strap or cane to her. Outrage scorched at the image, flaming higher from memories of his own beatings at the hands of the earl. During his youth he had been the family whipping boy, receiving the punishment no matter who instigated the transgressions.

The idea that she had experienced the same brutality wrenched some-thing inside him. Whippings could be the least of it, of course. A father's coldness could lash in a thousand ways without a hand being raised.

A pained expression flickered, cracking her composure. "You are wonder-ing if it worked. It did. I brought witness at the court against that young man, about what I had seen in that clearing and what he had told me."

"He was a criminal and Alistair was your father. To anyone's mind, your choice was clear."

"I sent him to hell, Burchard."

The maid entered with the water. He instructed her to place it on the washstand and go and wait outside the door. He removed the cloth and checked the cut. "It does not look as if it needs sewing. The maid can get it cleaned and bandaged. I do not think you need a surgeon."

"I am relieved to hear it. I would not like to be delayed by it."

"If you still think to leave tonight, you are mistaken. I have told your coachman that you will not be departing until morning after all."

"You had no right to do that."

"You can hardly travel with that wound still fresh, and you should rest."

"I will wait until morning to depart, but I intend to be off at dawn."

"Dawn it will be. There will be one other change, however. You will not go to Portsmouth so you can sail back to France. I am keeping you in England, where I have some control over your safety."

Reference to her safety checked her argument. Either that or acceptance that her plan had failed.

"You will sleep in my chamber," he said.

"I will not." She pointedly looked him over, reminding him that he was dressed informally, to say the least.

"This is not a contrivance to spend the night with you. You will use my chamber and I will take this one. Whoever did this knew which window was yours. I do not think that we will see any more drama tonight, but we will not take the chance."

She began to protest, but thought better of it. Her shoulders sagged. "You think that I am a coward."

It wasn't clear if she meant because she had intended to run away, or because she refused to share a chamber. The notion that the two were related occurred to him.

"You said at Marleigh that you would try taking up the reins. Why did you decide to flee to France?"

"I changed my mind. Frivolous women like me do that all the time." She spoke flippantly, but her gaze met his eyes and then slowly descended. It lingered for a moment on the gape in his shirt that exposed his chest. For one delicious moment he expected her to lay her hand on his skin.

She looked away. "I will have the maid clean up the glass. It is dangerous."

Her retreat into practicalities did not fool him. He understood why she had decided to flee. It had not been the act of a frivolous woman, because she was not frivolous, despite the mask that she often showed the world.

She was frightened of him, and of what had started. Nor was she indifferent. She would not have to run away if she were.

"Would you prefer if I separated from your entourage? Will this duty be easier if I am not with you?" The words were harder to say than he expected.

She thoughtfully toed at the letter on the floor. "If something happened to me, Wellington would have your head. Also, it appears that I may need some protection after all. Under the circumstances, it may be best if you come along."

"Will you promise that I will not wake one morning to find you have taken the coach to a seaport?"

"I will see this part of it through. Leaving was a foolish impulse. The enormity of it all overwhelmed me suddenly, that is all. I will manage it in the future."

She shot him a glance that clarified her declaration. *I will manage you in the future.*

The carriages and wagon lumbered back into Devon. Each mile took them closer to a storm.

Heavy black clouds announced the oncoming tempest, but it was not a spring rain that kept Adrian alert. Other signs of a different kind of storm claimed his attention, and, on occasion, his intervention. The *thud* of a clod of dirt against the carriage. The curse of a wagoner when he saw the ducal crest. The milling of farmers along the fields' edges, and the hateful shouts that they yelled at the passing noble.

There had been trouble on the way from Portsmouth to Marleigh, but this was more consistent. It was as if someone had guessed the duchess's route and was riling the people deliberately.

Adrian knew who that person undoubtedly was.

The last stop of the day was Haford. This was not a rotten borough, but a largely populated one in the shadow of one of Everdon's coastal manors, Staverly.

A steady rain greeted their arrival. The whole countryside seemed to have congregated in the town. Silent tension quivered off the congested streets in a way that made the earlier demonstrations seem benign.

Harvey Douglas, the M.P., appeared oblivious to both rain and danger. He met the carriage with a broad-toothed smile parting his tawny mustache and beard. It turned out that the duchess knew him.

"It is good to see you, Mister Douglas. When I saw the list of candidates, I was delighted to recognize at least one name."

He helped Adrian guide her to the local inn. Already the wagons were being unloaded there. "Saved enough as your father's steward at Staverly to buy some property, I did. Was proud as a man can be when he offered me the seat. I'd like to think that I've done the job as well as any man could."

He grinned at Adrian for confirmation. Douglas had indeed been the consummate puppet M.P. He never expressed an opinion and probably did not possess any. Other "owned" members of the Commons sometimes chafed at their obligations, but Douglas thrived on them because politics did not interest him at all. His position gained him entrée into drawing rooms otherwise closed to him, and he got to play the big man at county assemblies. He was understandably grateful to the dead duke for the gift of social elevation.

And also grateful to Gerald Stidolph. Adrian remembered that it had been Stidolph who had recommended Douglas for the seat when its last occupant passed on five years ago. Stidolph's influence in the matter had made his own position in the duke's favor very clear to everyone.

"The town is unusually busy considering it is not market day," Adrian observed as they all shook off the rain.

"They're curious. Haven't seen the duchess in years. It's all Everdon land around here. I had the husting put up near the church. I expected a crowd, what with the duchess returning, and thought they would want to see it. I hadn't thought it to rain, of course."

"We will go to the church shortly," Adrian instructed. "I will tell you now that the duchess is making no formal statement regarding reform."

"I don't understand. The duke—"

"It is for the duchess to decide now."

"But I've already let it be known how we stand. He made it very clear on the last bill how we were to vote. You know that, Burchard. You are the one who gave us the word."

Sophia cocked her head. "It was not for you to let it be known without my saying so, Mister Douglas."

"Of course, Your Grace. But people have been asking, and Mister Stidolph explained that Everdon would stand against any new bill as it did the last one."

She stood, assuming the formidability that she could summon unexpectedly. "Do not assume that Mister Stidolph, or anyone else, knows Everdon's mind now. No one will give you the word on this except me. Until I do, you are not to speak in my name. Now, if you understand that, I am ready."

The main coach had already been taken away, but the servants' open carriage still stood outside the inn. Adrian requisitioned it from the groom and handed Sophia in. He took reins in hand and trotted quickly to the church. The farmers and townspeople formed a river behind them.

By the time they had all taken their places on the platform, at least three hundred men and women had gathered to hear their landlord speak. Adrian wished they were not so quiet.

Douglas introduced the duchess with a long speech that extolled her father's benign rule in the region.

Sophia stepped forward to speak. Silence fell until only the splattering rain could be heard. She launched into her standard nomination.

She never got past the third sentence. The tension in the crowd snapped, releasing a barrage of emotion.

It was as if someone had given a signal.

"Support reform!" a man called.

"We want our due!"

"Go back to France!"

Sophia persevered, finishing the brief announcement while the crowd transformed into a mob. Political sentiments of every color mixed freely with personal grievances in the uproar. Some yelled at landowners, some at the government, some at reformers, and some at Sophia Raughley herself. She stood straight as a rod, letting the swells of anger crash against her.

Adrian stepped close to her. "Time to go."

She ignored him and raised an arm against the tide. "My good people. This is no way to settle differences or to influence events."

"*Now,* Your Grace."

"Only rational discourse will help us find common ground." Her voice barely penetrated the uproar.

The agitation grew physical. The crowd milled and surged. Fights broke out. Sweating with fear, Douglas bobbed his respects and disappeared.

"My apologies, Duchess." Circling her waist with his arm, Adrian pulled her to the stairs. Amidst the increasing roar of resentment, he hauled one indignant, squirming duchess away.

He pushed her into the carriage and jumped up to take the reins, cursing Douglas for being too stupid to fathom what had been brewing right under his nose.

He moved the horses, aiming for the closest edge of town. Most of the crowd peeled away, but some bolder men clutched at the reins. He whipped them off. A scream from Sophia shot his head around. Hands were grabbing for her.

"Up here," he ordered.

She furiously slapped off the dragging arms. Half-crawling, half-tumbling, she managed to climb over the seat. Adrian grasped her arm firmly with one hand while he maneuvered the horses with the other. When she had all her limbs beside him, he slammed her down where he could keep an eye on her. He whipped the horses into a gallop, trusting Providence to move people out of the way.

He careened past the church and onto the northern road while rain poured down on the huddle of black cloth, white face, and flaming eyes beside him.

A mile out of town he pulled the horses to a stop.

She rose, the drenched bow of her bonnet sagging over one of her livid eyes. "I had things well in hand back there. They were coming around. Now there will probably be a riot and all of England will hear that I was run out of a town on my own property."

"The riot was underway before you left. That is what we call a crowd of three hundred fighting in the streets here in England. I need to walk the horses, so sit down."

"Where do you get the notion that you can manhandle me whenever you feel like it? I will not have you picking me up and carting me about at will, especially not in front of all those people. Paris was bad enough, but this was inexcusable."

"None of those people noticed or cared. Now, sit or you will fall." He grabbed her arm and pulled her down.

He got the horses moving. She sniffed with indignation, still beautifully angry. Drops of water dripped off her bonnet's edge, right onto her nose.

"How are those people ever to take me seriously after what you did?" she fumed. "It was extremely presum—"

"Don't say it," he warned.

They drove past sodden fields for a few more miles.

"Turn around now. I am sure that things have calmed down," she said.

"The hell I will, and the hell they have. When a mob gets its blood up like that, it doesn't calm for hours, unless the yeomanry enforces order. With any luck it has been called up."

"If you are not returning to Haford, where are you going?"

"Someplace dry and safe. I am taking you to Staverly."

"No. I forbid it. I will not go there. As the Duchess of Everdon I order you to turn this carriage around."

"For someone who claims not to want the position, you throw out ducal orders easily enough when it suits you. I don't care about your noble prerogatives right now. I suspect that your Captain Brutus was on that street, managing the whole thing. Staverly is the closest place where you will be safe and that is where I am taking you."

The road met the coast and curved east along its edge. The rhythm of crashing waves joined the faster beat of pounding rain. Sophia retreated into a simmering anger, ignoring the downpour that had drenched them both to the bone.

The gates to Staverly were closed, but a man stepped out of the gatehouse upon their approach.

"No one goes in here," he announced as Adrian pulled up the horses.

"This is the Duchess of Everdon."

The old man peered beneath the bonnet. "Miss Raughley! I got no word you would be visiting, Your Grace."

"It was a sudden decision, and not mine, Martin."

Martin looked down the road. "Are the others following? None to do for you here, Your Grace. You know how the duke left it."

"We are alone," Adrian explained. "There was trouble in Haford. Are you saying the house is closed? There are no servants here?"

"Just me, as Her Grace could have told ye."

"Then we will have to make do. Close and lock the gate behind us, then go to a nearby farm and buy some provisions." He handed over some shillings. "You are to sleep here tonight. If anyone tries to enter, come and get me."

The drive wound through a quarter mile of overgrown park before stopping in front of an old Tudor manor. Chipping plaster and high weeds announced that no one had tended the estate in years. The sea roared louder here, and Adrian surmised that the cliffs began not far from the garden doors.

He handed Sophia down. An overhang waited five steps away, but she remained in the rain, gazing up at the half-timbered facade.

"We used to come here every summer when I was a girl."

"It is a charming property. Why did your father let it go to ruin?"

Gathering her drenched skirts, she headed to the door.

"It is a wonder that he did not burn it down. This is where it happened. This is where my brother Brandon died."

chapter 13

She supposed that she always knew that she would have to come back to Staverly. Perhaps it was fitting that it would be on the day when she had made such a magnificent failure of being Alistair's heir.

She paced around the library, pulling covers from the furniture. Puffs of dust rose like specters following her progress.

Adrian lit a fire to burn off some of the damp that had claimed the house years ago.

"We should see if there are some dry clothes for you," he said, poking at the coals.

"And you too. Follow me."

She led the way up to the bedchambers, grateful that Adrian was much larger than Brandon and she would not have to go into the room her brother had used.

"You will find that this is not a very large house. Mother would not let Father add to it. She wanted it reserved for family life."

A few items remained in the duke's wardrobe. They reeked of Alistair. The whole house did. Marleigh was so large that one could find places where he had never gone much, but that was not the case here.

"You can sleep here. Martin has kept it clean, in case my father should ever come. You should build a fire here as well. This chamber was always cold, even in the hottest summers."

She left him and entered her mother's old room through the dressing chamber. Unlike Marleigh, where Celine had methodically obliterated the memory of the first duchess, nothing had been changed here.

Nostalgia squeezed her heart while she rummaged through the personal items still imbued with that gentle woman's scent. Finding a high-waisted muslin gown and some underclothes and slippers, she scurried out as fast as she could and sought her own small chamber.

Memories bombarded her. She gazed out the small northern window. Every summer she had played in the garden below. When she was seven she had learned to swim in the surf. She could spot the rocks near the sea that her imagination had transformed into a castle.

She remembered starlit nights sitting at this open window, dreaming about a pure and passionate love.

A shelf held the items collected in the course of twenty summers. They contained the story of the girl she had been once. She had left them all when she and her father hurriedly departed that last summer, just as she had left behind the girl herself.

She opened the wardrobe and tossed them all into it. The tokens of play with Brandon. The book of romantic poems written her fifteenth summer. The radical tracts toted here the season before Captain Brutus, when the idealism of youth had excited her intellect much as her Robin Hood would soon excite her womanhood.

She slammed the door closed, as if she could silence the memories if she hid their remnants. She began peeling off the black weeds.

The old-fashioned, scoop-necked muslin gown would not cover her stays, so she stripped naked and then slipped it on over only her mother's chemise. The damp had turned her hair to ringlets. She gathered most of them into a topknot and let the rest hang around her face. Turning to the long oval mirror, she surveyed the results.

A ghost stared back at her. Long and willowy, wearing this same high-waisted white gown with its scattered violets, it approached with a gentle smile and comforting arms. She could not remember why her mother had come to her that afternoon, but suddenly it might have been yesterday.

She had never realized how much she resembled her mother. The nose and chin were Alistair's, but the rest, the eyes and hair and face, were not.

She suddenly realized that she could not run away from the ghosts. They did not exist in objects and places that she could avoid. They were in her, all of them, waiting to be recognized. Good ones had been ignored along with the ones that brought pain.

She ran to her mother's chamber again and grabbed a long fringed shawl. Passing the main bedchamber she saw through the open door that Adrian had built the fire.

She found him bending to the old hearth in the kitchen. Pails of water had been brought from the nearby pump house and he had wiped the dust off a table where some cheese and ham waited.

"You have not changed your clothes," she said.

He rose and combed his damp locks back off his forehead with his fingers. "I took care of the horses."

"You had better take care of yourself now."

He gestured absently to the food, began to speak, then stopped. He looked her way with a serious expression. "I apologize for making you come here. I did not know what this place meant to you."

"You could not know. Your decision was sounder than my denial."

"The rain looks to be stopping and there is at least an hour before dusk. I will ride back to Haford and see how things stand. If it has calmed, I will come and get you. I know the road now and once the clouds break there will be some moon, so it will be safe enough even at night."

She found a knife on a shelf and wiped it with the damp cloth. She sliced a bit of cheese and nibbled. As soon as she tasted, she knew which farm Martin had gone to.

"It will be dawn before all those trips are made. Do not look so worried. I am not going to turn into a madwoman on you. I never thought to return here for many more years, but now I wonder if it was a good thing to come. There is a sweetness to the sadness. Also, I had forgotten how beautiful it is here."

She fetched some crockery cups and poured the home-brewed ale that had arrived with the food.

"You are sure that it will not distress you?"

"No, but it occurs to me that if I am not going to live my whole life getting back at him, as you put it in the park, this is a good place to start. Besides, the ghosts will come whether you are here or not. I'd rather not face them entirely alone."

The rain had stopped, and rays from the low sun peeked golden light through the clouds. Sophia opened the door to the kitchen garden so the fresh breeze could enter. Through the growth she spied the roof of the Chinese gazebo that perched on the cliff at the end of the gardens. One could see the sea and rocks of the whole cove from it.

Not yet. She would enjoy the good memories first.

She inhaled the clean scent of a newly washed world and admired the sparkling droplets on the high grass before turning back to the table.

She looked beautiful standing near the open door. The breeze fluttered the tendrils around her face and the late sun bathed her pale skin in hazy gold.

The dress must be at least twenty years old, but it suited her perfectly. The low neckline displayed delicate bones and the thin muslin curved around her soft breasts, emphasizing them with its cinched high waist. The ethereal rays made the cloth vaguely transparent, showing her legs and the absence of any petticoat underneath. Adrian had seen her in black so much that he had forgotten how fresh and vibrant and youthful she could appear.

She took her seat. "What will you do first? Eat or get out of those wet clothes?"

"I had thought to eat, but if Your Grace demands the latter, I will oblige." He teased even though she had not asked him to stay for lovemaking. The request had been much more flattering than that.

He broke some bread and cut some ham.

"I have been thinking," she mused as she munched more cheese. "Mister Hawkins may be right. From what we have witnessed, reapportionment may be inevitable."

"Do you want the people who attacked you today to make English law? Did they strike you as suited to the task?"

"You must admit that the way things stand is unfair."

"Much in life and government is, but the system works well with its checks and balances. It is not clear that the alternative would."

"The French and the Americans have fairer systems."

"The French system gave the world Napoleon and a generation of war. The American system permits the continuation of slavery. The influence that the upper house exerts on the lower one here maintains stability and avoids governance by the mob."

"It does more than that. We both know it preserves privilege too."

"Your privilege, Duchess. Even so, there have been some reforms that were not in the lords' interest. Voices for change are heard."

"So you really believe it should be stopped? If you would neither win anything nor lose anything by your vote, would you vote reform down?"

He met her frank gaze. "What are you asking me?"

"I am asking what you really believe about this. And I suppose I am asking just how thoroughly you are Wellington's man."

"In other words, am I a toadying sycophant? I regret to say that those of us who must make our own way are, to one degree or another."

She looked down quickly. "I am sorry."

"Do not be. It was a fair question. I did not form my opinions and persona in order to gain a powerful man's favor. Wellington would see right through that, for one thing. I do not always agree with him or the ministers, and I present my own arguments. However, if you are asking if I have ever cast a vote for a position with which I did not agree, the answer is yes. Politics always involves compromise. And if you are asking if my general agreement with the party leadership has benefited me, again the answer is yes."

He spoke more sharply than he wanted, for reasons he did not care to explore. She grew subdued while she watched him. He had the sensation that he had revealed more than he knew, and that she was comprehending something he did not fully grasp himself.

"You must think I am insufferably spoiled," she said. "Childish and self-absorbed and resentful about a life that most would kill for. How unfair it must seem to you that a woman who knows only parties and gowns should be given the kind of power that belongs to Everdon."

"I do not judge its fairness at all. I do not think that you know only parties and gowns, and I only find you a little spoiled, and not much at all when it comes to the things that truly matter. As to your self-absorption, I think that you are salving wounds that I cannot know about."

"Can't you? I look at you and find myself thinking that if I had been required to make my own way, the achievement of doing so might have healed those wounds, or at least made them less significant."

The quiet observation unsettled him. He had not expected the ghosts confronted here to be any from his own life.

He rose. "I will go and change now. If when you next see me I am too informal, you must forgive me. It remains to be discovered what of the duke's wardrobe will fit."

She laughed and picked at her muslin skirt. "At least your garments won't be twenty years out of date."

He lifted two buckets and paused to look at her. He memorized the image of her smiling, with bright eyes and the hint of sadness behind that glitter, and the shadows of her feminine curves still visible in the last of beautiful light.

"It is a lovely gown," he said, turning away. "And you look beguiling in it."

She was gone when he came back down. Dark had fallen, and he guessed that she had sought solitude in her chamber, perhaps to sleep after the day's tumult, perhaps to hide because of last night's advances. He had thought it would be pleasant to spend the evening with her, and so he entered the empty library with some disappointment.

The shelves mostly held popular novels and the lightest of poetry, the kinds of things one might read during a holiday by the sea. He tried to pass the time with one of Humboldt's travel portfolios, but the exotic engravings could not hold his attention. He wondered if the ghosts were upstairs now, and how Sophia was dealing with them.

Putting aside the portfolio, he made his way to the whitewashed kitchen and out to the gardens. The night sky was perfectly clear and a refreshing breeze blew through the shirt that he wore without coats. He headed toward the cliffs.

The sloping roof of a Chinese gazebo loomed against the star-speckled sky. He began to walk around it when he noticed a shadow move inside. Sophia rocked back and forth against the balustrade as a child might, stretching away on extended arms and then pulling forward until her head stuck up toward the sky.

She stopped suddenly, bending out. "Burchard?"

He stepped onto the planked floor. "I did not intend to disturb you. I assumed that you had retired."

"I decided to come out here first and look at the sea." She pointed down at dark masses. "Even at night you can see all the way around the little cove. That big shadow is a point of land marking its eastern curve. The water near the land is very placid, except over there. We used to swim every day. Everyone except Father."

"You came to visit the memories?"

"I suppose so."

"Good ones, I hope."

"Not entirely."

He could not see her face, but he knew that distracted tone. "Do you want me to leave?"

"I think that I was hoping you would come." She resumed rocking, angling back and then pulling forward until her hips hit the balustrade. He pictured her doing that over the years, learning each summer that the wood hit differently on her growing body.

"Do you know what Jenny said about you that first night? That you were the sort of man one wants to hand things to because you will make it all come out right in the end. That is why the Foreign Secretary found you useful, and why Wellington depends on you, isn't it? It was rude of me to suggest otherwise today."

He should probably tell her that foreign missions and political plans were one thing, and the hidden pain of a woman was another. He had no idea at all how to manage that.

"What would you have done?" she asked. "If I had not nominated you? You said in Paris that you would have occupied yourself with your other interests."

He suspected that she posed the question only to avoid something else.

"I have been asked on occasion to manage other than ambassadors, M.P.'s, and duchesses."

"Businesses?"

"Sometimes. More appealing have been the offers to accompany scientific and archeological expeditions. The latter in particular require extensive organization, much like a military campaign. They make use of native workers, and in my travels for the Foreign Secretary I learned how to be accepted by them."

"Then perhaps you would make a good ambassador, if you are sympathetic to foreigners and their ways."

"Ambassadors are too visible. They must be Britain personified. For important posts, they are always drawn from the nobility and mostly serve a ceremonial role. It is left to their staffs to conduct the more subtle work."

"Were you good at being less visible and more subtle?"

"My appearance helped with the first."

"I hadn't thought about that, but I imagine that it did."

The fact that she did not think about that, and had never found him especially exotic, was one of her appeals. After Greeks and Hungarians, a half-breed Englishman would not be very distinctive.

"The Foreign Secretaries were lucky to have you. Do you still do that sometimes?"

"On occasion, when Parliament is not in session. Since taking my seat in the Commons, I mostly just serve as a fancy messenger boy."

She seemed to accept that. She turned back to the sea.

Abruptly, as if some inner decision had been made, she pointed to the east. "He drowned there, where the rocks make the water churn badly. He was twenty years old. We were twins."

He could sense her fragile hold on her emotions, and wished that he could do more than stand like a silent witness. Whatever ghost she had decided to face here was bigger than his protection. In the things that mattered, he was worthless to her.

"It was my fault," she breathed the words so low the crashing surf almost submerged them. "I swam too close to the eastern edge, and got into trouble. I almost died. I remember fighting the water with a ghastly panic and then losing consciousness. I came to on the shore. Gerald was here, and he and the steward saw me washed up and pulled me out of the surf. Brandon must have seen me going down and came in to help. They found his body a few hours later on the other side of that promontory."

"It was not your fault."

"It was. In this one judgment my father was right. I was angry and hurt that day and I swam like a madwoman, not caring where I went. It was my brother's misfortune to be walking on the rocks where he could see me struggling."

"You would have tried to help him, too, I have no doubt."

"It was my carelessness."

Her body swooned subtly. Her battle against the anguish twisted his heart.

"The wrong child died," she said, her voice strangling on a swallowed sob.

Those were Alistair's words. He just knew it. Anger blazed at the realization that the man had been so cruel as to actually say that, no matter what was thought. He pictured the duke, stern and accusatory and unforgiving. No comfort had been given to her that day, or later.

She pressed her hands to her eyes. "This is so embarrassing. I'm sorry. When I asked you to stay I did not expect to get like this. I think it would be better if you left after all."

He did not move. He could not leave her like this, balanced on the brink.

With deep breaths and a rigid stance she fought valiantly for composure. "I realize now that I never mourned him. Not properly. I could not. Thinking about it at all made me feel as if I were being physically torn into pieces."

He reached for her and pulled her into his arms. "Then mourn him now, Sophia. I will hold you together."

She struggled but he held tighter. Her fingers stretched and twisted into the fabric of his shirt.

With a moan of defeat, she gave up.

He had never seen a woman cry as she did then. Soul-wrenching, groaning sobs racked her, sapping her strength until only his arms kept her upright, clutched to his chest. The shredding pain that she feared tore through her, and into him. Throat and chest burning, he buried his face in her hair and prayed that she would not emerge shattered forever.

Slowly, her explosive grief calmed to a quieter sorrow. Her clawing fingers relaxed against his chest and she lay against him, weeping gently. He kept her wrapped in his arms, giving what feeble comfort he could, hoping this confrontation with the past had helped her.

After it passed she stayed resting in his arms, her spent breath warming his body between her flat palms. He fought a swelling awareness of her soft femininity beneath his hands. A flowing sensuality bathed the poignant intimacy that her emotional outburst had created.

He angled his head and kissed her brow, telling himself that he intended no more than a single gesture of friendship and solace. She tilted her face up and suddenly his good intentions came undone. A soul-shaking desire flared. His lips tasted the salty tears on her cheek and then met her mouth.

She accepted his kiss with an assenting sigh that obliterated good sense. Hoping that he gave as well as took, he lost himself in the taste of her mouth, the scent of her body, the signs of her climbing arousal. Her palms caressed up his chest to encircle his neck, their pressing paths inciting a ferocious hunger.

He knew how to manage a woman's pleasure and mindless passion led him to exploit hers. His caresses brought her closer, trembling against his length, gasping with helplessness. No stays or petticoats interfered. His hands explored soft curves of hips and back and thighs, pressing, feeling, and stroking her to a needful delirium that left her rising up into his body until his erection buried in her stomach.

His mind was already taking her in the damp grass outside, against the post of the gazebo, on the wood floor beneath their feet. His imagination already had her naked, pliant, accepting him any way he wanted her. His body responded to the expectation with an eager fire. Easing his knee between her thighs he caressed up to her breast and stroked the erect nipple straining against the muslin.

Arm around her waist, he lifted and carried her to a nearby bench and pulled her onto his lap. He trailed kisses down her neck and found the rapid pulse that throbbed in time with the one pounding in his head. He tasted the smooth warmth of her skin down to the gown's low neckline.

He caressed her breast and she melted. Kissing her again, claiming and exploring her mouth the way he planned to learn all of her, he released the two tapes on the back of her gown.

She straightened and gazed at him in the dark. For a few seconds she did not move. He waited for whatever she was deciding while her short, shallow breaths prodded his desire so high that he thought he would burn if she pulled away.

Then she surprised him in the unpredictable way that she had. She removed her arms from his shoulders and he thought that she intended to leave. Instead her hands bent to the shoulders of her gown, and then slid down as she lowered the bodice.

He peeled off her chemise and took her lovely breast in his hand. As he had wanted to do since that first night in Paris, he dipped to kiss it while gently palming the hard nipple. Her head lolled against his neck. Her desperate kisses heated his skin while her gasps of pleasure scorched his brain.

He took his time, caressing those full swells and teasing at the hard tips until she grew impatient and the gasps turned to cries. The sound of her need sent his own arousal soaring. Taking a breast in his mouth, he licked and drew. He caressed down the length of her flexing, rocking body and then retraced the path under her skirt.

Again she paused, as if he had confused her with an unexpected question. He kept his hand on her legs, stroking ever higher, his mind blank to any thought but of soon following the path of his fingers with his lips. He took her breast again and this time she held it to him. He did not wait for a sign of assent this time, but moved up her thigh and slid his hand to his goal.

He stroked the secret, soft flesh. A tremor shivered through her, into him, shaking his control. She suddenly went as limp as she had been in her grief. A low, melodic cry of submissive passion broke the breezy night.

Its desperate, helpless note touched him. It resonated with the night's earlier defenseless emotions.

A spot of lucidity reemerged. He lifted his head and stilled his hand.

Her mouth sought his impatiently, almost angrily. "Don't stop," she gasped, pressing him down to her breast and moving her hips against his hand.

"Sophia—"

"Don't. Please don't."

He pulled his hand away from her undulating body, cursing the chivalry that was asserting itself. "This will go too far." With the fevered, biting kisses they kept giving each other, he barely got the words out.

"You said that you wanted me. Last night . . ."

"I do want you. Too much to start it like this."

"But I want this."

"For the wrong reasons. This is not the way to bury your pain. You are vulnerable and if I take advantage of that you will hate me for it, with good cause."

She stopped showering kisses on him. Her body stilled and her forehead sank against his shoulder. "Damn it, Burchard. Why couldn't you just use me like you were supposed to? For once I wouldn't have minded."

"I do not want to use you at all."

She sat upright and turned her face away. "Yes, you do." She sighed deeply. "All men do. I do not mind so much anymore. In Paris I learned how to manage all of that."

That provoked an edgy resentment. He had just rejected an offer his body did not thank him for refusing, and she had responded by lumping him in the same group as the duke and Captain Brutus and those artists.

Furthermore, she implied that she managed a man's use of her now, which meant that in reality she used the man. She insinuated that tonight had not been under his control, and out of hers, quite the way he thought.

Still, he would have gladly held her in his embrace all night, but he sensed her retreating emotionally. As with her recent child's game at the balustrade, she kept swinging into intimacy and then pulling back. This time, however, he suspected that he knew why.

She scrambled off his lap and hurriedly drew up her garments. She would have bolted immediately but he rose and blocked her escape. Turning her, he fixed the gown's tapes.

"I should thank you for being so honorable. And for before, when I spoke of Brandon," she said.

"I do not want your thanks."

"Then what do you want?"

"I want you. I can offer you nothing but affection and pleasure, but when the ghosts do not interfere as they do today, I want to make love to you. If I can make it happen, I will."

She turned to him. "Then you should have done so while you had me at a disadvantage, because now it will not happen. You see, I know that is not all you want. I know why you are here."

"Sophia, politics is the last thing on my mind this evening."

"No, it isn't. I know what you stand to gain. I know about the Treasury position. It is a stepping stone, isn't it? To a ministry someday."

"Are you convincing yourself that this was about my career? Do you assume every man is only moved by self-interest?"

She stiffened at the accusations. "I did not like this. I will not let it happen again."

"You liked it. Too well. That frightens you, doesn't it? It complicates the game of who uses whom that you worked out so neatly in Paris. Keep control, keep it shallow, and there are no risks. That is how you want things with men, isn't it?"

"That is right. That is how I want it."

"Sorry, darling. I am not one of your boys looking for a frivolous friendship, or an artist offering the great lady amusement in return for a chamber. It will not be that way with us, even if you prefer the safety of it."

"It will not be any way with us."

"The hell it won't."

A renewed, pounding desire ached to show her how it would be, right now, and to hell with the restraint provoked by her grief.

He forced himself to turn away so that he would not act on the impulse. "Return to the house now. I will wait until you have retired before I follow."

She had the good sense to obey. She ran away, up the garden path.

chapter 14

S uch a pity that you have to wear weeds all through the summer,"
Dorothy said. "Although I think that an argument can be made that you
should attend the coronation ball come September. After all, you are Everdon. Don't you agree, Adrian?"

"If the duchess seeks a rationale, I am sure that we can devise one."

Adrian strolled beside his willowy aunt, and glanced past her cloud of
white hair to Sophia. The duchess's broad bonnet, laden with black sweeping feathers, obscured his view, so that only her nose and chin were visible.

Adrian had invited his aunt on this walk, knowing that they would most
likely meet Sophia, since she took a morning stroll in the park each day at
this time. He was reduced to these machinations because Sophia had been
avoiding him. She had dismissed him at the end of the journey to nominate
her candidates. Since coming up to London three weeks ago she had arranged
that someone else was always present if she received him.

Sophia managed to engage Dot in a conversation that did not include
him. The two of them pulled ahead by a few steps, and the Earl of Dincaster
paced alongside them. That the earl had tagged along this morning was,
Adrian suspected, not good news.

Adrian turned his attention to the other members of their party. Daniel
St. John and his wife, Diane, had also taken a morning stroll, and Adrian had
introduced them to the duchess upon meeting them in the park.

"She seemed to recognize both of you," he said to Daniel.

"We have been introduced before, several years ago, while we visited our
home in Paris."

"Then you know something of her life there."

"Miss Raughley and her Ensemble were well-known in Paris." St. John's
voice carried no censure or sarcasm. "She built another life there. Another
identity. Pity she could not hold on to it if she preferred it to the one here."

Adrian knew that St. John spoke from experience. Daniel St. John himself now lived a different identity than the one to which he had been born. Adrian was one of the few people in England who knew that secret and why the mystery had been created. He was not entirely sure why St. John persisted in the deception when the reasons for it had long ago been resolved.

"She appears very tired," Diane St. John said, her soulful eyes fixed on the duchess's black dress. "I expect coming home has been a trial."

"Yes, and coming to London has made it worse. A steady stream of visitors has been calling on her. Every woman in society wants to conduct an independent inspection before agreeing with the growing consensus that Sophia Raughley really isn't very suitable for her position."

"Let me guess. They also think that the right husband would go far to redeeming her, and she would be much improved if she just married the visitor's perfect son, brother, or nephew," St. John said.

"Undoubtedly. I arranged this accidental meeting with Dot because she could use a friend who is formidable enough to protect her through the next few months of social hell."

"That was thoughtful of you, since she has no family to help her. She must do this all alone," Diane said. "Perhaps she could also use some friends who are not a part of that particular hell. I will call on her, to reminisce about Paris, if you think it would help. Unless you think she would find us beneath her."

"I think it would help enormously. Nor does the duchess hold strict notions about who is suitable for her circle, as she proved in Paris." Nor would the friendship of Daniel and Diane St. John be much of a step down. St. John had become incredibly wealthy through shipping and finance, and could buy most of the peers of the realm.

"Then I will make the overtures and see if she is amenable." Diane lengthened her stride just enough to fall into step beside Dot.

As she did so, the earl slowed enough to trail the ladies a bit.

St. John noticed. "It appears he wants some conversation with you."

"There is no other explanation for his presence here this morning. I don't think he has seen this much exercise in months."

"I will make myself scarce, then." St. John joined his wife and extricated her from the ladies. The two of them turned and retraced their steps.

That left Adrian walking with the earl, who sidled up closely.

"Is it done, then?" he asked, slowing even more so the ladies could not hear.

"They were all elected and are arriving for the Parliament even as we speak."

Sophia's candidates had been voted in, but not enough other Tories had won. Whigs elected on a mandate of reform firmly controlled the lower house by a huge margin.

Wellington and Peel and the other Tory leaders now faced a delicate situation. The goal would be to see that the bill was very moderate at worst, and that the vote was very close so that the House of Lords could kill it without too much public outrage.

Which meant that Sophia's twelve votes still mattered, and that Everdon's empty seat in the upper house had become more critical.

"Heard talk out of Cornwall. Seems she didn't tell them how to vote."

"That is her choice for now."

"Heard she started a riot."

"A very small riot."

"Damn it, you were supposed to manage it, keep her in hand, control the ribbons."

"She is not a horse to be steered by a bridle."

"No, she is a woman to be steered by a husband. Stidolph still doesn't know, although I think someone should tell him. Thinks he still has first claim, when in fact the filly is tethered in someone else's corral. Hell of a situation. Why couldn't Everdon have sired a nice, demure, obedient colt?"

"Maybe he did, but pulled too hard on the bit and ruined her mouth. Now, don't you think that we have butchered the horse metaphor enough?"

It was the lengthiest conversation they had suffered in years, and Adrian waited for the rest. What had been broached thus far was not important enough to force the earl to arrange for it.

Suddenly the earl pivoted, placing his body in front of Adrian, forcing him to stop.

Adrian squarely met the gray eyes so different from his own. The earl's pale skin had flushed from the unaccustomed exercise. His swept-back white hair, once fair like Colin's and Gavin's, poked out the back beneath his hat. The face, once angular, and the chest, once fit and strong like his sons', had gone soft and puffy from too much indulgence. As had the mind.

Adrian considered that if the House of Lords were made up entirely of Earls of Dincaster, he would vote for reform in an instant.

"She went to a radicals' meeting last night," the earl confided.

"Did she?" Adrian was amused that the earl thought this would be news. He could himself recite where she had gone everytime she had left her house these last weeks. He could relate what she ate every day. He could tell that she had embarked on a frenzy of extravagance that had modistes all over the city elated.

He could report that she had received two more letters from Captain Brutus, and had not called for Adrian to discuss them.

"Laclere gave a speech. The duchess met with him afterwards. She's to visit his house tomorrow."

The Viscount Laclere was one of the few Tory peers supporting reform. He was also a member of a circle of Adrian's friends that included St. John and a few others, men with whom he had experienced events that forged bonds that transcended social rank or politics. When young they had dubbed themselves the Hampstead Dueling Society, and they still congregated on occasion at the Chevalier Corbet's fencing academy, to spar with sabres.

It was, in essential ways, the only social circle where he had ever really been accepted, and to which he ever truly belonged.

"Laclere's wife is an artist," Adrian said. "The duchess is probably more interested in that than Laclere's political views."

"Artist! Hell, the woman is an opera singer. American at that. Laclere used to be solid, but she's ruined him. Everyone knows that he dabbles in trade now too. I think that you should find a way to go tomorrow, to keep an eye on things and make sure the duchess doesn't get bamboozled."

Adrian forced an expression of agreement. Wellington had already made this suggestion, and seen that an invitation had arrived the past evening.

"There is something else," the earl began, looking uncomfortable but determined.

Adrian almost didn't hear him because he became distracted by activity seen out of the corner of his eye. In the distance behind them on the carriage path a curricle approached, careening back and forth from inexpert handling. A dark figure stood in it beside the driver, wobbling off balance, waving its arms. A shout just barely made it to them on the breeze.

Sophia.

"Whatever else you need to say, let us discuss it while we catch up with the ladies," Adrian said.

"It is best discussed in privacy."

Sooo . . . pheee . . . aaaa.

The Earl cocked his head. "Did you hear something?"

"Not at all. Now, what is this other matter?"

"I could have sworn . . . It has to do with the duchess as well. Stidolph spoke with me. Thinks that you have been attending on her far too much. Won't do, will it?"

Oh, sweet Sophia, my lady.

"First you instruct me to keep an eye on things, and now you say to stay away."

"See here, Adrian, you know what I am saying."

They were almost alongside Dot and Sophia. Adrian glanced back and watched the curricle weave precariously. The waving figure tumbled into the seat.

"I am not sure that I do know. Perhaps you had better say it more clearly."

The gray eyes turned to flint and the puffy face found some angles. "It won't do. A liaison would be scandalous."

"Any liaison, or just one with me?"

"I do not want my family to be the entertainment of the summer gossips."

"In other words, you want me to remain as invisible as possible. That has never been very easy."

The earl scanned his face with a cold appraisal that Adrian had resented since he was old enough to understand what was reflected in his mirror. No response came to his oblique reference to what his face revealed, however. None ever had.

He caught up with the ladies and herded them away from the carriage path toward some trees. He could hear the curricle bearing down on them, but its noise broke and obscured the continued shouts.

Soph . . . stop . . .

"There is a lovely pond back here," Adrian said. "There are swans, and one is black. You really must see it."

"I have seen it already and none of the swans are black," Sophia said. "Why are we hurrying? I will ruin my skirt if you do not slow—"

Wait. Come back.

"What was that?" She glanced around.

"The black swan must have been hiding the day you visited. Come along."

"I am sure that I heard . . ."

Sophia! Kedvesem, wait!

She pivoted. "Attila! Look, Burchard, it's Attila and Jacques."

"By Zeus, so it is."

She ran the seventy yards back to the carriage path. Adrian followed with Dorothy and the earl in tow. By the time they arrived, a display of hugging and kissing was underway. Dorothy watched with a curious smile. The earl's face puffed.

"*Kedvesem!* Oh, it is so good to see you again," Attila cried. "Jacques and I were so worried about you. There we were, sitting around Paris, talking about our wonderful Sophia, and then inspiration struck. Why not go and visit? When we went to your house this morning Jacques cajoled Charles into telling us where to find you." He bowed to give her hand another big kiss, then turned to Adrian. "Mister Burchard, we meet again. I hope that you do not mind. Jacques said that you might want more time alone with Sophia after all those years . . ."

Hell.

". . . but I said you would not mind old friends coming to make sure that she was happy in all her new responsibilities, not only to her country but to you and that . . ."

Fortunately Sophia interrupted the effervescent flow to make introductions, and neither Dot nor the earl noticed the odd references to Adrian.

"Is it just you two? Where is Dieter?" Sophia asked.

"Dieter got word that a countess back home will pay to have his latest novel printed, so of course he had to return for that," Jacques explained. "Stefan just disappeared one day. A new composer arrived in Paris from Poland. His name is Chopin, and he really *is* of their nobility, so of course things got a little warm for poor Stefan."

"Did you just disembark?"

"Yesterday. Jacques found us a charming little inn for last night, and we came looking for you at once this morning."

"An inn? I will not hear of it. We will send for your things at once. There is plenty of room at Everdon House."

Attila grinned with delight. "Wonderful. It will be just like old times."

Jacques smiled smoothly. "We would be honored, dear lady. Of course, that is if Monsieur Burchard does not mind."

"Burchard?" Sophia frowned. Adrian watched the potential disaster dawn on her. She glanced askance at Dorothy and the earl. *"Oh."*

"The duchess is more generous than prudent," Adrian said. "We would not want to affect her position, especially since she is so recently returned, would we, gentlemen?"

"I cannot countenance having my friends stay in some inn with flea-bitten beds." Sophia was getting that formidable, determined, the-world-be-damned look about her.

The last thing Adrian wanted was the Ensemble living with her again. "May my aunt offer you both accommodations? Dincaster's town house is on the same square as Everdon's."

"Yes," Dorothy said. "You must both stay with us."

The earl absorbed that his hospitality had just been extended to these two foreign persons. "I say . . ." he blustered, but Attila moved in with a flow of gratitude that submerged his objections. Overwhelmed, the earl inched away, mumbled about an engagement, and headed down the path.

Jacques eased next to Adrian and tilted his head conspiratorially. *"Pardon,* but am I correct in surmising that you do not live at this Everdon House and that the marriage is still a secret here?" he muttered.

"Yes."

"But why? Surely now . . ."

"Politics."

Jacques' expression cleared. "Ahhh, *bien.* Politics. Of course." He nodded knowingly.

"We will go to my house and send for your things at once," Sophia announced. She let Jacques hand her up into the curricle before he settled in and retook the reins. Attila climbed onto a footboard in the rear and bent to pour an enthusiastic description of their crossing into her ear.

"I will send a carriage in the afternoon to collect you," Dorothy called after them.

"I love England already. What warm and wonderful people," Attila effused as the wheels rolled. "See, Jacques? We should have come sooner."

"Thank you, Dot," Adrian said after they had driven off.

She raised her eyebrows. "Who are they?"

"Artist friends. Try to keep them away from the earl, will you?"

"I suspect he will take his dinners at his clubs while they are in residence."

"That will not be necessary. She will probably insist that they dine with her."

Dot looked to the shrinking curricle. "You did not want them staying with her, and I do not think it was only concern about the harpies' gossip."

"Not entirely."

"Am I correct in assuming that you will not join us at the house to help me entertain them, but remain at your private chambers?"

"The earl would prefer that, don't you think?"

"How much do you want me to divert them so that you can be alone with her?"

He smiled at Dorothy's perception. "That remains to be seen."

She slipped her arm in his and they continued their walk. "I do not think she is as sophisticated as her Parisian *savoir faire* suggests. Having witnessed you work your charm before, I daresay she does not stand a chance if you are determined. I would admonish you to be discreet, but I know that is not necessary."

"No, that is not necessary."

She narrowed her eyes on the tiny, disappearing speck that was Sophia's bonnet. "I trust that you will be kind too. For all her brave front, she is very frightened. Of you?"

"Partly."

"Then perhaps you should retreat. After all, she must marry and you may only make it harder for her."

Perhaps he should retreat. Sophia obviously had, with determination. But he would not. He had spent years sensibly doing that. He had spent a lifetime being the discreet, as-invisible-as-possible third son of the Earl of Dincaster, but this was different.

He wanted Sophia Raughley. He wanted her in his arms and in his bed.

He wanted to slay the ghosts and soothe her quiet sadness and protect and take care of her for as long as their world would let him.

Mostly, however, he wanted what she was afraid of. Unfortunately, he suspected that she would never again trust any man enough for that.

"When she decides to marry, I will retreat, Dot. I will not make it harder on her."

chapter 15

T he house slept and he moved in silence. He made his way to the servants' stairs *and got to work.*

Sophia was proving more resilient than he had expected. She was not acting like the little mouse he remembered.

She knew he was watching and what he was demanding. He had made that very clear. Even if she had not realized he had been in Haford, her protector surely had. She was not reacting the way he wanted, however. He kept waiting for a sign that he had won, that she had broken, but she remained ambiguous about the vote and everything else.

Perhaps she thought he was bluffing. Well, she would learn differently tonight.

He pulled some of his broadsheets from his coat, crushed them in his fist, and piled them on the bottom step. He slipped to the kitchen hearth and lifted some glowing coals on a small shovel. Toting them through the dark, he mounted the stairs again, and slid them into the bed of paper.

Lines of hot orange slowly formed around the coals.

Charles opened the door just enough for Adrian to slip in out of the night. With a finger to his lips and a criminal's glance over his shoulder, the butler gestured for Adrian to follow. They stole their way through the sleeping house to Charles' chambers off the silver pantry.

His sitting room was tiny but comfortably appointed. Adrian settled into a chair and held out his hand expectantly.

Charles hesitated. "Still doesn't seem right, sir. Telling you what she's been doing doesn't seem as much a betrayal, since she isn't doing much at all. This is different, and I'm of two minds, I am."

Charles' unease pricked at Adrian's own. He was unaccustomed to using such subterfuge in England. "It is different and it isn't right and under any other circumstance I would never ask it. However, I did not lie when I said she might be in danger. If she is being threatened, I want to know."

Charles debated, then extracted two papers from his Bible and handed them over. "She'll release me if she finds out."

"You can return them shortly to her desk."

Adrian held the sheets near a brace of candles. Like the first letter from Captain Brutus, these were neatly printed in anonymous block letters. However, they contained much less restraint than the other, and bore an accusatory, demanding tone.

The first called on her to support the most radical of the proposed reform plans. It ended with a reminder of their "intimacy" years ago, and a demand that she not display the weakness again that she had so ignobly shown during that episode.

The most recent one was more explicit. "You have the chance to expiate your betrayals and crimes, Your Grace. What you did to me is nothing compared to the blow you struck at the hopes of the people, the hopes that I embodied. My own life is nothing in this. Nor is yours. History calls, and it is time for you to rectify what occurred. I must call in the debt, and you must pay it. One way or the other."

That the next paragraph read like a lover's appeal, remembering her "soft warmth" and "kind heart" and "generous affection," did not dilute the implied threat. Adrian reread those endearments more often than he needed to.

Why hadn't she shown him, or anyone else, these letters? Were the overtures of affection touching her more than the warnings were frightening her?

"Do you have any reason to think that she has met with him?" he asked Charles. "Have any men visited, whom you wondered about?"

"None that I saw. But she does go out, doesn't she? On those walks alone. And last night she went to that political meeting."

"It was a meeting of reform supporters, but not of Captain Brutus' ilk. The Viscount Laclere does not associate with revolutionaries."

He quizzed Charles more specifically on the callers, but only learned that they were all well-known members of society. The park was busy enough in the mornings that he doubted she would arrange an assignation there.

He read again the most recent letter. The mind that wrote it couldn't decide if it wanted Sophia for revenge, for love, or for political advantage.

He rose. He would have to have a firm talk with the duchess.

Charles ducked around to open the sitting room door. He escorted Adrian through the silver pantry and out into the corridor.

Almost immediately they both stopped short.

Charles cocked his head. Adrian sniffed.

"Sir, do you? . . ." Charles began warily.

The sting in Adrian's eyes told him for sure. He ran to the stairwell. Puffs of smoke billowed up from the lower level. "Rouse the footmen to fight it, then go and raise the cry in the neighborhood," he ordered.

Already the smoke was thickening. Turning on his heel, Adrian headed for the chambers above.

He ran right into Gerald Stidolph, who was exiting the library.

"What the hell are you doing here, Stidolph?"

"*My* presence is not at all irregular. I visited with Sophia and paused for a glass of port after she retired."

"Making yourself at home prematurely, aren't you?"

"I do not care for your impertinence."

Adrian brushed past him and started up the stairs at a run. "No time for this, Stidolph. Follow me. There is a fire below."

"A fire! My God, Sophia . . ." Gerald was at his heels in an instant.

"Go above and alert the servants," Adrian ordered.

Gerald pulled at Adrian's arm. "The hell I will. You go up. I will save Sophia, not you." He slammed Adrian against the wall, almost making him topple.

Cursing Stidolph's determination to be heroic, Adrian followed to the third level and saw him aim for Sophia's chambers. Flying now, because acrid smoke already wafted through the house, Adrian continued up to the attic chambers.

Sophia stared around her dark chamber. This house still felt foreign to her, and the shadows' shapes unsettled her. She reached down beside her bed and let her fingers drift along Camilla's fur and pretended that she was back in Paris.

Near the hearth Yuri and his brothers snorted in their dreams, and she could make out Prinny snoozing in his wooden cage near the settee. The presence of her animal friends provided some comfort of the familiar, just as the arrival of Attila and Jacques today had created a welcome distraction from the silent turmoil that she carried inside her.

Her emotions were at war about many things, including Captain Brutus and the elections and Gerald and so much else. However, all of those pressures had become secondary to the battle that her heart waged over Adrian Burchard. Her loneliness so badly desired the comfort that he offered that yearning perpetually stung like a new burn.

She wanted desperately to lie to herself and embrace the closeness for whatever it was worth. But that night at Staverly had proven that she could not control things with him the way that she needed in order to be safe from scathing disappointment, so she had been hiding from the intimacy entirely.

Which only left her more alone at a time when she could use his friendship and advice very badly.

She drowsily considered the last weeks of false smiles and critical eyes and threatening letters. Everyone was waiting for her to make choices she did not want to face. Wellington had called and obliquely broached the issue of her marriage, letting her know he did not believe the story of the husband. It would not be long before he and others ceased being subtle.

The image of Gerald entering this house this evening, of him sitting in the drawing room as if it were his own, and loitering in the library later, too comfortable by far, began intruding.

Her mind took refuge by drifting off to sleep. A mild commotion from below barely penetrated. She became drowsily aware of her chamber door opening.

It was Prinny's squeal that snapped her alert. And Yuri's growl. And the sudden rise of Camilla's back under her fingers.

A tall presence loomed beside her bed.

"Gerald? How *dare* you."

"Wake up, Sophia. You must leave at once. There is a fire."

"A fire!"

With one hand he hauled her out of bed. With the other he grabbed her dressing robe off a nearby chair. She heard running footsteps on the boards above her head, and shouts from below.

"Do not worry, my dear. I will save you." He pushed her toward the door.

"The dogs . . ."

"There is no time."

"Prinny . . ."

He pressed a hand on her back and shoved. "Move quickly, down to the front door."

She could hear servants pouring down from the upper levels with shouts and screams. Frightened and agitated, the dogs howled and Prinny squealed.

"I cannot leave them."

"The fire is in the lower stairwell and if it isn't contained it will shoot right up to the attic."

"Just let me go and—"

"No!" Gripping her arm, he dragged her to the door.

She dug in her heels and yanked free. "Go, if you must. I will be right behind you." Currents of smoke stung her eyes shut. She bumped into the dogs' cages and bent to open them. She groped her way back toward Prinny.

Gerald opened the door and smoke billowed in. "Sophia, there is no time!"

She felt for the cage's latch.

"Sophia!" His shadow took one step toward her, but the sound of wood

crashing below stopped him. His head turned to the chaotic sounds of a terrified household and the obscuring smoke, then back to her.

He ran, swallowed by the darkness.

She frantically reached for the monkey, but he lunged past her, over to the
window. Calling to him, she felt for the dogs' leads. Yuri and his brothers
paced in the dim light by the windows, barking at the danger they sensed
all too well.

Her chest burned. The upper levels of the house grew quiet but the street
below her window had filled with noise. She began to panic. She grabbed for
Prinny but he jumped away.

Suddenly the door closed. The air cleared a little. She startled as an arm
encircled her waist.

"Burchard." Relief swept her. "The animals . . . they will not obey and
come."

"That is because you indulge them too much, as I do you." Releasing her,
he called sharply for the dogs and Camilla. Silenced, they all filed forward.

He brought them to the door. "Out. Run," he commanded, opening it.
The dark line lunged with a fast patter of paws. He slammed the door after
them.

He took Sophia's arm and guided her to the window. "They are fast and
will be in the street within moments. You, however, cannot go that way now.
The smoke is too thick."

She had already guessed that. Despite the closed door, she could smell it.
Feel it. Her chest began constricting again, both from smoke and from fear.
She stuck her face to the fresh air and gazed into the torch-lit street.

The fire had drawn the whole neighborhood and men of all classes worked
the water line. She made out the forms of the dogs and ocelot pouring out
the building, into the arms of Attila and Jacques.

Dincaster's house was also on St. James Square and the news of the fire had
brought the whole household. The Burchard family craned inspecting gazes
up at the building. Colin noticed her and Adrian at the window, and tore
toward the entrance.

Adrian bent out and yelled for his brother to stop, then ducked back in.
He grabbed a heavy chair. "Stand back," he ordered. He shouted the same
command to the people below and then crashed the chair into the window.
Glass and wood splintered and flew. He battered the remnants away until a
large hole gaped.

"You expect to go out this way? If we jump it will kill us."

He strode over to her bed and began tearing it apart. "I will climb down
and you will hold on." He began tying the bed cloths together.

"This is not going to work."

"Of course it is. I've done it before."

He sounded so confident. Her terror retreated a little, and she helped him shove the heavy bed over near the window and tie the escape line to its base.

"Up on the chair. Arms around my neck and legs around my waist."

"You are sure that you know what you are doing?" she asked, assuming the embarrassing position.

"Absolutely. Hold tight now."

He threw down the line of sheets. A cry went up from the onlookers.

"At least we will give London some entertainment tonight." He backed her out of the window and climbed out legs first.

Night air sucked at her and suddenly she was clinging to his dangling body forty feet above the street. A squeal tore her attention from her precarious hold to a desperate little face peering out above her.

"Prinny! Adrian . . ."

"God forbid we should leave His Majesty behind." Twisting one arm in the sheets, he plucked the monkey and threw him onto her head. Prinny screamed and grabbed her, much as Sophia clutched Burchard.

They began to descend. Very slowly.

"You are sure that you have done this before?" she whispered.

"Well, the last time there was no woman and no monkey. And it was a rope, not sheets."

"No woman . . . you do not know for sure that this will work, do you?"

"Of course I do. We have made it at least five feet closer to the ground already."

He bumped against the facade with each lowered hand hold, skinning her legs against the stone. Swallowing a fear that wanted to suffocate her, she clutched tighter and hitched her legs more snugly.

Adrian paused. "Move your right leg just a bit."

"It is all I can do to hold on at all."

"If you do not move your leg, I will be the one to let go. We would like all of my concentration and strength centered in my arms."

She realized with a jolt what he meant. Under her lower calf a ridge of hardness had emerged. "Really, this is not the time or the place."

"I am all too aware of that. Now, try and move your leg. Please."

Burning with humiliation, she tried. She managed something of a rub instead of a move.

"Hell," he muttered. They just hung there, supported only by his strained arms.

"We are both going to die if you don't get hold of yourself. Think of something else, Burchard."

"Why don't you distract me by promising to repay the debt you are incurring by having your life saved?"

She ventured a peek to the distant street below. The height made her head swim. "What prize would instill the resolve to hold onto those sheets?"

"You know what I want."

"It is yours. I will direct my M.P.'s to vote against all reform bills unless directed otherwise by the Tory leadership."

Hand over hand he continued his descent. Each move jerked them precariously. He wound his legs in the sheets and that seemed to stabilize them a little.

Their slow progress made the crowd restless. Encouragement and advice shot up through the night.

"Halfway, Adrian," Colin called.

"Good heavens, Adrian, couldn't you have found a simpler . . ."

"Oh, Jacques, look at our poor Sophia. Do not worry, my lady. We will catch you."

Finally the rusticated stone of the house's first level moved into view. Then a window. Finally came the heavenly sensation of feeling Adrian's weight land on the ground.

Gerald was the first of the closing crowd to reach them. He helped Sophia off Adrian's back. "Awfully dramatic, don't you think, Burchard?"

"Less so than a funeral," Sophia snapped. "If you had helped me with the animals and not run away—"

A huge hug from Attila separated her from Gerald's seething reaction. "Oh, my lady, we saw the smoke and came, never knowing it was your house. Thank God that Mister Burchard was staying with you tonight."

The closest onlookers, the Burchard family and Gerald, inhaled a collective breath. Colin and Dorothy exhaled exclamations and congratulations to blunt the absorption of Attila's insinuation.

The *faux pas* pricked Sophia's mind. How had Adrian come to be in the house to save her?

The crowd milled and pressed, sorry that the spectacle was over. Adrian plucked Prinny from her shoulders and handed him to the earl. The monkey embraced his neck and settled into the crook of his arm. The earl, flustering with indignation, was left holding him like a child.

"Don't let Prinny get away or we will spend all night scouring London for him," Adrian said.

"Prinny? By Jove, that is treasonous."

Prinny smiled up beatifically. The earl froze. "What the hell is he . . . the damn ape has . . . My coat is ruined!"

Adrian shook off his frock coat and threw it around Sophia's naked shoulders.

"The fire is contained and almost out," Colin reported. "The damage was significant and the building is still filled with smoke. That was a close call, Duchess. Bravo, Adrian."

Adrian dusted himself off. Sophia sensed that he would brush off the attention if he could. "You had better take the duchess home with you, Dot."

"Of course. You will stay with us, my dear, until things can be assessed. Will you escort us, Adrian?"

"Colin, would you do it? I need to see about some things here. I will speak with you tomorrow, Duchess. We have some things to discuss."

"We certainly do." Including what Adrian had been up to tonight in her home.

A man from the water line pushed through to Adrian. He handed over a charred scrap of paper. "It was found where the fire started."

"What is it?" Sophia asked.

"Part of a broadside used to start the flames," Adrian said quietly. "Robin Hood's calling card."

Adrian knew how to blend in with the night. After learning what he could from the charred evidence at Everdon House, he disappeared into the shadows of London's streets for several hours.

He poured ale down the throats of talkative men and paid barmaids and whores to tell what they knew. He ventured into a house across the river that served as a lair for smugglers and petty thieves. The denizens accepted him because two of their members had once made his acquaintance when they were acting as privateers in the eastern Mediterranean. Finally, in the hours before dawn he called on the shabby home of a political radical with whom he periodically shared arguments and wine.

None of them could point him toward Captain Brutus. The man was only a name to them. They had never met him, nor heard talk of whom he hired to distribute his broadsides and do the more criminal work such as the fire.

Adrian headed home frustrated. Normally London's netherworld was rife with rumors. Captain Brutus must be very intelligent and careful to remain so obscure. He decided it was just as well that he had not tracked down the man tonight. With Sophia's mortal danger still fresh in his mind, he might have killed him.

He let himself into the building where he lived and went up to the rooms he leased on the second floor. This had been his home since the day fifteen years ago when he had endured his last big row with the earl.

It occurred soon after he left Oxford and a month after his mother died. Summoned like a retainer, he had received the announcement that the earl had procured a position for him with the East India Company. The earl was severing all financial responsibility for him, but had arranged this, ostensibly so he would be provided for.

If he had been a normal son he might have been grateful, but he knew that this was really the earl's way of removing his presence from society. This employment would render him invisible. Banished to the other side of the globe. It had been the final, blatant example of the repudiation that he had suffered in countless ways over the years.

Boiling with resentments only exaggerated by his mother's death, and determined to take no gifts from the man, he had refused.

Anticipating that, the earl had then offered an army commission. As a boy Adrian had dreamed of redeeming the accident of his birth on the battlefield, but he could see no point in being an army officer if there were no wars in which to demonstrate valor and patriotism. He did not doubt that the earl would see that he was assigned to a unit in some distant colony too.

Again he refused. So the earl had fallen back on a third alternative that would at least demand periodic long absences from England. He offered to intercede to procure for Adrian a minor post with the Foreign Secretary's office.

This time he had accepted. It had been a chance for travel and a small role in government. He soon discovered that it also provided opportunities to prove his loyalty to England. His countrymen might find his face vaguely foreign, but much of the world found it very familiar. His natural disguise allowed him to blend into countries in ways he had never been able to at home.

It never bothered him that his risks and successes remained a secret, never to be publicly celebrated like the great battle victories he had dreamed about in his youth. The men who mattered knew all about what occurred on those missions.

Using his salary and the income from the portion left to him by his mother, he had removed himself from Dincaster's homes and all but the most formal relationship with the earl. He had taken these rooms. He had never felt the urge to move to more expansive and fashionable quarters. If he conducted an affair with a lady of society, he did so elsewhere.

And so, when he stepped into the sitting room of the masculine, comfortable chambers, he was surprised to find a duchess waiting for him.

Not the one he wanted to see.

The Dowager Duchess of Everdon barely acknowledged his arrival while she surveyed the items on his shelves.

"How did you get in?" He poured himself a glass of sack. She had already helped herself to one.

"Your manservant did not want me lounging around the entrance."

No doubt Celine had played the grand lady to the hilt. His manservant could hardly stand against that.

He did not bother to ask why she had come. The way she held herself, and the way that she looked at him, and the way that she made the black gown sway when she strolled, told him the answer to that. The real question was, why now?

"I heard about your daring rescue tonight. Very heroic. I wanted to make sure that you had not been harmed."

"How considerate." He wondered who had gone to Celine in the dead of night with the story.

"You do not sound as if you appreciate my concern. Perhaps if I was helpless and lost I could provoke more interest. Maybe if I was too stupid to leave a burning building and thus precipitated a public spectacle . . ."

Gerald must have visited her. He knew about Sophia staying behind for the animals.

"You have decided to visit London during the summer sessions?" he asked.

"I may live here permanently. I do not care for that Cornwall manor that is my dowager property. Sophia made me leave, I'm sure you know. Sent me away from Marleigh." Something between a girlish pout and a very calculating glare played over her lovely face. "It was insulting for her to do that. Marleigh is large enough for us both."

"I seriously doubt that."

"She did it to diminish me. To set me down."

"I doubt that as well."

"It is mine too! I gave up quite a lot to have it."

"Yes, I expect that you did. Your youth. Your chance for love. Certainly you gave up whatever softness was once in you. But Alistair is dead and Sophia is duchess. If you have come for advice, I can only offer that it is time to move on."

"I did not come for advice."

He already knew that. She strolled around the chamber, examining and fingering the oddities brought back from his travels. She acted very absorbed in the Greek icon and Turkish bronze, and studied the primitive African carving with its distorted features and jutting breasts. Every move, every tilt of the head and pose of the body, was intended to entrance a man.

"Since you did not come for advice, perhaps you should explain why you are here."

Swishing across the room like it was a stage, she took a chair and he sat in another. "I am told that you have some influence over her."

"You were told wrong."

"You have a friendship."

"A very formal one."

"Still, you could speak with her. Explain that she could use a friend and companion to help her at Marleigh. I could be a great aid to her."

"Everyone can use a friend. If you propose to be hers, your actions will speak louder than my words. However, anything less than sincerity will be a waste of your time. The duchess is very sensitive about people using her."

She did not like the insinuation. She glared with a defensive smirk. It passed quickly. She relaxed into the chair.

"I went to great risk to come here. If anyone finds out, my reputation will be ruined."

"Since your husband is barely cold, that is probably true. In fact, it would be best if you left."

She kept her blue eyes locked on him. She was beautiful enough to affect any man, and he was not completely untouched. Ten years ago he had been thoroughly bedazzled. Age begets some wisdom, however, and in him that was especially true about the Celine Laceys of the world. His reaction now was a thin, superficial thing that he could easily contain and ignore.

"I will never forget the time you kissed me. It was a wonderful kiss."

"If I had known that you were to become engaged to Everdon the next day, it never would have happened."

"He was a duke, Adrian. A *duke*. And you were . . ." she caught herself and smiled apologetically.

"Yes." He usually did not resent that anymore, but he did now. Not because of Celine, but because of another duchess and what it implied about the limits of his relationship with her. The flare of annoyance provoked a bluntness that normally he would have suppressed. "Tell me, when did you conclude that you were unable to have children?"

Her face fell. "What an extraordinary thing to ask. I am not—"

"When you began taking lovers I assumed it was the duke, and that you sought another way to provide the son that he could not sire. I suspect it began that way."

"I did not take lovers."

"I know about Laclere's brother Dante. And a few others." *Stidolph?*

She did not even blush. "Alistair was old. I knew after two years that he would never get me with child. If there were lovers, I was not the first wife to solve the problem thus."

"Except that after a few more years, you realized it was not him, but you."

"You are determined to insult me."

"There is no insult in it. I know because the pattern was obvious. Dante and the others were fair or brown-haired. Their bastards could have passed muster. When you offered yourself to me it was clear that you knew there was no danger of a child. You would hardly risk presenting Everdon with a son who had my eyes and hair."

She rose and began her stroll again. "I wish I had known at once. Before you became his M.P. and felt honor-bound to him."

"If it is any consolation, I would not have been any more agreeable earlier."

He might have slapped her in the face, so immediate was the reaction of shock. Evidently Celine had never faced the notion that any man would not succumb.

Unfortunately, shock turned into determination. She smiled as if a gauntlet had been thrown. "That is a blatant lie. You wanted me."

"Once I did. It passed quickly."

"Such things do not pass."

"You are a lovely woman and you can incite a physical reaction in any man. It has been many years since I *wanted* you, however."

Sharp of eye and sensuous of smile, she eased toward him until she stood close to his shoulder. "You think that you *want* her now?"

He did not answer.

"You see what she can do for you, that is all, but she is just prickly enough to resent your expectations that she advance you. I, on the other hand, understand such things perfectly. It is the least that a lover can do." She reached down and stroked one fingernail gently along his jaw. "I know many powerful men. They owe me. In a year we will not even have to be very discreet anymore."

He grasped her hand and pulled it away from his face. She twisted her wrist until she held his hand instead. Looking down like an angel, she placed his palm on her breast.

He met her eyes and let her see his indifference. He removed his hand and stood. He walked to the door and opened it.

"As you said, you risk your reputation coming here. You should leave now."

Unlike Sophia, Celine did not appear at all beautiful when she was angry. The emotion distorted her face into something brittle and ugly and dangerous.

"You dare to dismiss me?"

"I worry for your reputation, as you should. He is no longer alive to blunt the talk. You should be more discreet now that your circumstances have changed."

She collected her shawl and breezed past. "Do not lecture me, Burchard. My circumstances have changed but my position is unassailable, and I did not become Everdon's duchess by being stupid."

He closed the door on her beauty and fury and returned to his sack.

What the devil had all of that really been about?

"It is early to be calling, Gerald," Sophia said as she entered Dincaster's morning room to greet her guest.

"The events of last night render propriety unimportant, to my mind."

"Gerald, you are the sort of man for whom the approach of an invading army would not render proprieties unimportant. So, to what do I owe the pleasure of this unseemly visit at ten o'clock?"

"We need to speak, frankly and directly. Please sit."

She perched on a chair. He paced around her, giving her a hard gaze like one would to a naughty child.

"That spectacle last night was beyond the pale."

"Do you think so? Now that I have had some sleep, I am beginning to see it as quite humorous." That wasn't true. With the passage of shock had come an insistent fear and a helpless confusion about how to protect herself.

"Climbing down that building, dangling like that, you barely clothed . . . it is all over town. The entire episode is highly embarrassing."

"I would rather endure an embarrassing rescue than a discreet death. I am grateful that Mister Burchard chose to risk his own neck in order to help me save mine. I daresay that he could have been on the ground in a minute without me on his back."

"If you had not been so willful about those stupid animals—"

"You would have gotten me out. I do not blame you for running when I refused to obey. It was the sensible course. I have told no one, if that is your real reason for coming. Society will not brand you the coward in contrast to Adrian's hero."

His flush revealed that that had indeed been one of his concerns, and that he resented her articulating it so baldly. A defensive sneer twisted his mouth. "What was he doing in your house?"

"Not visiting me, as you well know. You were present when I left the library and retired. You found me alone in my chamber. I assume that he was passing the house and noticed some smoke and found a way in."

"That strange walrus of a man, the Bohemian, assumed otherwise."

"Attila is Hungarian. Unfortunately, his mouth runs ahead of his brain. Considering that Adrian was lowering us both from my chamber window, his assumption is understandable even if it is incorrect."

"Only if he knows you for a woman who takes lovers. Who is this Attila, anyway, and what is he doing here?"

"He is a friend from Paris. He and Jacques have come to visit me."

"Are you saying that you have imported your lovers? Is it your goal to humiliate me before the whole country?"

"Really, Gerald. I have no intention of answering any more of your impertinent questions."

"My future bride is the center of a public spectacle that will be the tattle of drawing rooms for weeks, she has her virtue publicly compromised by the

indiscreet yapping of a hairy foreigner, and you call my concern impertinent?"

"I call your concern self-centered. You have expressed no interest in my
health or disposition after last night's shock, but only in how things affect
you. However, your continued assumption that we will marry is indeed
impertinent."

Anger brought out something icy and hard in Gerald. He stopped his
pacing and looked her over with his best Alistair inspection, instantly giving that ghost physical substance. The similarity sucked the strength right
out of her. She barely suppressed a tremble. *So this is what I am left with,* that
expression said. *And a sad specimen it is too.*

"Harvey Douglas has come up for the sessions. He said that you visited
Staverly."

"He no doubt also told you why I took refuge there."

"Another spectacle. They follow you wherever you go, don't they? I would
not have expected you to ever go back to Staverly, let alone so soon after your
return."

She knew that he could see that broaching this subject made her composure wobble. He was glad for it. "It was not as difficult as I expected."

"Wasn't it? Are you that heartless? I would think that being there would
overwhelm you with guilt."

She could only glare at him while her heart filled again with the dismay
she had felt in the gazebo.

Unlike Adrian, he did not seek to comfort her, but cruelly pressed his advantage. "You accuse me of impertinence for assuming we will marry, but
Everdon was everything to Alistair. With the succession secured by Brandon,
he knew some peace. You robbed him of that."

"I did not."

"Have you blocked the memories that well? You killed him. Your willfulness and rebelliousness killed him. Call it an accident if you want, but you
were the direct cause of his death, and the death of your father's dreams."

The way he ruthlessly spelled out her guilt, giving voice to her own horrible thoughts, left her boneless and nauseous.

"The notion that you would be the heir distressed him to no end. Your
behavior in Paris only confirmed his fears. In your childish, extravagant
hands, Everdon's status would be ruined in a generation. So he gave you to
me. Not to some earl or marquess, but to me. He did not want the power of
Everdon to be swallowed by being joined to another great title. I would be
its caretaker until your son could assume his position. The legacy would continue whole, just delayed by a generation."

"I do not care why he did it. It was not my choice."

"Your choice? How like you to think only of yourself. It has always been like that. Your shocking friendship with a revolutionary ruined your reputation. Your recklessness killed your brother. Your father sought a way to rectify the disasters, and all you could think about was whether he had pampered your childish sensibilities by giving you a choice."

The relentless picking at the scab of those memories was driving her close to tears.

"You owe it to him, Sophia. You owe it to him, and to Brandon, to obey him in this. For once in your frivolous, intemperate, and thoughtless life you must do his will. There will be no peace about your brother's death until you expiate the damage that you caused."

She was beyond defending herself. The browbeating had worn her down, just as Alistair's always did. There was too much truth in what he was saying. She could not even look him in the eyes anymore.

He picked up his hat and walked to the door.

"One more thing. I would not put too much faith in Burchard's friendship. I heard a rumor that he had a visitor at his chambers last night. Celine. He was one of her suitors before she married your father, you know." He opened the door and threw out his last punch with a vicious smile. "As you once said, if he is interested in a pleasurable liaison with a woman, he can do better than you."

She did not move for a long while after he left. She felt as if she had been pummeled by fists. The final blow, the information about Celine, had knocked the life right out of her.

Maybe Gerald was right. If she married him, she might bury the ghosts and the guilt. With Everdon's power transferred to her husband, probably Captain Brutus would lose interest in her and the letters and danger would cease. There might be some peace. Finally.

She pictured a life as Gerald's wife. The images left her queasy. They might make an arrangement, of course. One that permitted her to go back to France. She had him at a disadvantage and he would most likely agree. But would he honor that solution once he had her? The husband of Everdon would be much diminished if Everdon was in Paris.

With a weary sigh she pushed to her feet. The coercions would only increase. In a few days the Parliament would start, and the demands that she choose her political course would get more insistent. The calls for her to marry would mount. All the time that she tried to discover the right decisions, Captain Brutus would be watching and waiting.

What had been his intention with that fire? To frighten the duchess into obeying his political demands? Or to harm the woman who had betrayed him years ago? His letters implied that he might not know for sure which he desired more badly.

She wanted desperately to hand this all over to someone else. Someone who would manage it for her and make it come out good in the end. Someone like Adrian.

She had woken this morning much softened toward him. Last night had moved her to reconsider the judgments that she had formed. She had even decided to show him those letters and ask his advice.

How stupid of her to read genuine affection into that rescue. How very childish to grasp at the excuse it offered to make a fool of herself. How ridiculous to experience this excruciating disappointment on hearing how he had spent last night.

Do not put too much faith in Burchard's friendship. It had been weak of her to ever do so. He had been managing her to his own ends from the start. He had tried to make love to her even while he cast his lure for Celine.

She coldly looked into the future of demands and expectations and threats and confusion. It was unfair that her life should have been disrupted like this. She wanted none of it. By what right did all these people, these *men,* pull her in several directions like a criminal to be quartered?

Simmering annoyance gave her back some spine. She left the drawing room and headed in search of the only two friends she had in England.

She remembered that first conversation with Adrian. *I am nothing in this.* How true. It was Everdon that they wanted to control, not her.

Well, damn it, let them have it.

The gathering at Laclere's house in late afternoon was a political meeting, which was how Sophia justified attending despite being in mourning. Fortunately, the conversation did not completely revolve around Parliamentary reform.

Perhaps that was because Laclere's wife had invited some friends who were not in the government. Maybe it was because Sophia herself did not encourage the few overtures to political discussions that wafted her way. Most likely, however, it was because many of the guests had an interest in the arts and found that topic more pleasant.

She attached herself to a group that did. It included the St. Johns, whom she had met the day before in the park, and members of Laclere's family.

The viscount's handsome younger brother, Dante Duclairc, began charming her after their introduction. Dante displayed absolutely no interest in politics, which she found refreshing. He was also handsome as sin, with thick brown hair and heavily lashed, beautiful eyes.

"I had expected a more formal gathering," she said to him when he sought reassurance that she was enjoying herself.

"Would that have pleased Your Grace?"

"Not at all. I have been spared formalities for years, and do not relish living with them again."

"Then you have come to the right place. My brother's wife possesses a spirit that undermines most social rituals through her mere presence. No matter what my brother's intentions in this gathering, Bianca will not permit it to be boring."

"We will be spared speeches, then?"

The Viscount Laclere's sister, the Countess of Glasbury, had joined their conversation. She now glanced at Laclere. "No speeches. If you notice, however, my brother is speaking quietly with the M.P.'s present who straddle the fence."

Sophia had noticed those private chats. The tall, imposing lord with his harsh good looks and piercing blue eyes was using the assembly to work his persuasion individually and subtly.

She wondered when he would make his way around to her.

"I apologize that I have not called on you, Your Grace. I thought it best to be introduced first," the countess said.

"I hope that you will call now. Your interest in the arts matches my own, and it would be a joy to have friends with similar sympathies. I count on you to introduce me to others of like mind."

Sophia felt guilty making the overture, since it was unlikely that friendship would have a chance to blossom. Still, she understood the unspoken allusion in the countess's comment, and wanted to reassure her that the new Duchess of Everdon did not judge women as harshly as others might.

The countess appeared surprised and grateful for the invitation. With a smile, she allowed her attention to be claimed by Diane St. John.

"That was kind of you," Dante said.

"You mean, because she is separated from the earl?" Sophia had been pointedly educated by several imposing and annoying arbiters of society on how that scandal had affected the countess's social status.

"Penelope did not want to risk criticism because of it."

"Such things are common in France, and I do not hold them against a woman."

"Not criticism from you. *Of* you."

"I daresay that with all of the criticism *of* me filling the drawing rooms these days, any I might receive for receiving your sister would be the least of it."

Dante laughed lightly, and gave a warm look that indicated he found some of that criticism both interesting and intriguing.

Any inclination he had to explore how intriguing was thwarted by a new presence in their midst. Adrian Burchard had arrived, and was suddenly standing right beside Sophia in a manner that crowded Dante away.

Adrian looked tousle-haired and a little tired and handsome as the devil. He managed to separate her totally from the group. She could not tell if he eased her away or if the others retreated, but suddenly it was just the two of them talking alone.

"I see that you have met Laclere's family," he said.

"The countess is very sweet, and his brother is very charming."

"You are not the first woman to think that of Dante Duclairc. Do not even consider adding him to your Ensemble, however. Dante has no artistic pretensions, and prefers married women."

"He spoke earlier as if you are his friend, but you do not sound like one."

"He is a very good friend, as are Laclere and St. John. That is another reason why you should not consider him for your Ensemble." His scrutiny snapped from Dante to her. "You appear none the worse for last night's adventure. I am relieved to see that you have recovered so well."

"I slept soundly and woke much refreshed. And you, Mister Burchard? Did you sleep well?"

"Passably."

"That is good news. After such strenuous activity, the wise course is to rest. However, I am told that some men seek more exertions after such occurrences, as if their blood does not know how to calm."

"That is true, but considering your shock, it did not seem polite to pursue further exertions last night."

He had a lot of brass to make such insinuations after exerting himself all night with Celine. His quiet, slow tone lacked the playful flirting of their earliest exchanges. It caused an unwelcome sensation to tingle through her, despite her pique.

"I assume that you managed to solve the dilemma," she said.

"Again, passably."

Really!

"I will escort you home after this, Sophia."

"My coach will be waiting, so I must decline."

"I will escort you. The fire was deliberately set and your danger is no longer in question."

"Again, I must decline. However, I want to say that I am grateful for your help last night. I truly am. Although I have come to wonder how you were in my house when the fire began."

"Are you implying that I may have started it?"

The question astonished her. "In no way did I intend to suggest that, although someone other than Captain Brutus could be responsible, of course. I am merely curious about your timely presence. What were you doing in my house last night?"

"Reading the letters that you have received from Captain Brutus." He did not so much as blink.

"You dared to intrude on my privacy in such a dishonorable way?"

He studied her with sharp deliberation, standing too closely, towering above her in a very male manner. "I found them interesting, and I find your willingness to believe he was not responsible for the fire astonishing. The threats in those letters were unmistakable. Maybe you did not absorb the danger because you were distracted by his references to your past intimacy with him. He writes to you as a lover, and now you consider excusing him from this criminal attack on you. It is enough to make one wonder if you welcome his return into your life."

"You cannot seriously believe that."

"I can think of no other reason for your keeping those letters to yourself."

"Perhaps to share them would embarrass me. How did I come to be making the explanations? You are the one who stole into my house and read my private correspondence."

"You can voice your displeasure about that on the way back to Dincaster House. No matter what your feelings toward this man, you should not be about alone, considering your apparent danger from him."

"Why do you assume that I will be alone? Every woman in society is intent on throwing eligible men my way. If I need an escort, I daresay I can find another one. I would not dream of delaying you from pursuing whatever pleasures and diversions await you this evening."

His jaw tightened at her crisp tone. At least she hoped it sounded crisp, and not shrewish and hurt. "In the best of circumstances you are a vexing woman. It has its charm, but your demeanor today does not amuse me. I must demand your company for the evening. You and I have some matters to discuss."

"I do not think that we have anything to discuss."

"Of course we do. Captain Brutus, for one thing. The way that you have been hiding from me, for another."

"I have not been hiding from you. I have been discouraging you."

He began to respond, but stopped because their hostess approached. Lady Laclere bore down on them with a tall, dark, brooding man in tow.

"I see Julian Hampton is here," Adrian muttered dryly. "Do not consider recruiting him to your Ensemble, either. He is far too old, and is a lawyer despite his poetic appearance."

The viscount's wife, Bianca, possessed a distinctive face that managed to combine youthful innocence and worldly sensuality in its wide blue eyes and full lips and firm little chin. "There you are, Duchess. I want to introduce Mister Hampton. He is a dear friend of our family, and has served as solicitor to the St. Johns as well."

Sophia was relieved by the interruption, and delighted to meet the solicitor. His presence reminded her that she had not taken care of a few details about her inheritance. It was past time to rectify the oversight.

"Mister Hampton, are you willing to consider new clients?" she asked after a few pleasantries had been exchanged. "I ask because I have relieved my father's lawyer of his duties."

Julian Hampton appeared vaguely surprised by the question, but if he thought it in bad taste to broach the matter at this assembly he did not allow his expression to show it. "I would be happy to discuss the matter at your convenience, Your Grace."

"That would be right now, I'm afraid. It will not do to have the estate matters left drifting. Would you meet with the previous solicitor and procure the documents and such? I will contact you soon regarding anything that needs my attention."

Julian Hampton took it in stride, and Lady Laclere appeared delighted that her introduction had borne fruit so quickly. Adrian, however, gave Sophia a very peculiar look.

Mister Hampton requested some conversation with Adrian, and the two men wandered off. That left Sophia with Lady Laclere.

In no time the viscount found them. Sophia suspected it had all been planned, and that Mister Hampton had been asked to get Adrian out of the way.

"I am sorry to hear about the damage to your home, Duchess," Laclere offered. "There is a rumor that it was deliberately started. I trust that is not true."

"There is evidence to that, but I hope that you will help me to quash talk of it."

"Do you think it was politically motivated?" Lady Laclere asked.

"It may have been."

Laclere sighed with annoyance. "The more impatient radicals do not understand the fruitlessness of violence, I am afraid. Nothing will be accomplished through intimidation. Rather the opposite."

Sophia could not agree. She was feeling thoroughly intimidated on many fronts, and it had definitely borne fruit.

"I risk being overbold, but how is it that Adrian Burchard attends this meeting?" she asked. "He is firmly in the antireform camp."

Laclere glanced to where Adrian and Hampton spoke near a window. "Burchard is an old friend of mine. He is also an intelligent man. I am hopeful where he is concerned."

"Vergil is quite the optimist," Lady Laclere said.

"Decidedly, my dear. Those of us who support reform are optimists who think that men are capable of understanding issues and acting in the common good. Those who oppose assume that the general population is weakminded, just so many children to be led by their parents."

"I think that your optimism is misplaced where Mister Burchard is concerned," Sophia said. "He did not attend today to listen to reason, did he? Nor did you invite him in the hopes that he would."

"As I said, I am hopeful. But no, his attendance was arranged by certain ministers in my party. Because of you?"

"Probably."

"For romantic reasons, or because they feared that I would corrupt you?"

"They think that I am one of those children, to be led by my parents."

"Just like men," Lady Laclere said, "to assume that a woman is incapable of determining the right course on her own."

The viscount eyed her more sharply. "Have you been able to determine your own course, Duchess? Despite the overbearing influences that certain powerful men are trying to exert?"

"Yes." And she had. Not the course that Laclere meant. Nor the one that Adrian tried to manage. She had most definitely decided her own course, however, and it was time to act on it.

The viscount chatted a bit about Paris and then excused himself. Sophia turned to her hostess.

"That was very mild. I expected more exhortations."

"My husband is too clever for that. It is enough that you know that there are men of principle with other points of view. He assumes that you will seek him out if you need him."

"His restraint is welcome, I assure you."

Lady Laclere examined her with a naked interest. As if making a decision, she guided her over to sit side by side on a bench. "Vergil says that they are exhorting you to marry."

"Yes."

"Not the man whom you want, I assume. It never is."

"I suspect that they would welcome any man who agrees with them. I would prefer to remain unmarried, however. I know that sounds odd."

"You will receive no censure from me. If not for falling in love with Laclere, I expect that I would still be unmarried. Without love, marriage has little to recommend it if a woman can provide for herself through property or employment."

The viscountess spoke with a familiarity that Sophia had rarely shared with a woman. She warmed to this young American woman who did not seem to know how to dissemble.

"I am told that you are an opera singer," Sophia said. "That must be very exciting."

"Thus far the roles have been in theaters in England, but I have been offered a major one in Italy next year." She gazed toward her husband. "Laclere married someone quite unsuitable. Not only an American, but a performer. You cannot get much more unsuitable than that."

She stated it matter-of-factly. Sophia surmised that here was a young woman who dealt with society on her own terms, and who had found a man who did as well. The Viscount Laclere rose significantly in her estimation.

"Has it mattered?"

"Of course. You learn who your friends are, and who the fools are. It has not been as bad as it might have been. Vergil is seen as a bit eccentric and that makes me almost interesting, like an outrageous extravagance."

Their conversation had been refreshingly frank, the sort out of which true friendships are sewn. Sophia risked pushing the intimacy further. "I have a peculiar request to make of you. I would like you to occupy Mister Burchard when I depart."

"You do not welcome your rescuer's attendance? After my husband, he is the most handsome man in the room, and from the way he was watching you earlier I assumed that he was in love."

The offhand observation startled her. "His attendance would be intrusive this evening, and it is his management that I do not welcome."

"Yes, he has that tendency, much as my Vergil does. It can be comforting and charming sometimes, but . . ." Lady Laclere patted her arm conspiratorially. "When you take your leave, I will see that Mister Burchard is distracted. He will not impose, not that the attention of a man who looks like that is ever a complete imposition."

How in blazes had she left without his noticing?

Had it been when Lady Laclere engaged him in that private conversation that probed none too subtly about his affections for the duchess? Or when Laclere cornered him to conduct a quick assessment of his true sympathies in the upcoming political debate? Both exchanges distracted him, and it was only after Laclere walked away that he realized Sophia was no longer in the house.

He commandeered his curricle and snapped the horses toward Dincaster House. Sophia might prefer to avoid talking about Captain Brutus, but it needed to be done.

The way she had given him the slip darkened his mood, which had been shadowed enough from her attitude earlier. He had not realized until their exchange just how jealous he had become of the elusive Captain Brutus.

He arrived at Dincaster House just as the earl was exiting the dining room. "A fortuitous visit, Adrian. I was just about to send for you."

Adrian did not welcome the distraction, but the earl appeared pursemouthed and serious and he had no choice but to follow him to the study.

The earl settled in the chair behind an elaborate desk that had not been the site of any serious study for decades. Adrian sat across its polished, inlaid expanse.

The earl tossed a scandal sheet across to him. "Have you seen it?"

Adrian perused the only story that could have possibly interested the earl. It described the famous rescue of the Duchess of Everdon last night, only the building was higher (five stories), the descent more precarious (sheets shredding from the weight), the hero more romantic (a dark, brooding, man of the world), and the duchess more naked (barely covered by tattered silk). Three times it mentioned that the window had been that of her bedchamber.

"It was inevitable, I suppose."

"Damned embarrassing."

"I could have let her roast and spared you this. It was inconsiderate of me not to do so."

"Your flippancy is not amusing. What the hell were you doing there?"

"Stealing a look at her correspondence."

"Her correspondence! See here—"

"I will not be lectured by you about my behavior. I apologize for the attention that last night has directed at me. I know how much you dislike anything that reminds the world of our relationship. Short of letting the duchess stay in that burning house, this spectacle could not be avoided, however."

The earl did not like his tone, but Adrian had not liked the earl's tone for most of his life, so he did not care.

"You are not without your debts to me, Adrian," the earl said, suddenly flinty-eyed.

"I am *fully* aware of *exactly* what I owe to *whomever* I am indebted."

The earl blinked surprise at the emphasis, and retreated. "Yes, well, that story is not the actual subject that I want to discuss. I had a most peculiar conversation with that Frenchman today."

Any conversation between the earl and Jacques was not good news. Only being informed of a chat between the earl and Attila would be worse. "I hope that you found it enjoyable."

"Not bad, not bad. If you can get that Hun out of the way, the Frenchman can be almost presentable. He is very curious about our ways and our government. Can't hurt to educate 'em to the superior culture here, that's what I say. If the whole world were English, it would be a damn sight easier to manage."

"Definitely. On what points did you educate Jacques?"

"That was the odd part. It began normally enough, but then he asked some questions about the peerage. Very detailed. Wanted to know if we could marry without the Crown's consent, and if we did if the marriage would stand. The more I thought about it later, the more it struck me that he knows about the duchess being married. Maybe he knows who the man is."

He would kill Jacques. "It may have only been a passing curiosity because he knows the King wants her to marry Stidolph."

"Possibly, possibly. Then he quizzed me about marital rights here. Asked how marriages could be ended."

"Again, just curiosity, I am sure."

"Then he asked what would happen to someone who helped a woman to leave her husband. Whether they could be jailed if caught. I explained that the biggest danger came from the husband, and that the French may think nothing of absconding with another man's wife but that we take a much dimmer view of such behavior here." He said it forcefully, as if to emphasize a moral rule.

Adrian ignored the lesson. His mind had completely focused on the implications of Jacques' last question. *He would hang Jacques by the . . .* He rose to leave.

"Then he asked the most peculiar question of all," the earl continued, stopping him. "He inquired if you were a spy."

"A spy?"

"A spy. An agent provocateur."

"What did you say?"

"That it was preposterous, of course. The very notion. I explained that when you go abroad you are nothing more than a secretary or clerk. Good heavens, a *spy*." The earl chortled at the idiocy of the idea.

"What did Jacques say to that?"

His brow puckered while he searched his memory. "He muttered something about assuming that I would know, which of course I would, and we spoke a bit about the weather and then he removed himself." He leaned over the desk. "The point is, I think he knows who the husband is. We should try and get it out of him. Whomever she married is probably influencing her, and not to the good. Perhaps we should think about getting the husband out of the way if he is about, for the time being that is."

The "we" part of this made Adrian uncomfortable. Almost as uncomfortable as the various revelations embedded in Jacques' questions. Adrian experienced a profound gratitude that the earl had long ago given up the habit of deep thought and calculation.

"An excellent idea. Leave it to me. It would be best if you do not broach the subject with him. It might warn him off. I know the man quite well and will worm it out of him quickly."

"Thought that you would want a go at it. It will give you a chance to fix things. Haven't been too successful with getting her in line, have you?"

"I am grateful for the opportunity to redeem myself."

He strode down the corridor to the dining room. He found Colin there, smoking a cigar.

"Glad you came, Adrian. Join me." He pushed a box toward him. "Just me and Father for dinner tonight, and your company will help me recover from the tedium."

"The duchess was not here? Nor her guests?"

"Just the two of us."

"Have you seen her at all in the last few hours?"

"Her carriage went to Laclere's sometime ago to fetch her. Jacques and Attila rode along to escort her home. She should return shortly, I expect."

Adrian swore and slammed a chair hard against the table. "She will not. She has bolted, I am sure of it, and those damn artists are helping her."

"Bolted? To where?"

"She could be headed to India for all I know."

"Not by ship. The tide won't be right until the morning."

Adrian turned to go. "I will have to check the docks."

Colin laid down his cigar. "That could take hours. I will help. It will spare me the boredom of listening to political yammering in my club. I think that I can find some friends to join us. It sounds like a splendid diversion. We will have a duchess hunt."

"I welcome your aid, Colin. However, when we run this particular fox to ground and trophies are being claimed, her tail is *mine.*"

chapter 18

Y ou should rest, Sophia. Go to your cabin and sleep. This boat does not leave until close to dawn. We will wake you after the crossing," Attila said.

Sophia peered up at the starlit sky. Jacques and Attila flanked her, leaning against the railing of the small ship that would take her to France. "I will retire shortly. Thank you again for helping me."

"It was Jacques who found these berths for hire. I am only sorry that the tide meant we could not depart at once."

"A few hours will not matter too much." She did not add that now that she was here, waiting to leave, she welcomed the delay.

A melancholy filled her. It was ridiculous, but she could not shake it. They had spent the last hours laughing about her great escape and anticipating the wonderful times waiting on the Continent. She had already planned the next year full of balls and diversions and a long sojourn in Italy. It would be like old times. But her merriment had been a facade to hide an inexplicable heartsickness. She should be excited and relieved, not aching and sad. This mood made no sense at all. She hated England.

"You do not think that he will interfere?" Jacques asked.

She knew who "he" was. The same "he" who intruded on her thoughts while she gazed into the night sky. Without even knowing what she was up to, "he" had already managed to interfere. Although Attila had agreed to this plan after a little cajoling, Jacques had resisted, because to his mind they would be stealing her from her husband, which could have dire consequences.

She had explained again and again that she and Adrian were not married, but neither artist believed her. Adrian's performance in Paris had been too effective, and the old lie about a husband had come back to haunt her when she asked for their assistance this morning. In desperation she had pled horrible unhappiness and had even, she recalled guiltily, made a few ambiguous accusations about Adrian being the cause of it. That had finally swayed Jacques, which was just as well. She doubted that Attila could have managed this on his own.

"I am worried about Camilla and Yuri and the others," Attila said. "You do not think that he will take vengeance against them or hold them hostage? Such a man might."

The lie's details about her husband's vile temper had not made this any easier. "He is kind to animals, and will see to their care. When I write and ask for them, they will be sent, along with Charles and Jenny."

"Just like an Englishman to be more kind to dogs than to a woman," Jacques said.

"He was not actually unkind to me."

"Do not speak of it, Sophia. It is an indelicate matter, but I understood you well enough. I was hesitant to help you escape, but when I comprehended your situation it became a matter of honor for me to see that he does not touch you again."

"It is not as if he hurt me. I hope that you do not think that."

"There are deeper wounds than those inflicted by a fist or weapons. Like all women, you are resilient about such things, but you are free of him now. The clumsy, selfish brute did not deserve you."

Adrian, clumsy and selfish? She was quite sure that she had never said that about him. She scoured her memory to remember exactly what she *had* said.

Jacques' relaxed body suddenly tightened. "What is that?" he asked, cocking his head. "Do you hear that? There. At the far dock." He pointed.

They all turned to the rail and bent over to watch. Torches danced in the night around two carriages overladen with passengers. Bodies began pouring off their sides and tops and out of their compartments. Soon a raucous crowd milled around a distant dock.

"Good heavens, not another demonstration," Sophia said. "It is the middle of the night."

"Maybe they plan to burn all the boats," Attila said. "Maybe a revolution has begun, and they want to make sure the aristocrats cannot escape the country. It would be the perfect time, with all the government here for Parliament."

"It does not look like a revolution to me and I should know, having just been in one," Jacques said. He squinted at the crowd, which had moved to the next nearest dock. "More like a group of drunks looking for some sport."

That dock ceased to amuse them, and the crowd milled to the next one. Sophia could make out some details now. They were apparently in high spirits, playing some game. Flames briefly illuminated bits of them. Some wore army uniforms and others evening clothes. They swarmed over the piers onto the boats, disappeared for a spell, then swarmed back onto the dock.

"You should go to your cabin, *kedvesem,*" Attila warned.

She barely heard him. One of the men had gone onto a small ship alone and spoken with someone there.

Her gaze locked on that man. He was no more than a dark blotch amidst the jumping torch flames, but . . .

They were only three docks away now and it was clear what was happening. They were searching the ships.

The merry crowd jostled forward. The uniforms became distinct. The officers among them were not common army, but Royal Guardsmen.

The dark blotch strode in front of them all. He suddenly took distinct form.

"*Merde,*" Jacques hissed.

"It is *him.* And he is wearing a sabre." Attila gulped. "We are dead, Jacques."

Jacques narrowed his eyes. "Go to your cabin, Sophia."

"Once he sees you he will know I am here anyway. Let me handle this. He must listen to reason."

"There is no reason in such matters."

The crowd approached their dock. The gangway was down and they could not board. Sophia recognized Colin, carrying one of the torches, and a few other gentlemen to whom she had been introduced during the last few weeks, including Dante Duclairc. Unmarried, all of them, and right now totally foxed.

Except Adrian, who stood front and center. He appeared completely sober. And furious.

They collected in front of her on the wharf.

"There she is! At the railing!"

"Run to ground in two hours. By Jove, we're better than hounds."

"Two men with her, Adrian. Do we lynch them?"

Attila frowned. "Lynch? Lynch? What is this lynch?"

"Hang," Jacques said.

"Hang!"

"They are not going to hurt you," Sophia said, not entirely convinced of that herself. Adrian, for one, looked fit to kill.

The noise brought the captain from his cabin. Well into his night gin, he staggered forward and peered over the rail.

"What the hell is this about?" the captain yelled.

"Raise the gangway," Adrian called. "The woman desires to disembark."

"I do not," Sophia countered. "Do not permit them to board, Captain."

The poor man shook his head, as if he tried to clear it. "You've Royal Guardsmen with you. Were you sent by His Majesty?"

"Of course he wasn't."

Adrian muttered something and the officers tried to line up neatly and look steady. "Would these officers be with me otherwise?"

"He is tricking you. He collected them out of taverns and brothels, and not at the King's command. I have paid for this ship, and I demand that you not raise the gangway. I order you to cast off at once."

"I can't cast off. Nowhere's to go, and night is no time to be navigating down river, not to mention the crew ain't on board."

"Just drift for an hour or something, as long as you get me away. I will pay you double."

That made him pause. He faced Adrian. "What do you want with this woman?"

"She is the Duchess of Everdon and the King requires that she remain in England."

The Captain debated and sighed. "Damned situation. See here, Your Grace, if that is who you are, better you go and settle this with the gentleman and the King. Tide is at five if you will still be wanting this ship, but I don't take any passenger against the Crown's pleasure, no matter how good the silver." He lumbered over to the winch and began raising the gangway.

Adrian waited patiently, glaring at her. The officers tried to maintain an official stance, but kept wobbling and giggling like the besotted fools they were. Colin and the other gentlemen joked and enjoyed the spectacle.

Sophia seethed.

With the gangway in place, the captain ambled away. One very annoyed third son of an earl strode onto the ship.

He marched right up to her. She instinctively took a step back before she dug in her heels.

"Going somewhere?" he asked coolly.

"Yes."

"Not tonight, you aren't." He turned to Jacques and Attila. "I am left to conclude that you two only came to England in order to abduct the duchess."

"Abduct?" Attila cried.

"Worse, you have dishonorably taken advantage of my family's hospitality even while you plotted against the realm."

"Plotted against the realm? Oh, no, Mister Burchard, there has been no plotting. Why, Jacques and I would not know how to plot, would we, Jacques?"

"Speak for yourself. I am weary of being threatened by this man. The English win one little war and they think they are masters of the world. As to how we came to accompany Sophia, that is none of your concern."

"It is very much my concern."

"She is a free citizen. Even a husband's rights do not nullify that. She does not want you anymore. Her decision to leave makes that clear. I cannot say that I blame her. She does not belong in England, or with you. After experiencing the glory that is France, she could never be happy again on this provincial island, or with one of its men sharing her bed."

A very tense silence fell. Adrian's stance relaxed. Somehow it made him seem more dangerous.

"What do you mean by that?" he asked ever so calmly.

"Nothing," Sophia inserted quickly.

"Please, M'sieur. We broach a topic best left alone, don't you agree?" Jacques' finely hewn face pursed into a bored, knowing smirk.

"Yes," Sophia said. "Especially with a lady present."

"I am interested in broaching it. Compelled, actually."

Jacques sighed with exasperation. "It is well-known that Englishmen do not know how to handle women."

"Is it?"

"Oh, yes." Attila concurred apologetically. "Jacques is too frank, but what he says is true. The rest of the world does not throw it in your face because that would be impolite."

Adrian glanced to the crowd of Englishmen on the wharf. "And dangerous."

Jacques ignored the warning. He made a disdainful gesture. "The English have no great art, no great music, so it is not surprising that their imagination fails in love. A woman is like a new rose, beckoning all the senses. An Englishman sees it, plucks it, and then crushes it."

Sophia felt her face burning. This was no time for Jacques to wax poetic.

"This is fascinating," Adrian said.

"Eh, *bien*? Listen and learn. The right way to enjoy that rose is to gently sniff. To carefully peel the petals apart. To caress and nibble its velvet layers and lick its nectar."

"I am entranced, Jacques. Although I would like to interrupt here and say that if I ever learn that you attend the duchess in the hopes of licking her nectar, I will kill you."

Sophia rushed in. "I assure you, neither Jacques nor Attila has ever licked . . . that is to say . . ."

Jacques threw up his hands. "You are hopeless. What did I tell you, Attila? I generously try to help this Englishman by imparting the secrets of my heritage, and all I get is threats. You do not deserve her, and unless you plan to use that sword, we will not let you force her to return."

"Then I will have to use the sword."

"If you use it with the skill that she says you deploy with your other weapon, we are safe."

Utter silence this time. Not a sound, not a movement. The air stilled around them. Sophia tried to speak, but her wide-open mouth would not move.

Finally Adrian shifted his weight and scratched his brow, as if checking to be sure that he was really standing on this ship and had just heard correctly.

"Are you saying that Sophia told you that she is leaving because I am a poor lover?"

Jacques struck a brave pose and made a shrug that answered more eloquently than words.

Attila tried desperately to smooth things. "We hesitated helping her. To come between a husband and wife is a serious offense. She repudiated you as she did in Paris, and we could see her unhappiness and desperation, but of course we knew that when she said again that you were not married, that she was lying to enlist our assistance. I even tried to intercede on your behalf. It was then that she blurted the truth."

"Did she?" Adrian asked silkenly. "What did she say?"

"Nothing!" Sophia's voice returned so abruptly that the cry startled her.

"I insist that you tell me, Attila, so that I can correct my ways."

Attila missed the ominous undertones. He looked relieved that Adrian was being reasonable. "She said that you are domineering, too aggressive, and that you only manage her to your own interest and pleasure, and that you manhandle her almost daily." He smiled sympathetically. "We do not blame you. As an Englishman you cannot help being prone to the quick, crushing style that in reality most woman only enjoy every now and then. It is your misfortune that in your absence she went to Paris and discovered that love can be pleasurable. There were all those years apart."

"And all those artists to teach her."

Attila coughed nervously. "Our hearts went out to her to have to suffer such clumsiness, and we could not leave our sweet Sophia in such a situation, since it had so distressed her."

She wanted to die. She would grab Adrian's sword and fall on it and that would be that.

He looked down at her. "Well, my dear, I stand admonished. I can see that I will have to endeavor to do better in the future."

"See, Sophia, he is contrite. I suggested this morning that you speak honestly to him, did I not?"

"Gentlemen, the duchess will not be staying on this ship tonight. I will see that she is back by sailing time. There is a second carriage that will take you two back to Dincaster House if you choose, or you can stay here. You can all sail to France in the morning, if you like. In fact, you can sail to hell, for all I care."

"We will accompany Sophia back to Dincaster House," Jacques said.

"She will be coming in another carriage with me."

"I will not leave this ship," Sophia said. "You have no authority here, and no right to interfere. Collect that rabble down there and be on your way."

"Foolish of me to think that you would obey so that we could do this with some dignity." He stepped up to her. "Time to go, Duchess."

With a quick move he bent and embraced her legs. The world flipped and she was facing his back, slung over his shoulder as she had been in Paris. He strode down the gangway, and Colin and the others went wild.

"I will have you drawn and quartered," she said, thumping his back.

The young men made the most of it by hooting and cheering. The Royal Guardsmen stood smartly as they passed.

Adrian toted her to the first carriage and set her down at its open door. Burning with mortification, she considered refusing to enter. One look at the dark eyes glaring at her said that he would bodily throw her in, if necessary.

She surveyed the little mob with her best ducal stare. That quelled them a little. Turning away with what poise she could muster, she entered the carriage with her head high, determined to give Adrian a piece of her mind.

"That was inexcusable," she snapped as he stepped in behind her.

"You left me no choice."

"Do not act as if some mandate from God required you to interfere. Coming after me was *presumptuous.*" She emphasized the hated word.

"Probably, but I am in one hell of a presumptuous mood. Who knows where it could lead if you do not behave."

They headed away from the wharf with the second carriage close behind. Adrian sat across from her, his dark mood filling the compartment. She decided it might be wise to wait a few minutes before continuing to upbraid him.

His silence became a thick cloud that the night breeze could not penetrate. She got the sense that she was the one being scolded, and he wasn't even speaking.

He was probably brooding about Jacques and Attila's little misunderstanding.

It might be best to explain her innocence.

"I want you to know that Jacques completely mistook what I said to him this morning. About you. I never . . . that is, I couldn't criticize . . . after all, we haven't . . ."

He didn't respond.

"I may have mentioned something about your managing me and man-handling me, which, of course, you have just done again, but it had nothing to do with . . . well, that."

He just watched her.

"I want to make that clear, since we took this carriage in order to discuss matters that require privacy, and that is definitely one of them."

"It certainly is, but we will not discuss that or the other matters here."

"We are unlikely to find more privacy at Dincaster House."

"I never said that I was taking you to Dincaster House."

As if to emphasize that, the sounds of the second carriage peeled away.

"Are you abducting me?" She laughed nervously.

"I am collecting on your debt."

Of course he would not want to risk losing the great prize. She should have thought of that. "There was no need for tonight's dramatics. You have removed me from my ship for no reason. As I promised last night, I have directed my votes the way that you want. I left letters with Jenny that give my M.P.'s the word."

"Very honorable. Only that was not the payment that I referred to last night."

"It certainly was."

"You offered anything in your power to bestow. You assumed it would be the votes, but I never agreed to that payment."

"You did not disagree either."

"I was preoccupied."

Their isolation on the silent streets suddenly pressed on her. "Where are you taking me?"

"To my home."

"Exactly what payment did you have in mind, Mister Burchard?"

No reply.

"You are a scoundrel."

"Considering the insults that I endured from your Ensemble, I am barely resisting the temptation to be one. Right now. In the quick, crushing style preferred by clumsy Englishmen. Provoke me and I may lose the battle."

His tone suggested the threat was real, but her outrage knew no prudence. "You intend to take advantage of something I said while facing the jaws of death, while dangling thirty feet above a street?"

"You offered me whatever I wanted, after I had specifically told you on two occasions what that was. Your assumption that I would claim those damn votes instead of you is charming. Maybe you really convinced yourself that I only wanted you in order to get the votes."

"Do you really intend to hold me to this debt? Do you think that I will agree to make love with you under such a condition?"

"If I require it, you are bound by honor to do so. The devil of it is, I cannot convince myself to be enough of a scoundrel to press my advantage that far. So I only demand an hour of your company for some conversation, and one kiss."

"Some conversation, and one kiss?"

"That is all."

"After this conversation and kiss, you will allow me to return to the ship and leave England?"

"I will even arrange that your Ensemble, your servants, and your animals join you."

That seemed awfully fair. Suspiciously so. Still, if he promised, he would abide by it. She would be off to the Continent as she had planned, with only this brief diversion.

Some conversation with him was probably in order too. It had saddened her to leave without saying good-bye.

The only snag was the kiss. She remembered his kisses too well. The dangerous but compelling intimacy they offered. The potential they embodied. It would tear her heart to experience that again, only this time in final parting.

It might be best to manage that part of the debt her own way.

Clutching the door, she pulled herself up and bent over him. She quickly pecked him on the lips and then plopped back into her seat. "Now we have only to deal with the conversation."

He leaned forward and took her chin in his warm hand. "The kiss is mine to collect, when I want, how I want. I will choose the time and place." His fingers caressed her jaw and chin before releasing her, leaving her tingling from the contact. He might have embraced her whole body, so thorough was her reaction.

The carriage stopped on a street of large houses on the edge of Mayfair. Adrian escorted her up the four stone steps to the door of one of them. Her stomach did a strange lurch as they passed the threshold and climbed the long marble staircase to the second level.

Every instinct told her to balk. He appeared as relaxed and coolly elegant as ever, but his eyes held an expression that was sharper and deeper than normal. He looked as if he had accepted something as inevitable. Her departure and the failure of his mission?

Just one kiss. She wasn't a complete fool where he was concerned. She could handle that.

He ushered her into a sitting room. It struck her as deliciously comfortable. Good chairs for reading and a large hearth for fires. Dark patterns and dark wood everywhere. A polished desk in one corner. A shelf of exotic oddities.

"So this is where you bring your women."

"This is where I live. I bring my women elsewhere."

"This conversation will probably be our last. I think that we should be honest, or there is little point to it. I know that you bring Celine here. Gerald told me."

"It appears that Stidolph gives no quarter and takes no prisoners. That is good to know." He came up behind her and lifted her shawl from her shoulders. "I did not bring Celine here. She came on her own."

"Well, goodness, that makes all the difference."

"I threw her out."

"You expect me to believe that you rejected one of the most beautiful women in England?"

"Celine's celebrated beauty is a superficial thing. Unlike you, she possesses very few layers, and they barely conceal her selfish vanity."

A manservant appeared and Adrian sent him for some wine.

They sat in chairs across from each other.

Seeing him in his home created an unexpected intimacy. It occurred to her that she had never ventured into a man's private spaces before. Her Ensemble were always the guests and intruders, not her.

"Your hour is ticking away," she said.

"If I choose to spend it only looking at you, that is my prerogative."

An hour of being looked at by those dark eyes would be more than she could bear.

She was grateful when the wine came. She was more than happy to have someone else in the room for a few minutes. But the little ritual of pouring and presenting ended quickly, and then they were alone again.

"Why are you running away?" Adrian asked.

"I am not running away. I am returning to my life."

"You are returning to the place where you hid for eight years."

"I did not hide. Everyone knew where I was."

"You hid from yourself there."

The comment dismayed her. Its insight pierced her like a shaft of light. She retreated from its illumination.

"If I am running away, I think that I can be excused. Someone did try to kill me yesterday."

"Someone tried to frighten you yesterday. If the goal had been your murder, there were more efficient ways to affect it. Captain Brutus counted on that fire being discovered before you came to harm. You are of no use to him dead." He glanced at her over the rim of his glass. "Did you enter into a secret marriage with him?"

"No."

"Were you his lover?"

"Our intimacy did not go that far."

"Has your affection survived all these years, or been rekindled with his return?"

"You ask because I did not show anyone those letters?"

"I ask because I want to know if he owns your heart."

"It was not his reminders of our affection that touched me. It was the rest."

"His threats? Surely you know that I would have seen to your protection if I had known."

"Not the threats. It was his reminders of my sympathy for his cause. When I was younger, I believed and cared about such things. I confess that those letters, coming from him, called forth the idealistic girl."

"Which only made your situation here more difficult. So you are running away from having to make a real decision about reform. Leaving those letters to your M.P.'s, but only in payment of a debt, absolved you of that responsibility."

"You make it sound as if I slyly construct excuses for myself. I am not that clever."

"You are very clever. I had not realized until now just how clever you have been in finding ways to run and hide."

His frankness made her uncomfortable. "I cannot decide if I have just been complimented or insulted."

"What else are you running from? Stidolph?"

"I do not choose to talk about Gerald. Spend your hour elsewhere, what is left of it."

"He has been intimidating you, hasn't he?"

"I can manage Gerald's calls to duty and responsibility."

He studied her as though he sought to read her soul. "My mention now of his name disturbed you, and simple calls to duty would not affect you like that. He has been using the past to get to you, hasn't he? Brandon and the rest."

When she had suggested that they be honest tonight, she had not expected it to go this far. His perception astonished her. The mention of Gerald had indeed disturbed her, and summoned again the horrible confusion she had experienced during that conversation this morning.

"He says there will be no peace until I rectify what happened by fulfilling my father's wishes about Everdon's future. That peace would be a delicious thing to know. It may be worth any price, I think sometimes."

"So you ran away from the temptation to pay the price, because you know that you would only exchange one hell for another."

She resented the way he kept peeling away, exposing her heart. "You seem to know my mind better than I do. If I ran from that, it was a sensible course. I am not very strong. Not like you."

"I think that you are one of the strongest women I have ever met."

"Then your knowledge of women is pitiful. Those memories leave me weak. You have seen it yourself. Gerald came and threw my guilt at me this morning and within moments I had no will. Yes, damn you, I am running away. From him and the ghosts and Everdon and Captain Brutus."

He set down his glass. "Aren't you forgetting something?"

"I think that you have forced me to thoroughly admit my cowardice. What more is there?"

"You are also running away from me."

She struggled to phrase an offhanded denial, but the truth of his comment flowed like a thick current between them. The air was full of him suddenly, as if he physically reached across to her.

Trembling, she shot to her feet and paced to a window to break the effect. It didn't help much. He rose, too, relaxed and confident. She could feel him watching her, calmly waiting for a response.

"I trust that you do not intend to force a discussion of that now too," she said.

"I had, but I have changed my mind."

"That is generous of you, and probably very wise."

"Not generous or wise. It is selfish and calculating. We will talk about it later."

She turned in surprise. "Not much later. Your hour is almost passed."

He removed his frock coat and laid it on the chair. "Later. After I have made love to you. Surely you know that is why I brought you here."

He strolled around the chairs and leaned against the back of one with his arms folded over his chest. He reminded her of how he had looked that first night in Paris. *This is how it will be,* his expression said. *This is what will happen.*

His aura of calm decision contrasted starkly with her own demeanor. Her heart had grown into a heavy weight whose deep pulse shook her body.

He looked so splendid with his dark hair mussed over his brow. Long lines angled from his broad shoulders to his hips. And those eyes. His gaze practically scorched.

Running away might be a good idea at that.

"You said only one kiss."

"Only one kiss as payment of your debt. I would not enjoy it if you felt obligated about the rest."

"There will not be any of 'the rest.' " She tried to adopt an authoritative tone, but it came out tremorously.

"If you are determined, that is how it will be. I am hardly going to force you."

He pushed off from the chair and came to her until he stood just inches away. His masculinity assaulted her like a force, pinning her against the window. A primitive response inside her reveled in the power he projected. Sensual expectation fluttered through her body.

He gently took hold of her shoulders with firm, exploring caresses. She shuddered from the warm pressure of those splaying fingers. So appealing. So unnerving.

He tilted his head to see her face. "You are afraid."

"I am not." But she was afraid. Afraid of that kiss and where it might lead. Frightened of the vulnerability that the passion would create. Fearful of discovering that this was just a more dishonorable way of manipulating her.

"You still worry that I only want you as a way to gain something else."

He possessed a second sight tonight. "You do seek a way to gain something else. Do not deny it."

"You would prefer it if I did, but I told you it would not be that way with us." He eyed her bonnet for pins, and pulled them out. "That hiding place is denied you. I could have gone and fetched those letters once you told me about them. Now you can destroy them. You can even write others, directing us to vote for reform, before you leave on that ship."

He lifted off the bonnet and set it aside. Night air from the window cooled her head. She felt that she had just been deprived of an essential piece of armor.

He tilted her chin up with one finger. "What happens here has nothing to do with controlling Everdon's power, nor will I ever speak to you about those damn votes again. This is only about you and me."

"I think it best if you do not do this."

"If I do not do it now, I may never get to."

"I do not know why you persist in this."

"Yes, you do. That is what really frightens you."

He stretched his fingers into her hair along her nape. He guided her head toward him. "I will have that kiss now."

It was a kiss of a lifetime, full of slowly ascending demand. Deliberate and determined and merciless. She did not begin to know how to defend against what it did to her. Cradling her head, arching her into his embrace, he turned that "one kiss" into a long exploration of arousal that left her alight with shivery, spiraling sensations. The loneliness groaned with gratitude that he possessed the skill to make capitulation almost inevitable.

He ended it with a tender bite on her lower lip. Caressing her face, he looked down at her. "Another? I must warn you that it is the last time I will ask. After this you are on your own to express your will."

Decision time. She knew what she risked. She would be giving this man the power to use her and hurt her as none other had. The disillusionments of her youth could one day pale in light of what might await her with him. But maybe he was right. She had been running and hiding from that danger for too long.

She neither agreed nor disagreed. His mouth suddenly fascinated her. Maybe one more. She reached up and grazed her fingertips along his lips.

He clutched her hand and held it there, kissing her palm and inner wrist.

His tight expression enthralled and dismayed her. His reaction to her gesture left her light-headed and confused. He pulled her back to him and the river of her emotions flowed with renewed turbulence.

.   .   .

He had lied.

He had said that he had no ulterior motive for seducing her, but he did. He had implied that they would share one night before she left for France, but he had no intention of bringing her to that ship for its dawn sailing.

He planned to bind her to England. Not because of Everdon or the promise of a Treasury position. He would do it for the simple reason that he could not let her go, and wanted much more than one night.

She felt so good in his arms. Soft and feminine and trembling with her touching hesitation. He kissed her again until the last of the stiff caution melted, caressing through the black gown and rigid stays, seeking the curves of her body. Angling his head, he tasted the sweet skin of her neck. The shortening rasp of her breath flurried against his ear, a melody of desire that instantly drowned out his own inner chant that exhorted control.

The hunger that had been building for weeks suddenly roared for release. He barely suppressed the urge to take her at once against the wall. Pulling her tightly so he could feel her along his length, he kissed her again with a devouring mouth as impatience overwhelmed him.

Her arms slid around his body in a shy embrace. Her tongue darted in play with his, but retreated at his demanding reaction. Both responses possessed a caution that checked him. Her body might be bowed into his, and his caresses might be raising gasps of pleasure, but she was surprised and frightened.

He wrapped her in his arms and nuzzled her hair and forced some restraint. He did not need Jacques' lessons to know that this was no way to make love to a woman the first time.

When he kissed her again he did so carefully, slowly luring her. She joined him in her tentative way. He reveled in her soft curves as she grew relaxed and pliant beneath his hands again, but arousal still surged and retreated, as if she feared the sensations and kept forcing control on them. Something inside her resisted knowing again the abandon she had experienced in the gazebo.

Her breasts, hardened with passion, pressed against his chest. He drew his hand forward and smoothed at their fullness. A deep sigh breathed from her, a lovely sound, and her whole body trembled. He set her away from him against the wall and cradled both breasts in his hands. When he rubbed their hard tips with his thumbs, she grasped at his arms as if to steady herself.

He watched the soulful battle as she alternately gloried in the pleasure and fought it. Her clutching fingers on his arms both held him to her and pressed him away. His own need burned fiercely at the image she presented, liquid-eyed and beautiful, tottering on the brink of ecstasy.

Dipping his head, he kissed her breast. He slid his hands to her back and released the closures of her gown. Her heavy lids rose with renewed alertness.

If she was going to change her mind, it would be now.

He knew how to stop that from happening. He slid the gown's bodice down, determined to subdue any misgivings with his hands and mouth.

The relief in her expression stopped him.

He realized that it was what she expected and wanted. Defeat instead of surrender.

They faced each other, their breaths the only sounds, both resisting for their own reasons the pull of desire. They held each others' arms in an odd, distant embrace. Her gown hung around her hips and her lovely breasts strained against the thin fabric of her chemise. Their swells peeked erotically over the hard encasement of her stays.

He traced one finger along the neckline of her undergarment. "Remove it. Offer yourself to me as you did at Staverly."

Surprise flashed in her eyes. She glanced away in embarrassment. He fought the urge to trail his hand lower and provide the excuse of seduction she wanted.

She looked back. With the charming awkwardness that claimed her at times, she pushed the straps of her chemise down her arms.

The small cooperation ended her fragile resistance. When he caressed this time, skin on skin, her head lolled back against the wall with a sensual sigh of acceptance.

He took her hands and placed them behind her neck so that her bent elbows flanked her head and her lovely breasts rose to him. He caressed and licked them, teasing at the hard tips, drawing out her passion. She arched against the wall in growing delirium, and finally stroked one hand into his hair to encourage him to draw more aggressively.

His thoughts blurred to everything but the smell and taste and sounds of her. Chaotic need crashed through him. He stroked to her thighs but the armor of petticoats interfered. Exploring ineffectively but unable to keep his hands off her, he took her mouth in another kiss.

She rose to it with an eagerness that equaled his own. They sparred with biting, impatient mouths. He grasped her head steady and tamed her cascading kisses with a deep joining that eased his burning even while it stoked it.

He broke away and took a step back. She looked wonderfully wild and dishevelled. Her eyes gleamed with the primitive sensuality of her arousal.

Taking her hand, he eased her forward. "Come to bed."

Her slight pull of resistance surprised him. She was long past retreat. He knew that even if she did not.

He released her hand and opened his arm. She stepped into it. Lifting a brace of candles from a nearby table, he brought her to the bedchamber.

She walked within that guiding arm, against his warm strength, almost tripping over her hanging skirts in her clumsy breathlessness. Electrifying emotions gave their progress an unreal quality.

Decorated like the sitting room, the bedchamber spoke of comfort created
by a man with no one to accommodate but himself. The carved, draped bed
impressed her as incredibly inviting. And frightening.

He explored her neck with kisses while he loosened the fastenings to her
gown and petticoats. Acres of fabric billowed down to the floor.

He knelt to lift her feet out of the heaping fabric. "So many layers. Unlike the ones reflected in your eyes, these are a nuisance."

"You see more in my eyes than what is there."

He slid off her hose with tantalizing palms. "They are there, and they are
intriguing."

Their talk barely distracted her from the shocking reality that she was
down to her stays and underclothes. "Perhaps more intriguing than what is
under them."

"I already know what is under them. You are the one who does not."

He stood and embraced her in a long kiss, then parted and began to
loosen the sleeves of his shirt.

She tried to be a bold lover. She plucked loose the tie of his cravat and
fumbled at the buttons of his waistcoat. He watched with warm amusement
and did not seem surprised when her shaking hands stopped. He shed his
waistcoat and shirt on his own.

Which left her standing with her nose an inch away from his bare chest.

His hewn beauty left her mouth dry. She laid her hand on the tautness and
warmth. Her fingers stretched up a chiseled muscle and a sensual stirring
purred through her. She had never thought that seeing a man's body could
be so engrossing.

She looked up. Searing eyes watched her tentative explorations. Self-
conscious suddenly, she let her hand fall away.

He sat in a chair, removed his boots, and began on the trousers that she
had been too cowardly to deal with. Flustered and excited, she turned away
and tried to unlace her stays.

"I will do it." Strong hands grasped her waist and guided her back until
she sat on his knees. His bare knees, she realized with a jolt. He was naked.

She balanced awkwardly on his legs, facing away from him. Flush after
flush tingled her skin while his hands released and removed the stays. She
looked down at the thin fabric of her drawers and the chemise falling around
her hips. Her naked legs dangled along his shins.

She made to scoot off but he pulled her back, into the astounding physicality of his arms and body. The sensation of his nakedness shocked her. It was also wickedly exciting.

Not as wicked as his hands. Slow, languid caresses raised waves of sensuality that drowned her embarrassment. She relaxed into him, her head against his shoulder and her face turned toward his handsome profile. His gaze wandered down her at will, while his strong hands traced delicious lines of pleasure around her breasts.

"How beautiful you are," he said. "Your skin is so luminous and your form so feminine. I could look at you for hours."

She watched him look at her. His hands moved and circled her breasts with trails of excruciating anticipation. He touched the tips in ways that forced cries to rise to her throat and her body to arch for more.

His head turned to kiss her while he gently rubbed and palmed. Anxious hunger churned through her, down deeply, pulsing with excitement. The craving pleasure created by his slow, patient hands was driving her mad.

A groan passed from her mouth into his. "That's right, darling. Let me know what you like," he whispered.

One hand pressed lower to her hips and thighs. With smooth slides he removed what was left of her clothing, leaving her atop him completely naked.

He parted her legs until she straddled his lap. The change left his phallus nestled erotically against the cleft of her bottom. He lifted one of her knees and hitched it over the chair's arm, spreading her into an exposed position.

Punishing her mouth with a savage kiss, he stroked the soft flesh of her raised thigh while his other hand continued arousing her breast. Desire veered into a screaming need for him to explore her open vulnerability. Her entire consciousness focused on how badly she wanted him to touch her down there.

He did, and she arched and cried from the magnificent shock of it. He kept his hand to her, exploring her reactions, arousing astonishing pleasure and tension. His voice spoke lowly, praising the beauty of her abandon, but she barely heard him through the primal sounds springing from her primitive essence. Every gasping breath came out a moan or a cry. Her hips rose and fell, shamelessly begging.

He moved the caresses to a specific spot of sensitivity. She shot to an unworldly height of pleasure, a frightening place of excitement so sharp that it was almost painful. She tried to retreat and grabbed his hand to push it away.

He would not let her. "You do not run away tonight, darling. Not from me," he said with his mouth pressed to her temple.

She could not fight the intensity. With a helpless groan she surrendered and with a throaty scream she died. Only the death was a blissful moment, full of pure pleasure and heavenly release.

He carried her to the bed and laid her down. His body came over hers and she clutched him, joyed to finally embrace him and grateful to hold on to his reality amidst the unworldly sensuality in which she floated.

He was as careful and gentle as one could expect, but not careful and gentle enough.

She winced at the quick stretching. A burning tear brought her back from the edges of paradise.

He froze. Her gaze drifted up the naked chest suddenly motionless above her on taut arms. She ventured a glance at his face.

"You should have told me."

"Perhaps you should not have assumed otherwise."

"I can be excused, I think."

"Would it have made a difference? Would you have gone all honorable on me?"

"I don't know."

She caressed his chest. "Are you angry?" He looked it, a little.

He dipped to kiss her. "No. I am flattered." He moved. "I will try not to hurt you more."

He didn't hurt her at all. He entranced her, enthralled her, and mesmerized her. The physical joining astonished her heart and soul even more than his hands had amazed her body. Something beckoned to her much like the release had. Something spiritual and glorious and promising heaven. It stirred in her emotions and whispered in rhythm to his body. *Give yourself. Lose yourself. Believe. Trust.*

Toward the end, she knew astonishing pleasure again. Not with the physical fracture of before, but instead with an emotion-drenched joy that reveled in absorbing his demanding need and accepting his erupting passion and finally enfolding his spent strength.

He moved off her and pulled her into an embrace that connected their whole bodies. She savored the eloquent silence, and marveled at the new awareness of herself and him that had just been born.

He had lied. He *was* angry. Not at her, but at what she was and how that framed the implications of what had just happened.

He brushed damp curls away from her face and tucked her closer. He had not been nearly as surprised as he should have been. Maybe he secretly had not assumed otherwise at all. The truth fit with what he knew of her life and saw in her depths. But admitting the possibility would have made tonight impossible, and so he had chosen to accept her pose of worldly sophistication.

He rose on one arm and looked down at her serene contentment. "Why me?"

"Maybe I trusted you to do England proud." She smiled impishly, but her eyes met his with a silent request that he not insist that she search her heart for a serious answer.

"All those years. All those permanent guests and French gentlemen. Did nary a one touch your heart?"

"One or two. I would have never given them such a hold on me, however. It was not me they wanted. Not really. It was always something else."

Yes, she would assume that. Her own father had used her as a way to get something else. She would take it for granted that anyone's attention had ulterior motives.

It pained him that she had lived so many years with the loneliness that must have created. What must it be like to accept that every offer of friendship or love was really an attempt to procure your wealth or patronage or even Everdon itself? She had gone to France convinced that she had no value except for those things.

She may have finally accepted that was not the case with him. He would have to be very careful not to disillusion her.

Which restricted his reaction to tonight as surely as her position as the Duchess of Everdon did. It was that which angered him.

With any other woman he would be honor-bound to offer marriage now. The bastard son of an earl's wife did not propose to a duchess in her own right, however, even if he had just taken her innocence. Nor could Adrian Burchard do the right thing by Sophia Raughley, because the prize of Everdon would taint the purity of his motives.

She nestled snugly, her expression one of utter peace. He tightened his embrace on her soft body and kissed her cheek. "You are a beautiful, magnificent woman."

She blinked surprise, then smiled skeptically. "It is gallant of you to say so."

"Not gallant. Stay in England and I will say it again, often, until you believe me. Until you see your own worth and understand who you really are."

She looked troubled, as if facing who she really was must surely lead to disappointment. He would have gladly killed Alistair right then if the man was not already blessedly gone.

"Are you offering me a liaison, Adrian?"

"Yes. And affection and friendship and help, if you want them." He could not include more, nor could she accept it.

"You can do better than me."

"There is no one better, and no one else I want. I am not just being gallant, but if you think I am, humor me for a few weeks at least. You can always leave later if you doubt my affection, or decide an affair is not worth the risks."

Or decide to choose an appropriate consort for the Duchess of Everdon. No, in that event, he would be the one to leave. He had told Dot that he would not make it difficult for her, and he wouldn't.

She turned in his arms and clung to him. "Maybe I am magnificent when I am with you. I feel as if I might be."

"You surely are."

She nestled her face into the crook of his neck and breathed deeply. "Show me again, Adrian. Make love to me again. Can we?"

He could. With his body he showed her just how beautiful and magnificent she was to him. With more emotion than he had ever known before, he called forth her glorious passion from beneath the layers and then lost himself in it.

Afterwards he watched the contented peace reclaim her as she believed in herself for a while once more.

She did not make the tide. When the ships in port set sail, she was nestled asleep in his arms.

chapter 20

I have been thinking about the Marquess of Northford," Dot said. White wisps blew around her head from the little gale raised by her snapping fan.

"For what reason?" Adrian asked, appreciating the bit of breeze wafting to him. Parliament had adjourned early and he had ridden over to Dincaster House in search of Colin, only to find him visiting Dorothy in her dainty private sitting room. He had joined them, and at Dot's generous invitation had stripped down to shirt and trousers like Colin, so as not to swelter on this unbearably hot August day.

"For Sophia. Surely you saw the letter in today's gazette, calling on the lords to gird for battle to slay the dragon of mob rule. It pointedly referred to a certain peeress who needs to ensure that a certain seat in the House of Lords is filled soon, in case a Reform Bill passes the Commons."

"Why the marquess?" Colin asked. "In case you don't know, Dot, he's—"

"Exactly. He has not even done his duty to his family line and the succession. If he ever married, he would accept that his wife had a lover."

Silence greeted this casual observation.

"It is one solution, is all that I am saying. Not an ideal one, I will admit, but not unheard of."

"I think that we should let the duchess manage her own affairs," Colin said.

Adrian agreed. In fact, Sophia was proving adept at managing her affairs. She had arranged her two-month affair with him with fastidious discretion.

She had moved to a leased house while Everdon House was being repaired. She had chosen one several streets from his chambers, and made sure that it was small enough to require only Jenny and Charles and a few servants whom Charles assured would be discreet. Besides those retainers, only Colin and Dot knew that many nights Adrian walked down an alley and through a walled back garden and into Sophia's arms.

It was often midnight when he slipped into bed beside her. Night debates at the Commons kept him late. Endless, raucous debates. Traditional alliances had begun to crumble. Demonstrating crowds daily reminded him and his colleagues that they held the fate of a great nation in their hands. One misstep might plunge the country into massive bloodshed.

The knowledge that Sophia carefully studied all the speeches as reported in the newspapers had something to do with his new willingness to listen to the other side.

He would have liked to talk to her about it. Conversation might help him to work out his chaotic ideas. He had promised never to do so, however, because she might think that he was not seeking a sympathetic ear, but instead trying to influence her. She might then conclude that he had seduced her only to continue his old mission.

It was one of the sore points that kept their affair from being perfect. Another was the pressure on her to marry. Those exhortations had now become public. More worrisome was the concern that their lovemaking invited a pregnancy that would make her future precarious.

He hoped that they would dodge that. If they didn't, the only way to avoid horrible scandal would be for her to negotiate a quick marriage to a man appropriate to her position. Eventually that would be inevitable, but he had no desire to hasten the day when they had to part.

"If it came to it, Northford might be a solution," he said, thinking aloud.

"And you would become the intimate family friend?" Colin asked. "It would be a humiliating arrangement for everyone. You deserve better. In fact, I don't see why you don't marry her yourself. You are far better equipped to exercise Everdon's power than the Marquess of Northford, or the other men being shoved at her."

"You know it isn't possible," Dot soothed.

"The reasons why are stupid ones. What could anyone do? Burn her at the stake? As to Adrian's birth, Father did not repudiate him. In the eyes of the law, Adrian is an earl's son."

"In the eyes of the law, but not in the eyes of the world," Adrian said.

"To hell with the world."

It was the retort of a man who owned the world, and so could easily dismiss its importance. The security to do that was the only thing about his brother's superior fortune in life that Adrian envied.

Dot changed the subject by asking about the day's debate. Adrian regaled them with a description of the outbreak of fisticuffs that had led to Parliament's early dismissal.

After a half hour, he and Colin took their leave. They went to Colin's chambers to fetch fresh cravats and make themselves presentable.

"I came to ask some favors of you," Adrian said.

Colin tied his neckpiece while he gazed in the mirror. "Something time-consuming, I hope. Aside from the fun when the new London Bridge opened, this summer has been boring. I'd go down to the country, but everyone is here."

"The first favor will only occupy one night. I would like you to escort Sophia to the coronation ball." King William was due to be crowned in several weeks, now that mourning for the last King had ended.

"I think that you should, not me."

"I expect to be unwell that day."

"I do not agree with how you are handling this. She is not some child. If an affair is suspected, it will not be the undoing of either of you. Besides, there is no declaration in merely walking her into a ballroom."

Adrian went to work on his own cravat. "My request has nothing to do with what is between Sophia and me."

Colin frowned in perplexity, then his brow suddenly cleared. "Is he coming? For the coronation?"

"I received word from the embassy that he is."

"Doesn't seem fair that you should miss the ball."

"The palace is planning a modest affair, so there will not be that much to miss. I can hardly be in the same room with him. Despite his age and beard, the resemblance might be noticed if we are seen together, and a coronation ball is the last place where I would want to reinflame that scandal. Our mother asked that I never embarrass the earl and you and Gavin."

"That promise has proven a stranglehold on you, and it was unfair of her to demand it."

"It was part of her agreement with the earl, made while she carried me. To refuse to honor it after her death would be selfish and inexcusable."

"That agreement was for my sake and Gavin's. So that she would stay and we would have our mother."

"And mine. So that I could stay and have *my* mother."

"Still, we are all grown now, and she is gone."

"I do not owe the earl much, Colin, but I do owe him this. I will not invite speculation about either my birth or my relationship with the duchess by attending with her on my arm while a man with my eyes stands among the foreign dignitaries. You know that my choice is the right one."

"Probably so, but I do not understand your equanimity about either situation. Your feelings for the duchess are very obvious to me. I would like you to have some happiness, and how happy can you be if you conduct an affair of the heart assuming that it will end?"

Happier than I have ever been in my life, Adrian thought. As happy as the situation will permit. However, Colin had touched the biggest sore point in the affair, and one that Adrian carefully avoided pressing, because doing so might destroy the joy.

Although it was certainly an affair of the heart, she was not in love with him. She needed him and trusted him and felt great affection. In her own careful way, maybe she even loved him, but she was not *in love*. She would not let herself take that final step.

Sometimes when they embraced he could sense it in her, like something fighting against restraints, but she was too afraid to let it free.

Just as well. It could not last. Sooner or later something would convince her of that. Then he would retreat as he had sworn to himself that he would. Doing so would be difficult, however, because he *had* fallen in love with her.

Colin broke into his thoughts. "There was another favor?"

"One that will give you something to do. I want you to look for Captain Brutus. I do not have the time, and it is vital to track him down."

"An investigation? Sounds almost as diverting as our duchess hunt. I will take up the charge with enthusiasm."

"I will explain what little I have learned, then, and hope that you can do better."

It was all Burchard's fault. Her protector was giving her more confidence in her safety than she had any right to have. The man had become an unacceptable interference. The solution was obvious. Get rid of him, and she would be helpless.

He considered that as he slipped into the garden and crept toward the duchess's house. Beside him another figure crept too. He had thought long and hard before getting help this time, but he would need someone keeping watch. This house was not so large as the other, and there would be no place to hide if a cry was raised while he was inside.

Still, he preferred acting alone. No one knew better than he did what could happen if another person knew one's secrets and plans. Betrayal was always a possibility. He had no intention of being vulnerable again if he could help it.

His companion felt the door's latch, and made a gesture to indicate it was unbolted. Now, that was convenient. And irritating. Sophia acted as if Captain Brutus represented no threat at all. By now she should know better.

He pulled a letter out of his coat. Well, this missive would make it explicit, even if the fire had not.

He began to turn the latch.

Adrian slipped through the portal of Sophia's garden well past midnight. The Commons had sat very late, due to an upcoming adjournment because of the coronation festivities.

The hour had made him contemplate not coming. She would be asleep, and it would be selfish to disturb her. But he needed to find some peace in her arms. Holding her would soothe the inner turmoil churned up by the day's events.

Three Tories had moved to the reform camp this afternoon. Two of them held seats sure to be abolished if reform passed. One was a protégé of Peel. He had watched them cross the aisle, knowing as well as they that the act was political suicide. He should have been furious with their defections. Instead he had admired their independence and adherence to principle.

As he ambled through the garden to the house, he contemplated that unexpected reaction. His thoughts occupied most of his mind, but an essential, primitive part remained aware of his surroundings.

It was that part that made him abruptly halt halfway to the house.

Something shifted in the dark up ahead. A shadow moved near the building. His blood instantly pounded with alarm for Sophia. Easing over near the wall, he slid forward.

A man crouched near the door. Adrian could barely make out his shape, but it appeared he was trying to enter.

The black fury that he had known after the fire broke again. He rushed forward, determined to catch the culprit. With any luck it would be Captain Brutus himself. Even if it was only a minion, he would at least have a lead to the elusive radical.

He lunged at the shadow and grappled him to the ground. They sprawled and fought in a melee of confusion. Quickly getting the upper hand, he forced the intruder onto his stomach and pressed his knee into his back while he twisted and imprisoned one arm.

The air stirred behind him. His instincts snapped alert, but it was already too late. A hissed curse floated to his ear just as something slammed into his head and the dark night swallowed him.

A gentle yank pulled Sophia out of her dreams. Blinking, she looked up to see Jenny and Charles flanking her bed.

"You had better come downstairs, Your Grace," Charles said.

His gentle tone had her wide-awake in an instant. It was the voice one used for bad news. She knew immediately that it was about Adrian. She reached to the empty place where she expected him to be sleeping and her heart dropped into her stomach.

Tears flowed down Jenny's face while she held up a wrap. "Oh, my lady, he is badly hurt. Cook found him this morning outside the garden door."

She jumped out of bed and thrust on the wrap. Not bothering with shoes, she ran down to the kitchen with Charles and Jenny in her wake. The garden door stood open and she plunged into the dawn's soft light.

He still lay on the ground. Someone had fetched a blanket to cover him. Servants stood around helplessly.

"We dared not move him," Charles said. "He has been badly beaten. I thought him dead at first."

He did look dead. Pale and lifeless and eerily at peace.

Dread choked her. She sank to her knees and used the edge of her wrap to wipe some thick blood off his brow.

"We found this by the door," a footman said.

He handed her a folded paper. She opened it and scanned down its threats. Captain Brutus.

She crushed the letter in her fist. Eyes blurring, she bent and kissed Adrian.

She had caused this. Her recklessness and willfulness had hurt him.

She should have given Captain Brutus what he wanted. She should have kept Adrian at a distance, so he would not become a target of that man's twisted plans.

Stupid, vain woman. It had been madness to think she might have any use in this world besides being a means to an end.

She caressed his face and battled an anguish that threatened to unhinge her. He had only tried to give her friendship and protection, and now he might die because of her.

Just like Brandon.

"We cannot leave him here," she said. "The damp will do more harm than the blows. Two of you find something firm to put him on. Take down a door if you have to. Charles, send to Dincaster House for Colin Burchard, and get a physician here at once."

They moved him to one of the footmen's chambers on the lower level. With Charles's help she stripped off his clothes. Horrible bruises covered his chest and stomach, as if he had neglected to defend himself. His breath rasped lowly and she worried that they had worsened his injuries by lifting him.

Weeping at her helplessness, she washed the blood from his head and placed cold towels on the worst of his blows and prayed desperately that he had not been mortally harmed.

Colin arrived alongside the physician. So did Daniel St. John.

"Do not worry. St. John knows how to keep secrets," Colin reassured her. "We were about to ride out to Hampstead when your servant came for me."

"Adrian and I have an old friendship, and I am in his debt, Your Grace," St. John said. "I welcome the chance to aid him, if you will permit it."

She did not really care who knew what now. She only cared about Adrian.

They watched the initial examination and heard the ambiguous description of Adrian's wounds. The physician then ordered everyone but Charles from the chamber.

Colin and St. John brought Sophia up to the library. Colin poured her some sherry. The little crystal glass seemed terribly heavy in her hand.

"Drink it. You look ready to swoon."

"It is my fault," she said. "He was coming here. Someone must have followed him, or been waiting."

"It may have only been a thief."

She withdrew the letter from where she had tucked it away. "This was near the door."

Colin read the missive. His face hardened when he got to the part that specifically spoke of Adrian as a Tory pawn and warned that her intimacy with him would not be tolerated.

"I will kill this man when I find him," Colin said.

"He knows about us. He must have been following Adrian, or watching this house. When Adrian arrived last night, he must have been hiding and overcame him."

"No one follows Adrian without his realizing it, and no one hides from him either," St. John said. He spoke with authority, as if he knew Adrian's abilities in this area very well. "More likely this letter was being left, and Adrian chanced upon the situation. This was hardly written in the dead of night while Adrian lay on the ground."

"I do not see that it matters how it happened. He is lying below, terribly battered. Maybe dying. Because of me."

"Do not blame yourself," St. John said gently. "It would wound him even more to know that you did. If he confronted those men, it was his choice. The only blame here lies with the animals who would do that to a man after he was down."

It took her a moment to hear him through the guilt fogging her perceptions. "Men?"

"There had to be at least two. One man could never succeed in rendering Adrian defenseless."

They stayed with her until the physician came up to make his report.

"Two broken ribs, undoubtedly a concussion, and possibly some internal bleeding," the man said while he adjusted his frock coat. "It should be worse. He should be dead. I gave the servants instructions for his care."

Colin's eyes asked the question that Sophia could not bring herself to voice.

The physician flipped his hand in the air. "Impossible to say. If an organ was badly damaged . . . but my impression is that he will recover."

A tentative relief flooded her, but the guilt still rippled, a current waiting to sweep her away.

"I brought him around. He asked for you, Your Grace."

She ran out of the room while Colin began a quiet explanation of the need for discretion.

Charles slipped out of the chamber as soon as Sophia entered. Adrian's smile of greeting was a valiant, incomplete effort.

She sat in a chair beside the bed and took his hand in hers. "The physician thinks that you will be well soon."

"It is not my first fight, so I can assess the damage. A few days and I will be up and about."

She ventured a light caress on his face. "Are you in pain?"

"My chest is bound so tightly that I can barely breathe, but aside from that it isn't bad." He glanced down her body. "They pulled you out of bed. You look beautiful. Very provocative. I feel better already."

Tears puddled in her eyes. It was such a typically Adrian thing to say. It sounded so normal, and so out of place in the mood of dread that had fallen on the house.

His attempt at levity had the opposite effect. The fear and guilt rose so quickly that she could not control them. Keeling forward, she buried his hand between her face and the bed and wept into it.

He spoke words of reassurance while the worst of it poured out of her. Eventually she managed to stifle the sobs with ragged breaths. She rubbed her tear-soaked face against the rough skin of his palm, grateful that he had not been taken from her.

Sliding his hand from beneath her head, he stroked her hair with the gentlest caresses. Calmed by the soothing tranquility of that hand, she told him about the letter.

"St. John is right," he said. "No one laid in wait for me. My untimely arrival caused this. And my carelessness. I should have suspected another man might be there, keeping watch."

"Your friendship with me caused it. The letter is very explicit. He threatens to remove you and your influence. He found the chance last night and tried to kill you. He may have only failed to do so because in the dark he did not know you still breathed. Next time—"

"There will be no next time. I will be on my guard."

She gritted her teeth and clutched the bed cloths beneath her cheek. She struggled for the strength to do what needed to be done.

Regret tore and burned her heart. She had been given a few weeks of happiness, but had not been brave enough to use them very well. How would she manage without him? How would she live with that void again?

How like you to think only about yourself. It has always been like that. The condemnation pierced her memory. Alistair's words? No. Gerald's.

She could do this. For Adrian she could do it.

Her voice came out on shaking, broken breaths. "I cannot risk you. I could not live with the guilt if I caused more harm. I think that we—"

"No."

She rose up on her arms and looked at him. His severe expression had nothing to do with pain.

"He wants to kill you."

"Then he missed his only chance. We do not end it because of this. I will not accept that."

She verged on weeping again. "Adrian, think . . ."

"No." He had that look in his eyes. *This is what will happen. This is how it will be.*

She had never been able to defeat that determination. She suspected that no one else had either.

He took her hand and pulled her forward. "Now, sit here with me. I may as well enjoy my infirmity by having you dote on me."

She found a spot up near the bed board. Bent around him, half-reclining, she nestled his head gently with her breasts and stomach. Stroking his brow, she tried to give back some of the comfort that she so frequently took from him.

chapter 21

The evening was a success?" Adrian asked. He lay propped up on his bed, still enduring the three weeks of immobile boredom to which the physician had condemned him.

Colin gestured to the hose and pumps and short breeches that he had worn to the coronation ball. "Except that we all looked like actors in a play from the last century. It really is time for Court dress to accommodate the changing fashions."

Adrian laughed, which did not hurt nearly as much as it had a few days ago. He had been back in his chambers for two weeks now. As much as he had enjoyed Sophia's unflagging attention, he would not compromise her by remaining at her house. Nor would he risk her safety if Captain Brutus had decided to make "the Tory pawn" his new target.

"Your duchess was lovely," Colin said. "Her pale grays were a welcome rest for the eyes in that sea of jewels and bright plumage. She could not dance, of course, so she sat in elegant nobility to the side. The other women looked like cyprians in comparison."

Adrian shifted uncomfortably. His infirmity had begun to annoy, a sure sign that he was practically healed. "You personally escorted her home?"

"Of course. Before you ask, let me assure you that the men whom you hired to protect her continue to make their watch very discreetly."

"That is more than I can say about the men whom *you* hired to protect *me.*"

"Damn it, how—"

"I saw them from the window. They lounge in the same spots all the time. I certainly hope that my men are being more professional."

"You are supposed to be staying in bed, not spying out windows."

"Call them off. I can take care of myself."

"The men outside are not hired. They are friends of yours. Julian Hampton, Dante Duclairc, and some others. Even Laclere has taken watches. St. John is in command and told them to be visible, so it is obvious you have protection. I doubt that I *can* call them off. You are stuck with them."

"Do they know what happened?"

"Your absence from society was noticed, so St. John and I came up with an excuse. We told a select few that you were waylaid in a dark street. Some of the chaps who suspect about your missions concluded that it must have been agents of some unfriendly government seeking revenge."

"That is preposterous."

"I cannot account for the vivid imagination of others. Your pride will have to swallow it. Besides, that pistol you have under the sheet will hardly help you if there is another fire." He held out his hand. "Give it here. It could go off accidentally in your sleep."

"I am never that careless." All the same, Adrian extracted the pistol and gave it to his brother. Just then the sounds of a carriage stopping at the building blew in the window on the night breeze.

Colin peered out. "It is the duchess. No wonder she wanted to leave the ball early. She is still in her ball gown."

"You should have told her there were men watching."

"Hell, most of them were all at the docks that night. Besides, when it is really necessary, we all know how to be silent."

Colin left the bedchamber, to let Sophia in. Adrian heard the mumble of their brief conversation and then the light *swish* of petticoats approaching through the sitting room.

His heart leaped at the sight of her. Her silvery gray gown of raw silk barely reflected the light and cast off the most subtle of shimmers. Three discreet plumes in dark gray adorned her hair, but he could imagine how she had looked in the ducal coronet. She wore no jewels, but the fashionably cut ball gown showed off her luminous, beautiful skin. The Duchess of Everdon had turned the restraint required by mourning into an opportunity to enhance her subtle beauty.

She bent to kiss him. He captured her head so it lasted a long time. They had only been apart two weeks, but he had missed her badly.

"You should not have come, but I am grateful that you did. Colin said that you made the other women look like courtesans on parade and I can see what he meant."

"Dot advised me on the color and fabric. We think that I am sufficiently subdued, although there were many who questioned the appropriateness of my going at all. Attending the coronation was one thing, but showing up at the ball was quite another. The Queen greeted me warmly, however, so that was that."

"The ladies were just jealous that even subdued you could outshine them." He patted the bed beside him. "Sit here and tell me all about it."

She perched carefully. He inhaled her perfume and the underlying scent of Sophia the woman. His body responded to her closeness in a way that announced he definitely had almost healed.

She described the night, focusing on amusing confrontations and detailed menus, with occasional digressions about outstanding jewels and gowns. The tale animated her. While he watched her bright expression and excited giggles, his heart kept rising with delight and falling with foreboding.

She had finally taken her elevated place as a duchess in her own right. She had held her own among the highest of the high, and she knew it. He could practically see her spirit assessing what it all meant to her life.

Suddenly he wanted her. Desperately.

"Of all of the women besides the royals, I was introduced first to the visiting princes and dignitaries, of course. I confess that I enjoyed taking precedence, after all of the critical scrutiny these last months. Was it too naughty of me?"

"Not at all."

"I could not have pulled it off without Dot. She has spent the last week exhorting me to flex my power a little, and to use this opportunity to put certain ladies in their place."

That certain other ladies had learned their place would be good for her. That she was beginning to learn her own worried him. Not that he would change things. He was glad that the day had been a triumph. Glad for her, that was. Not necessarily for himself.

She darted him a pointed glance. "There were dignitaries from all over. Several from the Ottoman Court in Turkey. They wore magnificent robes. When I met them I almost giggled, because all I could think of was my silly *seraglio* in Paris."

"It must have been very colorful."

"One spoke with me, beyond the usual polite exchange. I gather he is an important member of the Sultan's government. His English is fluent. He told me that he has been here several times before, on embassies." She spoke casually while she drew little patterns on the back of his hand. Inflaming, torturous designs.

"That would be my father."

"I saw a resemblance. The same eyes. I expected to have to worm it out of you."

"About a dozen people at the ball knew. You may as well too."

"Have you always known about him?"

He lined his fingertips up her bare arm, entranced by her skin's glow in the candlelight. "My mother told me when I turned eighteen. She should have done so earlier. I had only to look in the mirror to know that I was not the earl's. His coldness to me told the tale as well."

He let his fingers trail higher and lower, enjoying the sensation of her skin. Its texture and warmth were acutely tangible tonight. It affected him as if he used his lips. "When my father learned that my mother carried me, he went to the earl and offered to buy her. Fifty horses, I think it was, and ten thousand pounds."

"I can imagine Dincaster's reaction to that."

"There was no way he would let my mother leave. The humiliation would have been insurmountable."

"Did she want to go away?"

"I think she considered it, but Gavin and Colin would be lost to her. So she forged an agreement with the earl that guaranteed I would not be repudiated and that he would accept me as his own before the world and the law."

His gaze and light caress traveled over her shoulder to the skin exposed by the flaring top of her gown. It felt so soothing to touch her. She subtly angled for more, like a cat encouraging petting.

"He did not really accept you and give you a father's love, did he? Even now he does not treat you like a son."

"His generosity did not extend that far. In return for being allowed to keep me, my mother agreed to stay. And, of course, she gave up her lover."

His touching had raised a lovely tint on her cheeks, but she kept to the subject. "Have you met him?"

"The first time I was in that part of the world, he made himself known to me. I have spent some time with him."

"I am glad for that, Adrian. It saddens me to think of you as a boy, receiving only sneers from the earl."

"It was not as with you and Alistair. Dincaster had his reason, and it was a good one. I will not say that I was not wounded, but knowing there was a reason made it easier." She looked distracted and sad. He slid his hand along her back. "Now, I do not want to talk about it anymore. Actually, I discover that I do not want to talk at all." He found the gown's fastenings beneath a flap of silk and released them.

She straightened with a start. "You are in no condition."

"I am in superb condition. Astounding condition. In fact, I am astonished at the heroic proportion of my condition."

"I am sure it is not advisable."

He laughed. "It is damn close to being essential."

He reached for her and she scooted away. "Heroic condition or not, you know it is not wise. Besides, I want to talk even if you do not. I need to tell you something."

"Tell me while you get undressed."

"After I tell you, you may not want me to stay."

His playful mood drained away. "What is it, then?"

She bit her lower lip. "I have decided to leave London for a while."

"If you are running away to France, I will stop you as I did the last time," he warned.

"Not to France. I have decided to visit Marleigh. I am leaving in two days."

"Wait a few more. I should be able to travel soon."

"In a few days Parliament will begin sessions again, and you must be there."

"I can miss a week of debate."

"You do not understand. I do not want you to come."

She grimaced when she said it, as if she expected him to react badly. That was exactly what he began to do, but her expression checked him.

"I do not like it. It could be dangerous. We do not know that Captain Brutus has fully turned his attention on me."

"I will take an escort of four footmen as guards, and Jacques and Attila will ride in the coach with me. Jacques is very good with a pistol."

"I still do not like it."

She moved until she sat very close to him. She took his face in her hands and touched her cheek to his. "Do not be angry with me. This is something that I have to do. It is time to face it all, and make some decisions, and find out who I am and who I will be." She kissed him. "It is only because of you that I can do it. You have carried me halfway down the road. Now I must walk the rest of the way myself."

She was right, but he resisted accepting it. She might not know what she would find when she looked for herself, but he did. He had seen it from the start, beneath all of those layers.

He doubted that the woman who returned from Marleigh would have any need of him. Once she came to terms with Everdon, she would *be* Everdon, and duty to Everdon would rule her life.

Hadn't he brought her back from Paris so it would be so?

He stroked his hands into her hair and gazed into her eyes. So many interesting shadows played in their glow. He held her head to a deep kiss and tried to keep her from sensing the apprehension of loss that drenched his climbing passion.

This might be their last night.

He lowered his hands to her shoulders and slid her gown down. "Get undressed."

"Adrian . . ."

"I want you to lie here with me. You can hardly do so in these clothes." He turned her so he could unlace her stays and release the petticoats. She glanced over her shoulder to begin a protest, but he gave her a look that warned her not to bother.

She got off the bed and slid the gown lower. "I suppose if you just intend us to lie beside each other . . ."

He said nothing to that, but watched as she stepped out of the gown and petticoats and shed the stays. She had been beautiful in the luxurious gray silk, but he drank in the sight of her feminine form emerging. The low light hinted at her curves beneath the chemise.

He memorized every inch of her, and every move she made while she carried the gown and laid it over a chair.

He let her climb in beside him still wearing her undergarments and hose, because to order them off would only set her scolding.

She snuggled under his arm and gingerly rested her head on his shoulder and her hand on his chest.

"I thought about you constantly through all these days of coronation festivities. I wished you were with me today," she said. "However, this makes up for it. This is very nice."

It would be nicer soon, but he needed to know something first. "No more letters from our Captain?"

"None at all. Maybe what happened frightened him. Did you think I would not tell you?"

"That is exactly what I thought, since you insist on treating me like an invalid."

"I am only worried about you. The physician said three weeks of quiet bed rest."

"The physician is an ass. As I said earlier, I am practically good as new and am in fine condition." He closed his hand on her breast. "I'll prove it."

He silenced her startled objection with his mouth and conquered her brief resistance with his caress. She melted and her pliant body curved into him.

"That is wickedly wonderful," she whispered as he played at her through the thin fabric. "But if you exert yourself we will probably have to call the physician again."

"I do not plan to move much at all. All of the exertion will be yours." He went to work on her ear. "I will tell you what to do. As a beginning, curl up facing me so I do not have to twist like this."

That made it easier for him to kiss her properly and to reach her whole body, to finish undressing her. He plunged into the bliss of pure sensation and expectant hunger. Her arousal escalated beautifully, until she was with him kiss for kiss and breath for breath in their private world of emotion and pleasure.

He wanted, he wanted . . . all of her. All that he had known with her and all that he hadn't and all that he might never know again. The images of what he desired sent him veering toward the breaking point. He took her in a gentle, exploring kiss while he forced some control. Her mouth smiled against his.

"My need amuses you?" he asked.

"No more than mine does. No, that kiss made me remember Jacques' lessons in love on the boat. I will have to tell him that you are not at all clumsy and crushing when you peel apart a rose's petals and lick its nectar."

"Jacques' metaphor was not about a woman's mouth, Sophia."

She went still for a moment. He sensed her working out what it *was* about.

"Do you want that?"

"Yes."

Another moment of stillness.

"Tell me what to do."

He told her. After he had brought her to a thunderous climax he slid from between her kneeling legs and came up behind her and took her while she hung limply against the bed board.

It destroyed whatever restraints still existed between them. He did not leave the exertions to her after all. All night long he made love to her, oblivious to his healing ribs and bruises. He molded her recurrent arousals to his explorations while a ferocious, aching hunger tried to have enough of her to last a lifetime.

Such an impressive palace." Attila's cry echoed from where he stood gaping in the middle of the immense ballroom. The room's dimensions turned his bearish form into a diminutive spot of astonishment. "Your home is as big as the Louvre."

"As always, our friend exaggerates," Jacques said while he strolled beside Sophia, inspecting the luxurious appointments. They had arrived an hour earlier and she was giving them a tour. "However, you are more important than I ever imagined. Everdon must be one of your country's great titles."

"Let us just say that if it had been a French title forty years ago, the likes of you would have sent me to the guillotine in the first wave."

"It appears that your countrymen seek to cut off some heads of their own now, only the weapon will be this new law instead of a blade. The result will be a half-measure, and incomplete."

Sophia could tell that, like all young men of radical disposition, Jacques found half-measures unpalatable. Captain Brutus had been like that.

"Perhaps we are fortunate that you are French and not English," she teased.

"The condition of men anywhere is everyone's concern."

"I hope that you have not been instigating riots while you are here." She made it a mock scold, but admitted the possibility of outside interference that she had never considered before.

"I would never misuse your hospitality that way. However, it is inevitable that men have come here from other countries to use the turmoil to their own ends. Your husband, I think, can tell you how it works."

"What do you mean by that?"

"You told me yourself that your husband is a spy and agent provocateur. A dangerous man."

"I made that up, Jacques. It was a silly tale."

"Silly tale or not, I think that you touched the truth. Perhaps your heart suspected." Jacques fingered a gilt candelabra. "Magnificent. All of it. How many chambers, did you say? Eighty-four?"

"You disapprove."

"I prefer your house in London, and your *maison* in Paris. This is majestic, but empty. Cold, and full of echoes. Perhaps when you and Monsieur Burchard fill it with children it will be different."

She had come here to settle things for herself. A good first step would be to set Jacques and Attila straight about her relationship with Adrian.

She stopped his stroll and looked him in the eyes. "As I told you before, I am not married. Not to Adrian, or to anyone else. I lied to you about that, just like the part about my husband being a spy. Adrian exploited the lies so you would not interfere when he came to bring me back to England. I had never seen him before that night of my *seraglio.*"

Attila joined them in time to overhear the last few words. "You plan another *seraglio*? Here? The cost of the silks for the ceiling would be exorbitant. Perhaps the east drawing room would be better. Much more intimate."

"Sophia is not planning another *seraglio,*" Jacques said. "She is explaining again that she is not married to Monsieur Burchard. This time I find myself believing her."

Attila's happy expression fell. "It is so? You have been playing a very dangerous game. When your true husband learns what has transpired with Burchard, it could be very ugly."

"There is no husband at all," she said.

"No husband? But Jacques said that you told him . . ."

"She lied to me."

"And a few others," Sophia admitted.

"You lied to Jacques? But why? I will admit that I was wounded to learn that you took him into your confidence and not me, too, but if it was a lie, you only insulted him."

"She lied to me and others to discourage us."

Attila turned on Jacques with wide eyes. "Discourage you? Are you saying that you tried . . . ?"

Jacques responded with one of his shrugs.

"I am speechless, Jacques."

"I doubt that I will be so blessed."

"To think that you would take advantage of our sweet lady's generosity. Have the French no shame? To have pressed her to the point where she took refuge in a lie . . ."

Sophia slipped away while Attila continued his harangue. Jacques bore it patiently, looking to the ceiling with resignation while the lecture poured down on him.

.   .   .

She had debated all the way to Marleigh just when to do it. By the time she arrived she had laid out a schedule that would not require confronting the ghosts until a few days had passed. Therefore it surprised her when a fit of cold resolve gripped her as she left the ballroom.

Why not just face it now? It was why she had come. Best to get it over with. Delay would not make it easier, and might give her too much time to lose her courage.

Steeling herself, she wound through the house's chambers and up its grand staircase. At the third landing she looked at the door to Alistair's suite of rooms.

Sickening dread made her turn away. She would face a gentler ghost first, even though it would probably be more painful.

She made her way to Brandon's chamber. A mellow sadness swelled with each step. She could only contemplate this because she had already faced the worst of it at Staverly. She had only succeeded in that because Adrian had helped her.

Adrian. She wished he were here to hold her together again. But she knew, she just knew, that it was important to do this on her own.

She thought about the man whose passion could make her feel beautiful and magnificent. The thought of him pierced her heart with regret. She was not giving him everything like she wanted to. She loved him, but the deepest level of her spirit held back. Was there a sadder pain in the world than aching to believe and trust and love without question, and discovering that you are incapable of it?

That was why she was here. To reclaim the part of her soul that had learned to hide too well. There was a danger in the quest. She could discover that it was not hiding, but was dead.

She turned the latch and stepped inside the chamber. Its starkness startled her. Fury split her mind.

Nothing of her brother remained. She had always assumed that Alistair had left it as it stood on that summer day. Instead he had wiped it clean of Brandon's life.

He had done it on purpose. He had known that one day she would want to feel Brandon's presence again, and he had deliberately robbed her of it. He wanted to make sure she could never reconcile what had happened. He needed her to wallow in guilt.

Scathing resentment maddened her thoughts, turning them harsh. *I can do the same, Papa. I can go into that suite and wipe out your years there. I can burn the clothes and furniture and sell all the items that you used. I can even refuse to have a child. I can obliterate you.*

She stiffened with sudden self-awareness. The ugliness of her rage shocked her. The internal voice had sounded horribly familiar. Its cruelty reminded her of Alistair himself.

She forced some calm and blocked out the thought of him. Not yet.

She sat on the bed and closed her eyes and pictured this chamber as it had once been.

The image that came to her was from childhood, during the years when she and her twin lived one life. They used to make a fort out of a velvet quilt and bounce a ball down the chamber's long length. It was how she remembered this room best. After they had begun to mature, she had rarely ventured in here.

Memories flew by, and she embraced them all. Heartrending nostalgia made tears drip down her cheeks. She saw him as a little boy and as a young man. She had forgotten how much he looked like their mother, bright-eyed and dark-haired and quick to smile. There had been little of Alistair in him, much to their father's annoyance. Too soft. Too kind. *Weak,* Papa had called him.

Not weak. Thoughtful and sensitive and giving, but not weak. A good person, full of their mother's quiet strength. No, there had been little of Alistair in him. Unlike her.

Brandon's childish face suddenly froze in one of those memories. He was looking at her after learning that she had gotten him into trouble for something he had not done. She forgot the crime now, but remembered the lie. She had implicated him because she did not want to face their father alone.

His eyes focused on her, gazing with a wisdom beyond his years. In them she saw understanding. And forgiveness.

The image held. Her eyes and throat burned. Then the memory was gone.

She looked around the vacant chamber. A peaceful elation moved her. She had not needed his clothes or books or toys. Opening this door to the past had brought more comfort than pain. She should have known that it would.

She walked to the door and glanced back at the emptiness. Maybe Alistair had not erased Brandon's history because of her, but for himself. Perhaps he had feared remembering even more than she had.

There would have been no images of happiness and forgiveness waiting on the other side of the door if it ever blew open for him. He probably knew that.

She did not need clothes or objects in Alistair's chambers either. They were all there, of course. Not even Celine would dare to erase the late Duke of Everdon from his home. Sophia had rarely seen him in this inner sanctum, however, and its contents held no special meaning for her.

That disappointed her. She had counted on it just happening when she walked in the door.

She sat in a chair near the cold hearth. She would have to do it on her own. Of course she would. None of this really had to do with Marleigh's chambers. It was all inside her.

She let the memories come, steeling her composure to face them.

Alistair critical and harsh and cutting.

A thousand little hurts when she was too young to understand anything but that Papa was busy or angry.

The nagging suspicion as she got older that it was not just his manner.

The eventual admission that he really did not love them much at all.

The more recent ones were harder, and she cringed against their cruelty. She watched his triumph when he captured Captain Brutus. She relived his blunt satisfaction in throwing the truth of all that in her face. She mentally turned away from his expression during the fierce browbeatings and terrible whipping that he had used to force her to speak at the trial.

Finally, she called forth the steely coldness with which he treated her after Brandon died, as if he would gladly exchange her for the body in the grave.

She did not cry. Alistair never evoked that response. It had always been something much worse. He killed her confidence and joy. He made her feel worthless and insignificant. He sucked the strength and life out of her.

It was vital not to let him do that today. She battled to hold on to the woman Adrian had helped her to begin discovering.

"They say you were a good duke," she said aloud to the memory.

I executed my duties better than most.

"Did it consume you? Is that why there was nothing left for us?"

I did my duty to you too.

"I am not speaking of duty."

You have always been sentimental and emotional, Sophia. It does you no credit. Such things are not for the likes of us. You must learn to control those tendencies, and your willfulness and impetuousness and extravagance and . . .

"I am well aware of my deficiencies. You cataloged them for me often enough. Did you not love us at all? Were we only duties?"

I cared for you in that way, to the extent that I was capable.

"Which is your way of saying very little. Did Everdon make you that way, or were you born thus?"

Your question is impertinent. Another failing that requires self-discipline.

"The question is important to me. You see, I have come back. It is mine now. I want to know what goes with the power and precedence and wealth."

You are unsuitable and will fail. A duke is born to the title, but his sense of duty is molded. I educated your brother for it, not you. He was too soft, but I had him shaping up. That you are all who is left . . .

"I am not afraid of the duties. I will not fail if I accept them. But will they turn me into what you were? Or was your inability to love a part of your nature?"

Which answer would you prefer?

"The first, I suppose. I can always run away from Marleigh. I can never get rid of the other legacy, the part of you that is in me."

Running away. You are good at that. It took your half-breed lover to get you to admit it.

"Do not insult him. Adrian is good for me. He sees wonderful things in me."

It is in his interest to do so.

"That is not true."

So he gives you affection and pleasure and asks no more in return? A rare man, considering your position. Except that you do not truly believe that. Which is why you cannot love him.

Her jaw clenched against the accusation.

Ah. So that is what this is about. All of this talk of love. I dared to hope for a moment that we were having an intelligent conversation. Listen carefully. I only bother because you are all who is left. You are Everdon now, and Everdon is a power to be used. Others will want to control it, and will try to use you in order do so. You know that. It has already happened. There is no place for sentimentality in any of it. You must be nimble, clever, and sometimes ruthless. Love will only leave you vulnerable. Imagine how much more I would have been disappointed in you if I had loved you.

"So it was Everdon that made you what you were."

I was molded to become Everdon, but I was bred to be a duke. Since you do not understand, I will answer in a way you might comprehend. I was born unusually free of the sentiment you call love, and that helped me become a strong Duke of Everdon.

"I think that is sad."

You would. Because there is much of me in you, and you were hoping for a different answer. However, I have never held with telling people what they want to hear instead of the truth.

"Then hear some truth from me. You were not a good man. You were cold and hard. That is not strength. I will show you how it can be done another way. I will be nimble and clever, but never ruthless. Nor will I permit duty to turn me to stone."

Then I must watch the deterioration of the prestige and power built over centuries.

"Your confidence, as always, gives me heart."

I am finished with you. I had hoped these last few months had taught you something.

"There is one more thing, Papa."

What is that?

"I forgive you."

There is nothing for you to forgive.

"There is much to forgive."

Have it your way. But, Sophia, never forget. I do not forgive you.

"I did not expect you to. But I will forget. I intend to start forgetting today."

The next day after breakfast Sophia found two men cooling their heels outside the study. One was her new solicitor, Julian Hampton.

"Mister Hampton, I am glad that you could arrange to come. Have you been examining the papers?"

"I have, Your Grace. With Mister Carson's aid, we should know the state of things very quickly."

She turned to the other man. Aging and gray, he appeared ill at ease. He smiled cautiously while he made a bow. "Your Grace."

She led the way into the study. "Mister Hampton has convinced me that perhaps I was too rash in releasing you, Mister Carson. After all, you have been my father's secretary for over twenty years. Are you content to live off the bequest he left you, or are you interested in continuing your duties here?"

"The bequest was generous, but service to Everdon has been my life. I would prefer to serve until my abilities fail me."

She paced along the wall lined with mahogany shelves holding registers and portfolios of documents. Other walls displayed sedate oil landscapes. Some fox tails and other trophies of the hunt were tacked between the long windows. Besides some plain wooden chairs, the huge dark desk and smaller secretary were the only furnishings.

A man's study, and very much Alistair's. Alistair the Duke, not the father, and the part of him contained here did not disturb her too much. Still, she flung open the windows so the sultry summer air could decimate the vague scent of him.

"This is what I propose, Mister Carson. The three of us will go through my father's correspondence from the last two years and you will explain what every letter was about and what my father's plans and intentions were. If I perceive that you are forthright and honest, I will consider keeping you on. If you are not, you will never cross this threshold again."

"That is acceptable to me, Your Grace."

"Is it? We will be looking at his letters to me and about me, too, I should warn you."

"I can see where that could be awkward, but I will do my duty."

"Then let us get started."

They spent the next three days sequestered in the study while Jacques and Attila made free with the luxury of Marleigh. Her friends went riding and played tennis, while she pored over contracts and leases. Attila began composing a new sonata on the pianoforte, while she learned about Everdon's investments. After dinner the second night, Jacques read a new love poem. It employed the rose metaphor. Sophia barely heard it. Her mind was on items of unfinished business that Mister Hampton had brought to her attention.

The last day she discovered a thick green portfolio tied with red ribbon.

"That contains copies of the duke's private letters, Your Grace," Mister Carson explained. "The ones he wrote himself, and that I never saw."

"It might be prudent just to burn it," Mister Hampton advised.

Probably. That would be the wise choice.

She pulled at the tie of the ribbon. "Occupy yourselves. I will review this alone."

The portfolio spanned Alistair's adult life. She began with the oldest letters and worked her way through the years. There were notes to old friends and a series of political missives. She discovered epistles of instruction to Brandon at school. Most of their contents were as distant and cold as the duke himself.

Early on she began finding some personal letters of a different tone, however. Love letters. Not to her mother. The Duke of Everdon had enjoyed a series of mistresses. There were few names on them, just salutations of "my dear."

She skipped their contents, but could not ignore the periodic flurry of them that indicated a new affair, and then the eventual silence that said that woman was history.

It surprised her how much they saddened her. She had assumed that she was beyond such a reaction where Alistair was concerned. Maybe she had hoped that with their mother at least . . .

She flipped quickly until she got to the most recent letters. Near the top, among the correspondence written the month before he died, she found the only letter addressed to Gerald Stidolph. Her cousin stayed so close to Everdon that most communication could be verbal.

When she read the letter she understood why Alistair would have wanted to convey its news from a distance.

In it the Duke of Everdon admitted that he was getting concerned about his age and the succession. He had concluded that his daughter would never be agreeable to marrying Stidolph. He was pursuing alternate matches in the hopes of luring her home to do her duty.

Then, at the end, he confessed that their plan to make her wed Gerald had grown distasteful to him, in any case.

She focused on that line, and read it again and again. It was the only evidence that she had ever had that her father had considered her feelings in anything.

Gerald's disapproving expression filled her mind. She remembered how he had been harping on her need to satisfy her father's wishes. The abusive way that he had played on her guilt had even been more insidious than Alistair's.

She removed the letter from the portfolio and folded it. This one would return to London with her. After Alistair's death, Gerald had conveniently forgotten that it had been written.

Mister Carson stacked some portfolios and carried them back to the shelves. Those endless documents represented an important part of Everdon's power and most of its wealth. The lessons of the last few days had not overwhelmed her. She could do it. She could make the myriad decisions if she chose to.

Only she did not want to. She did not want to spend her days deciding what the rents should be next year, and whether to hold or sell the investment in those canals. She possessed the head for it, but not the nature. She would much prefer to hand it all over to someone else who would manage it for her.

If she accepted Everdon, she would have to decide who that someone should be. There were important decisions and duties waiting, besides those filed on that shelf. Foremost was the one to produce an heir, and she wasn't getting any younger.

The spirit of the house suddenly saturated her. The dukes down through time clamored for attention. She sighed at their silent demands.

She had come to decide what to do, but of course there had never really been any choice. Hadn't Adrian warned her of that the first night in Paris?

But I will do it my way, not Alistair's way and not yours, she said to the house.

While dressing for the coronation, Dot had ceremoniously placed the ducal coronet on her head. Now Sophia mentally repeated the action, using her own hands.

She closed the green portfolio and finally laid the previous Duke of Everdon to rest.

Well, maybe not to rest. She suspected that before she was done, he would turn in his grave.

chapter 23

T he invitation to share tea arrived in the morning post. It was inscribed on the finest cream-laid stock and bore the ducal crest. Sophia had not written it. Adrian recognized the hand as that of Carson, Alistair's secretary.

Tea? *Tea?* She had quietly returned to London three days earlier, had not contacted him, had moved out of the small house nearby, and now she had sent a formal invitation to share *tea?*

The message could not have been clearer if she had given him pearls as a parting gift.

Time had been fanning a slow burn since he had learned from his runners that she was back. Now it flared into scorching resentment.

He had been creating pitiful excuses to avoid facing the truth. He had rationalized that of course she would want to move back to Everdon House now that it was repaired. He had almost convinced himself that once she had resettled herself he would hear from her.

Hell, he had been right about that part.

Crushing the paper in his left hand, he scratched out an equally formal note of regret and sent it off.

He barely heard the debates in the Commons that afternoon. Since he was due to give a speech the next day, he knew that he should pay more attention, but his mind was full of Sophia. A thick, melancholic regret clouded his perceptions. Sometimes spikes of caustic rage penetrated it, but little else. Certainly not the histrionics of his fellow Tories, valiantly fighting a losing battle.

Which was why James Hawkins had to nudge his arm to get his attention after the session adjourned.

"Shall we go together?"

Adrian was in the middle of a mental lecture in which he was accusing

Sophia of cowardice in letting a grand passion simply fade away. At the very least he had the right to a dramatic confrontation and clean break.

"Go where?"

"To call on the duchess. Surely you received the summons. We all did."

The slow burn instantly turned to white heat. "Are you saying that *all* of her M.P.'s were invited this afternoon?"

Hawkins backed up a bit. "Don't know why you are angry. Makes sense, doesn't it? Past time for us to get off the fence. Especially you, what with your speech planned for tomorrow."

Adrian came close to punching Hawkins merely because he was the nearest target.

"Of course I am going. Hell, I wouldn't think of missing it. It would not do to insult my patroness, would it? We will take my carriage." He grabbed Hawkins by the shoulder of his coat and hauled him away.

"I say," Hawkins muttered, stumbling to keep up. "This is most undignified."

"We must hurry. Don't want to be the last there, do we? She may think we don't have the proper respect. She may surmise that we take her damn favor the hell for granted. She may even conclude that we mistook her for a soft and caring woman instead of the great Duchess of Everdon."

Hawkins tripped along, more aghast with each step. By the time they claimed the carriage, he looked like he feared he had fallen into the hands of a madman.

"You seem out of sorts, Burchard. I heard that you had been conched on the head a while back. Perhaps you should beg off and get some rest."

"Get in."

"By Jove, the afternoon is fair, isn't it? I think that a walk would be very pleasant after—"

"Get in. Duty calls, Hawkins. Lesson number one in being an owned man is that Power should never be kept waiting. I trust that you brought some of your poetry to read in case the duchess wants to pretend that this is a social engagement."

Hawkins reluctantly climbed into the curricle. "Actually, I do have a few sonnets with me."

"That will be a rare treat for us all."

They were not the first to arrive. Harvey Douglas already fawned over the duchess in the drawing room when Adrian and Hawkins were announced.

Adrian almost forgot his annoyance upon seeing Sophia. She had dropped the mourning. She wore a pale green gown with a rose sash and its broad neckline exposed her shoulders. A discreet necklace of gold filigree lay on her luminous skin. She appeared serene and happy and at peace.

He knew at once that the visit to Marleigh had been good for her. She had accomplished what she set out to do. He had never doubted that she would. Hadn't he told her that she was one of the strongest women whom he had ever met?

Pride swelled in him, making an odd mix with his resentment. She had discovered who she was. The implications for her love affair with Adrian Burchard had been inescapable.

Still, she should have done it differently. Now he would always wonder if he had imagined the best parts.

She rose and came toward him. "I am grateful that you were able to attend after all, Mister Burchard."

"I was able to rearrange my appointments." He briefly took her hand and made a formal bow. She looked startled at the gesture. He glanced into her eyes and let her see his resentment.

Her gaze turned frosty. He still saw the depths and layers, but self-confidence had replaced the flickering guilt and fear.

She greeted Hawkins and then foisted him on Douglas before easing Adrian away.

"Where have you been?" she hissed.

"Where I always am."

"Why haven't you come to see me?"

"I received no request to do so."

"Since when do you wait on a request?"

"When you have left the city and I have no way of knowing that you are back."

"Of course you knew. Those men you had secretly watching my house saw me return. I waited up that whole first night, expecting you. I needed to speak with you and tell you what I planned to do."

Two other guests were announced just then. "It appears that I will learn with everyone else."

"I am not speaking only of politics and you know it. Why are you so cold? Are you that unsympathetic a friend?"

"I am not amused by the circumstances of our reunion."

"It is your own fault. You should have come. What was I to think when you did not?" She glanced to where her guests waited expectantly. "I need to explain things to you."

"This is hardly the place for it."

"Stay after the others leave."

He felt his jaw stiffen. He looked away so anyone watching would think their exchange a casual one. "Ask sweetly and I will consider it."

"You came here determined to vex me."

"I came here because I was obligated to do so. I am not obligated to stay when this is over. If you have accepted your position, I am glad for you. If you are feeling your oats, that is understandable. But I am the man who has possessed you and who knows your body better than you do, and you *will not* command that man to attend on you."

She flushed so red that everyone must have noticed. "My apologies, Mister Burchard. *Please* stay after the others leave." She bit out the request before sweeping away to her backed-up arrivals.

He wasn't sure that he would. He suddenly realized that he did not want a dramatic confrontation after all. He did not want to endure the regretful explanation.

The drawing room filled. Tea was served. They spent an hour pretending that it was mere coincidence that the duchess had invited her twelve M.P.'s to her house on the same afternoon.

Hawkins read his sonnets. They weren't half-bad, which made them barely half-good. The last was a flowery tribute to the duchess. Sophia beamed appreciation and Hawkins began looking roguishly hopeful again. The other men felt obliged to praise and discuss the poems for a quarter hour.

Finally, Sophia got down to business. "I know that all of you have been waiting for my word on the bill being discussed in the Commons. I expect that you are being pressed by your colleagues for your position."

"Hardly pressed, Your Grace," Douglas said. "Rumors have been about all summer that we will be with Wellington and Peel and the Tories."

"I trust that you are not behind those rumors, Mister Douglas. I made very clear at Haford that only I would give the word."

"Not me. I heard that Wellington himself has been counting us in. Some say he got reassurances, and I just assumed you had spoken with him."

Eleven heads nodded. Sophia's glare came to rest on the one that did not.

Adrian sipped some tea. She should have known that he was lying to Wellington when the Iron Duke didn't press her.

"Not that it will matter much," Hawkins said. "A bill is sure to pass soon."

"We still need your official word, of course," Douglas said. "The closer the vote, the easier it will be for the House of Lords to hold the line and kill it."

Sophia's gaze scanned the room. Talk dribbled off. Everyone knew that a ducal announcement was coming.

"I called you here to let you know what I have decided. I have thought long and hard about this, and I suspect that some of you will not agree with me, but it is how I choose to go."

Bodies angled toward her. Silence reigned. Her dramatic pause stretched. Adrian succumbed to a childish urge to ruin the show. He set his cup down, very noisily. It wobbled and tinged and clattered, distracting the audience.

He had a thousand things to resent today, but the evidence that she had decided this without once discussing it with him was the last straw.

"Your decision, Duchess?" he asked.

"It is very simple. I have decided not to decide."

"Excuse me for stating the obvious, but deciding not to decide is not a decision."

Hawkin's perfect brow puckered. "He has a point there."

"The implication is obvious, if you will only consider it. I will not decide. You will. Each of you, according to his conscience. There will be no word from me. There will be no block of twelve votes."

The M.P.'s reacted with shock. Douglas's mouth gaped so wide that his tawny beard hit his chest.

Adrian stared in astonishment. She was throwing it away. She had accepted Everdon's power only to destroy it.

"There is something else that all of you should know," she said. "Your votes will not affect your relationship with me in any way, no matter how you go. In the future, Everdon will no longer be nominating candidates and requiring its tenants to support them."

Stunned amazement greeted this final surprise. It held for a solid minute while everyone absorbed the full implications.

Then chaos erupted.

The M.P.'s broke into noisy groups. One converged on the duchess to explain with strained politeness how this simply would not do. Adrian strolled over to the windows to contemplate the astounding development.

He was furious with her. Livid. Explaining this to Wellington would be nigh impossible. No man would understand why the duchess had just diminished a power carefully accumulated over generations. The Iron Duke would have apoplexy when he learned just how badly she had been managed.

He looked to where she calmly deflected the exhortations heaped on her. She had given them a freedom that they did not want.

Adrian realized that he did not want it either. He had been counting on her making a decision that he did not want to make himself. The choice would not really be his, and no one would really hold him responsible. His conscience would be clear, and his political future still bright.

Hawkins hustled over. "Hell of a thing. You brought her to the boroughs in May. Go explain how things work."

"It appears that they will work differently now."

"Easy for you to say. Stockton is a solid borough. I'm in a damnable situation. If I go with the bill, I vote to abolish my own seat."

"Then vote against it."

"Don't know if I can. She's gone and left it to me now, hasn't she? Changes things, doesn't it?"

It certainly did. Damn it.

"There are other boroughs."

"Not for a Tory who sides with the opposition, nor is there much need for a Whig whose friends are all Tories."

Adrian agreed. Solid borough or not, there was little political influence for an M.P. of those colors. She had put all of them in a hellish situation. Especially Adrian Burchard.

The crowd around her had gotten thicker. He strolled over and interrupted. "Gentlemen, it is clear that the duchess is resolved. May I suggest that we assess our squandered fortunes elsewhere."

He exited the drawing room first but did not leave. After instructions to Charles to send his carriage down the square, he nipped up the staircase before anyone else got away.

His entrance into her sitting room sent the animals into throes of excitement. He wasn't in the mood to play. After greetings and scratches, he ordered the dogs, Camilla, and Prinny to their cages.

It took her a half hour to follow. She finally slipped in, catching him pacing with impatience.

"From your expression, I gather that we will not be falling into each other's arms," she said. "I do not believe I have ever seen you so angry."

"The hell of it is, I cannot decide which angers me more. Being summoned here like the lady's serf, or learning that I have been freed of my bondage."

"You were not summoned. The others were, but not you. If you had not been so stubborn, you would have known about the vote three nights ago. And my decision to cease nominations. And about the rest."

"Whatever the rest is, let it wait. You have given me enough to swallow for one day."

"Seeing your mood, I may let it wait forever." She strolled to a chair and arranged her skirts to sit. "Why didn't you come?"

"Why did you move out of the other house?"

"It was time for me to come back here. I would have explained if you had visited that first night."

"I could not visit without your requesting it. You know that."

"I know nothing of the kind."

"Sophia, you went to Marleigh for a reason. We both knew what it was. We both knew what it may mean about us."

"I did not know. If I had, I might not have gone."

"But you did go. And I am right, aren't I? You are Everdon now, of your own choosing. You must marry, and soon."

She looked to her lap. After a pause, she nodded.

So there it was. Ended. Finished. A sick weight filled his chest.

Her gaze rose and met his directly. She did not even look very sad about it.

That sliced him to his core. He had concluded that she was not in love with him, but he had thought there was more than that calm acceptance suggested.

"Do not blame me for foreseeing the end and avoiding the indignity of learning about it after sneaking in your garden door."

"And do not blame me for being who I am."

"I do not blame you. I love who you are. Runaway or duchess, fearful or strong. However, right now I am infuriated by how thoroughly you have disrupted my life."

"You are speaking of the vote now, and not us."

"I am speaking of both. I apologize if I cannot match your own noble equanimity."

"That is not fair. You misinterpret my mood and my feelings, but I do not think that today you will hear anything that I say about that. As to my announcement downstairs, I do not understand how I have disrupted anything for you. You are free to vote against the bill, as you have always wanted to."

He turned away in exasperation.

Her skirts rustled. She came up behind him. "Oh."

"Yes. Oh."

"You never indicated . . ."

"How could I? To have brought up the subject would have left you wondering if I still tried to manage you. Influence you. *Use you.* Nor did you seek discussion or advice. I never imagined that you were deciding not to decide, as you put it. Or that you were contemplating throwing the futures of twelve men to the winds."

"If it means anything at all, I did not choose this course until I was at Marleigh. Then I just knew what I had to do. It is not right, my controlling those seats. There are few enough votes among the people without my stealing the voices of so many. Please try to understand."

He turned to see her worried frown. The ducal facade had cracked. She looked earnest and concerned. And absolutely beautiful. His duchess. His Sophia.

"I understand. A damn sight more than I would like to at the moment."

Tilting her chin up, he kissed her. He intended it to be brief and light, a small gesture of parting. The warmth of her lips captivated him, however, and flowed like a balm through his veins. He lingered, and the melancholy that had suffused him for days pitched high with nostalgia.

He pulled away. "You must excuse me now. I have a speech to give to-morrow, and I need to decide what I will say."

"Speak against reform, Adrian. Even if you believe otherwise now, it will make no difference. The bill will pass no matter what you do."

"It is not that simple. My patron's last command was to vote my conscience. It is time to decide what that is."

He kissed her hand and went to the door.

"Please come and find me. After. I would like to tell you about Marleigh, and what happened there," she said.

He could not promise that he would. That kiss left him thinking that he dare not.

He opened the door. "There is one thing that I need to know now. Tell me it will not be Stidolph."

"It will not be Gerald. I would kill myself first."

He did not return to his chambers. He walked the city, watching the people at their work, not thinking much about anything.

His feet took him through rich neighborhoods and poor ones, along lanes of fine shops and market streets full of smells. He tried to walk off his feelings for Sophia, but that didn't happen. He struggled to weigh his options about the bill, but his thoughts remained scrambled and incoherent.

Somehow, despite the lack of rational argument, he decided what to do. After two hours he turned on his heel and headed back. He did not return to Sophia. Instead he visited another square, seeking out the home of a man who had already faced the choice that he confronted now.

A footman admitted him and accepted his card. "The family is about to sit down to dinner, sir. Perhaps tomorrow afternoon . . ."

A door opened off the hall and a tall man emerged. He saw Adrian and approached.

"Burchard, it is good to see you."

"Laclere. My apologies. I know it is an odd hour to call, but . . ."

The viscount waved his explanation silent and turned to the footman. "Mister Burchard will be joining us."

"I do not want to intrude."

"Nonsense. We are informal here. Bianca's bad influence, I am often told." He guided him toward the dining room. "Besides, now that you have finally come, I do not intend to let you get away."

"I only came for advice, but I would be honored to join you for dinner. And as for women and their influence, I have recently learned that they can exert it so subtly that a man does not even know it is happening."

Laclere's blue eyes pierced him. "If you take the step that I think you are contemplating, there will be no protecting you. Wellington will see that you spend your career in Parliament on the back benches."

"I know that."

"We will talk of it after dinner. Now come and eat. I warn you that Bianca insists that the children dine with us when there are no guests, and you were not expected. You have a good hand with animals, though. Perhaps you can get them to behave."

The next afternoon Adrian gave the speech of his life, supporting moderate reform. Since he was Wellington's protégé, and since everyone knew that his stand was on principle and would not affect the outcome, it caused a stir. The newspaper scribes did not miss a word.

While he spoke, his gaze swept the gallery. It stopped on a broad pink bonnet plumed with blue feathers. Its owner's green eyes never left him while she listened intently.

When he finished, the third son of the Earl of Dincaster moved his seat to join the dissenting members of his party, treading a short path that effectively ended his political significance.

It might have been a lonely path as well, but nine of Everdon's other M.P.'s rose and joined him.

After the session adjourned that afternoon, he went looking for Sophia Raughley.

chapter 24

As Adrian rode his gelding along the river, another horse fell into pace beside him.

Gerald Stidolph smiled over with malicious glee. "A remarkable performance, Burchard. Like a soliloquy in a Greek tragedy."

"And here I thought it was the most English speech that I have ever given."

"Douglas told me what transpired yesterday with the duchess. You made a mess of it, didn't you? Wellington would have had your head. Did you decide to fall on your sword instead?"

"The Commons is not debating whether to raise a tariff by three pennies, Stidolph. I decided to do the right thing. I do not expect you to understand that."

"What I understand is that I will not have to waste my time breaking you as I intended. You have done it for me. I overestimated you."

"Your estimation of me has always been irrelevant. However, your opinion of Sophia is also off the mark. That is why you will fail."

"Do not force me to finish the job that you started today. Fifty well-placed pounds and your borough will vote you out. Fifty well-placed words about your true blood and no decent house will receive you. Without the protection of Dincaster or the patronage of Wellington, you are nobody but a half-breed bastard with no family and no fortune. Have anything more to do with Sophia and I will reduce you to the nonentity that you were born to be." Gerald turned his horse and trotted off.

Adrian rode on to Everdon House where Charles grimaced his regrets that the duchess was not at home.

"Is she truly not here, or is she refusing to receive me?"

"Not here, sir. She has gone to the shops. It is not uncommon for her to do that when she is out of sorts, as you know. She went to the other house and got the artists to accompany her, I believe. They have been living there since we returned here."

Adrian already knew that. The Ensemble was making free with the love nest. One more decision by the Duchess of Everdon that he didn't much like.

Charles assumed a doleful expression. "She took the grand coach. She had that look in her eyes, sir. I think that this may be a very expensive afternoon."

"Then I should stop her before she has to mortgage the estate. It will be easier if I walk. Have my horse dealt with."

It wasn't hard to find her. Everdon's coach stood on Regent Street, already bursting with packages. Adrian imagined the bonnets and gloves and jewelry they contained. The visit to Marleigh had not changed everything. Sophia still buried her strongest emotions beneath a mountain of extravagance.

He discovered her in a tailor's shop, poring over fashion plates with Attila and Jacques. A blond English head bent with the two dark foreign ones. Hawkins had joined the Ensemble.

"These three waistcoats, I think. With gold buttons."

"You are too generous, *chéri*. Brass would be fine."

"They will look poor with the design. No, gold it must be."

The tailor nodded with professional agreement. "The lady is right. Only gold will do. And for the frock coats that you have ordered, as well. Now, gentlemen, may I show you some plates for riding coats?"

Adrian strolled up behind them and peered down at the fan of plates that displayed the Ensemble's expanding wardrobes.

Hawkins saw him first. The pup looked guilty as hell at being caught accepting a woman's support. As he should.

"Dressing up your dolls, Duchess?"

They all turned at his voice. Attila looked wounded and Jacques insulted. Sophia pursed her lips.

The artists prudently decided to go inspect the other designs.

Adrian sat beside Sophia.

She returned her attention to the plates. "I did not think that you would come. You did not say that you would."

"I expect that I will always come if you ask me to."

She flipped through the colored engravings, and stopped at one. "I can picture you in this, but you would never let me give it to you. You have never taken anything from me."

"That is not true. I took the most precious things that you had to give. I will always be grateful for your gifts. At least as much as Hawkins will be. What is he doing here?"

"He stays with a sister while in London. She has three children and he can never find the quiet he needs for his poetry. He has moved in for now with Attila and Jacques at the small house."

"Those sonnets needed more than silence to improve them. So you are giving him a home and today you are buying him new coats."

"I could hardly leave him out when I stopped by for the others."

"Does he understand how this works? That you purchase only friendship with these favors?"

"I can see that your mood is not much improved from yesterday."

"It was until five minutes ago."

She sighed heavily and threw the plates down. "I want to leave. This doesn't amuse me the way it used to."

"How unfortunate for our blond friend. To only catch the tail end of your fascination with collecting young men."

"Now you are getting insulting. Are you going to take me away from here or not?"

He went to the artists and informed them that the duchess was leaving. He collected Sophia and escorted her to the coach. He had to restack some packages, to make room for them both.

"Do not look like that and do not scold. I can afford it. I was astounded to learn how wealthy I am."

"I would never think of scolding. Since coming to London you have provided employment for countless seamstresses and milliners. The economy of England has grown dependent upon you. I trust that you ordered a dozen new gowns today, as well?"

Her eyes narrowed on the tower of luxuries. "I know what you are thinking. It is cowardly. Another diversion and distraction. Another means of running away."

"I thought that the reason for going to Marleigh was to put that behind you. What are you running from now?"

She regarded him with stark honesty. "You. Us. From the knowledge that you are all too aware of how pitiful those gifts were that I gave you. I am also running away from seeing the rest of it through. I am afraid."

Her bluntness stunned him. He had never expected to hear her admit that she had not given as much as he wanted.

Her regret moved him more than a declaration of love. He wanted to soothe her and say that it hadn't mattered. Except it had.

The coach still stood in front of the tailor's shop.

"Where do you want to go?"

"Take me to the park. Show me the black swan that you mentioned the day that Attila and Jacques arrived. I have heard others speak of it."

"There is no black swan. It is a tale men tell to lure women to a secluded spot."

"How secluded?"

Her gaze burned into him. The invitation surprised him. It instantly fired the desire that he was still learning how to smother.

"Not that secluded."

"Then take me to your chambers."

"Another diversion, Sophia?"

"Yes. I want to run a little longer. Into your arms where I am beautiful and magnificent. I want to hide for a while before I learn if my life will be heaven or hell."

Memories of their lovemaking filled his mind. His blood craved to agree even though his heart knew he should not. For his own sake, if not for hers.

"Your coach will be recognized."

"You think my future consort will know about us? I do not care. In fact, if he does not, I will tell him. If I must marry some lord, he will be getting Everdon, not me. Never me." The determined line of her mouth trembled and her eyes grew moist. "Please. Before the Duchess of Everdon faces the reality that she will create for herself."

Her sadness and need touched him like it always had. He rapped the coach wall and gave directions. Then he closed the curtains and lifted her into his arms.

Her love cried for release, resenting its confinement. It screamed like a physical thing trapped in a box made of glass. Her spirit reached to free it, but the invisible panes intruded.

As she climbed in her passion, she beat against the barrier with her frenzy. The yearning became so painful that she begged for the sensual climax that would obliterate the emotional battle.

He did not give it to her. His mouth stopped its torture and he came up over her.

It was a joining drenched with emotions deep and unspoken. His embrace and movements told of his sadness and anger.

She sensed his resolve that this would be the last time. She could tell that he planned to keep her maddened and aching to the end. She tried to bare her heart so that he could brand it as he wanted to, but fire cannot penetrate glass.

He paused, leaving her tense with unbearable pleasure, one step from the highest peak that she had ever known. He rubbed his face against hers, as if he sought to inhale her essence.

"You will always be in my heart."

They were the parting words of a man who accepted the end.

He moved again. She clutched him frantically and soared with him, riding their desperate need to a moment of bliss.

For an exquisite instant she believed that there could never be loneliness again. His own beauty and magnificence saturated her. He filled all of her, all of the voids. The power of utter completeness suddenly cracked that glass, and the sweetest peace began dripping into her heart with a slow, cautious rhythm. *Trust. Believe. Give.*

She held him and listened and felt, overwhelmed by the fragile fulfillment. Was it real? Would it last after his embrace ended and she was left with herself? The glass had not totally shattered. The old hurts might yet repair the barrier.

He rolled off and gathered her into his arms. She rested her cheek and hand on his chest and listened to his heartbeat, happier and more afraid than she had ever been in her life.

"Thank you for coming to the Commons today," he said.

"I could not stay away, especially after disrupting your life."

"Maybe I should thank you for that too."

"Why did you do it?"

"I realized how much I have permitted my birth to dictate who I am. I have always felt the need to be more English than most, in order to make up for the half of me that is not English at all. It molded me as surely as Everdon molded you. Maybe I thought that if I allied myself with England's great hero and supported the old traditions, no one would notice that I do not fit in."

"Does England's great hero know?"

"I met with him this morning. He does not like it, but he understands. He did not insult me by spelling out the cost, but of course that relationship cannot continue now. I find that I do not mind very much. I had renounced my independence in making my way more than I had realized. I despised Harvey Douglas, but I was no better. Worse, since I began being a player and not just a pawn."

"You said once that compromise is essential in government. Couldn't you have justified one more?"

"There are times when compromise is dishonorable. Every man knows when those moments arrive."

"What will you do now?"

"Maybe I will agree to manage one of those archeological expeditions. Some time away might be good."

A long time. Far away. From her.

"I made a mess of it, didn't I? I wanted you to be free to do what you thought best."

"Which is exactly what happened. You did not make a mess of it at all."

She nestled closer. The matching pulses of their hearts beat out the passing of their final hour together. The expectation of parting soaked their intimacy with heartrending tenderness.

For three days she had put off learning how it would be. His restraint in coming to her had undermined the confidence that she had carried back from Marleigh. But she could not wait any longer.

"Adrian, you have never spoken of marriage to me. I have wondered why."

"You know why."

"Because of your birth?"

"It is an insurmountable barrier, but actually, I never contemplated that much where you were concerned."

"Then why? Did you never even consider it?"

He shifted abruptly, flipping her onto her back and bracing above her so he could look her in the eyes. "Do not imply that it was lack of honor on my part. If you want to run for a while, I will let you. I will even hide you. But not to endure insults afterwards. What if I had spoken of it? What would you have thought?"

"That you wanted to take care of me and protect me."

"I have never needed marriage to do that."

"That you loved me and wanted to stay with me."

"Would you have found my motives so pure? Nothing less than complete selflessness can win your trust, and no man proposing to the Duchess of Everdon can claim that."

"You sound bitter. You said yesterday that you do not blame me for being who I am, but you do."

"Who you are is one thing. How it stands between us is another."

"That is because of me, isn't it? Because of my suspicions. Because of how the past strangled my ability to believe, unless the selflessness was explicit. That is what you really mean."

He swung away angrily and landed on his back beside her. "Yes, damn it. Are you satisfied now? I do not know why you have forced this. Neither of us has learned anything that we did not already know."

"Haven't we? I have learned that you did consider proposing. You should not have assumed that I would know that you wanted me in that way. I am not nearly that self-confident. When you did not come to see me when I returned, I began imagining that I had misunderstood everything. We women have a tendency to do that at the slightest provocation."

"You may have imagined it, but I refuse to accept that you believed it. This has hardly been a casual affair, Sophia."

"It was enough to make me hesitate, and wonder, and worry about how you would react to the vote and the nominations and to the rest of it."

"Ah, yes, the rest of it. You wanted to tell me about that. If it refers to your plans to marry and execute your duties to Everdon, I must warn you that I will react badly. It would be best not to ruin our time together by speaking of it."

Our time. Our last time.

"I'm afraid that I must risk it. I want to tell you."

He exhaled with the exasperation of a man cornered by a woman who did not have the sense to sidestep a painful topic. It was not a very promising sound. She lay beside him, looking at the ceiling, frightfully aware that this was not how she had imagined it at all.

His arm rested beside hers. She sought his hand and entwined her fingers through his.

"I want you to work out the rest of it with me, Adrian. I want you to help me to see it all through."

"If you expect me to advise you on your marriage, you ask too much. Speak with Dot. She probably knows more about the suitable prospects than I do."

"I do not want your advice. I have decided on my own. I already know who I want it to be. All I need is for you to agree it was the right choice."

He turned so that he could see her. "What are you saying?"

She took a deep breath, and prayed that he wasn't completely selfless after all.

"Will you marry me, Adrian?"

She suffered the long minutes of silence, not daring to look at him. She could tell that he was surprised.

He cupped her chin and turned her head so that she could not avoid his gaze.

"Taking in another stray, Duchess?"

"That isn't fair. I decided this long before today. I knew I would ask even before I went to Marleigh. It is why I wanted to settle things with the past. If you had come that first night, I had planned to ask you then. Although I am proud of your stand today, this has nothing to do with it."

"Then why? Are you so intent on destroying Everdon that you seek to pollute its bloodline?"

"You credit me with cruel motives. That was a harsh thing to say."

"No more harsh than what you will hear from others."

"I don't care what is said."

"You will. A marriage to me will be the scandal of the year. I know that your motives are not cruel, but I wonder what they are, nonetheless."

"I can trust you to take care of Marleigh and the other estates. To manage them well."

"A good employee can do that."

"I would have more confidence in you."

"Then hire me. At the moment I might accept, with my future being ambiguous."

"It isn't just that. I want my children to have a good father."

"There is no evidence that I will be one. I have no experience with children, or even with good fathers."

"You will be a wonderful father. There is the rest of it too. The seat in the House of Lords, for example. I know that you will use Everdon's place there well."

"Where I will speak in your name?"

"In Everdon's. We will discuss matters, but I would not expect to dictate to you. I would know better than to try."

She had not only been giving her reasons, but also enumerating the benefits and power. She could tell that he was waiting for more. She suddenly wished that he had compromised his political principles. It might have made him less obliged to adhere to others.

"I do not want to marry anyone else. You are my best friend, Adrian. In a way, my only friend."

"You have other friends. Attila and Jacques are true to you, and would be so even if the largesse ended today. However, you have created a habit of buying affection, Sophia, and I find myself stuck with the notion that you will now buy mine."

"I cannot help that Everdon comes with me."

"No, but you can help that duty to Everdon motivates this proposal. And I can wish that it did not."

Frustration made her eyes blur. "What more do you want from me, Adrian? I am offering you everything that I have."

"That is not true, damn it."

He was going to refuse her. The realization flooded her with desolation. She pictured the dry, formal, dead life she would be forced to lead. The thought of marrying some carefully chosen, appropriate man left her nauseous.

She closed her eyes to hold in the tears, but they dripped down her temples. She wished that she were half as impetuous and emotional as Alistair had always accused.

The cracks in the glass were still there. The perfect emotion dripped in, continuing its rhythm. How long before the trickle filled her and turned the

love that she felt for Adrian into something free and peaceful and unques-
tioning?

Too long.

She wished that she could lie.

She wished that he did not know her so well that he could tell if she did.

She turned and embraced him desperately. "Listen to me. Please listen and
believe me. It is not duty to Everdon that makes me ask this. It is not. It is
keeping you with me. It is holding you like this, and being magnificent and
not knowing the loneliness again. It is being loved, and loving as much as I
am able, more than I ever thought I could. It is about tasting heaven and not
wanting to find places to hide in hell."

His arm encircled her and pulled her closer, along his whole body. He
kissed the tears on her temple, and then her mouth.

She ached for that complete intimacy again. She caressed him and deepened the kiss, urging his arousal while her heart cried with longing.

"I have never had much defense against your sadness, Sophia. But I need
some time to think about this. I have to consider what you are offering, and
whether we can be happy together."

His passion showed her again what that could mean, and why she dared
not lose him.

The next morning Adrian met Colin at an auction called to sell the horses of a profligate lord whose gambling debts had gotten out of hand. He found his brother near a corral on a Kent estate, examining a tall chestnut gelding with handsome lines.

"There you are, Adrian. Hope I didn't drag you away too soon. I would have come in last evening instead of leaving the note, but I saw her carriage around the corner."

Adrian did not need Colin to remind him that it had been an indiscreet night. And an infuriating one.

He did not know why he was reacting to her proposal like this. Only a fool would hesitate. If a duchess in her own right was foolish enough, brave enough, to marry a man with his shadowed history and lack of fortune, that man would have to be an idiot not to agree.

Instead he kept viewing the proposal with caution. He did not doubt her affection, and his heart welcomed the chance to stay with her and take care of her. A simmering annoyance, however, would not permit much happiness with the other opportunities that she had offered him.

He could not shake the notion that this marriage would make him a more intimate and expensive version of Attila or Hawkins, and that she would actually be more comfortable with their relationship if it did. The power and wealth that she gave him would tip them back to her old way of managing men and interpreting their interest. The small, impossible distance still separating them might never be breached, and he would resent that gap every day of his life.

Perhaps he would view it differently in a few days. Right now, still heady with the liberation embraced in the Commons, he did not fancy looking in the mirror ever again and seeing an owned man.

"Your message made it very clear that we should meet here, Colin. Was there a reason for that besides your desire to bid on that gelding?"

Colin patted the chestnut's rump and then motioned Adrian aside. "Unfortunately, yes. I did not want you going to Dincaster House."

"I take it the earl is displeased with my speech."

"Displeased does not begin to cover his humor yesterday. He has given orders that you are not to be admitted. Ranted about your traitorous face never darkening his threshold again. He cursed himself for not having repudiated you at birth, and declared that he was disowning you."

"He essentially did that long ago."

"Dot is sick about it, and plans to work on him once things calm down."

"I will arrange to see Dot and reassure her that this is not the catastrophe it seems."

"He has ordered her to plan a ball as soon as possible. One to which you will pointedly not be invited. His way of declaring things to society at large."

"I have lived on the edge of society for so long that falling out will be a very small drop."

They began walking toward the auction circle. "If it means anything, I was very proud of you yesterday. I was out of town, but got back in time to hear you. I was in the gallery, but I doubt you noticed anyone but her."

"I noticed. Thank you."

"A damn fine speech. Everyone knew what it cost you. Even the conservatives were moved. When those other men rose and joined you . . . well, you will long be remembered for it."

How long? A year? Five? What was the name again of that promising young man who threw away his future on a matter of principle?

"I did not just rouse you to warn about the earl, Adrian. I've some news."

"What news?"

"I have found him. Captain Brutus."

The chestnut gelding was led into the auction circle just then, so Adrian had to wait impatiently until Colin finished bidding.

"I am feeling smug about how brilliant I have been," Colin explained while they walked to a tent to settle the bill of exchange. "I remembered how you said the duchess had described him as educated, so I took a chance and went to the universities. I found a don at Cambridge who remembered a student from about that time, blond-haired and radical, average build. Guess what his name was?"

"John Brutus."

"Damn, how did you know?"

"I have wondered if it could have been his real name."

"John Brutus Marsham, to be complete. Son of a clergyman from York. I rode to York and looked up the father and there he was, in the sitting room, as if he had been expecting me."

"The father?"

"Aren't you listening? Captain Brutus himself was there. I said that I found him."

"Did you warn him off? Tell him for me that it is worth his life to stay away from Sophia?"

"Well, that is where it starts getting confusing. Let me pay up and I will explain."

Adrian cooled his heels while Colin settled the bill and arranged for the gelding's move to Dincaster's stables. A quarter of an hour later they headed for their horses.

"He has been back in England almost a year," Colin said. "Came back a changed man."

"To be sure. Instead of burning threshing machines, he moved on to burning homes and threatening women. The hard life turned him into a hard man."

"It seems the opposite occurred. He studied for the Church at Cambridge and rediscovered the spiritual life while indentured. He has rejected all forms of violence. Still radical, but supports peaceful persuasion now."

"When confronted with the evidence against him, I do not doubt the scoundrel would claim that."

They stopped at the horses. Colin shrugged and ran his fingers through his blond hair. "I believed him."

Adrian had been indulging in a fantasy of beating Captain Brutus bloody. Colin's statement cut it short.

"I do not question your ability to judge a man, but events indicate he lied to you."

"Perhaps. It is not only my judgment, however. He swears he hasn't left York since he returned ten months ago, and his family supports him. He was troubled to learn that his name has been used on those broadsides, and that someone has threatened the duchess. If he is a liar, so is his father, and they both lie very well."

Adrian absorbed the implications. If Colin's impressions were correct, it cast a new light on what had been happening to Sophia the last few months.

"If not John Brutus, then someone else sent those letters and lit that fire, Colin."

His gaze met Colin's in a mutual acknowledgment of who that someone might be.

But it made no sense.

Of course it didn't.

His mind laid it out, and it all fit together like a cobblestone path winding

into a dark maze. That path led to dangerous conclusions and sickening suspicions.

His blood chilled. If he was right about half of it, they were dealing with
a monster.

He didn't have a dot of proof. Unless . . .

He swung up on his horse. "I have been blind, Colin. You have my heartfelt gratitude for discovering the truth."

"If you are going where I think, let me come with you."

If his ugliest suspicion was true, he would not want Colin learning of it.
Or anyone else. "Better if you are not involved."

"Damn it, if he is cornered he could be dangerous. Rats usually are. He
almost killed you once. At least tell him that I know, too, so he doesn't think
that removing you will solve it for him."

"I will not confront him until I have enough proof that nothing will solve
it for him."

He turned his horse and went looking for the only person who might provide that proof.

chapter 26

Attila's head flew back in a passionate swoon while his fingers evoked a flamboyant melody from the pianoforte. Jacques, who had provided the lyrics to the new song, watched anxiously while their collaboration unfolded in front of its first audience. The Viscountess Laclere warbled the love poem that the Ensemble had set to music.

The third verse veered into the rose metaphor. The viscountess blinked at the words on the sheet that she held, but did not miss a note.

Sophia reddened. Oh, dear. And at her first dinner party too. She should have demanded a rehearsal before she allowed Attila and Jacques to plan the entertainment. She had not realized that it was *that* poem.

The twenty guests listened attentively. Few reacted in a way to indicate they understood the symbolism. She glanced to her left. Three chairs away, Gerald Stidolph's tight lips barely held in his disapproval. His shock made her feel much better.

The song went on and on. The form and sensuality of the rose was described in amazing detail. The lovers in the song grew rapturous with their memories.

A few guests shifted uncomfortably. Several coughed.

Jacques beamed. Attila let the music transport him to a higher plane of existence. The viscountess persevered.

They got to the nectar-licking part.

The professional stance of the viscountess cracked. She shot a glance to the man sitting on Sophia's right and bit back a conspiratorial smile that only an idiot would not understand. Dozens of eyes followed her sensual acknowledgment. The Viscount Laclere, who had been maintaining an expression of cool passivity, closed his eyes and sighed at his wife's indiscretion.

"My apologies," Sophia whispered. "When I cajoled her to perform, I had no idea."

"It is an ancient metaphor with a long pedigree. There is a famous English medieval romance on the same topic. Should I tell Monsieur Delaroche that he digs well-tilled ground?"

"Maybe you shouldn't. He may decide to make his longer and more creative, as a form of competition."

"Heaven forbid."

The song finally ended. The guests could not get up fast enough. Conversations were initiated with determination. As Sophia strolled past Jacques, she heard two ladies inviting him to visit and advise them on their gardens' poor blooms.

Sophia thanked the performers. Laclere smiled at his wife in a way that suggested a loving scold was waiting for a private moment.

Hawkins joined them, breathless at the marvel he had just witnessed.

"A rose. Who would think a poet could get such a long and magnificent poem out about two lovers admiring a single flower? I am undone and humbled. An interesting problem, though. An inspiration. As an exercise, I may try it myself." He narrowed his eyes, an artist awaiting his muse. "Bluebells. Yes, I think so. There is a lot of soul in bluebells. At least forty lines worth, don't you agree?"

Laclere crooked his finger. "Come with me, Hawkins. All magnificent poems deserve serious analysis. Let us leave the ladies while we consider this one."

Sophia did her duty to her guests, but her heart was not in it. This dinner had been planned for a reason. Last night she had asked Adrian to attend and stay by her side. None of these peers and their ladies would have missed the significance of that.

When he had said that he needed to consider her offer, she had hoped that he would do so quickly. Right up to the moment when she had led the way down to the dining room this evening, she had prayed he would arrive. Evidently it took Adrian Burchard longer than one day to make up his mind.

Or not long at all. Maybe his absence announced his decision.

That possibility had been creeping into her mind all evening, making her listless. The party had become a chore.

Gerald Stidolph appeared at her side.

"You sent a letter that you wanted to speak with me," he said.

"Yes, I do. It is of some importance."

"Among all these people? I expect that it requires more privacy."

"It certainly does. Will you come with me to the study, where we can find some?"

"I would be delighted to, my dear."

She led him to the study. She had intended to inform him tonight about marrying Adrian. Doing so would have made this easier, and much more satisfying. *I have chosen the man whom I want, Gerald, and it is not you.* Now she was left with only half that declaration, and she doubted he would hear the same finality.

She sat behind the desk, in her father's chair. That left Gerald across from her, like a petitioner. She enjoyed that more than she ought.

"I visited Marleigh last week."

"So I was told when I called on you."

"It was a good visit. I had been avoiding Marleigh and what it meant. I am more at peace with it now."

"It is understandable that you avoided it. It is a heavy burden for a woman. As were those memories, and the duties required by them."

"You do not understand, but then you never did. I did not resist it because I am a woman. We are not nearly as stupid and helpless as men think. I am not nearly as useless and frivolous as *you* think."

"I do not think—"

"It does not matter, Gerald. I went. I accept the title. All that it is and all that it means."

He smiled broadly. "I never doubted that you would, Sophia. Your dramatic decision about the M.P.'s showed the world that you do. An eloquent gesture, but perhaps an extravagant one. We will wait a year or two before reestablishing Everdon's power in those boroughs. Everyone will understand that with proper council you reconsidered."

"By proper council, you mean yourself."

"Of course, my dear. It has always been my only goal to help you."

He appeared very contented. Very pleased about the power that he assumed would now fall into his hands.

She remembered his expression that day after the fire, while he beat her heart with the cane of her guilt.

"It will not be you, Gerald. I accept all that it means, but I do not accept you. I will marry. I will give Everdon its next duke. But not with you."

A happy man one moment. A furious man the next.

"It is because of that interfering bastard, isn't it? He stole the affection that should have been mine."

"He stole nothing. He kindly accepted what little I gave him. He offered me comfort, while you only offered pain."

"I warned him. I'll destroy him, and if you have anything more to do with him, I will destroy you too. If you think for one moment that anyone will accept a marriage between you and that half-breed—"

"I did not say I was marrying Adrian. I merely said that I am not marrying you."

"I'll be damned before I accept this."

"Then be damned." She withdrew a folded paper from the desk and threw it across at him. "I only fulfill my father's wishes, as you always lectured me to do."

He scanned the letter that the late duke had written to him. "You read his private correspondence?"

"I read everything."

He gave her a blank stare. "Then you know all of it. That is why you repudiate me."

She understood neither his expression nor his words. He appeared defeated suddenly, like a man who knew he had lost. The depth of his vacancy made her uncomfortable.

"She does not know any of it. She repudiates you because she has always sensed what is inside you."

Sophia turned with a jolt. Adrian stood at the door. Absorbed in her confrontation with Gerald, she had not heard him enter.

"The game is over, Stidolph. Or should I address you as Captain Brutus?"

Gerald slowly turned to him.

"Captain Brutus?" she asked, completely perplexed.

"We found the real one, Sophia. Up in York. He never wrote those letters. It was Stidolph, counting on fear pushing you into his arms. He knew the route we would take to the boroughs, and went ahead, stirring up trouble. He was in the house when that fire started, too, ready to rescue you before it was too late. It would have been a dramatic, romantic gesture, if he hadn't turned coward."

"He is speaking nonsense."

"I am speaking the truth and she knows it. Look in her eyes and see who she really is. Not a woman easily duped. You always underestimated her."

"He is lying, to turn you against me. He wants you for himself."

"That is true. For herself. Not for Everdon. Not like you."

Adrian walked over and removed the letter from Gerald's lax fingers and read it. "This explains much. After all your patience, I wondered why you killed him. Alistair could not foresee that in sending this he had signed his own death warrant."

The accusation stunned her. She turned in shock to Gerald. "Is it true? Did you kill him? Just because he no longer wanted you to have me?"

He did not flinch. He did not move or look at her. He watched Adrian with a soulless, empty face, like a man made of stone.

"Your admission of that is not necessary," Adrian said. "But she does need to hear about Brandon. She has a right to it, after carrying that burden all these years."

Her brother's name had her grasping the desk's edge. Something was happening here that she did not understand. The air in the study had grown cold and heavy and stale, like that in a tomb. The sensation sent chills through her.

Adrian regarded Gerald with a determined expression. Gerald reacted impassively, but deep in his eyes the coldest lights sparked and suggested the mind still worked, cunningly.

The horrible atmosphere came from him.

"What about Brandon?" she asked, barely getting the words out.

Adrian waited. Gerald watched him. He watched so hard that she wondered if he had heard her question.

"You did not kill your brother, Sophia," Adrian said. "Not even accidentally. He was pulling you to shore when Stidolph arrived in a boat to help. He saw his chance and took it. An oar to the head. A wound that looked later like the rocks had made it."

Shock paralyzed her for one eternal, terrible, cold minute.

Then hot outrage flared.

She went over to Gerald and stood where he could not ignore her. She wanted to bloody his cold face. Scratch out his eyes with her bare hands. All of those years and all of that guilt. Dear, kind Brandon . . .

Frustration and fury blinded her. "It is true, isn't it? My God, what are you? *Why?*"

He looked past her, through her, to where Adrian stood. He cocked one eyebrow.

"He already had your father's favor," Adrian said. "With Brandon gone, he could hope to get the power of Everdon through you."

"You would go to such lengths? You would kill for it?"

"I deserved it."

"Deserved it! Because you flattered Alistair? Brandon is the one who deserved Everdon. You killed him, and then my father, too, when you saw the plan going awry? You let my father believe it was my fault, and you let me live with that guilt. You even used Brandon's death against me. You are a madman!"

The stone of his face creased into a confident sneer. "Burchard's work as a clerk in foreign countries leads him to see intrigue everywhere. He is wrong. He has no proof."

"I have proof. Not for the duke, but for Brandon. You were not the only one watching while he saved his sister. Another saw you row out and take Sophia into the boat. Saw the oar go down. Sophia said the steward helped bring her around on the shore. You bought him off with money and a seat in the Commons, but he was an accomplice through his silence and does not want to swing with you. Harvey Douglas has told me everything."

Gerald shrugged. "It is his word against mine."

His reaction unhinged her. No remorse or guilt. No fear. He wasn't even flustered.

She flew at him.

With a smooth movement he rose, caught her clawing hands, and thrust her away. She landed in Adrian's arms.

He embraced her tightly and glared at Gerald. "His word will be enough. He has no reason to lie, and it will cost him dearly. He will be believed. You will not be the first criminal who thought he could outsmart justice, only to find the gallows' trapdoor open beneath him."

Gerald strolled around the desk. "You expect a trial? I think not. After all, if I find myself in the dock and things are going badly, I may be compelled to explain everything."

Adrian's arms tightened protectively. The two men eyed each other. A terrible tension arched between them, as if their locked gazes exchanged silent threats.

Adrian's hold relaxed. He set her away. "Go back to your guests, Sophia. I need to speak with Stidolph alone."

"I will not. They were my brother and my father. I have a right to hear everything."

"Trust me on this. You must go now."

"I will not be dismissed."

"*Go.*"

She stood her ground. Adrian tore his gaze from Gerald and pulled her across the room. Forcing her out of the chamber, he closed the door behind her.

Her mind red with indignation, she grabbed the latch to reenter.

It would not budge. He had locked her out.

Gerald sprawled in the chair behind the desk. Comfortable in Alistair's place. Smug. He surveyed the room with a possessive expression. Finally his gaze came to rest on Adrian.

"You don't want her to hear it. That means that you know."

"I suspected."

"If you deduced that part, you are very good."

"She commented frequently that you reminded her of Alistair. Then there was the way that he favored you. As you get older, the resemblance is there. It also gives those murders a clearer motive."

Stidolph ran his hand over the polished desk, looking more like Alistair by the minute. "Of course *you* would suspect quicker than most. It is a story you know well, isn't it? So here we are. Two men cut from similar cloth. Except, of course, that I am all English wool, and you are half-primitive weave. Two men fathered by men other than their mothers' husbands."

"Everdon knew?"

"Of course he knew. When my mother's first husband died, he threw his brother at her because of me. He knew how to take care of his blood, even if I was sired on the wrong side of another man's blanket. He saw to my education and bought me my commission. He saw himself in me, more than in his legitimate children."

Adrian fought his profound disgust. It was too much to have hoped that Stidolph would lie, and have the decency to leave these secrets where they belonged.

"Whose idea was it? For you to marry your own half sister?"

"I think we both considered it separately. I certainly did. Otherwise, why do away with her brother? I sensed the duke would not be averse."

"So it was your plan. Your idea."

"It repulses you to think that our father suggested it? Sorry, but that is how it happened. He broached the subject after Brandon's death. He wanted Everdon to go to his son, and I was the one left. I would not get the title, but I would hold the power."

It did repulse him. It would sicken anyone. If Sophia ever learned that her father had planned this, if she ever suspected that Alistair had tried to force her into an incestuous marriage, it would be the final, horrible betrayal by a man who had given her little else. The wound might never heal.

"But he reconsidered. He remarried." Adrian tried to keep the hope for reassurance out of his voice.

"Ah, yes. Dear Celine. I reconsidered too. When no child came, I even tried to help out. If she had borne my son, I might have been satisfied. The title should have been mine. I was his blood. But if it went to my son . . . it might have been enough. But the bitch was barren. Wouldn't you know it. A sign, it seemed to me. Alistair thought so too. He revived the old plan. For a while."

"Then he reconsidered again, so you killed him."

"If you want to preserve your memory of him by thinking so, go ahead. It was not that way. He concluded that she could not be convinced, and that he was losing time. He decided to accept another match so that he could at least secure the succession before he died. Stupid man. To think I would settle for nothing after having it all within my grasp. He never would have stood down. He should have known I would not either."

So there it was. All of it, including the most insidious part. If the world found out what Alistair had tried to do, it would be a smear on Everdon for generations. It would also destroy Sophia's fragile truce with the past.

"You should not have told her. About Brandon," Gerald said.

"She deserved to know."

"Now I have only one card left. I will tell her all of it, and threaten to let the world know what her father intended if she does not marry me. I don't fancy marrying her if she knows. Her awareness that I am her brother will make it very sordid. Still, you have left me no choice."

"Do you think that she will submit to such heinous blackmail? Accept incest in order to protect her father's name from the accusation of plotting incest?"

"Not to protect her father's name. I doubt she would do it for that. But to protect the prestige of Everdon, maybe. What do you think?"

"That she would let you do your worst. Play that card, breathe one word of this to her, and I will make you wish you had never been born. Do not doubt that."

"If I am tried for murder, I will have nothing to lose. If I find myself in the dock, I will speak of it. Don't *you* doubt *that*."

So there it was. The real blackmail. Not of Sophia, but of him.

She would never agree to keeping silent about Brandon, especially if she did not know the reason. And her not knowing *was* the reason.

"It disgusts me to see you escape justice, but you have given her enough pain for one life. You have twenty-four hours to get out of Britain, Stidolph. I only make this concession for Sophia's sake."

"I have no intention of leaving. There is nothing for me on the Continent."

"Then flee to hell, where you belong. You have one day. Or I bring Harvey Douglas to the authorities and watch you hang."

Gerald drummed his fingers on the desk thoughtfully. "Without Douglas, you have nothing. Without you, Douglas has no coercion."

"Is that a threat?"

"It is an observation."

"Douglas is hidden where you will never find him."

"You are not."

"Others know."

"Not everything. If you offer me flight, they do not know about Douglas yet. Only Sophia does."

He spoke pleasantly, merely making another observation, but the conclusion was unmistakable. *I remove you and her and I am free.* Adrian's blood chilled as it had at the auction. A monster. Or, as Colin had said, a rat. Vicious when cornered.

Only, Adrian was cornered too. Bring Douglas forth, and Sophia would learn about her father's unnatural plans for her. Find a way to get Sophia to agree to keep silent, and Stidolph would one day try to remove the dangling threat of eventual disclosure.

He would risk his own safety. If Stidolph got to him, however, Sophia would be helpless.

"I have reconsidered. If you do not flee, I will not bring you to the authorities."

"I thought that you would see reason."

"Instead, I will kill you."

Gerald's smile froze. Then he laughed. "You don't have it in you."

Adrian placed both hands on the desk. He leaned forward, forcing Gerald back, and hovered while he looked him straight in the eyes. "I have it in me. Do you want the names of past ministers who can vouch for that? It was always self-defense before, but any one of the men I've killed had more right to live than you."

Gerald's face fell. Adrian swung away and strode to the door. "One day. After that, we begin an interesting game. Who will succeed in killing the other first? I think that the half of me that is a 'primitive weave,' as you put it, will give me the advantage. You will not even hear me coming."

chapter 27

Sophia paced furiously in front of the study door, blinking back tears of scathing anger. Her heart filled her chest, pulsing painfully, strangling her breath.

Her scrambled thoughts veered between plans for delicious revenge and terrible pictures depicting Gerald's crimes.

She glared at the door separating her from her enemy. She raised her fists to pound on it and demand entry.

The door suddenly opened. Adrian stepped out and closed it behind him.

Her fists found a target on his chest. Her emotions poured out while she pummeled him.

"By what right do you throw me out of that chamber when what will be discussed is all about Everdon and me? You reject the marriage that would have given you that kind of authority, and then you exercise the authority anyway. I *will not* be managed, especially when it is a matter so important to my family and to *me*."

The words did not emerge with the indignation she intended. Instead they wavered and broke and ended in a gasping sob that groaned out of her soul.

He pulled her into his arms.

He held her to his chest as he had at Staverly, keeping her together while the anger and grief engulfed her.

Slowly, within the security of his embrace, the tempest receded, leaving the profound calm that only comes after a dangerous storm.

Sounds of the pianoforte and conversation drifted and echoed. She looked to the music room.

"I cannot go back in there. I cannot spend the next hour speaking of stupid things after what I have just learned."

"You can send in word that you have taken ill."

She pressed her damp eyes against his shoulder. "I keep seeing Brandon. Over and over in my mind. All of the memories I blocked, have flooded into me all at once. It is breaking my heart. I can picture his face when Gerald came by in that boat. The relief, and then the shock. It is horribly vivid, as if I really witnessed it. I want to kill Gerald. If I had a weapon, I might have done so."

He caressed her hair with a soothing touch. A few distant footsteps intruded, then faded away. She jerked her head toward the sound.

"It was the viscountess. She will be discreet," Adrian said.

"I do not want to be discreet. I am sick to death of being discreet. Aren't you?"

"It has been a way of life for me, but, yes, sometimes I get sick to death of it too."

"Perhaps if it had been my way of life I would not find it so stifling. I suspect that is what I will hate most about Everdon. Never having the freedom of Paris again."

"You are freer at this moment than you have been in eight long years, darling."

His words made her look inside herself. "I am, aren't I? Free of the guilt and the past. Despite the heartbreak of learning about Brandon and my father, there is a kind of peace at the center of my soul that I have never known before. Thank you for discovering the truth for me."

The study door opened and Gerald stepped out. Adrian pulled her closer and wrapped his arms around her protectively.

Gerald smirked. "Charming. Very touching." With the air of a man who has no care in the world, he ambled back to the other guests.

Sophia could not believe her eyes. "He thinks to stay. He shows no distress at all, Adrian. He expects me to play the hostess to the man who murdered my brother and father."

"Go to your chambers. I will have Charles bring an explanation in to them."

She narrowed her eyes. "I will not give Gerald that satisfaction. He has seen me weak and enjoyed making me so, for the last time. I will go back in. Gerald Stidolph will be damned before he makes me hide again." She turned her back on the waiting party so she could see only Adrian. "I would like you to stay."

"You have the strength to do it yourself. You do not need me holding you up."

"I will not let him see me weak, but I am not feeling very strong at all. He frightens me. His coldness, his own lack of fear, chills me as if I have been touched by the hand of death. I may not need you holding me up in there, but I would like to be with you later. Please stay with me tonight, even if it is for the last time."

"We seem to have a lot of last times."

"I would settle for one more, but would prefer a lifetime without any."

"Until matters are concluded with Stidolph, I cannot give you an answer about that. I promise that I will, as soon as this is finished."

"That should be soon, though, shouldn't it? You plan to take care of it tomorrow, don't you?"

"Yes. Soon. Probably tomorrow." He kissed her hand and looked into her eyes. "In truth, the man chills me too. I think that only your embrace will warm me."

Already she was warming. His touch and gaze, the lights burning deeply in his eyes, had her flushing. Anticipation of the comfort of his arms would carry her through the next few hours even more than her satisfaction in showing Gerald that he could not break her spirit.

She turned toward the music room.

Adrian released her hand. "We may both be sick of discretion, but this is not the night to abandon it. I will follow you in a few moments."

She had thought that he intended to wait in her chambers, but he was going to come in. He would be there, not holding her up, but helping her to find her own strength as he always had.

She walked down the corridor to where Gerald Stidolph waited among her guests.

She could do this. She could stare evil and death in the face, because later she would heal her heart in the arms of goodness and life.

The next night Adrian sat with Colin, St. John, and Laclere at a table in Gordon's gaming hall. Only half of his mind participated in their languid rounds of vingt-et-un.

Colin was winning, Laclere was breaking even, St. John was up a huge amount, and Adrian was down twenty pounds. Adrian decided it was a good thing he was not a superstitious man.

Normally.

"That chestnut promises to be a good runner. With some work he may be up to Ascot," Colin said, continuing the forced banter that he had employed all day while he doggedly trailed Adrian all over London. Colin did not know what had transpired in Sophia's study, but he was worried and had not let Adrian out of his sight.

"It won a race in Sussex last spring, didn't it?" Laclere asked, picking up the cue.

Gordon's was not one of Laclere's normal haunts. Adrian suspected that he had arrived tonight specifically to sit next to him. The news of Dincaster's decision to socially repudiate his youngest son had spread very quickly. Since Laclere was hardly a paragon of acceptability himself, Adrian doubted that his display of support could break the fall much, but he was grateful for the effort.

Laclere may have come in friendship, but Daniel St. John had attended at Adrian's request. St. John made no attempt to enter the light conversation, and his eyes glowed with an internal distraction that echoed the tension that Adrian himself felt.

St. John's glance caught Adrian's own and a silent message passed. Soon. Very soon. Stidolph must realize that there really wasn't any choice.

A ten showed faceup on the table in front of him. His hole card was a seven. Adrian debated calling for another card.

A chill shivered down his back. A shadow fell on the cards. Adrian did not turn but his companions did. St. John's body tensed in a way that announced who had arrived.

"Stidolph," Laclere acknowledged in greeting.

"Laclere. Odd finding you here."

"I am more particular about my company than my surroundings."

"It would appear that you are not very particular about your company at all."

Adrian turned in time to see Laclere's blue eyes harden into crystals. "I am most particular, which is why I must ask you to excuse us."

"That is not possible at the moment. I need to speak with your half-breed bastard friend."

The men at nearby tables heard the insult. An oasis of silence instantly formed.

Laclere shot a questioning glance at Adrian, who returned a quelling blink. Colin required more direct restraint. St. John reached for Colin's arm, to prevent him from rising.

"Insult one Burchard and you must deal with us all," Colin warned.

"The way I hear it, I do not insult a Burchard at all. The word is that Dincaster will finally make that official."

The oasis of silence spread. Their table became the center of rapt attention. A few other gamers rose and sauntered closer.

Adrian met Stidolph's gaze with his own. "If you think to provoke me to a challenge, it will not happen. We will not do it quite that way."

"Then I must challenge you, although the evidence is that you do not have the honor to meet me."

Colin almost leapt out of his chair. St. John had to exert real strength to keep him in place.

Laclere summoned his best noble hauteur. "Unless there is good cause, there will be no excusing such a challenge, nor will any man here think badly of Burchard for refusing it."

"There is good cause, and he knows it. The best cause. The honor of a woman. The Duchess of Everdon."

"If the duchess believes that I have in any way harmed her, let her say so. It is not your place to interpret our friendship."

"Not that duchess, Burchard. The dowager duchess."

Celine.

Adrian had wondered if Celine had been a player in Stidolph's plans. No doubt if she had borne Gerald's son, she would have married him after Alistair died.

She had probably even encouraged Stidolph's marriage to Sophia when she found herself barren. If Gerald got Everdon through Sophia, he would permit Celine to stay. A wife in one chamber, a mistress in another. Celine would accept that. Keeping the position that she had bought with her beauty was all that mattered.

Maybe not entirely. After all, she had agreed to have her name used now in this desperate bid to save her lover's skin.

"The dowager duchess has no argument with me," Adrian said.

"She has confided in me. She told me that you pursued her before her marriage, and continued to do so dishonorably after it. She let me know that on several occasions you importuned her, and the last time, just this summer, crossed a line that cannot be excused."

"That is absurd," Colin said. "Of all the women to claim such a thing, she is the last to be believed."

"Keep that up and I will need to issue two challenges."

"I beg you to do so. I will demand that you meet them in order of precedence. Me first."

"My brother forgets that we are no longer boys on the playing field, and that I do not need his protection."

"Will you give me satisfaction, or will the world know you for a coward as well as a bastard?"

"I will definitely give you satisfaction. I would not think of disappointing you."

The silence in the gaming hall broke as word of the duel spread like a wildfire. At their table, utter quiet reigned for a solid minute.

"I would be honored to serve as your second, Burchard," Laclere finally said.

"Thank you, but St. John will take care of it."

Laclere's eyebrows rose faintly in realization that much of this had been prearranged.

St. John assumed his role with steely calm. "I will meet with your second tomorrow, Stidolph."

"Tonight," Gerald said.

"Yes, tonight," Adrian agreed.

"Tonight, then."

Gerald strode across the room and out the door. Dozens of astonished men watched, then directed their attention to Adrian.

He turned away, back to the cards.

"Damn the man," Colin muttered. "Whoever expected . . ."

"I expected."

"When you meet with his second you must seek to have the challenge withdrawn, St. John," Laclere said. "An hour or two and he will think better of it."

"I must insist that no one make any attempt to do that," Adrian said.

Laclere's brow furrowed. "May I assume, then, that this is about more than the dubious virtue of the dowager duchess."

"Yes."

"You are sure that it is necessary?"

"It is necessary, and the only way that I can see justice done."

Laclere called for a card. "I might remind you that it is illegal. Nor, after this public drama, will it be secret."

"Fifty men heard him challenge me in a way I could not ignore. No jury will convict me."

"Perhaps in France . . ."

"He will not agree to that either. It must be tomorrow, so it must be here."

Laclere turned his card with a troubled expression. "And if you fail in getting whatever justice you seek?"

"If I fail, there will still be justice. I am leaving a letter with Wellington, who will see to it. And if he cannot, another man will."

Laclere turned his head, suddenly very interested in the bland, calm presence of Daniel St. John.

"What weapons will you choose?" Colin asked, much subdued now. "You really are not a very good shot."

It was St. John who answered. "Sabres. Mounted."

Colin absorbed that. "At the risk of sounding like an older brother, may I point out that Stidolph was in the cavalry? He was trained by some of the finest swordsmen in England."

"A formidable man," St. John said. "Adrian, on the other hand, was trained by the greatest swordsman in Turkey."

Adrian gestured for a card.

It was a five. Twenty-two.

Hell.

She was dreaming about him one moment and awake in his presence the next. A swell of awareness gently raised her above the sea of sleep until she was alert to him.

It must have been the animals. They were silent now, as still as statues, but she could sense their eyes watching. They must have made a mild commotion when he entered, before he signaled them to behave.

She could not see him, but she knew he was in the dark corner by her bed, out of sight. His compelling aura filled the air.

"Adrian?"

"I am sorry. I did not intend to wake you."

"How did you get in?"

"This house has a garden door too."

"You have some experience with opening locked doors?" She had been wondering about those foreign missions ever since Jacques had suggested their purpose at Marleigh.

"Some."

"Will you tell me about it sometime?"

"Probably."

She turned on her side toward his voice. "Why are you here?"

"To see you. Just to look at you while you slept. To breathe the same air."

His quiet tone touched her more than his words. Something indefinable stretched and ached out of that shadow.

"Has something untoward happened?"

"No. Go back to sleep, darling."

She reached out her hand. "Come and sit with me. If you want to see me and breathe the same air, come closer."

He hesitated, then emerged from the corner. He shed his frock coat and sat beside her, his shoulders up against the board and his boots stretched atop her light coverlet.

She scooted up under his embracing arm. In the dim moonlight she imagined that she could see his serious expression, but in reality she only felt his deep, churning mood and could not see it at all.

"What is it, Adrian? Is it about Gerald? I understand that laying down information must have been difficult, no matter what his crimes."

"I will not regret Stidolph's death for one second, Sophia. I am not the sort to get sentimental about such a man. Justice will catch up with him tomorrow, and I will not regret it."

"Then what, Adrian? Your mood is troubling me. I have never seen you like this."

He nuzzled her hair. "A bad humor, is all. Too much thinking about the past and contemplating the future. Too much awareness of how fleeting life is, and how we waste it on insignificant concerns. I do not care to speak of it and infect you with my melancholy. Already it passes, as I knew it would if I came here."

That was not true. Whatever had brought him here in the night had not passed. She felt it in him like a dark, turbulent storm. He only contained it through his commanding strength of will.

It twisted her heart. This was Adrian. She had always assumed that he could snap his fingers and quell any inner turmoil as quickly as he did Yuri's rambunctious behavior.

It had been selfish and thoughtless of her to think that. He carried wounds as surely as she did. That he normally controlled whatever churned his depths and memories did not mean that those waters were placid.

Guilt pierced her. She had only learned about the parts of him that she needed to use. His strength. His passion. She had depended on him to fill her voids, but she had never thought that she might fill his. Maybe she should not blame herself too much for that, though. The Sophia Raughley that he had brought back from Paris would have laughed at the notion that she might have something such a man might want. Besides power and wealth, that is.

Well, she was not that woman any longer, thanks to Adrian. If he had come tonight just to breathe the same air, maybe she had more to offer him than she thought.

She turned and embraced him closer and let her heart reach out to his. Maybe she could hold him together a little, as he so often had done for her. Possibly she could soothe him like he comforted her.

He seemed to know what she was trying to do. He rested his cheek on her head. Invisibly, spiritually, without a word being said, he revealed his raw emotions.

They poured out of him and into her, creating a painful and poignant intimacy. Her heart both cringed from the dark onslaught and embraced it. She did not know what had provoked this in him, but she recognized the vulnerability too well. She tried to absorb it, hoping to make his burden a little lighter.

A long time passed silently. She felt him relaxing within her clinging embrace. The small sign that she was helping exhilarated her. He kissed her head gently, as if in gratitude.

A sweet, exquisite sensitivity bound them. Deep. Sacred. It suffused her with euphoria.

Easily, unexpectedly, love spread out from her heart through her whole being, and no barriers blocked its path.

It was her turn to give, and his to need. It had never been that way before. She had never known that the giving gave love its purpose and fulfillment. It obliterated the separateness and shattered the glass walls and created a world of perfect unity.

She trembled within the profound power of what she was experiencing. "I am so glad that you came," she whispered.

"I could not stay away. I knew that just being near you would make me feel alive."

Alive. Yes, that was what she felt. Totally alive, and alert to the reality of the moment. A kind of living that had nothing to do with breathing and heartbeats.

She tilted her head and kissed his neck. With glossing touches she caressed his face, sensing his essence as surely as his skin.

Giving. She was new to it, and fascinated. She had gotten it all backwards, this thing between men and women. Love made it different. In love, the taking became giving. Without it, the giving became taking.

She moved so that she could kiss his mouth. She embraced his need, both physically and spiritually, and reveled in the opportunity to take care of him.

She unbuttoned his waistcoat, kissing his chest through his shirt as the fabric gaped open. A soulful arousal quivered through her.

"I did not come here to make love, Sophia."

She plucked at his cravat and whisked it away. "Are you going to stop me?" Her fingers went to work on his collar.

It was still in him, that dark turmoil. Binding them now because she shared it and took some of its confusion off of him.

"No."

"Just do not speak of final times tonight, Adrian. I do not want to think about that."

A peculiar emotion surged out of him, but it quickly retreated. "We will neither speak of it, nor think of it."

She got his shirt off. He remained unusually passive and did not help her much. She liked that.

"Take off your nightgown. I want to see you."

Rising on her knees, she slid it up. His warm palm caressed down to her breasts. "You are so beautiful. Like a white flower in this moonlight. Beautiful and magnificent."

Hearing the words from their first night together wrenched her heart. Even then there had been little giving on her part. She may have surrendered her virginity, but the generosity had been all his.

She splayed her fingers over his chest and traced the wonderful ridges of his muscles. "I am only beautiful and magnificent with you. Only for you."

They caressed each other slowly, as if their hands could print the forms on their memories. Their mutual pleasure became a language shared in silent conversation. Her breasts and skin were unusually sensitive to his touch. Her new depth of emotion imbued the pleasure with shared ecstasy.

She moved down to pull off his boots. His gaze on her body made her breathless. She unbuttoned and lowered the rest of his garments, caressing and kissing his hips and legs as they emerged.

Giving. It drenched her delight in his body with an amazing richness. It made the desire tether their hearts.

She bent to lick his nipples and then trail her tongue down his chest while her fingers slid to encase his phallus. His whole body flexed in response.

She laid her cheek on his hard stomach and watched her caresses and felt the tension of his passion climb. Her own rose with it, toward a determined, yearning level.

"I want to make love to you, Adrian. You have never asked it of me. Do you want me to?"

"Yes. But I want to be inside you before the end. I need to hold you to my heart this time."

She moved her kisses lower and licked. He tensed, making her bolder. She explored more aggressively. A low affirmation escaped him.

Craving pleasure spread as his reactions absorbed her. Her own body began weeping with need. His hand warmed down her back and trailed her cleft to the spot that screamed for his touch.

They traveled a steep path of united sensuality. She kept expecting to shatter, only to pitch higher. Her consciousness blurred to everything except the release awaiting them.

Suddenly he reached for her. He flipped her on her back and bent her knees up to her breast. He lowered his head between her thighs and tortured her with intimate kisses that left her crying for him.

He rose up and came to her. The turmoil he had been carrying became a physical force. His thrusts left her gasping. She filled her arms with him, urging him to take whatever he needed.

At the end he rolled so that she straddled him. Arms wrapping her tightly, pressing her to his heart, he finally succumbed to a violent release. He brought her with him to that spot of heaven he had shown her before. Whatever drove him tonight simply disappeared in the peace of that special place.

He did not release her. Long after, he still embraced her. She grew drowsy in that contentment, and felt the relaxation that said he had fallen asleep.

Had he felt what was in her tonight? Did he know? She laid there and memorized every inch on his body against hers, focusing on the sensations bit by bit, the scent and texture and hardness of him.

"I love you, Adrian. You will always be in my heart."

His head turned slightly and he looked at her through the darkness. He was not asleep. He had heard her.

She woke to his presence again. He was standing beside the bed, looking down at her. His frock coat was slung over his shoulder, hooked on one finger.

She raised her hand and placed it flat on his chest. The first light of morning had turned his white shirt silver.

"Do you have to leave?"

"I have something that I must do this morning."

"Gerald?" She resented that seeing to Gerald's arrest would pull Adrian away before she could say what needed saying.

"Yes."

"Will you come back after?"

He kissed her hand and closed his eyes. "Of course. Now go back to sleep."

He lifted her chin and stroked her lips with his thumb, then bent and gently pressed his own to them. "I love all that you are. Hold me in your heart as you promised last night."

Turning abruptly, he strode from the chamber.

For some reason that she could not explain, that kiss shadowed her joy with a terrible foreboding.

chapter 28

She carried the love inside her all morning, fascinated by its novelty. She turned it this way and that in her heart, examining all its facets with delight. It was so enchanting that she could ignore the tiny worry that still pricked at her because of the way Adrian had taken his leave.

It changed everything, unfettered love did. The sun looked golden and the air smelled pure. All of the servants smiled more. When Jenny pulled her into the wardrobe, determined to cull the old gowns to make way for the new, the onerous duty actually sounded like fun.

Her mood must have infected Jenny. The maid kept smiling, smiling. Talking, talking. Gown after gown emerged for consideration.

"Take that one for yourself," Sophia said when a lace-trimmed yellow silk faced judgment. "You always liked it."

"But it is almost new."

"Take it. It doesn't matter. None of it matters anymore."

Jenny's smile disappeared. "What an odd thing to say, my lady." She set the yellow silk aside and pulled out the next gown. "What about this?"

"That I will keep."

"To be honest, the shade of rose never suited you."

"I will keep it. It is the gown I was wearing the first time Adrian kissed me."

Jenny turned away quickly.

"Is something wrong, Jenny?"

"No, of course not." She turned back with the smile in place and became all business again.

At eleven o'clock they were surprised by the arrival of Dorothy Burchard. Bright-eyed and happy, she intruded on the dressing room unannounced.

"Forgive me, Sophia, but I was out for a walk and decided to stop for a little rest. You don't mind, do you? I told Charles to dispense with formalities. What are you doing? Wardrobe? I promise not to interfere."

She sat next to Sophia.

Was it her imagination, or did Jenny look relieved to see Dincaster's sister arrive? The two of them exchanged one quick look and then Jenny persevered.

Dot had promised not to interfere, but she did. Constantly. Questions about the French modistes who had made the gowns. Admiration of the details and fabrics. Judgments as to practicality. All the while she regaled Sophia with humorous stories about sartorial disasters witnessed at balls down through the years.

Smiling, smiling. Talking, talking.

A half hour later word came up that the Viscountess Laclere had come to call.

A peculiar silence stilled Dot's prattling for a five count. She and Jenny exchanged a quick glance.

"The viscountess? How wonderful," Dot said. "Will you receive her? Why don't we go down and call for some cocoa? The air has a cool bite to it today, and I think cocoa would be just the thing."

Dot smiled encouragingly. Jenny beamed with agreement.

Sophia recognized what was happening. They were managing her. But why? The tiny worry that she had been ignoring suddenly demanded more attention.

They found the viscountess in the drawing room, decked out in a sapphire riding habit. She approached Sophia with outstretched hands and a chagrined smile. "Do forgive me for the uncivilized hour. I was coming back from a ride in the park and thought I would stop to call and congratulate you on your dinner party. Promise that you won't tell Laclere, or he will scold his errant American wife for presuming. Dorothy, what a happy coincidence to find you here. I had a brilliant idea about creating a ministry to support the arts that I planned to confide in the duchess, but your wisdom regarding the matter will be welcome."

"It sounds fascinating. You must tell us all about it over some cocoa," Dot said.

"Cocoa would be wonderful. The morning holds more chill than it appears. I fear that the last of summer is gone."

The cocoa came. They sipped it while the viscountess described an outrageous plan to petition to establish an entire government ministry dedicated to supporting young artists. The scope of the patronage grew while she talked.

As if she was making it up as she went.

Dot asked lots of questions. Sophia watched the spirited exchange. Too spirited. Too earnest. Talking, talking. Smiling, smiling. Except the talk struck her as oddly forced, and the smiles as too determined. They chattered around her and through her, as if a pause would be disastrous.

More unexpected arrivals were announced. Jacques and Attila. Probably a coincidence. Maybe not.

Jacques appeared as smooth as always. Attila exuded an exaggerated joviality. They joined the conversation. The viscountess began explaining her idea all over again.

The relentless chatter grew unnerving. Sophia wanted to sit quietly and savor her love, not be distracted by all this talk.

Distracted. She peered at the viscountess and Dorothy. Something dark shimmered beneath their bright expressions. Jacques looked more solemn than smooth, now that she examined him. Attila's smile might have been painted below his mustache.

Charles entered and bent to her ear.

Sophia listened to him and nodded. "It appears that the Duke of Wellington has come to call," she announced. "Perhaps I will start a new fashion. Morning salons."

That cut short the relentless talk. Jacques remained blasé, but Attila shot Dorothy a worried glance. Dot's cloud of white hair ever so subtly shook a vague negative.

The duke paused at the threshold and took in the collected visitors. "I feared that my calling so early might disturb you. I see that is not the case. Forgive my impertinence, but I was walking past and . . ."

"And the air was brisk and you thought some cocoa might be in order," Sophia said. "You are most welcome here. As you can see, this household is not rigid in its formalities."

She settled the duke down with Dorothy and the viscountess, and saw to his refreshment. A most awkward silence ensued, punctuated by small talk that only tightened the threads of tension weaving among the guests.

"Attila, I have been practicing that sonata that you gave me," Sophia said. "Come to the pianoforte so that I can show you my improvement."

Jacques did not want Attila to go off with her alone, that was evident. Neither did Dorothy. The viscountess leapt into the breach with a query to Wellington about the Battle of Waterloo. The duke grabbed the topic with gusto.

Sophia gestured for Attila nonetheless. Pasted smile wavering, Attila reluctantly joined her in the corner at the pianoforte.

"Wonderful. How you improve! Extraordinary, my lady," he said after she had tortured the first passage.

"Oh, nonsense. I am horrid, as I have always been."

"Not so. True, you miss a few notes still, and the hesitant tempo is a bit awkward, but your sympathy with the music touches my heart."

Her fingers persevered. The duke continued his stories. The viscountess wore an expression of rapt interest, but her gaze spent more time on Sophia than on Wellington.

"What is happening? Why are you all here?" Sophia demanded of Attila.

"To visit with you. Is that no longer permitted?"

"Attila, do not think me so stupid that I do not realize that this is most unusual. The Viscountess Laclere, with whom I am hardly intimate, has stopped by before noon. The Duke of Wellington is telling stories that must even bore him by now. You have agreed to listen to me play the pianoforte, when we both know that it pains you to do so. There is a shadow in this chamber, a dark shadow that everyone is trying to keep at bay with all this banter and amiability. Now, what is happening?"

He squirmed. "Nothing is happening. Jacques and I wanted to see you, that is all. We had no idea you would have other visitors. We came as friends. Is that so wrong? We did not want you to be alone."

Her gaze swept the little group. It *had* been a coincidence. They had not planned this. Each had come independently, because none of them wanted her to be alone. It was even why Wellington was here.

"Why didn't you want me to be alone, Attila?"

"Did I say that? I meant that we thought you might be lonely."

"It is something to do with Adrian, isn't it?"

She did not need to see his distraught expression to know the truth.

They did not want her to be alone in the event that bad news came.

The worry that she had been ignoring surged. The foreboding strangled her heart. She stopped playing and looked at her visitors. One by one they saw her expression. The talk drifted into silence. The careful smiles fell away.

She rose on trembling legs and rejoined the others.

She looked Wellington right in the eyes. "Where is Adrian?"

The duke's sharp expression donned a veil of sympathy.

Dorothy reached out and grasped her hand. "There was no choice. Colin assured me of that."

"Where is he?"

Wellington shook his head. "I do not know where the duel is happening. I received a letter from him this morning saying it would be done, but not where. The letter asked me to see to your protection if he did not survive. It also contained another, sealed letter, to be opened only in that event."

"A duel? He is meeting Gerald? Does everyone know except me?"

From their expressions she gathered that the whole city knew, except her. Even Jenny and the servants. It explained all those smiles this morning. That was the reason for the wardrobe duty. And for Dot's visit. And the rest. They had come to be with her in case bad news arrived, but also to make sure that she did not go out and learn what everyone else knew.

A duel. It was madness. Insanity. Gerald did not deserve the honor of it. He should be carried off in chains, not met one-on-one like a gentleman.

Adrian should have told her. Last night he should have shared it with her. Even if she would have argued to stop it. Even if she would have locked him in, to keep him from leaving. He should have told her.

Maybe he had. He had brought his fear to her, hadn't he? He had sought to share a night of life before facing death.

Death. It could happen that way. Every person in this room recognized that possibility. Gerald would not escape justice in the end, but he might take one more person from her before he faced it.

"Who is with him?"

"His brother, St. John, and my husband," the viscountess said.

"And at least a dozen others whose names will never be known unless it is necessary," Wellington added.

"You can stop this. If the Duke of Wellington demands to know where this is occurring, someone will tell him. You can prevent it. Instead you sit here and wait to learn the result as if it is some stupid vote in Parliament."

"I sit here as if I wait to hear the result of some action on which I have sent my best soldiers. If Burchard chose this way of resolving whatever stands between him and Stidolph, he had his reasons. He would not welcome this unless he thought it necessary."

"Do you know why they are meeting?"

"Stidolph issued the challenge over the honor of the dowager duchess, but no one believes it is really about that. I think that you know the reasons better than I. I daresay that they have to do with you."

"Those reasons do not require such risky heroics. You must stop it."

"I will not. I cannot. It is already over." He reached out and patted the hand that Dot still clasped. "I suspect that you do not know the fullness of it, Duchess. God willing, he will triumph and none of us ever will. If not, I will open that other letter, and see it through for him." His chiseled face softened. "He is a brave man. I could have used him in the old days. If I had chosen your champion myself, I could not have done better."

Her champion. Fighting the battle she could not wage herself. Risking his life in a cause that had nothing to do with him.

She felt so helpless. So terrified. So grateful that he had come to her last night, and that she had finally been brave enough to let herself fully love him.

"So I must sit here and wait. I must simply endure it until word comes."

A hand touched her shoulder. She looked up into Attila's gentle face. "We will all endure it together, *kedvesem*."

It was the worst hour of her life. A long hell of sickening anticipation. Her throat burned from swallowing back tears. Partway through, Dot entwined her arms around her so that they held each other, two women waiting to learn the fate of a man they loved.

A chill permeated the room. It had nothing to do with the brisk autumn air. Wellington called for a servant and had the fire built up in the hearth. They waited some more.

She thought that she heard a horse stop outside the house. She could not bring herself to run to the window to check. Nor could anyone else. They all froze, alert to the sound. It seemed as though everyone simply stopped breathing.

Boot steps approached. Charles opened the door and Laclere strode in.

He paused, taking in the group, surprised.

"Well?" the duke asked impatiently.

"I rode ahead. He is coming in a carriage, with his brother and St. John. He will be here shortly."

The wave of relief left her limp in Dot's arms. Her composure finally crumbled. Tears snuck down the sides of her face. "Was he hurt?"

"A gash on his thigh. Having it tended delayed us. I advised him to return home, but he insisted on coming here." He glanced pointedly around the chamber. "I do not think that he expects an assembly."

"Stidolph?" the duke asked.

Laclere said nothing, which said everything.

Wellington rose and bid his leave. He extracted a sealed letter from his coat. On his way to the door, he threw it in the fire. Jacques and Attila kissed her and departed in his wake.

"You must stay, Dot. You must see him," Sophia said.

"If you do not mind, just for a moment . . ." She wiped her eyes. "I never want to go through that again, let me tell you."

Laclere offered his hand to his wife. "Let us remove ourselves, my dear. I see that you have been riding. You rarely indulge in that pleasure when in the city. You used a sidesaddle, I trust."

"Really, Laclere. How can you be concerned about such silly little things on such a day? This has been about the great experiences. Life and death. Passions both grand and evil. Proper calling hours and proper saddles are of no account."

"In other words, no sidesaddle." He turned his attention to Sophia. "He may appear in a strange mood when he comes. It is not an easy thing, what has happened. Do not be surprised if he appears less than joyed with his victory."

"I understand. Thank you for everything that you have done for him today."

. . .

Sophia and Dot went to the library to wait for Adrian. Dot left the room as soon as the carriage sounded on the street. Whatever she said to her nephew was communicated privately in the reception hall.

Adrian entered the library slowly, carefully supporting some of his weight on a walking stick. He paused and faced her.

He wore no coats and his trousers stretched over the thick bandage that wrapped his thigh. His clothing was spotless, however. He must have traded with Colin in the carriage.

He looked at her with fiery eyes. Laclere had been right. No triumph. No joy. Just the stark awareness of what had occurred, and what might have. And deep lights of naked resolve.

Her heart ached with love and relief. She feasted her eyes on him, breathless with gratitude that he was alive.

He had never looked less English. His black eyes sizzled. His dark hair was disheveled. A thin, colorful sash belted his hips with its Eastern weave.

He carefully walked toward her. It gave him pain. A bad wound, then. He should have gone home, but she knew why he had come here instead. The reason showed in his eyes and the line of his mouth.

It had become a day for finalities. She prayed that she could convince him that there was no need of one with her.

"Laclere told you?"

"I already knew."

"I had hoped you would not, until it was over."

"That was not fair. There are some things that you should not protect me from." She stepped the few paces that separated them, to embrace and kiss him. He winced slightly, and she felt another bandage on his shoulder. Not only his leg had been wounded. He had changed his clothes so she would not see the blood.

She gingerly rested her head on his chest and listened to the sound of his heart. He pressed a kiss to her hair.

"Won't you sit?"

He shook his head.

She lifted the end of the sash. "What is this?"

"My father gave it to me. He is still in England."

"Did he come?"

"He was there. He stayed in a closed carriage off a ways, but I recognized the coachman and went to him. He gave this to me for good fortune. It is his. He suggested that I stuff it in my shirt. I decided that its power might not work as well that way." He looked down at the band of color. "He has thirteen other sons, but he stayed in that carriage to the end and prayed that I was fated to live."

She fingered the woven patterns that he had displayed to the world. It had been a day for declarations as well as finalities.

"Why did you meet Gerald?"

"He challenged me. Fifty men will swear that it came from him. I did not provoke him."

Maybe not directly, but he had managed this. It had worked out the way he wanted it to.

She still tasted the torture of waiting to learn if he was dead. "Why, Adrian? Why risk so much? Why not just have him arrested?"

He laid his hand against her cheek. "Do you trust me? Do you trust me enough to believe me when I say that it was better to handle it this way?"

She gazed in his eyes and knew that he would not explain more than that. Not now, maybe not ever. Wellington had been right. The reasons had to do with her. Adrian had done this to protect her, and she might never know why.

"Yes, I trust you. Completely. I believe you. I believe *in* you."

She began to embrace him again, but he slowly paced away, distracted by emotions dark and deep. "I have killed before. Not like this, though. Those were like military skirmishes. Country against country. Laclere warned me that it would be different. He has stood to a man, and confided that the memory is a hard one."

She felt the rawness in him and it wrenched her heart. He might know that there had been no other choice, but he still wrestled with the deed.

"Laclere has been a good friend to you. I am glad that he was there."

He nodded absently and paced some more. "I dined with him the night before I gave my speech. His young children were there. I had never seen him with them before. He spoils them. They have a little joke that it is Bianca's American influence, but he can deny them nothing. All the discipline comes from her, not him. Seeing that domestic joy, sitting amidst that love, moved me so much that I wanted to weep." It came out in bits and phrases, as if he gave voice to random thoughts. "I would like to have that."

"I am sure that we can have it. We may not know what to do, but we certainly know what *not* to do."

He shook his head. "You will never be forgiven if you marry me. It will never be forgotten, who I am. What I am. Nor will I ever pretend otherwise again. Many will never accept that."

"I can think of a few who will never forgive me if I do *not* marry you. The people who matter."

"Do not think lightly of it, Sophia. Your title will not protect you. Half of the people who attended your dinner party will cut you as soon as a marriage to me is announced. I was tolerated as long as I stayed on the edges. I will never be accepted in the center."

"Then we will learn who our true friends are, and who the fools are. I said before that there are some things that you should not try to protect me from. This is one of them. I will not let you ruin the happiness that we might have, in the name of shielding me."

He stopped his thoughtful pacing and turned to her. His expression made her breath catch. Vividly alert. Ruthlessly focused.

"It is not about that, is it?" she said. "You know that I do not care about being cut. I spent eight years ignoring those people. Their opinions cannot wound me now, and you know it. This really has nothing to do with your birth."

"Maybe it doesn't. I suppose I never thought that mattered much with you. But I cannot bear to think of your being hurt because of me."

"Why don't we admit what it *is* about."

He evened his weight, standing tall. He might have arrived unscathed.

His gaze penetrated her. "Do you love me? Not only need me, or want me, or depend on me. I welcome all of that, but I want to know if you love me as I love you. There is nothing careful and contained in my feelings for you. It is rash and hot and saturating and perfect. Nothing else really matters. Nothing. Not Everdon and the past, not scandal and the future. Not the assumptions we will face that I use you, or that you buy me. I do not love what you are, I love who you are. That will make all the rest insignificant, but not if I only have your need and your passion."

"I love you. I have loved you a long time. It frightened me, so I kept it contained and hidden. I kept giving it other names and kept trying to turn it into something else. Perhaps I did not believe that I deserved the happiness. I have failed people whom I had loved before."

"You deserve every happiness. And if you feared it, you had cause."

"Not from you. Also, it was more than that. I did not trust myself to love well. Last night you gave me the chance to learn that I could. Now I know that I can love you very well. Better than any other woman in the world. If you will let me give to you and protect you as you have done for me. If you will bring me your burdens as you did last night, and have done again today."

His expression softened. His eyes glistened. Last night's beautiful intimacy flowed across the ten feet of space that separated them.

She absorbed the emotions reaching her, afraid to move, lest she disturb them. She branded her memory with the sight of him. Strong despite his wounds. Mysterious in his dark, hybrid beauty. Brave and exciting.

In love with *her*. How astonishing.

"Didn't you feel it last night, Adrian? Didn't you know?"

"I felt it. I hoped. I carried that hope in me today. I came at once because I had to know that I had not misunderstood."

"You have always understood me. I do not think that you ever got it wrong. I only learned who I was by seeing my reflection in your eyes."

"The reflection of a beautiful woman, magnificent and strong. I am glad that you learned the truth of it."

His love made it true.

"I want us to fill each other's voids and end the loneliness forever, Adrian. I want us to make a happy family, where you can always sit amidst love."

His smile made the world sparkle. "If we are going to have a family, we should get married."

"Is that a proposal, Mister Burchard?"

He leaned his weight on the walking stick, and reached his free hand out to her. "We have both traveled alone for too long, darling. Will you complete the journey with me?"

Her happiness flew to him before her feet moved. She ran across the empty space and joined the man who had brought her home.

The man who valued and loved her, in her own right.

the
SINNER

chapter I

Utter ruin provokes soul-searching in even the least reflective of men.

Dante Duclairc was contemplating that unwelcome discovery when he heard the horse outside. He opened the cottage door to find one very annoyed physician standing in the moonlight at the threshold.

Morgan Wheeler peered severely over the top edge of his spectacles. "This had better be *very* serious, Duclairc. Your brother's land steward pulled me out of bed."

"It *is* very serious, and I am sorry that your sleep was interrupted."

"No one said you had come down to Laclere Park. Why haven't you called on me?"

"Only the steward knows I am here, so you must swear to keep this visit a secret. I should have sent for a surgeon, but you are the only medical man in the region I could trust to be discreet."

Morgan sighed heavily and stepped into the humble abode. "Why did you send for me?"

"There is a woman upstairs who needs your attention."

Morgan set down his bag and removed his frock coat. "She is alone here?"

"Except for me."

"Why does this woman require me?"

"The lady has been shot."

Morgan had been rolling up a sleeve. He stopped, arm outstretched and fingers engaged. "You have a lady visitor who has been shot?"

"Grazed, actually."

"Where was she shot? Excuse me, *grazed*?"

"In this cottage. Accidentally. We were playing a little game and—"

"I meant, where is the wound?"

"In the rear nether region of her trunk."

"Excuse me? Are you saying that you shot your lover in the buttock?"

"Yes. Come upstairs and—"

"One moment, my good friend. My dull life has feasted off the excitement of yours for years, but this is too much. You have secretly brought a woman, a *lady*, to a rustic cottage on your brother the viscount's estate, where you engaged in some orgiastic rite that resulted in her being shot in the buttock. Do I have the essential facts correct?"

"Her arm is hurt and she hit her head too."

"Not like you, Duclairc, getting rough like that. You surprise and disappoint me."

"I assure you that this was an accident. A little game gone awry."

"How? What? My imagination fails me. I try to picture it but . . . If I am going to debase myself by doing a surgeon's work, the price of my skill and silence is an explanation."

"As it happens, that is precisely what I can afford. Please come up now. The steward had some laudanum and we dosed her up so she is still out, and it would be best if you did this quickly."

"Details, Duclairc. I shall expect details."

As Dante led Wheeler up the stairs, he considered that details were exactly what his friend would never get. No one would. The woman awaiting Wheeler's attention had come to this cottage through bizarre circumstances. Dante knew in his gut that speaking of them to anyone would only cause him untimely trouble.

What had she been doing out there, dressed like a man and brandishing a pistol, on a night when the countryside was alive with a mob burning farming machines and a posse on the chase? Dante had taken his own gun to the highest hill of Laclere Park, in a nostalgic effort to protect the estate on his last night in England. When he had been surprised by a trespasser he had returned fire, only to discover to his horror that he had not shot a radical but a woman.

As it happened, not just any woman.

Dante paused outside the bedchamber. "If you ever reveal what has occurred here, or that she was with me, she will be ruined."

"Discretion is a physician's second name. I never failed you in the past, did I?"

Wheeler became all business as soon as they passed into the chamber. He walked to the bed, took the patient's pulse, and felt her cheek. Ever so gently, he turned her head toward him.

He froze.

"Oh, my God."

"Exactly."

"Oh—my—God."

"Now you know why discretion is essential."

"It is Fleur Monley, Duclairc. *Fleur Monley.*"

"So it is."

Wheeler collected his wits. Shaking his head, he proceeded to examine his patient. "*Fleur Monley.* Even I, who have seen women of highest repute faint at your smile, am thoroughly impressed. No one ever got Miss Monley to the altar let alone into bed, let alone playing games that get women shot in the buttocks. The closest was when your brother Laclere almost got engaged to her. . . ." The implications of *that* had Wheeler wide-eyed again. "He will probably kill you if he finds out."

"Another reason for discretion."

"Of course, of course. I promised silence and am bound by it, but it will be hell to honor my word. I will burst." He stripped away the bedclothes to reveal Fleur demurely dressed in one of Dante's nightshirts. "Charming, Duclairc, but why did you bother? She is drugged, I am a physician, and you are her lover."

He had bothered because he could hardly present her in those farm-boy rags, and because it did not seem dignified to leave her naked despite her unconsciousness and the ribald story he was feeding Wheeler. No matter what a man's reasons for stripping off her clothes, even a scoundrel did not leave the Fleur Monleys of the world naked for someone to see.

Morgan touched her bare leg. "She is damp. Did you bathe her?"

"She felt warm, and I thought that I should." It was one more bold-faced lie. Upon removing the rags he had discovered a very dirty body and had washed off the worst of it.

"Of course. Next time, do not give laudanum if the patient has a head wound."

"It wasn't much, and we dosed her some time ago when she began to moan as she came to. I am concerned that it may wear off, so you should get busy."

Morgan was not to be rushed. He touched all around her scalp. "It does not seem too serious. Fell, did she? Went out? She will have a bad lump. She will have to rest quietly for a few days."

"Surely she can be moved."

"Best not. You will have to make some excuse if anyone is expecting her return. She should stay here at least two or three days, in bed. *Resting.* It will give this arm time to repair too. Bad sprain. I can only guess how *that* happened. Some exotic position for coitus that country boys like me never get to learn, no doubt. Hindu?"

Wheeler's grin invited explication. Dante ignored him. Fleur Monley was going to create problems. He could not keep her here for several days, because he had no intention of being here himself. In approximately ten hours he planned to meet a fishing boat on the coast that would spirit him over to France.

"Help me to turn her so I can see about this gunshot. Gently now."

Together they turned Fleur on her stomach. Morgan pulled up the night-shirt. Dante turned to leave.

"No you don't. She was only nicked but you were right, it needs to be sewn. Get over here and hold her. The laudanum made her sleep but she is not unconscious. If she wakens while I am at it, I want someone backing me up."

Dante truly did not want to stay. In his thirty-two years he had seen more women nude than he could count. He had long ago learned to release or sup-press his sexual reactions at will, much like a canal lock controls water. Still, seeing Fleur like this was making him uncomfortable.

She was injured and needed care and he lied about being lovers only to protect her from the posse out there looking for blood. Having her in this bed, naked from the waist down and her face pressed in his pillow, appeared a desecration of sorts. All the same, he was annoyingly aware that stripping her and washing her and seeing her body had raised the lock's water level more than he would like.

That surprised him, because he had grown fairly jaded about such things. Furthermore, her reputation and condition made sexual reactions either ridiculous or despicable.

Then again, her very presence here indicated that the world may have got-ten that business about her unblemished virtue very wrong. The woman Fleur Monley was supposed to be would never run through the countryside in boy's clothes on a night when the radical rabble were out committing crimes.

What the hell had she been doing out there? For that matter, where the hell had she come from? The last he heard, she was visiting France.

He sat beside her on the bed and carefully placed his palms on her back. Be-hind him Morgan prepared the needle, sloshed something over Fleur's bottom, and went to work.

She gritted her teeth and held in the tears. She wanted to scream. If she did, however, these men would know that she was awake. That would be too hu-miliating to bear, and possibly very dangerous.

Where was she? The bed seemed clean but she could smell earth and damp and she doubted that she had made it to Laclere Park. That man who shot her must have given her up. She was probably in a farmer's cottage, be-ing tended before they carted her off to gaol.

Better that than Gregory, she supposed. Unless he learned about it and bribed them to get her back. In that case she would be right where she started.

The man holding her had not spoken much. She wished that he faced away. She would not have to swallow the pain so much if he were not looking at her. He was definitely doing that. She could feel his attention on her, despite his brief responses to the other's comments about horses and boxers.

A hand moved from her back to her head. She barely caught the cry of surprise that jumped to her throat. Fingertips gently brushed her hair back from the pillow and lightly stroked her head. She held her breath, cheek crushed against the down, and prayed that he had not seen her jaw clench or heard her shocked intake of breath.

That caressing hand should repel her. It implied dangerous interest and she was horribly defenseless. Instead, she found the light touch comforting and sympathetic and not at all insinuating. Who was this man who bothered to reassure an unconscious woman?

"I don't remember her being so thin," the voice near her rump mused. A painful skewer by the needle accompanied the comment. She tasted blood as she bit down. "I can see her ribs plainly. Normally people gain weight on the Continent, not lose it. I have to say that even so she has a nice, um, how did you so elegantly put it, rear nether region."

He spoke as if he knew her! If so, the night's risks had probably achieved nothing but more danger.

"Just sew," the man beside her muttered. "Aren't leeches supposed to be above noticing such things? Rather like artists?"

"I am a physician, a man of culture and learning, not a leech. If you think artists grow immune either, you are doubly a fool. All the same, I accept your correction. Although, coming from *you* . . ."

"I do not like my lady friends discussed by other men, that is all."

Her ears were half-smothered in the pillow, but that voice sounded familiar. Why would he be claiming she was his lady friend? A dreadful possibility opened. Could this be the man she had heard speaking with Gregory last night?

"Considering how quickly you tire of your mistresses, I have always thought your reticence in talking about them a little priggish and ungenerous," the physician said. "Although it has never been the ladies who interested me but the strategies for winning and loving them. You could save yourself a lot of curious questions by writing a treatise as I suggested years ago."

"Maybe I will do that. I will have plenty of time in France, and it may pay my keep for a few years."

The rhythm of the needle stopped. "France? My good man, you are not! Has it come to that?"

"Afraid so."

"How bad?"

"Very bad. They are on my trail."

"Surely your brother—"

"I have been to that well far too often, and I will not go again. Once settled in France I will write and explain to him."

"Now I am distraught. You have ruined my humor completely."

"Well, finish up here, come downstairs, and I will tell you all, but it is such an old and tired story that I am sure you have heard it often before."

Efficient hands bound a bandage to her hip. More gentle ones slid the nightshirt down and carefully tucked bedclothes up around her shoulders.

They left. She exhaled the strain of keeping her composure and stillness. Her rump hurt badly now, even worse than when she had first woken in shock to that sewing needle. Still, the pain both existed and didn't, like something floating in part of her mind while the other parts daydreamed and slept. She did not know how long she drifted around the edges of consciousness.

She wondered if only the physician had recognized her or whether the other man had as well. He spoke in the cultured manner that said he moved in the sort of circles where she could have met him at some point over the years.

She clung to the hope that he was not anyone who had anything to do with Gregory, and certainly not the man who had spent last night bargaining for her like she was some four-hoofed animal.

A door below closed on mumbled farewells. Boot steps sounded on the stairs. Someone entered the chamber. She closed her eyes but she felt the warmth of the candle near her face.

"He is gone. Let us see if we can make you more comfortable now, Miss Monley."

She heard his voice plainly this time. Jolting up on her good arm, she twisted in shock.

And looked right into the resplendent brown eyes of the most charming wastrel in England.

The women of English society could bicker and argue with the best of them, but on one point they had always been in total agreement.

Dante Duclairc was a beautiful man.

That was the word they used. Beautiful. His luminous eyes, thick, lustrous brown hair, perfect face, and devilish smile had mesmerized any female he chose to conquer since he turned seventeen. Fleur knew three ladies who had committed adultery only once in their lives. With him.

The years had added some hardness to his countenance, but they had not dulled the heart-skipping effect that his attention provoked.

Even in her, and he wasn't even trying.

His expression bore curiosity and wry amusement. He smiled with warm familiarity, instantly bridging time back to that period ten years ago when his brother Vergil, the Viscount Laclere, had courted her. And yet underneath his cool, refined composure there shimmered a dangerous, exciting energy. With Dante it was always there.

Right now it frightened her speechless.

Somehow she knew without asking that they were alone. There was no female servant in this cottage, which meant that Dante had probably undressed her and put her in bed. What he had seen while the physician tended her had been the least of it.

"You are uncommonly brave," he said. "Wheeler never suspected that you were awake." His tone implied that he had known the exact moment when she had come to. He had caressed her head aware that she would feel him do it.

"It was my hope to avoid giving explanations to strangers."

"Since I am hardly that, you should not mind giving one to me. Let us get you comfortable first."

Her reaction to the Dante Duclaircs of the world had always been to run away, but she could not do that now. She suffered his lean strength hovering over her bed, propping pillows and arranging to her comfort. When he began to ease her onto her side, she stopped his hands with a freezing gesture and managed it on her own.

That left her looking up at him and him looking down at her. He had removed his coat and collar, and his shirt gaped open above his waistcoat. As an unmarried woman, she never saw men this relaxed in their dress.

Her vulnerability hit her with force. She said a quick prayer of thanks that of all the libertines in England, she had been fortunate enough to fall into this one's hands.

After all, they had come close to being related. That should count for something. She hoped.

He crossed his arms and regarded her. For a man with a reputation for being good-natured, his scrutiny appeared more critical than one would expect. She tucked the bedclothes around her neck.

"This is a remarkably singular occurrence, Miss Monley. Finding you, of all women, in my bed."

He wasn't going to make this easy.

She eased back against a pillow and winced when her bottom stung from the pressure. "I trust that you did not hit your target."

"Of course I did. Be glad I did not aim for your head, which is where you almost got me."

"Only because you veered to the right. I did not aim anywhere near you and was just trying to scare you off."

"Why? I expect you to explain what you were doing with a gun, in those clothes, running around this county."

"I would rather not."

"Then you leave me no choice but to assume that you are part of the mob burning machines and fields. Their leader? I hope so. There is a considerable bounty on that head, and, as it happens, I could use the money."

Yes, he probably could, if he was fleeing to France. Gregory would probably pay handsomely to get her back too. Best not to let him know about that.

"Is your brother at Laclere Park?" she asked.

"He and Bianca have been spending a few months in Naples, where she is performing. My sister Penelope traveled with them. Since Charlotte and I prefer London, there are only servants at the house here."

Despair stomped out the small flame of hope that she had been carefully stoking for two months.

Dante's tall form towered over the bed. "Is that why you are here? You came looking for Vergil?" One finger gently slid under her chin. He tilted her head until he could see her face. "Are you in some trouble, Fleur?"

She could not answer. That last bit of hope had been very fragile, but it had sustained her. With its destruction all her strength simply disappeared. All was lost now. Her freedom, the Grand Project, her dream of having her life mean something—If Gregory entered the chamber right now she would agree to whatever he wanted.

Dante gazed down at her. He owned the most beautiful, clear eyes, and the concern in them surprised her. She had never seen him look serious before. He was the sort of man whom one assumed did not care about much at all.

He had called her Fleur, which he really shouldn't do, and was touching her, which he definitely shouldn't do, but she *was* in his bed, wearing his nightshirt. There was nothing insinuating about his behavior, in truth, and the breach in formalities comforted her. She was relieved to be able to respond in kind. "I am very tired, Dante. My head is still swimming. Perhaps in the morning I will feel up to explaining."

His hand fell away. "Of course, Fleur. My apologies for pushing you."

She fell asleep almost immediately. The laudanum must still be making her drowsy. Dante walked around the bed to get the candle.

He held the light closer to her face. As a girl Fleur had been the epitome of fashionable beauty with her dark hair and ivory skin and bowed red mouth. She possessed a willowy grace and demure demeanor too, along with a significant fortune. All of that had made her one of the most prized girls on the marriage mart. When it looked as though his perfect brother Vergil was going to win her, it had seemed evidence that the world indeed functioned like a well-designed clock.

Then Vergil had married an American opera singer and Fleur had disappeared onto the Continent for two years. Upon her return she had been a changed woman. She withdrew from society and shunned balls. She grew indifferent to her beauty and dressed unfashionably. Charity work, not pleasures and diversions, absorbed her interest and income.

The mumble that she had lost her looks was untrue. Dante thought her still extraordinarily lovely.

She was in trouble and frightened. Frightened enough to walk cross-country during the night to seek refuge with his brother.

Foolish of him to think that she would confide in him instead. Just as well that she had not. She would be trouble enough without entangling him in whatever misadventure had involved her.

He left the door open and went down to the sitting room to contemplate providing for her protection after he left tomorrow. While he did so he cleaned both of their pistols. No sooner was he finished than he heard the sounds of horses and dogs that said the posse was approaching.

Tucking the pistols away in a cabinet, he strode to the door and waited on its threshold.

Ten horsemen thundered into the little clearing and reined in their animals. Pearson, the steward, flew off his mount and ran to Dante.

"Had to bring them. They stopped at the big house and demanded entry. Said the dogs had a scent of one of them on the big hill, heading this way." He lowered his voice and tipped his head closely. "They demanded to check every damn cottage, especially the vacant ones. I insisted on coming to keep an eye on them and to reassure the tenants."

"Good man. Try to stay when they leave. I need your help."

Sir Thomas Jameson, the county justice of the peace, heaved his considerable bulk off his horse and paced forward. "Who is that there?" His beefy face jutted toward the door's shadow as he tried to see in the moonlight.

"It is Mr. Duclairc, the viscount's brother," Pearson said.

"Duclairc? Didn't know you had come down. What are you doing here?"

"I am visiting the family seat. What are *you* doing here?"

"Damn question to ask. Someone's got to protect the property and uphold the law while the likes of you waste your time in gaming hells and brothels. Now step aside. We are searching for one of them seen coming this way."

"I have been here all evening, so I can assure you that one of whatever you hunt is not in here."

"Still, got to check. Last month the men of the county decided it was how we would do it, no exceptions."

"I must insist upon one."

"I said step aside, or we might get suspicious about why you refuse."

"My good man, politics bore me and everyone knows it. I would not know the difference between a radical and a radish."

Another man left the horses and joined Jameson. "Humor him, Duclairc, so that we can all do our duty and get home to bed."

Upon hearing the sardonic voice, Dante immediately lost his sense of humor. "You are a long way from London, Siddel."

"As are you. An odd coincidence to meet you here so soon after our last encounter."

Dante's blood flowed hotter at the reference. Their last encounter had been at a card table two weeks before and, he was almost positive, Siddel had cheated. "Laclere Park is Duclairc property, Siddel. You are the one with no ties to Sussex."

"I was in the county visiting a friend and decided to join the fun. A rare treat, hunting man instead of fox."

Icy currents of ill will flowed between them. Jameson did not seem to notice. "Can't wait all night, Duclairc. Step aside."

There was nothing to do but try and contain the damage. He backed into the cottage. "Surely two of you will be enough. I am not prepared to host a county assembly."

Jameson nodded. He and Siddel stepped inside.

The search did not take long, since the cottage held only a sitting room and kitchen down below. Jameson conducted some ridiculous poking into chests.

Dante lounged in his chair but kept one eye on Siddel's dark hair and thickening form. He had been a sportsman in his youth, a regular Corinthian, but excess and drink had taken its toll and turned him soft.

It was hard to believe that the man had a shrewd head for investments, as was reported, and counted great financiers and wealthy aristocrats among his associates. The style in which he lived confirmed those rumors, however. His despoiling cynicism proved, to Dante's mind, that the belief that virtue and success went together was nonsense.

Jameson plodded to the stairs.

Dante wished that he could spare Fleur this, but he saw no way out. "Gentlemen, I must warn you that there is someone up there sleeping. Not him whom you seek, but a lady."

Siddel grinned. "I doff my hat to you, Duclairc. Even as the bailiffs sniff for your trail, you dally for your pleasure. That is true style."

"Thank you."

"Still, while we are all gentlemen and your word should be sufficient, it would probably be best if we verify your description of the person above." Siddel headed for the stairs with unseemly anticipation.

Jameson had turned to come down and he flushed furiously when Siddel blocked his path. "Yes, of course. Needs to be done. Damn embarrassing though," he muttered as Siddel shooed him up.

"She is sleeping," Dante called after them. "I trust that you will do nothing to disturb her. She is very tired."

Siddel laughed. Jameson stumbled.

Dante listened to their boot steps on the boards above his head. He heard them pace over to the bed. He heard Jameson exclaim in shock.

Both men beat a retreat to the sitting room.

Jameson gaped at him. "It is . . . it is . . . ."

"I doff my hat again," Siddel said dryly. "What brought her here?"

"My charm, I assume."

"I meant, what conveyance. There is no carriage outside."

"I hired one and fetched her when I heard she was back in the country. My last indulgence."

Siddel's lids lowered. "Most definitely that."

The threat was unmistakable. Dante recognized the tension pouring off Siddel, because he had provoked it often enough before. The man twisted with suppressed fury, just like a husband who had been cuckolded.

Jameson was so flustered one might have thought *he* had been caught with a saint in his bed. "Very good, very good. Done here. All finished. Out we go. The soul of discretion, that we are, eh, Siddel? Our lips are sealed. Good night to you, and give the viscount my regards. . . ."

His words rambled out the door after him. Siddel did not follow immediately. He turned on Dante from the threshold, limned in moonlight.

"You will regret touching her," he snarled.

This more blatant threat piqued Dante's annoyance. "I did not realize that you had an affection for her, Siddel. If I had but known . . . Well, it actually would not have made any difference at all. You will see to Jameson's silence, I trust?"

Siddel muttered a curse and swung out of the cottage.

Horses began pouring down the lane. Pearson eased in through the garden door as the sounds receded.

"Where is my sister Charlotte?" Dante asked.

"She is visiting Brighton with the St. Johns."

"First go to the house and find some women's clothes. See what Charl or Penelope have left there. Then I need you to ride to Brighton immediately and tell Charlotte that I need her here at once. Get St. John to come too. Tell him it is important."

The steward ducked out to claim his mount. Dante gazed up toward the chamber where Fleur slept.

If he had any sense, he would take Pearson's horse and ride himself. To the coast. The disgrace waiting if he did not would be worse than anything he had ever visited on his family. However, he could not go until he handed Fleur over to someone he trusted to protect her.

She was in trouble, of that he was sure. In the morning he would make her tell him about it. It would give him something to think about while he languished in prison.

Fleur opened her eyes to the whitewashed walls of the cottage and the sun streaming through simple curtains.

Last night's despair tried to submerge her again. She forced it down. Actually, if one looked at it a certain way, her situation was quite humorous. She had come looking for help from the one man she trusted, but he was gone, living his life as he should be. Instead of the viscount, the paragon, the rock of authority, she had found the brother, the rake, the wastrel. She needed the protection of a man who could intimidate judges and lords. Instead, she had been shot in the bottom by one who could not pay his tailor.

She struggled to sit. Movement sharply reminded her of her infirmities. She managed to get to her feet and inch around to take care of necessary business. She was contemplating how to get back into bed when Dante appeared at the doorway.

"You should have called me."

"I can do it. Please go away."

Strong arms braced under her shoulders and knees. He swung, lifted, and lowered. A sheet billowed down to cover her.

"Where are my clothes?"

"You mean the rags that you were wearing while armed men tried to hunt you down? The ones that led me to think that I was shooting a man? I burned them."

"What am I supposed to wear?"

"If you have grown fond of trousers, you can have a pair of mine. Or you can use the dress that the steward secreted out of Laclere House."

"Does the steward know why you wanted it?"

"I am sure we are both glad that he knows it is not for me."

Fluttering panic beat in her chest. "Did he see me?"

"He knows you are here. Several people do, I am afraid." He pulled the chair over and sat, propping his boot on the bed's edge.

"We had visitors last night. Jameson—the justice of the peace—and his men. They were searching the whole estate. I could not keep your presence a secret. I assumed that you would not want them to know how you really got here, so I let them think that you were my guest."

"Your guest? That is putting it very finely. Surely they did not believe you."

"Well, Fleur, they did not want to, but the evidence was rather damning. Their shock almost brought this roof down when they found you in this bed."

"Are you saying that they saw me? In this bed? Men whom I do not know witnessed this?"

"I regret to say that they did."

"How could you permit such a thing?"

"A better question is how could I have stopped it." He fixed her with his brown eyes. "Did I err, Fleur? Should I have told the truth instead?"

"Of course not." She said it too quickly. "Only, the idea that people would think that we . . . Who saw me?"

"Just Sir Thomas Jameson and Hugh Siddel."

"Siddel! He knows? Oh, dear Lord." That promised to be very humiliating. Her mind began filling with the potential complications Mr. Siddel's discovery could create.

"Forgive my impertinence, but do you have some relationship with him? He acted as if our love affair directly insulted him."

"When I came out as a girl, Siddel briefly courted me, but that was years ago."

He did not seem to notice that she had not answered his question. "My instincts on this are well honed by experience, Fleur. He was in a fury at the evidence that we were lovers. I half-expected him to call me out. As it happens, right now a duel is the least of the trouble the man can cause me." Suddenly his attention focused on her face. "Which is why you need to explain things now. I find myself involved in a situation not of my making or understanding. I must insist on knowing why you acted as if you were running for your life last night."

He had settled comfortably in the chair. A contained man, unruffled and smooth. A handsome man, at ease with his body and presence, confident of his physical impression.

A determined man, whose clear eyes watched her with patience. He was prepared to wait her out. *Take your time,* his whole pose said. *We have all day, if you want to do it that way.*

"I would like you to bring up the dress that you spoke of, Dante. I will put it on and leave."

"You are to rest, and I could not permit you to walk away on your own even if you were well."

"I will go to the house and ask for help. It will be better this way."

"No." He folded his arms over his chest.

The temptation to tell him, and pretend that there was some hope that he would know what to do, almost defeated her.

He watched her. Too much and too long. It became a compelling examination. She grew uncomfortable in a strangely exciting way and embarrassingly aware of that frightening something that shimmered around him like a subtle force.

"I think that we will pass the time with a game," he said.

"What kind of game?"

"You do not have to look so suspicious. Not that kind. Although having you in my bed, but in a condition that prevents me from trying to breach your defenses, is enough to make me weep."

"I doubt that you will weep when you are so clearly laughing. At me. Now, what kind of game?"

"The rules are simple. I ask you a question and you answer it honestly. Then I ask you another one and you answer that. And so on until I run out of questions."

"It does not sound like a fun game at all. At the least I think we should take turns. You ask a question, then I ask one of you. And so on."

"Sounds almost too sporting. I think that I should be allowed to press my advantage in some manner, since you are indisposed and cannot be seduced."

"Stop teasing me like a clumsy lothario. Everyone knows that you are much smoother when you are really after a woman."

That caught him off guard. "Does everyone know that, indeed?"

"Yes. Everyone," she said, pleased that she had tipped the balance in this game, whatever it really was.

"Are you saying that a few of my lovers have been indiscreet?"

"You have been discussed in retiring rooms for years. I heard all about you when I was a girl. It is a wonder that you continue to be successful, what with every seductive strategy of yours so well documented by personal testimony."

"I find this disconcerting. *I* have never discussed what occurred between myself and any woman."

"As a gentleman, you are prevented from doing so. Women are not so constrained."

"How naughty of you to listen to such things." He smiled devilishly, and she realized that his dismay had been a ruse. He had deliberately led her into a very inappropriate conversation.

And, it appeared, was not going to let her out.

"I do not think that I could seduce you now, no matter how darling you look in my nightshirt, Fleur. I would be expecting you to be fresh and ignorant. Instead, you would be checking items off a list as I progressed."

She swallowed hard. This conversation had gotten too personal all of a sudden.

His head angled. His lids lowered. He regarded her with a man's warmth. That something shimmered. Right into her.

"I can see it now. I would be caressing up your bare leg and you would remind me I missed the sensitive spot behind a woman's knee that I discovered that night with a certain duchess."

He had definitely crossed the line with that. If she could find her voice she would give him a good scolding.

"Or I would be kissing your back and you would instruct me not to forget the trick involving the hollow at your spine's base, as related by the wife of a prominent M.P."

This had become outrageous, but his shocking descriptions of loveplay cast a spell. She could not take her eyes off him. Her pulse beat so loudly in her ears that she worried he could hear.

He angled forward in the chair until his face was not far from hers. "Perhaps if my performance did not meet expectations, you would demand that

I show you how some parts of a woman's body could be even more sensitive after lovemaking than before, as an indiscreet baroness confided I once showed her."

"You are a depraved rogue."

"And you are flushed and ready and I have not even touched you."

He took her hand in the warmth of his. She gaped as he raised it to his mouth and kissed her fingers. Her body gave a physical shriek that scared her out of her wits.

She snatched her hand away. "How *dare* you."

He relaxed back in his chair, bright eyed with dark amusement. "A very small dare, to remind you that I am not a fool. You are safe from me, but only because I choose to make it so. Do not goad me, because if challenged the choice of weapons is mine."

Her heart, her blood, her very breath badly needed to settle. She struggled to keep him from seeing the horrible internal strife that his touch had provoked.

An exciting, mounting euphoria had crashed headlong into a sickening, numbing dread.

She stared down at the hand he had kissed and felt again the warmth of his breath. Her warring reactions left her nauseous.

This had never happened before. The fear had never permitted it. Not when she was a girl, and certainly not since she had put herself on the shelf.

"I have badly frightened you, haven't I?" He reached toward her face, but stopped himself. "I should not have done that. Your virtue is really very safe with me. However, if I am to keep you safe in other ways, I need to know what this is about."

He did deserve an explanation. She had involved him, now that others had seen her here. She had not had time to come up with a good lie, however. She would have to give him the truth. Or at least part of it. She would simply have to skirt any references to the Grand Project.

"Last October I left England to visit some friends in France. I stayed through the new year. I returned two months ago, in February."

"February? No one ever mentioned your return or seeing you in town."

"That is because my stepfather, Gregory Farthingstone, met me at the dock in Dover. I have been imprisoned by him ever since."

chapter 3

I had written that I planned to sail home on the *Sea Dragon* in February. Gregory was waiting in Dover. I was surprised but glad to see him. One can always use help after a long journey," Fleur explained.

"Then he imprisoned you?" Dante tried to keep the incredulity from his tone. The accusation was bizarre enough that one might wonder if the fall had affected her brain.

Gregory Farthingstone was a man known for good sense and moderate living, and a trustee of the Bank of England. It would be easier to believe that Fleur had imprisoned Farthingstone rather than the other way around.

Fleur had been fussing with the sheet, tucking it up around her neck as if his earlier teasing had left her naked. Now she forgot about that as resentment lit her eyes.

"He claimed that he was looking out for me, and protecting me, and ensuring that I got the help I needed. He said that as an old friend of my mother's family, and as her second husband, he was only fulfilling his responsibility. However, his intentions are far less benign than that."

"What intentions would those be?"

"He is trying to claim that I am irrational and incompetent."

"Why would he think that?"

"Because I have been giving my fortune away. That is how he sees my contributions to charities."

Fleur's generosity to schools, hospitals, and reform causes was well known. "Have you risked your own future with your largesse?"

"I have not given away all of it, but enough that Gregory thinks it is irresponsible. However, enough remains for me to live very comfortably. I am of age, and an independent woman. He is not my guardian and has no authority to interfere in my life. He says that he is the closest thing to family, and it is his responsibility to make sure that I receive the guidance and care that I need."

"Where did he bring you after he met you at Dover?"

"To one of his properties, in Essex."

"You walked here all of the way from Essex?"

"We were traveling. Gregory would not say where he was taking me, but I think it was one of those places near the sea where families put their problem relatives. I recognized that we were in Sussex and ran away, hoping I would find Laclere."

Yes, Vergil would be formidable enough to take on Gregory Farthingstone.

"I am not addled," she muttered, looking to her hands and their tense, entwined fingers. "It is not irresponsible to use money to help people. If I spent my fortune on ball gowns and jewels, no one would question it."

She should have done both. If she had bought those gowns and jewels, she would have been safe from suspicion. It had been her repudiation of society and marriage that had raised the specter of instability.

She kept gazing sightlessly at those twisting fingers. He got the impression that there was more to tell and that she was deciding whether to do so.

She had given him the explanation she owed him. He would not press for more, but he hoped that she would go on.

"There is something else," she finally said. "The night before last we stopped at an inn. As he has since Dover, he locked me in my chamber after supper. He did not realize that part of the wall had been removed to build in a wardrobe. When I opened the door of that wardrobe, I could hear a muffled conversation in Gregory's chamber. Another man was there late at night. They were talking about me, I think."

"Would it not have been obvious if they were?"

"At first I thought that they spoke of a thing, not a person. You see, the man was offering to buy the thing. Only later did I realize that maybe it was me."

Now she *was* sounding a bit strange, like one of those people who thinks everyone plots against them. "Fleur, Farthingstone cannot sell you. If he did, what good would it do the buyer? As you said, you are an independent woman of mature years."

"No, he cannot legally sell me. But then, he cannot legally imprison me, yet he has done so. 'It will be over before she knows what happened, and she will be the happier for it,' the man said. 'If she fights it, then we will put her away.' I do not know what you think, Dante, but that sounds like a forced marriage to me. For my own good, no doubt. To make sure someone has the authority to take care of me."

"Conveniently arranged before more of your fortune is gone."

"I never liked Gregory. I never understood why my mother married him after my father died. He assumes that I should defer to his judgment, but he is not my father, and no blood relation. It would not surprise me to learn that after this marriage he and that man intended to divide up whatever I have."

"Assuming that they discussed you at all. You do not know that." For a woman not addled, she told a bizarre tale. Still, it would not be the first time a woman had been used thus.

A frown puckered while she considered that. "I suppose. At the time . . . it was that which made me decide to run away. Gregory saw to it that I had no money. At his manor and on the road I was closely watched. Getting away would not be easy. But the idea that he might force me into a marriage gave me courage. Imprisonment I might have surrendered to, but not marriage."

"Certainly not. With that, he had definitely gone too far."

"The next evening I climbed out my window, got down the building, and snuck away. I stole those clothes and left my dress as payment. Outside a tavern I traded a ring I had for the gun. Then I ran. We must have been ten miles from here. When you shot me and I fell, I think that I went out as much from exhaustion as from the bump."

With the conclusion of Fleur's tale a peaceful quiet filled the chamber, as if the very telling of it had calmed her fears.

Dante rose and paced to the window. For whatever reason, she had chosen a different path than most. In a man such eccentricities would be accepted. But a determined Gregory Farthingstone might make a case showing sufficient instability that would convince a judge to take away a woman's independence.

"I ask a favor of you, Dante." She appeared so helpless in that bed. Small and fragile and very alone. "When Laclere gets back, please tell him. Perhaps he will find me to see if things turned out all right."

"Of course, Fleur, but it will not come to that. Whether you understood that conversation or not, he still has no right to confine you. If you went to such risk to get away, we should see that you do not go back."

"Since I have been seen here, Gregory will learn where I am. I have been waiting for the sounds of his carriage."

"If you hear a carriage, do not assume it is Gregory. I sent the steward for my sister Charlotte and Daniel St. John. They are in Brighton and should be here after noon."

Her eyes brightened with something that might be hope. She relaxed into the pillows. "Even last night you thought to do that? It was very kind of you, Dante."

"Nonsense. I do things like that every time I shoot a woman in the bottom. You rest now. I will go down and see about some food for you. You are not to worry."

He reassured her with more conviction than he felt. Charlotte and St. John had better not tarry in leaving Brighton. If Farthingstone learned where she was, this could be a race to the finish.

She slept after breakfast, and Dante paced the lower level while the hours passed and the sun moved.

Most likely her concerns were not founded on anything real. Possibly she had behaved erratically in ways a chance acquaintance would not notice. Maybe Farthingstone just wanted to be sure she rested after her voyage. Undoubtedly she had misconstrued what little she had heard through that wardrobe.

Still, Farthingstone's connection to her through marriage to her mother gave him the semblance of authority. Worse, he could put her away with no one knowing, since it was thought she still traveled the Continent.

Ridiculous, of course. She was in no danger.

He removed both pistols from their cabinet and loaded them.

A little before midday he heard her moving around on the bed. He went up and found her sitting on its edge, trying with her good arm to spread out the dress he had procured.

"I do not want them to find me like this," she said. "I will dress, at least."

"If you wish." He brought over the undergarments that Pearson had found. He lifted her from the bed and set her on her feet.

She realized his intentions. "I can manage."

"I know that you cannot. I will help you."

"You must not."

"Do not let my earlier attempt at wit discomfort you. The repetition of pleasure has dulled my susceptibility. I must deliberately light the candle or there is no flame. I am utterly indifferent. Like a physician or an artist."

"The physician yesterday said they are not indifferent, but I can see how *you* might be. The first naked woman would be exciting but the thousandth would be boring. A bit like too much marzipan."

"Precisely. Except you are not the thousandth. I only recently passed eight hundred."

She turned shocked eyes on him.

"I am joking, Fleur. Now, left arm up."

He assumed the bland countenance of a valet and averted his eyes, but the candle glowed all by itself when the nightshirt dropped to the floor. Indifference hardly described his reaction when he glimpsed her ivory skin and feminine curves and high breasts. She looked away and blushed as he slid the chemise over her shy, trembling nakedness.

Getting the rest of the garments on was a clumsy process, due to their mutual attempts to pretend the other wasn't there.

He roughly made the bed and then lifted her back onto it.

"See. No liberties. It was your lucky day when you got shot by a sated, jaded rake like me."

She laughed. It was a beautiful sound, like the watery notes of a harp.

"My lucky day, Dante, but not yours. Now, I am all arranged, and dressed and fed. I think that you should go to the stables, get a horse, and ride to the coast as you had planned."

He sat in the chair. "I cannot do that, Fleur."

"I will be safe. Someone will be here soon."

"It could be the wrong person. What if someone does not come? Tonight could be like the last, and those marauders might choose to burn this cottage or come in and hide here. I cannot leave you alone."

"You could get someone from the house to stay with me."

"The servants cannot stand against Farthingstone if he arrives looking for you. We will wait for Charl and St. John together. I said that you would be safe, and you will be."

"I am sorry this has happened," she said. "Are the bailiffs really on your trail?"

"Certain creditors sold my notes to a man, Mr. Thompson, who demanded payment. A bad night at cards ruined any chance of negotiating."

"Couldn't you ask Laclere to help you?"

"I could, and he would. It is probably what Thompson hopes for. But I will not. Verg has already been too generous."

He wondered why he spoke so candidly. Maybe dressing her had deepened their familiarity. Maybe taking care of her had.

He experienced a peaceful companionship with her. Probably the survivors of shipwrecks developed friendships quickly too, while they shared a raft and tried not to watch the horizon.

"I would say it was unfortunate that things did not end happily between you and Bianca, except she and Laclere are so obviously right together," she said.

Fleur was referring to the time when she was Vergil's intended, and the plan had been for Bianca to be Dante's. "I was not disappointed about Bianca wanting Vergil. She and I did not suit well, and she is good for him. However, I would lie if I denied that I have on occasion regretted losing her fortune."

She laughed again. "I have smiled more this last hour than I have in the last year. Odd, that. After all, sooner or later I must face Gregory, and you must get away. If you miss that boat, how will you escape?"

"There are other boats."

"How selfish of me, to be so caught up in my own problem that I did not see sooner how I had made yours worse. Please do not delay for me."

"Until I know that you are safe, I will remain here. Any gentleman would, and despite my circumstances I hope that I am still that."

"You are most definitely that, and much more, dear friend."

Her gratitude touched him. The serenity he remembered in her from years ago had settled on her.

He should probably leave her to her privacy, but the bedchamber was airy and pleasant and her company pleased him. A day of waiting stretched out ahead of them.

He made himself comfortable. "I will tell you how I wasted my life, if you tell me how you have been flourishing in yours."

The harp played again while she laughed.

She had never realized that he could be so kind. She should have guessed. His lovers always spoke well of him. They knew going into the affairs that he was inconstant and that the passion would be brief. If hearts had been broken, and some had, she suspected it was not because he promised more than he gave.

Not all kindness, however. A little ridge of darkness lurked within the charm. She could see it in his eyes sometimes, and hear it in his voice. It could manifest itself unexpectedly, as with his threat to turn her in, or with that toying flirtation this morning. She sensed that it wanted to become something bigger, but he controlled it. Most of the time.

He amused her with stories of daring at the gaming tables and horse races, and of fortunes won and lost. He appeared contrite when he admitted the times he had turned to his brother when he had gotten in too deep.

She already knew the details that he did not add. She knew about the disastrous finances that his brother Vergil had inherited when their older brother, Milton, died. Only *déclassé* ventures in trade had saved the Duclairc family at all. Still, Dante's allowance might have been adequate for a different sort of man. He could have devoted himself to some employment and not just pleasure.

All the same, she envied him. Here was a man who had truly lived for the moment. That doing so had led to ruin was one of those moral tales that one was supposed to nod at approvingly. Instead, she couldn't help resenting it.

Her own story, of charity and good works, should shine in comparison. Instead, it embarrassed her to have so little real joy to describe. In certain essential ways, she was the one who had lived a wasted and barren life.

She might have told him about that. About the loneliness and emptiness. About her plans to find some fulfillment through her Grand Project. She came near to doing so. The ease with which they spoke encouraged confidences. But their few hours of friendship were too short. Sounds on the lane in mid-afternoon heralded their end.

Dante went to the window as commotion filled the clearing outside. "This should be interesting," he said as he slid on his frock coat. "It was a dead heat. Both Charl and Farthingstone have arrived together."

Her peace disappeared in an instant. "I will come down. Please, help me up."

"If you insist on coming, I will carry you." He lifted her into his arms.

She began to object, but it felt very safe and secure to be nestled in his arms. She realized with a start that she had embraced no person since her mother's death, and no man for over ten years.

He bore her down the steps. Their visitors had just entered the sitting room, arguing.

His younger sister, Charlotte, her dark hair a little disheveled and her pert face most distraught, fretted beside the darkly handsome Daniel St. John. Gregory's aging, freckled face turned pink with consternation while he queried them on their sudden arrival.

Dante's boot on the bottom step caught Gregory in mid-bluster and everyone turned in surprise. More horses were arriving outside.

"No need to put her down, Duclairc. You can just carry her out to my coach," Farthingstone ordered.

Dante set Fleur's sore rump carefully down in a chair.

"See here—" Farthingstone began.

"No, you see here. Charl, I thank you for coming. Miss Monley is injured, and in need of both care and sanctuary. Whatever else happens, St. John, I ask you to promise that you will not allow Farthingstone to take her away."

St. John made a slight bow in Fleur's direction. "We met many years ago, Miss Monley, here at Laclere Park."

"I remember. Thank you for interrupting your visit to Brighton."

Charlotte hurried over to her. "Fleur, what are you doing here? I thought that you were touring the Continent. You are injured? What has happened?"

"She was grazed by a bullet," Dante said.

"Grazed . . . she was shot? Where?"

"Actually, in the rear nether region."

Charlotte blinked. "In the rear nether . . . you mean that she was shot in the . . . oh, my."

Gregory's face had gone red beneath his white hair. "How she was wounded needs investigation, but one thing is clear. Duclairc kept her here so that he could compromise her."

"Dante, you didn't! Not Fleur too! Vergil will have apoplexy."

"His plot is obvious," Farthingstone sneered. His bulbous nose made the expression more comical than disdainful. "However, it will not work, sir. There're men outside wanting to see you, and my stepdaughter is not in her right mind and cannot be held responsible for your dishonorable use of her. I will take care of her now."

"My honor is my business and not Mr. Farthingstone's," Fleur said, ignoring Gregory and speaking to Charlotte and St. John, who were her only hopes. "Your brother has seen to my care and protected me. I beg you to hear him, and to refuse Mr. Farthingstone his demands. He has no legal rights to me. I will not go with him of my own will."

The door stood open. Two large, rough-looking men darkened its threshold.

"Ah, our salon is complete," Dante observed. "Would you be Mr. Thompson's bailiffs?"

"Aye," one mumbled. "You be coming with us nice and easy now, Mr. Duclairc. Don't want no trouble."

"No trouble at all, I promise. Can I ask how you found me?"

"Word came up to London during the night. We rode hard and it will be a long ways back, so let's be going."

"Dante, now what is *this*?" Charlotte cried.

"Destiny, sweet sister."

He turned to St. John. "I leave Miss Monley in your protection. She should not be traveling, and her complaints against Farthingstone are well founded. Promise me that you will at least hear her out."

"She will be safe." St. John glanced meaningfully to the waiting bailiffs. "Allow me to see to this other matter for you, Duclairc."

"No. It is an amount I could never repay."

Fleur knew a thing or two about the fate that Dante faced. "Mr. St. John, Dante has no horse. They will make him walk all the way to London."

"Stop by the stables and get a horse for him," St. John ordered the men. "I will settle it with Laclere."

"Dante," Fleur whispered frantically, reaching toward him.

He bent over her. "St. John will see to you now, Fleur. He is not nearly so strict as he appears. Tell him and Charlotte what you told me."

"It is not that. Those men . . . How much, Dante? How much do you owe?"

He raised her hand to his lips. "An obscenely high amount. Do not even offer. I have never dunned friends, and I would never accept a penny from a woman."

"But it is my fault."

"No, Fleur, it is mine alone."

Assuming the cool elegance for which he was famous, he walked out of the cottage.

Fleur stepped out of Daniel St. John's carriage and accepted the footman's escort to the gaol's front door.

There was one great convenience to being a twenty-nine-year-old woman on the shelf who devoted herself to charity. When you told little lies, people believed you. Mr. St. John and his wife, Diane, thought that today she was attending a meeting to plan a new school for workers' sons.

Fleur knew all about London's gaols. She supported the reformers like Elizabeth Fry who sought to improve their condition. She noted with distaste that Mr. Thompson had arranged for Dante to be put in one of the worst of them. The narrow, crowded street smelled of rotting food and offal, and a din of voices poured out of the old buildings. The crumbling plaster of the gaol, black with age and damp, depressed her spirits.

It would hurt Dante's pride for anyone he knew to see him in such a place. She rehearsed once more the plan that had brought her here.

The gaoler's wife let her in with a display of bowing, indicating that the care Fleur had taken with her appearance had been successful. She had sent to her house for her only fashionable dress, a broad-skirted one in ice-blue muslin. Considering her mission today, she did not want to look too much the dowd.

The woman brought her into the sitting room of the fetid inn that housed debtors while their creditors tried to extract payment. The chamber's few windows let in little light, but she could see the negligible attempts at providing comfort. Considering the squalid environment, the high spirits of the men playing cards and wagering with pieces of straw surprised her.

In the thick of it, joking and laughing, still playing the games that had brought him here, sat Dante Duclairc.

In contrast to the poor appearance of his comrades, Dante looked impeccable. His cravat showed several days' wear and his frock coat needed pressing, but he had shaved and dressed for a day on the town even though he would never leave these walls.

"You've a visitor, Mr. Duclairc. A *lady*," the woman called.

They all looked at her. Dante's smile froze. He threw in his cards and came over.

"Miss Monley, this is surprising." His tone conveyed disapproval. "I will take her out back, Meg."

"For ten pence you can use my chamber if you want," Meg offered with a bawdy grin.

"We will go out back, Meg."

He led her out to a garden. Three pigs grunted in a pen at one end and chickens pecked around the almost-bare ground. A crude bench sat against the far wall.

"You should not be here."

"Do not scold, Dante. I have seen such places before. I brought you something from Charlotte."

"She already sent enough money to pay for meat. Tell her I do not need any more."

"It is not exactly from Charlotte herself." She sat on the bench and extracted a small purse from her reticule. "A lady came to visit your sister once we got back in town last week. She said that you had given her these jewels recently, as a parting gift. Having heard of your circumstances, she does not feel right keeping them."

She opened the little purse and revealed two amethyst earrings.

He gazed at them. "No doubt you think it reckless of me to have used my last guineas in such a way."

"I think that you decided those guineas would not make much difference, and it was important to maintain standards."

"Very open-minded of you, Fleur." He took the purse. "And very good-hearted of the lady. Now you must go. This is no place for you."

She refused to budge. A night of debate and panic had driven her here, and she would see it through. "I also came to visit with you, Dante. It is rude to throw me out."

"My apologies. Of course Saint Fleur would want to bring comfort to the imprisoned. I have not even asked after your health. You are better now? If Charl brought you to town from Laclere Park, I assume that you are healing properly. You look lovely today. That blue brings out the color of your eyes."

The courtesies tripped off his tongue in a slightly sarcastic voice. The dark ridge had bared itself. Yes, his pride was hurt to be seen here. He clearly wanted her gone.

"I am well healed, thank you. I have been staying with the St. Johns while I recover."

"And Farthingstone?"

"St. John held him off. For now."

His hard expression broke. The man she remembered, the Dante who had been her friend for a day in that cottage, looked down with concern. "What is he up to?"

"He is going to Chancery to ask that all my finances be put under his control, due to my erratic emotional state and my inability to make sound judgments. St. John's solicitor thinks he may succeed. The way that I ran away, and the discovery that I was with you in that cottage will not help my case. Along with control of my finances, he also will request guardianship over me."

He sat beside her. "Damn the man. If it comes to it, maybe you should request someone else get the authority. My brother should be back in a month. He will agree to do it."

"While I would trust Laclere with my life, I do not like the idea of putting those responsibilities on his shoulders, or of being answerable to him. I have been thinking of a different solution."

"If I can help in any way, I am at your command." He rose with solicitous grace. "Now, this is an unhealthy place, and if it is learned that you came, Farthingstone will only have more odd behavior to describe. It was good of you to visit, Fleur. I confess that I have worried about you a bit during my days here. However, you really must leave."

"Please sit, Dante. I want to tell you my solution and hear what you think of it."

He complied with a sigh. She angled away from him so she could watch the chickens and pigs and not his reactions. She was very sure that she would not want to see them.

"Dante, did Laclere ever tell you why he and I never married?"

Stillness instantly occupied the space where he sat.

"Of course not," he finally said. "I assumed it was because of Bianca."

She had known Laclere would never speak of it to Dante, but she had rather hoped he had anyway. It would make this easier.

"It was not because of Bianca. There was never a true courtship between Laclere and me. It was all a pretense. I did not want to marry, and acting as if we were going to wed each other spared me for a year."

"That explains quite a lot. I always thought that Verg treated you badly. Love excuses much, but you and he were all but engaged before Bianca came to England."

"It was a feint from the beginning. I planned never to marry. Ever since I was a girl, I have been very sure of that." She closed her eyes, took a deep breath, and plunged forward. "Except, as our friendship grew, it occurred to me that there might be an alternative. A very special kind of marriage. I offered it to him and he refused."

"What are you saying, Fleur?"

How did one say it outright? She never had to with Laclere. Somehow, he had just known what she meant.

"Fleur, did you offer my brother a white marriage? One without physical intimacy?"

She felt her face burning. "I was not surprised that he refused. I think that my fortune made it tempting, but as viscount he would want a son."

"Why are you telling me this? Are you thinking of marrying?"

"Last night, after meeting with Gregory, I began to contemplate it. A husband would have authority that Gregory could not violate. I am thinking about a marriage such as I offered your brother. Such an understanding would end all of this. I am right, aren't I? Don't you think so?"

Stillness again. Total silence for a long pause.

"What I think is that you had better be very, very careful about the man whom you choose, Fleur."

A resonance in his tone made her face him. He regarded her with a thoughtful, speculative gaze.

"Yes, very careful," she said. "It would have to be someone I trusted. Someone who accepts that I cannot be a true wife to any man. The understanding on that would have to be very firm."

He just watched. She almost lost her courage, but the memory of Gregory's florid face demanding her return from St. John and of the unctuous, patronizing way he had spoken to her, as if she were a stupid child, kept her resolve together.

"It would have to be someone who has a full life already, and interests that the marriage would permit him to pursue freely," she continued. "A man who would accept half of my income and live within its means, and who would agree to permit me to use the rest as I choose. We would both have separate lives in reality. You might say that we would not really be married at all."

"You are describing a man of undisputed honor, like my brother. A paragon among men. There are few like him."

"I am describing an honorable man, but not a paragon. Maybe I am describing a man who would never accept a penny from a female friend but who might accept an extremely high amount from a wife. A man whose vast experiences mean that the candle does not burn unless he lights it. A man who need not seek pleasure with a wife because he can find it anywhere for a smile. A man like you."

There. It was said.

His expression grew more intensely contemplative. He studied her as if he tried to decide if she was serious.

It seemed an eternity that they sat there with their silence broken by the sounds of city life and yard animals. She prayed that his enigmatic reaction did not hide abhorrence.

She had to look away. "I never thought to make this suggestion to another man, Dante. I know that you must think me unnatural, in ways that make Gregory's accusations pale."

"Not so unnatural, Fleur. However, are you sure that you have not outgrown your girlhood fear?"

"It is not a girlhood fear. My blood turns to ice at the thought of . . . When I heard that man bargaining for me . . . I could not breathe." Her voice sounded frantic to her own ears. Her chest and mind filled with panic as it had that night.

He reached over and lightly stroked her hair. "Calm yourself, pretty flower. If you say it is so, I believe you."

The silence stretched again. She closed her eyes and prayed he would not reject her outright.

"You have mentioned two agreements, regarding intimacy and money, that are out of the ordinary, Fleur. Are there any other unusual terms or specifics that I should hear?"

His willingness to listen gave her hope that the life she knew, the plans she had laid, would not be stolen from her. "The income derives from the trust my father left. I have lands and other funds, however, mostly inherited from my aunt. I want a promise that I can use or dispose of that property and income as I choose, if I want to. I want an agreement that you will not interfere and will sign any documents as become necessary."

His reaction indicated he found these particular terms most unusual, as indeed they were. By law, husbands were supposed to get everything and control any lands. Reserving property to her own discretionary use was almost unheard of, but she desperately needed him to agree to this. She had lived independently too long, and had gone too far on her Grand Project, to be subject to any man on her decisions, especially to a husband who really wouldn't be a husband.

"Even without that independent fortune, my inheritance is significant, Dante. Half the income from the trust is a handsome amount."

"How handsome?"

"Your share would be three thousand, to use as you please. I would continue to maintain my household with my own part."

He laughed. "That is certainly handsome, Fleur. However, look where we are. Where I am. Forgive me, but it is not very sensible for you to make this proposal, with all of these private financial understandings, to a man in gaol for debt. Don't you worry that someday I will be in too deep again and will take all of it?"

"All of our arrangement will be grounded on your honor, Dante. That is sufficient guarantee for me. I do not doubt that you will keep any promises that you make. Even if someday you want all of it, I do not believe that you will take it. I also think that you will never incur debts that would jeopardize what is not yours."

His expression turned enigmatic again. She could not decide if he was flattered or if he tried to hide his opinion that she was a fool.

"You must be thinking it odd that I do not jump at this offer. It is very generous, and solves my present problem very neatly."

"As it solves mine. The mutually beneficial aspect of the solution is the best part of it, I think."

"It is far too optimistic of you after our brief friendship. You do not know me, Fleur."

"I trust you. I know you are honorable. I also enjoy your company, and that is a rare thing for me with a man."

"You can do better."

"I do not think so."

He rose abruptly and paced away, his arms crossed over his chest and a thoughtful scowl on his handsome face. A burst of laughter from inside the gaol reminded her of how peculiar a place this had been for a proposal. But then, the proposal itself was so odd that no place would have really been appropriate.

He returned to stand in front of her. Propping one booted foot beside her on the bench, he bent over his knee and lifted her chin with his dry, warm fingers, forcing her to look into his luminous eyes.

"It is an astonishing idea. Totally unexpected. I am not exactly the marrying kind, Fleur."

"This is not exactly a typical marriage. I will never ask you questions about your lovers, Dante. I know that I will have no right to. There will be no jealous scenes."

"The freedom to have lovers is not what concerns me right now. We speak of a lifetime. Just how separate do you expect us to be? It would raise questions if we are never together."

"We need not be strangers. We can share a house, and entertain mutual friends if it suits us."

"I think that we would have to at first, don't you? It would not do to make people suspicious, especially Farthingstone."

"You can move to my house in Mayfair after the wedding. There is enough room for one more."

His expression went serious, and she knew that he was deciding her future in that moment. His gaze fell to her lips. For an instant that special energy shimmered intensely.

His thumb brushed her mouth. "Will I be allowed to kiss my wife some-times?"

"Friends do, don't they?"

He touched his mouth gently to hers. The softness and warmth of the kiss caused a bright light to blink through her.

"When do you plan to hold the wedding, Miss Monley? As it happens, my social diary is without commitments at the moment."

It was the money that swayed him. He would have been an idiot not to grab for it.

Dante told himself that many times over the next few days while he contemplated why he had accepted Fleur's offer.

He had agreed because the marriage would rescue him from dire straits, but he confessed that her appeal had touched him in other ways.

She trusted him. It was a novel notion, and a surprisingly compelling one. So it was really about the money, but the flattery of her trust may have nudged him a little.

It was an unusual arrangement, but in many ways ideal. The day-to-day coexistence would not be unpleasant. He would have every freedom he had ever had, but now with the blunt to pay for it properly. He would finally be free of his dependence on his family.

Yes, financially speaking, he had done very well.

The only cloud on the bright horizon, and it was a very small cloud to be sure, was that while Fleur was indifferent to men, he was not indifferent to Fleur.

In that backyard, while the chickens pecked around his boots and he weighed her offer, that part of the agreement had struck him as rather dismal. When he had held her hand in acceptance, it had taken some strength of will not to pull her into a very different kind of kiss from the one she had just permitted.

That should take care of itself, however. Once he was back to his old life, his attraction would pass quickly. It rarely settled in one place for long.

Even though it was all about her money, she had made it clear that it was not about *all* of her money. Therefore, when the Duclaircs' solicitor, Julian Hampton, arrived at the gaol to discuss the settlement, Dante did not quibble over the three thousand a year that would be his free and clear, even though in a normal marriage he would have much more.

He did not blink when Hampton explained that the land would also be at Fleur's disposal and that Dante would be agreeing to permit her to use it and its income as she chose.

He even remained impassive when Hampton explained that he could leave the gaol. The solicitor had already spoken with Thompson on Fleur's request, and informed the creditor that Dante's bride would be paying the outstanding debt of fifteen thousand pounds in full.

After itemizing Fleur's terms, Hampton moved on to a fuller discussion of the matter.

"As your family's counselor, I advise against this marriage." Hampton spoke in his most formal tone. He had been a friend of the family for years, but signaled with his voice and demeanor when he fully assumed his occupational role.

"The terms are unusual, but not ungenerous. I am unlikely to do better."

"You are promising to agree to financial decisions even if they are unsound. She could squander the entire fortune not in trust, and you would have no authority to prevent it."

"Then we will live on the trust income. However, I think it unlikely that she will squander all the rest."

Hampton rose and paced over to the grimy window of the gaol's tiny bedchamber. This time Dante had paid Meg the ten pence for some privacy. As Hampton gazed out on the scrubby yard, his entire demeanor was that of a tall, dark pillar of professional responsibility. One would never guess that they had played together as boys, when Dante tagged along during Hampton's visits to Vergil.

"The private agreement has no standing in the law, of course. If you conclude she is not acting sensibly, or break it for other reasons, no judge will uphold it. I explained that to her," he said.

"I think she understood that risk already."

"Yes. It will be a matter of your honor. So she said. I would prefer it only be words on paper. Those can be interpreted and argued. If you promise these provisions on your honor, there will be no recourse except acting dishonorably."

Hampton turned, his face impassive, his dark eyes enigmatic beneath his tousled dark hair. One rarely knew what Hampton was thinking. He was a silent foil to others' wit and verbal excess, an observer of the world. Dante knew that many women found Hampton mysterious and romantic, although men were more likely to think him merely proud and reserved.

"I still must advise against it, for other reasons. I have been making inquiries about her."

"I did not ask you to make any inquiries." Dante kept his pique at the presumption under control, but his jaw tightened.

"St. John and I thought it best to find out if Farthingstone's accusations had any basis."

Hampton was also St. John's solicitor, a position acquired through their common friendship with Laclere. They were all part of a circle of friends who

for years had fenced together. When young men, they had dubbed themselves the Hampstead Dueling Society, and Dante had been absorbed into
the group after he left university.

"How fortunate for me that you and St. John are my guardian angels."

"With Laclere in Italy—"

"To hell with St. John, and *you*."

"We are your friends, Duclairc. Be angry if you want, but hear me out.
Miss Monley refused to explain some of the matters I asked about, and I have
doubts whether there were any explanations to give in any case."

"You spoke with her during these inquiries?" The image of Fleur being
examined by Hampton's precise, probing solicitor's questions angered him
further.

"I also spoke with Farthingstone."

"Damn it—"

"Just listen." Hampton traced the edges of the window's rough stone sill
as he spoke. "The change in your future bride after she broke with Laclere is
well known. However, recently she has gone much further in her largesse. It
is no longer a matter of spending her income. She has sold out some funds
not in trust and donated the money to a variety of causes. Most are predictable charities. However, last year she sent a goodly sum, at least a thousand, north during the work stoppage in the coal mines. It was used by the
colliers and the keelmen to support their families."

"That only means she does not like to see people starve."

"It also means that she has connections to some radical groups, and not
those who work through normal channels. Which in turn raises the question
of whether she was only running away when you found her or was actually
involved in what was happening on the estates that night."

"I do not believe that."

"It also means, at the very least, that Farthingstone will have very powerful men who will not want that flow of financial support to happen again."

This latter point was worth knowing. No doubt some of those powerful
men had the ear of the judges in Chancery court.

"The diminishment of her inheritance has been significant the last two
years. The death of her mother appears to have something to do with her increased generosity. Farthingstone is in a position to know the details. He cal-
culates that fifty percent of the land is gone. *She sold it.*"

No wonder Farthingstone claimed she was addled. No one sold land.
They hoarded it and entailed it and coveted it.

"That still leaves a very large fortune."

"There is more. When asked how she decides which property to sell and
when, and which causes to support, she claims to have an adviser. She will

not name the man, however. Farthingstone thinks there is no adviser, only a fantasy of her imagination."

"He claims she is hearing voices now? Seeing invisible friends? Surely you do not believe—"

"She is currently planning to sell her largest tract of land, a significant estate in Durham. She inherited it from her aunt Ophelia. Did I mention that her aunt was quite an original? It is in the family, it appears." Hampton continued as if the anger pouring toward him was not there.

"It is in my family too. I don't see anyone trying to label my sisters incompetent."

"There was another aunt, also deceased. That one was strange enough that even the eccentric Aunt Ophelia kept her in seclusion." Hampton just kept talking in that damn, flat, factual voice. "Miss Monley would not say to whom she plans to sell the Durham property, and neither I nor St. John can discover the name of the purchaser. We fear that she is about to be the victim of a swindle. Secrecy is often demanded in such cases, and on this transaction she will not disclose anything at all."

"Perhaps that is because she does not think you have the right to demand the details, just as Farthingstone does not."

"No, but you do, no matter what the private terms of this marriage will be. I suggested that she write the facts down, seal the letter, and allow me to bring them to you. She refused. It is, and will be, none of your affair, she said."

Her response did not shock Dante. Hearing it stated so bluntly, however, made forcefully clear what Fleur had meant when she proposed. His anger retreated as he absorbed the implications.

Separate lives, she had said. Not really married. She had meant it.

"Again, I must counsel you not to agree to this marriage," Hampton said. He did not use the solicitor's voice this time, but the friend's.

"I have already agreed to it, Julian."

"She is in no position to claim breach of contract. St. John will pay what is owed Thompson, and Laclere will reimburse him upon his return."

"Fifteen thousand is a large sum even for my brother."

"I am in a position to know that he can afford it. The viscountess's income alone can cover it."

"So now I am to be bailed out by my brother's wife?"

"It is an alternative solution to your current dilemma. As for your acceptance of the proposal, I can take care of that."

Except Dante did not want Hampton to take care of it, any more than he wanted to rely on St. John and then Laclere to pay this debt. He did not want this alternative solution.

He realized he did not want it for the simple reason that he did not want to let Fleur down.

She needed help, had come to him, and he had agreed to her plan. Maybe she was addled, or maybe she was rational as a clock. In either case, he had promised to protect her.

"Much of what you describe is merely the action of a good-hearted woman, who may be a little eccentric or overly generous, Hampton. If she says she has an adviser, I'm sure that she does. If that adviser is taking advantage of her, I will find out and deal with him."

"What if she will not confide in you? The day may come when she demands your signature on documents you know nothing about, or of which you do not approve. That agreement may mean that you one day contribute to a plan to defraud her."

"I will not sign anything that has not been explained to my satisfaction as financially sound. In the hierarchy of honor, my duty to protect her comes first. No matter what our agreement, she will still be my wife and I will take responsibility for her."

"You are determined then? If so, as both your friend and solicitor I will aid you, even if I think it unwise. Laclere may have my head, but that is a problem for another day."

Dante had to laugh. "When my brother gets back, I will explain that you did your best to save me and that, as always, I am a victim of my own recklessness."

chapter 5

F arthingstone learned of the pending nuptials with surprising speed. Fast enough to convince the archbishop to delay in giving the special license.

Soon enough to request a meeting with the chancellor, Lord Brougham, so he could lay out his claims that Fleur Monley's emotional condition rendered her incapable of entering into a contract of marriage.

Three days after Dante left gaol, Fleur found herself with him and Julian Hampton in the garden of St. John's house, getting the bad news.

"It will not be an official hearing," Hampton explained as they strolled through the plants wakening to the spring. "However, Brougham was sufficiently concerned that he will advise the archbishop to refuse the license until the matter is settled. He is sure that you will agree that it is best not to wed until Chancery can assess Farthingstone's claims."

"I don't agree at all," Fleur said.

"It is not your agreement he assumes, Miss Monley, but Duclairc's. Brougham is sure that no man would want the world thinking he took advantage of a woman's weak condition."

"I have no *condition*, least of all a weak one."

She was not convinced that Mr. Hampton believed that. He was so enigmatic, one never could tell what his own opinion was. Also, she doubted he had fought Gregory very hard on this. He had not approved of the private settlement and had asked too many impertinent questions about her affairs.

Dante appeared less than distraught by this development. So much that she wondered if he welcomed it. "When will Farthingstone have his meeting?" he asked.

"He is to give his argument in the high chancellor's chambers in a fortnight. Miss Monley will be asked to attend. I will recommend a barrister to accompany her."

Dante gazed at Mr. Hampton very directly. "Will Farthingstone succeed?"

"Possibly. I should tell you that among his other claims, he is using her choice of husband as further evidence that she cannot make sound judgments."

"I expected a husband to solve the problem, not make it worse," Fleur said.

"Farthingstone says no sensible woman would ally herself with Duclairc's reputation. He says no responsible woman would hand a fortune to a man she had to bail out of debtor's prison. Of course, he does not know of the private agreement, but if he did, it would only make things worse."

"So I will be at Chancery's mercy, after all." It vexed her that her life was being meddled with, by all these men who claimed to have her welfare in mind. Now it appeared that her attempts to thwart them had only expedited her doom.

Hampton stopped to finger some buds on a bush. "I am obligated to advise you to await Chancery's decision, of course."

Dante still appeared unconcerned by the entire conversation. "If we triumph at this meeting a fortnight hence, will that end it?"

"Farthingstone will still be able to bring a brief. He may persist in challenging her competence to contract a marriage, which means challenging the marriage itself. Such a case would be long and tedious and very expensive, in the way such things are. Also, if she is married, that compromises his position in all kinds of interesting ways."

"In other words, obeying the Lord High Chancellor benefits us little and leaves Fleur very vulnerable."

"One could say that."

"Thank you, Hampton. I think that Miss Monley and I need to speak privately now."

With a vague smile, Mr. Hampton turned and walked back to the house. Fleur almost stomped her foot in frustration. "I do not think he is very clever at all. He hasn't helped us much."

"He helped enormously."

"I did not hear him tell us anything except to wait."

"He could not give advice to disobey the Lord High Chancellor, but he let me know that we should. The course is clear, Fleur. We have to elope."

Dante had years ago accepted that if he ever married well, it would either be at the point of a sword or after a secret elopement. A decent family would accept him only if their girl's virtue had been compromised or if faced with a *fait accompli*. Therefore, sweeping Fleur away to Scotland seemed the fulfillment of fate.

The next day Fleur moved back to her house, and two mornings later her hired coach stopped in front of the building where Dante leased his chambers.

He settled in, pulled the curtains, and they were off.

"I think that we should not go to Gretna Green," he said. "Any place in Scotland will do. Once we are out of the city I will instruct your coachman to go north toward Newcastle. It will mean another half day's journey, but with Farthingstone bound to head west if he pursues, we can travel at our leisure."

"We will do it however you think best, Dante."

What a submissive, wifely thing to say. A pang of acute reality struck him. Wifely. *Wife*. The intended outcome of this journey suddenly demanded cold-blooded recognition.

No going back now. The sails were unfurled, the anchor was raised, and the winds would take them to the port of matrimony.

The journey was long and tedious. Even with spirited bouts of conversation and relaxed stops for meals, the hours weighed heavily. Dante fought a periodic tendency to lazily contemplate the delightful ways he could be spending the long ride alone with a woman if the woman was any other woman but Fleur Monley.

By the second day he occasionally lost the battle. Erotic images occupied his head.

. . . Peeling off the simple gray dress and petticoats . . . Sucking the pert tips of her round little breasts . . . Holding her soft, naked bottom as she moved up and down on him, while her slender knees straddled his hips and her fingers gripped his shoulders in her frenzy . . .

Sometimes she caught him looking at her during those reveries. She would break into her warm, trusting smile. He forced an expression of protective solicitation in return.

Both nights they stayed at inns and retired to separate chambers. Of course they did. However, with another woman . . .

The second night the inn was all but deserted. He lay restlessly, picturing the woman on the other side of the wall, hearing the sounds as she turned in her sleep. He imagined her body spread on his bed, naked in the moonlight streaming through the window, welcoming his hands and mouth as the night cooled the sweat of their passion.

The unbidden fantasy left him hard and hungry. He dressed and went for a long walk under the starry sky in order to break its spell.

So much for the flame only burning if he lit the candle. It had been insane of him to agree to this. He should direct the coach into Newcastle tomorrow, bid his leave of her, and hop a ship to the Continent.

He paused under an oak and debated that option. It would be a disgraceful breach of trust, but if he explained . . . Explained what? That the jaded rake found himself unexpectedly edgy with lust? That he lacked enough control to see it through and give her the protection that she had sought with this arrangement? That even fifteen thousand pounds and three thousand a year could not buy a little continence from him?

The abstinence forced on him by recent events probably had a lot to do with this hunger. Back in London he would find the necessary diversion. He would also no longer be in constant proximity to her. Even sharing a house, they would barely see each other.

He returned to his chamber convinced that he had matters in proper perspective. The low flame that would not die said otherwise. He threw himself on his bed, annoyingly aware that he had not wanted a woman like this in many years, and that the last time it had led to disaster.

But that had been an evil woman and Fleur was all goodness.

Still, it would be best to get back to London and out of her constant company as quickly as possible.

"On our return journey could we stop at my property in Durham? We passed nearby it yesterday, and it is not far from the mail road." Fleur made the request as the carriage crossed the northeast border into Scotland. "We could stay at the house there, instead of an inn."

"Whatever you would like," Dante said. "Do you intend to ask my permission about such little things now? It will be a senseless pretense, since I will have no authority in the big ones."

His fitful night had left him churlish, and her renewed presence had only made that damn flame burn hotter.

He saw her surprised reaction and regretted his tone. There she innocently sat, dressed in her blue gown, with a lovely silk shawl draping her delicate shoulders. He had turned his frustration on her like he was some randy schoolboy.

He realized that the shawl was probably new. The white kid gloves appeared fresh too. The bonnet with its blue bow near her right temple, bringing out the rosy tint of her cheeks, was more fashionable than her normal millinery.

She had not had time to have a wedding gown made, but in the two days before they left she had done what she could to deck herself in new finery.

It would not be much of a wedding, but it was all that she would ever have. He realized that her request had been the first thing she had said since entering the carriage this morning. He noticed now the worry glistening behind her serene composure.

She was unsettled, as well she might be. He gave up almost nothing in this marriage and gained considerably. She was the one taking all the chances.

He took her hand. "Of course we can stop and remain as long as you like. But today why don't we just cross back and go to Newcastle and stay over at the Versailles? It is one of the finest hotels in England, and contains all of the newest conveniences."

"That sounds like fun."

He held her hand in reassurance until they entered a large village. They pulled to a stop in front of a stone church. It was well before noon, and he sent the coachman off to find the vicar and another witness. While they waited they strolled through a lane of shops and he bought a hothouse rose from a flower girl.

He handed it to Fleur when they returned to the church door. "It will not be the prettiest flower present. You look even more lovely than usual today."

She blushed and looked down, biting her lower lip.

"You can change your mind. I will understand," he said.

"I do not want to change my mind."

Again he experienced that sense of sharpened reality. The immensity of what they were about to do pressed on him.

He took both her hands in his. "Inside we will speak the traditional vows, but I promise you now that I will take care of you and protect you. I will never raise a hand to you and will never knowingly hurt you."

She looked up. Her eyes moistened and her smile trembled. "And I will take care of you, and be a true friend and helpmate, and stand by you through times good and bad, as long as you want me at your side."

He offered his arm. "Ready, then?"

She took a deep breath. "Yes."

They strolled in the churchyard while they waited for the carriage.

"Married," Dante said. "Getting accustomed to the idea will require some time."

"It certainly will."

"Do you want to dine before we go?"

He could be a very considerate man. It was one of his appeals to women, she suspected. Did he show the same thoughtfulness when he made love? It would explain much. Other men who were just as handsome were not as successful.

"I could not eat now. Perhaps when we get to Newcastle."

They meandered down the path of the small garden. "You probably always thought that if you married you would have a grand wedding at St. Martin's," he said.

"I never dreamt of that. This was perfect."

It *had* been perfect. Just the two of them exchanging vows of friendship in a little stone church on a bright day. The quiet privacy had stirred her emotions.

She glanced to his hands and remembered how he had held her face at the end. Strong, gentle hands. No one else had existed but the two of them for that moment. His dark eyes had been luminous male depths that seemed to look into her heart. She had felt so connected to him, and her soul had filled with the honest affection of his two kisses. One on her forehead, the other on her lips.

She wondered if he kissed his lovers like that. She imagined that second kiss deepening, and those hands moving. The strange, scurrying excitement that she had known in the cottage scampered through her, followed by a poignant regret.

It seemed that her nature would permit vague wonderings. A fantasy posed no danger. Reality would leave her paralyzed.

Just as well. He did not want her like that. This marriage suited him because it left him free. That dark edge had bared itself this morning on the way to the church. No doubt he had been contemplating the potential restrictions on his pleasure if she did not behave as promised.

An alien pain stabbed at the thought of those hands on another woman's face. Soon, she had no doubt. She scolded the silly jealousy away. She had no right to it, and succumbing would only make her ridiculous.

Still, she had experienced something in that church that she had not expected. She had been given a taste of what some other women knew on their wedding day. She had felt a glimmer of the consummate intimacy that the true joining of two hearts and bodies could create.

She suspected that she would lick at the sweet memory of that moment for a very long time.

When they arrived in Newcastle they took a late luncheon in the Versailles's elegant restaurant. While Fleur nibbled her cold beef she kept looking past Dante's shoulder curiously.

"Does that dark-haired man back there know you?" she asked. "He keeps glancing our way."

Dante twisted to see a man his age reading a newspaper while he worked his way through a plate of cakes. "That is Ewan McLean. We were at university together. His estate is north of Berwick."

"Why hasn't he greeted you?"

Dante knew why. "Excuse me, while I go speak with him."

He walked over and took a seat at his friend's table. "Are you giving me the cut, McLean?"

McLean's black eyes twinkled. "Just trying to be discreet, Duclairc. If you came all this way north, I assume that the lady does not want to be recognized."

"Not discreet enough. She noticed you noticing."

McLean's face broke into a roguish smile. "Very lovely. She looks familiar but I cannot place her."

"Fleur Monley."

The smile fell in astonishment. He peered Fleur's way more obviously. "*No*. I'll be damned. You devil. If you are discovered it will be your undoing. I should upbraid you for corrupting an innocent, but instead I am moved to admire your audacity."

"Miss Monley and I have just been married."

McLean displayed genuine shock. "Say that you jest. You have no business getting married, and you damn well know it. We simply are not the type, Duclairc. Not to mention that if you have tied the knot, my visits to London promise to be considerably duller. I had planned one in a week, but if you have been domesticated there is no point in going."

"Your heartfelt congratulations touch me."

"Forgive me. Of course I am delighted for you. She is quite a catch and I only wish for your happiness. You must excuse me if I see this in symbolic terms that do not bode well for me, however. It is one of those watershed moments of history, like the Vandals conquering Rome. An era of pleasure is ending before my eyes."

"Well, compose yourself and come meet her. You are the first to know, by the way."

"You eloped? Stupid question. Of course you did. Even independent women have someone looking out for them that the likes of you and I would have to dodge."

He brought McLean to Fleur and introduced them. The Scot showed more tact in congratulating her.

"You are on your way back to London?" McLean asked, making himself comfortable in a spare chair and sending for his cakes. He pressed one on Fleur.

"We had planned to stay the night here at the Versailles first," Dante explained. "However, they are full, so we will find another hotel."

"I would say that is unlikely. Haven't you noticed how crowded the city is? A huge wedding is to be held tomorrow. The joining of two great coal families. Everyone in the north country has come for it. I doubt that you will find a stable with space to lay your head tonight."

"I suppose that we could push on until we are outside the city," Dante said. "Could you manage that, Fleur? You have been in a carriage for three days and I know that you must be tired."

McLean had been busy feeding his sweet tooth. "I have a better idea. As it happens, I was not invited to this great wedding, having once been discovered in a compromising situation with the bride's sister—" He caught himself and grimaced at Fleur. "My apologies."

"None are necessary, Mr. McLean."

"I assure you that it was only very slightly compromising. More a misunderstanding—"

"Your better idea," Dante said.

"I keep a suite of chambers here. It serves as my home in Newcastle. Why don't I be the one to push off, and the two of you can make use of it? I had planned to depart tomorrow anyway."

Fleur looked amenable to the suggestion. Dante shot McLean a meaningful glare. "Are these chambers similar to the ones that you keep in London?"

"Much more elegant. You will find them acceptable, I think." He belatedly understood the question's true meaning. "Oh. You mean . . ." He glanced at Fleur. "Not at all. For the most part, these are very traditional in their decor. And the library, while small, is almost entirely composed of the predictable classics."

Dante remained skeptical of "for the most part" and "almost entirely." Mclean's London rooms comprised a sexual play yard. And the library . . .

"You will not be embarrassed, Duclairc," McLean mumbled while Fleur was distracted by a server. "Nor will your bride be shocked."

"I would prefer to delay more travel until tomorrow, if we could," Fleur said, her attention returning. "If it would not inconvenience you, Mr. McLean."

"No inconvenience at all. I am joyed to be of assistance." He rose. "I will have the servants prepare for you. All should be ready in a couple of hours. Duclairc, I will let you know when I am next in London. Perhaps you will call on me." He took his leave.

"What a thoughtful man," Fleur said. "He is a good friend?"

"Yes."

"He appeared a little sad when he left. He thinks that you will have to repudiate your bachelor friends now that you have tied the knot, doesn't he?"

"It is often the case."

"He will be relieved to learn that it is not *your* case."

Her indifference to that unaccountably annoyed him.

Of course she would be indifferent. He wanted her to be. He certainly did not want her resentful and demanding. That would turn this white marriage into a farce worthy of the lowest opera house.

He knew why he was reacting like this. The little ceremony in the stone church had moved him in unexpected ways. It had left him both surprisingly happy and oddly melancholy. It had been the deeper part of him, a part he preferred to ignore, that had experienced the latter sentiment.

It stirred in him now again.

"Have you finished?" he asked. "If so, why don't we take a turn and see the old city."

His beautiful wife dabbed the last of McLean's cake from her lovely lips and extended her little feminine hand to him.

The staff of the Versailles were expecting them. When they arrived at dusk they were ushered into McLean's suite.

Dante quickly examined its entirety while Fleur went to remove her bonnet in the bedchamber.

The *only* bedchamber, he discovered.

He stood in the middle of the sitting room and examined the delicate furniture laid out around him. In London, McLean's sitting room was full of soft chaise longues and deep divans. Every seat invited sprawled comfort and provided convenience for seduction.

He would gladly exchange this room for the one in London at the moment. He would find a way to explain the swing hanging from the ceiling if it meant getting a good night's sleep.

"Oh, my, this is amazing," Fleur's distant voice exclaimed.

He followed the sound through the bedchamber and dressing room to a large tiled closet.

"Look." Fleur bent over a large tub shaped like a shoe and turned a handle on the wall above it. "It comes out warm. They must heat it on the roof before sending it down through pipes. What a novelty. I will have to use it."

She left him. He stared at the contraption and pictured a naked Fleur, slick with water, reclining in it.

"Oh, my," he heard her say again.

This time he found her in the bedchamber, holding a candle high and looking up under the drapes. "How very clever."

Dante strolled to the red, satin-covered bed. Luxurious. Huge. He peeked under the canopy to see what fascinated Fleur.

A large mirror hung directly over the bed and under the drapes, suspended on stiff wires.

"Do you think this is another of the hotel's new conveniences?" Fleur asked.

"More likely McLean added this himself."

She moved the candle around. She did not appear very shocked at all. "He is a very inventive man."

"He prides himself on it."

"Look how it reflects the light off this candle and makes it grow. Why, if you lit several you could read all night almost as if it were day. Mr. McLean must be devoted to books to have come up with such a brilliant solution."

"In his own area of investigation, the man is a renowned scholar."

Their gazes met across the glistening expanse of that satin bed. She froze, as if she suddenly realized where they were. Or as if she read in his eyes the images of reflected loveplay romping through his brain.

"Come to the sitting room and have some wine," he said. "McLean arranged for some to be sent up."

She walked around the wonderful bed. In the sitting room she perched herself on a little chair. "It was kind of your friend to do this for us. I am more tired than I had realized. These chambers are perfectly beautiful."

"Perfectly beautiful, perhaps, but not perfectly convenient, despite the piped warm water. There is only one bedchamber."

She glanced a sharp question to a door on the other side of the room.

He shook his head. "A study."

He handed her a silver goblet of wine, realizing belatedly that it bore relief images of satyrs having their ways with nymphs.

She did not notice. She was examining the fragile furniture of the room. "I don't suppose that there is a divan in the study?"

"Afraid not. I will take some blankets and make myself comfortable on the rug out here."

She peered down at her wine. "It is really not necessary for you to sleep on the floor. You could use the bed too."

It took a five count for him to absorb what she had said. "Excuse me?"

A deep flush rose up from her neck. "It is a very big bed, and we are both very tired and face a long journey. It will be a little awkward, I admit, but I expect over the years this situation will occur again. When we visit people, for example."

His body instantly announced that sharing a bed with her would be a mistake. The very idea had him hardening. Sanity demanded that he make do with the rug.

However, the notion of sleeping with her, even chastely, held an unexpected appeal. He could not explain why he wanted that intimacy, but he did. And just maybe . . .

"You are sure? I would not want you frightened or embarrassed."

"You never frighten me. I trust you completely."

So much for "just maybe." He would prefer she did not trust him. There was no reason why she should, and it was damn inconvenient that she did.

"This is very considerate of you. We will get a servant to help you with that bath. I will wait until you are asleep before I retire myself."

"That is very thoughtful."

She rose and disappeared into the bedchamber. When a manservant came to the door, Dante sent for a woman. He paced the sitting room until she arrived and went in to assist Fleur. Soon the sounds of splashing water drifted through the suite. Images of his wife washing her body lapped against his mind, defeating attempts to remain distracted.

He gladly would bathe her himself. And later lift her from the tepid water and dry her with the soft towel and carry her to that satin bed and take her slowly under the diffused light of that big mirror . . .

The water sounds stopped.

The servant emerged, curtsied, and departed.

After some movement, the bedchamber grew silent.

He checked his pocket watch. He would wait a solid half hour. That should do it.

He entered the study and perused McLean's library. Almost entirely the predictable classics, but not completely. He spied his friend's greatest prize, the only known surviving copy of *I Modi*, the series of erotic engravings by the Renaissance artist Raimondi. He flipped through the graphic images of sexual positions.

All of which were out of the question tonight.

Just as well. Changing that part of their arrangement would alter everything about it, and he certainly did not want that.

The half hour up, he entered the bedchamber. A candle burned on a table beside the bed, and the mirror spread its pale golden light, dimly showing Fleur's hair streaming down over the satin coverlet. She slept on her back. Her thick dark lashes feathered against her cheek.

He went to the dressing room and pulled off his clothes and put on the nightshirt that his recently rehired valet had sensibly packed. Trying not to wake her, he eased onto the bed.

He settled on his back and watched her in the mirror. She looked so peaceful and beautiful. He had never seen her hair down before. It flowed in thick waves over hands that were clasped atop the sheets on her stomach.

Her lashes flickered and her lids rose. They looked at each other in the reflection. A body's width separated them on the bed and they both lay almost rigidly beneath the mirror's moving light.

"I did not mean to wake you."

"I was not sleeping yet." She glanced down the bed. "This is a little strange."

"Yes."

"But not unpleasantly so."

"No, not unpleasantly so."

She looked at him again in the reflection. "Thank you for marrying me."

He had no idea what to say to that.

She closed her eyes. Her clasping hands relaxed and fell to her sides. He sensed her getting drowsy, but she looked up again. Her brow puckered into a thoughtful frown.

"Dante. This mirror. You don't suppose . . . It is a scandalous thought to have, but could it be that he put it there so that . . ." A blush deepened the rosy glow of her cheeks.

He reached over and patted her hand. "Most likely it was just to help his reading."

Her small hand turned under his. He left his atop it, enjoying the sensation of palm on palm. He reined in the impulse to roll toward her and make the connection one of mouth on mouth and body on body. There was a simple, pure affection in their handholding, and he enjoyed it more than he expected, but his blood wanted more.

"Good night," she muttered sleepily.

"Good night, pretty flower."

chapter 6

Ly aunt Ophelia owned this property," Fleur explained while the carriage followed a little lane through rolling Durham farmland. In the distance behind them a slow cart lumbered, carrying a few servants that she had hired at the nearby village.

"Her husband had died in the war, and her sister had disappeared, so she made my mother, her half-sister, her sole heir. It came to me through my mother."

"You have an aunt who disappeared?"

"Aunt Peg was not mentally sound. She was forever childish. Aunt Ophelia had her live in a little house within sight of the main one, with a servant who cared for her. Then one day she wandered off on her own and didn't come back."

She was talking too much, trying to fill the silence. Dante had been very quiet this morning, as if sharing that bed had made him uncomfortable with her. His manner had pulled back from yesterday's easy friendship.

"She was never found?" he said.

"Gregory and the men of the county searched for days, but to no avail. Ten years later her bones were found in a ravine miles away. She must have fallen and perished there."

"Farthingstone was your aunt's friend? Is that how he met your mother?"

"He has property that adjoins this on the north. Aunt Ophelia introduced him to my parents here years ago, and he became an adviser to them on financial matters. After Father died, my mother and I spent most of a summer here and he and she grew closer."

The coach brought them to an impressive stone house surrounded by tall trees. "I rarely visit here, but it should be presentable," she said. "There is a couple who care for it."

She was relieved to see that Mr. and Mrs. Hill had kept it very presentable. Dante strolled through the rooms on the first level.

"A lady's home," he observed, running his fingers across the light pat-
terned cloth on the drawing-room chairs. "Is this a large property?"

"Not so large. The income is not very significant."

She wondered why she said that, since it was not true.

She realized that she did not want him thinking that her decisions about
the disposition of this property were addled, the way Gregory claimed. It
might sound that way if she had to explain it to him. Once everything was
arranged and worked out, however, he would see the soundness of the Grand
Project and sign any deed necessary.

When the servants arrived, she sent one up to prepare two chambers. Two
chambers, two beds, two lives—that was the future they began this day. The
notion made her a little sad.

Last night had surprised her. She had never guessed at the comfort to be
had in lying beside a man. It created a special closeness that she had never
imagined could exist.

This morning they had lain there after she woke and sensed that he was
alert. She had kept her eyes closed, wanting it to last, not moving so that she
could drink in the cozy mood for a little longer.

She rather regretted they would not share that again.

After a light meal they made a walking tour of the property. The day was
crisp and a lovely breeze moved fluffy clouds across the deep blue sky. She
brought him to a hill about a mile from the house, from where one could
look out over surrounding land.

She stumbled on the way up. He righted her and gently swept the grass
off her skirts. She was very aware of the discreet pressure of his hand through
her petticoats. With any other man it would be improper, but he *was* her
husband and friend.

He took her hand to help her climb the rest of the way. The renewal of
contact warmed her, and she was grateful that he did not let go when they
reached the summit. They surveyed the countryside hand in hand, in something like yesterday's partnership.

"That cottage down there is where Aunt Peg lived," she explained, pointing east. "I am giving that building and the surrounding ten acres to a
school that will be built here."

She did not know why she impulsively confided this essential part of the
Grand Project. She only knew that she felt moved to share it with him.

"I thought that you were selling this property, not giving it away."

"I will be selling some of the rest, to create an endowment for the school."

"The income cannot be so small, if it can support a school."

Now she remembered why she never spoke of this. Explanations had a way of leading to the parts of the project she should not reveal because they would sound somewhat mad.

"The sale of the land will only provide part of the endowment, of course." It was the truth, but she did not like dissembling.

"It is out of the way for a school. I thought the ones you supported were in cities."

"This will be a special one, for colliers' sons."

"How will the boys get here?"

"There is a coal town about three miles north, and we expect some to come from there. Others will live here during the week and go home on Sundays."

He appeared interested. "Can their families afford to permit it? Not only the cost of the school, but the loss of wages if the boys do not work?"

"We hope to convince families of the benefits of educating boys with the talent and willingness to learn. This school will not just teach religion like most places for the lower orders, but practical things like mathematics and science. When the boys are grown they will be able to manage those mines, not just dig inside them. If the families are poor, the school will take the boys for no fees."

"We?"

"The Society of Friends will manage it. Their schools are well respected. They have agreed to my ideas of what should be taught."

He laughed. "I am sure that they will include a large dose of religion all the same. I approve, not that it did much good with me."

She squeezed his hand. "You are hardly the devil in disguise."

He looked directly at her. For a moment she experienced again that startling connection she had known in the church. She grew very conscious of the warmth of his palm and fingers encircling hers.

He looked away. "You do not know the half of it, Fleur. It would be a mistake for you to forget who I am." He pointed to the north. "Is that one of the school's buildings being constructed over there?"

She rose on her toes to see what he referred to. A rock below her shoe made her lose her balance. His arm caught her by the waist to steady her.

"No, that is Gregory's land. He must be having a new cottage built. Our school's property will stop right down here, on the field beyond the hedgerow, where those men are farming. I gave permission for a tenant to use the land and cottage until we begin building."

She came down off her toes. His arm stayed around her. That scurrying excitement fluttered. He inspected the field and appeared unaware that he still held her.

"Tell me where you will put the buildings."

"The main building will replace Aunt Peg's house because there is already a well there. The outbuildings will go there and there." She pointed out the spots and he leaned closer to follow her arm's directions. He did not seem to notice their physical proximity.

She did. It distracted her so much that her voice faltered twice. The excitement kept growing, filling her with an amazing elation. She waited for the freezing fear, dreading its inevitable claim on her.

"Why not move all the buildings closer to the house?" he suggested. "Then you would have plenty of space nearby for a playing field. Boys need to do more than study."

She said something about that being a good idea, but barely heard herself. The fear had not reared yet to kill the physical response now mesmerizing her.

The excitement awoke her senses. The breeze felt so fresh against her flushed skin, and the day looked so vividly clear. Dante's strength, close but still a little removed, called to her. The light weight of his arm around her waist absorbed her attention.

He still appeared blandly oblivious.

A silly euphoria swept her, as if the blood tingling through her limbs had rushed to her head. A foolish smile stretched without her willing it.

She had to stop this. If not, she would embarrass herself and insult him, and he would not even know why it had happened. She did not want him concluding that he had to stay ten feet away from her for the rest of their lives.

She forced herself to step aside, light-headed still. His vague smile made her wonder if he had known what was happening but had been politely ignoring it.

"Come, I'll show you a little drop in the next hill where there is a small waterfall," she said.

The steep decline was more difficult than climbing up. Once again her skirt interfered and she stumbled. This time his hand reached too late. She began rolling.

She could have stopped herself, but her intoxicated senses loved the dizzying spin. It reminded her of when she was a girl and had deliberately climbed hills just so she could descend like this. Over and over she tumbled, laughing with delight at the childish thrill of it, watching grass, sky, and hedge flip past.

She stopped at the bottom of the rise, near the hedge. She could hear the farmers working on the other side in the field. She gazed up at the white mountains of puffy clouds while she caught her breath and savored a glorious lightness of spirit.

A shadow fell over her face. Dante stood beside her, looking down.

"It has been a lifetime since I did that," she said, as she pushed up to sit.

"I think that I will include this hill in the school's property so the boys can play on it."

He slipped off his frock coat and sat down. He laid his coat behind her.

"They can roll down the hill and then lie here and find animals in the clouds. My brothers and sisters and I used to do that when we were children." He stretched out and pointed. "See, there is a dog."

She angled her head. "Its nose is wrong. More of a cat."

"No cat has a tail like that."

She fell back on his coat and raised her arm. "That one over there could be a horse if it had three more legs."

"It will be a unicorn soon if the breeze keeps stretching its head."

They played the child's game for a while, arguing and laughing. They lay side by side, placed almost identically to how they had been in the bed last night. Dante's easy manner had returned, and that delighted her. One of the farmers had moved closer to the hedge. She could hear him humming.

"I see a bear in that distant cloud," she said.

"I see a woman."

"It has to be an animal, Dante."

"I see a woman. A very beautiful woman, happy and free."

She turned her head to find him up on his elbow, looking not at the sky but at her.

His expression sent her blood tingling again. The farmer began singing the song he had hummed, his low melody drifting on the breeze.

Dante reached out and stroked the back of his fingers on her cheek. Wonderful sensations shimmered out from his touch. No fear stopped their path.

"A lovely woman, bright-eyed with a child's innocence, laughing in watery melodies."

She couldn't take her eyes off his beautiful face and luminous eyes. A man's eyes, watching her with a man's intensity. Waiting, no doubt, for her signal that he was crossing a line they had sworn not to approach.

She could not give it. She did not want to. The fear had miraculously not come and she wanted him to look at her like that, the way a man looks at a woman. She wanted him to touch her and give physical form to the connection she felt to him.

He rose on his arm and leaned over her, his head above hers, blocking the clouds. Expression serious and eyes fathomless, he watched his hand smooth down and gently encircle her neck. His thumb brushed a line along her jaw and chin before his fingers traced the skin at the top of her dress. Her breath caught at the force of her reaction to his slow, wandering caress. He looked into her eyes with a piercing acknowledgment of what he was doing to her.

"I am going to kiss you, pretty flower. Friends do, don't they?"

She knew it would not be a friend's kiss. The depths of his eyes warned her of that. She felt no fear at all, but only pulsing anticipation. The only thing that froze was time.

It was a wonderful kiss, more beautiful than she had ever imagined when she permitted herself to wonder. Warm and careful and restrained. Deep enough to speak his intentions, however, and long enough to make her body thrill.

He looked down at her while he caressed her hair and face. He knew exactly what she was experiencing, she had no doubt of that. This was Dante Duclairc. It would take more worldliness than she would ever possess to hide it from him.

He brushed kisses on her cheek and neck. Warm breath titillated her ear. He caressed gently across the sash of her gown, and the sensation of his hand on her stomach affected her whole body.

"If I frighten you, you must let me know."

She nodded, but it would not happen. Not here, not now. She just knew that, and the freedom filled her with indescribable happiness. There could be no room for that cold dread when such warm pleasure and affection saturated every inch of her.

More kisses, building in demand, pulled something wild from her depths. Wandering caresses, learning the outline of her body, left her trembling. A power flowed from him, as if his masculinity wanted to overwhelm her.

Astonishing sensations streaked and quavered, awakening yearning desires in the most womanly parts of her. Her awareness narrowed, focusing totally on those feelings and his command of them. Only the low song of the farmer intruded, reminding her that they were not alone.

He heard it too. He paused and glanced to the hedge.

His gaze returned and fell on her lips. With the gentlest strokes of his fingertips he cajoled them apart. He lowered his head and body and claimed her in a more intimate kiss and embrace.

The small invasion shocked her for an instant, and then a whirlwind swept her up. She embraced the man pressed against her chest, filling her arms with him.

Less restraint now. Deep kisses, skillfully seductive. On her mouth. Her ear. Her neck. Trailing to the skin exposed by the scoop of her bodice. Tantalizing her through the cloth of her gown until her breasts strained with a begging ache that left her whimpering.

Maybe he heard. Certainly he understood. His caress rose to cup her breast with an encompassing warmth that sent her spinning. Those fingers began exploring. Craving pleasure and hungry physicality pulsed down her body, building a shocking focus of need.

He rose above her. Her arms had to stretch to hold him and she pulled, wanting him back. She could see in his face and feel in his body that they were together in this passion.

He glanced once more to the hedge behind which the farmer invisibly worked and sang. He listened for a while before turning his inflaming gaze back to her.

His hand slid under her back. "Do not be afraid. I will make sure that you are not embarrassed. But I want to see you. I have been thinking of little else all day."

The bodice of her gown loosened. He slid it down her shoulders, then pushed down her chemise too.

The breeze shocked her naked breasts. The contrasting warmth of his hand comforted and aroused. He watched his caress follow her curves. She had never imagined she could want anything as badly as she hungered for that touch to continue.

It did, in wicked, devastating ways. The low sounds of her crazed desire filled her ears like a staccato rhythm against the deeper pulse of his breath.

He eased onto her, until his length covered half of her and his leg buried in her skirt between her thighs.

His head turned and lowered. Soft brown hair brushed her face. He kissed the fullness of her breast, and then the tip. Excruciating pleasure shot through her. He licked and nipped and drew, making it wonderfully worse. She grasped him tightly, clinging as utter abandon took over. Not thinking or caring about anything but her body's astonishing reactions, she pressed up against his leg, instinctively trying to ease the itching vacancy that was driving her to delirium.

A new tension stretched through him. He moved completely on top of her. "Part your legs, darling." The low instruction penetrated and she obeyed. "More."

He settled between her spread thighs. The many layers of their clothing could not obscure the intimate connection of their bodies. Like a wanton she leveraged to accept the pressure that afforded some relief.

In her daze she felt him stroke low on her leg. Her essence thrilled to it, welcomed it. If he did not cover her she would have torn the interfering petticoats off, so mindless had she grown. He did not need her help. His hand lined up her hose to her bare thigh, raising her skirt and petticoats as it ascended.

Even as her body welcomed that touch and moved into it, something of her essence retreated. A single drop of the old fear plunked into her euphoria, creating ripples of uncomfortable rationality. She cringed against the dreaded intrusion.

He sensed it. He stopped, and again that tension strung through him.

The farmer shouted to someone across the field just then. Dante looked to the sound and briefly closed his eyes, as if he focused his will on something.

He rolled off her and smoothed down her skirt. "You are right. Forgive me for going too far. This is not the place."

Relief drenched her. Then dismayed her. She realized with a jolt that she had counted on this. Even while she lost herself in the wonderful passion, she had assumed that it would never go too far on the grass behind a hedge while a farmer sang and worked nearby.

In seconds he had the gown fastened again. Stretching out on his back, he pulled her to him in an embrace.

The drop of fear had evaporated as quickly as it had come. She rested happily in the circle of his arm while they both once again looked up at the sky. She gazed at the clouds against the vivid blue, thinking it almost a vision of the heaven she was feeling.

Maybe. Maybe . . .

She knew that he intended to make love to her when night fell. All through the afternoon it was in his eyes and attention. During their casual strolls and light discussions that special something in him shimmered relentlessly, leaving her giddy and clumsy and excited.

She had never guessed that mutual attraction could create such a palpable, physical pull. She reveled in it, enjoying every moment of anticipation as much as she had relished the startling pleasure by the hedge.

But then, while they ate dinner on the garden terrace, another drop of the fear splashed onto her euphoria. Then another and another, until a faint drizzle of misgiving began to ruin her happiness.

She stared helplessly at some white flowers turning into ghosts in the dimming light. With all of her will she tried to control the horrible vise wanting to grip her stomach. A tremble of revulsion shook her.

Please, no. Not now.

Dante reached across the small table and took her hand in his. "Is the evening breeze chilling you?"

"No." Nor, for a blessed respite, was the fear. The warmth in his expression reduced the terror to something small and weak. And, maybe, manageable.

He rose and took her hand. "Let us go into the library anyway, so the servants can finish their duties."

She walked within his embracing arm to the library. A dance was beginning in which he would lead and she could only hope that she had the courage to follow.

They sat side by side on a divan, perusing a volume of archaeological engravings. Acute awareness of his closeness obscured any real study of the images. Did he feel it too? Could he also sense the ugly other thing in her, planted like a choking vine in the pit of her being, casting out a tendril now and then to remind her of its power?

It will not overcome me. I will not let it.

The door to the library stood open and they could hear the servants completing their work. She took comfort in the domestic sounds. They were not alone yet. But they would be soon.

I can do this. I want to.

Silence slowly descended on the house. Skirts swished by the door as the women headed to their chambers in the attic. One of them would wait for her upstairs, to help her undress.

Dante took the large volume from her lap and set it aside. He shifted to face her, embracing her shoulders with his arm.

A kiss. A lovely, sweet kiss. The fear withered under the light of affection, but did not disappear.

Another kiss. Deeper. The stirring of her body almost made the fear insignificant. Almost.

Please, please . . .

He caressed her face. He looked so beautiful in the candle glow. Beautiful and riveting and dangerous.

"I want to sleep with you again tonight, Fleur. Not as friends this time, but as husband and wife. It is not what we agreed to, but I think that we might make a real marriage out of this alliance. I would like to try."

His shimmering force flowed into her, and suddenly nothing mattered except feeling it forever. His luminous eyes captivated her, as if he saw into her soul. Had any woman ever refused him? Something in the depths of his eyes said that no woman had, but that he thought she might. She flattered herself that she saw something else too. Concern, as if her answer mattered.

I can do this.

"I would like to try too."

"That makes me very happy, darling." He stood and offered his hand. "Go up now. Your woman is waiting. I will follow soon."

Legs wobbling and heart pounding, she climbed the stairs to her bedchamber.

With every step, the choking vine cast out another killing tendril.

The woman helped her out of her clothes. She slipped on a pink nightgown and nervously fingered its thin silk. She'd had it made years ago, before she went on the shelf. Why had she brought this silly, lacy thing on this journey? To play a child's game of bride? Or because she had secretly hoped this night would happen? She pulled on its matching robe so she would not feel too foolish.

Please, please . . .

The woman brushed out her hair and then left her alone in the chamber. Alone, and defenseless against herself.

Like the monstrous enemy it was, the fear grew abruptly with cruel vengeance, wrapping her heart and panicking her soul.

Brutal images flew through her frantic mind. Filmy pictures of agony and blood and despair. No sounds accompanied them. The screams were silent, formed by mouths twisting inaudibly.

She ran to the window and threw it open to get some air. With more resolve than she had ever mustered before, she forced some control over her disquiet. The tiny corner of calm that she claimed instantly filled with anguished disappointment.

He would come soon. He would enter through that door, and all that she could give him was her rejection or her madness.

Better if she had kept more distance. Better to have not tasted a passion that she could never fully share. Better to have never seen what her deficient nature prevented her from experiencing.

Tears streamed down her face. The chill shaking her had nothing to do with the night breeze. The panic had retreated, leaving only the sickening dread that enslaved her body.

The door opened and she glanced over her shoulder. He had removed his coats and collar. His white shirt gleamed as luminously as his eyes. Her heart split into pieces. This fear knew no mercy at all. It permitted her to desire. It just forbade her having what the desire wanted.

She tried to speak but the words would not emerge. He came over to her and she turned back to the open window so he would not see her tears. He caressed her shoulders and arms and bent a kiss to her neck.

The panic surged. Her whole body involuntarily stiffened.

He stopped.

Neither of them moved for what seemed an eternity. She had never known such humiliation before.

She had to say something.

"I cannot do this," she whispered. "I thought that I could. I had hoped . . ."

"You do not have to be afraid. If you were told stories as a girl, they were probably much exaggerated. I am not going to hurt you."

"It is not that."

He stood behind her silently. She did not have to see him to know that the dark edge had emerged. She could not blame him. It had been heartless of her to do this to him.

"I do not understand," he said.

"Nor do I. I wish I were different. Normal. I have never wished it more than at this moment. After this afternoon, I thought maybe I could be. But I realize that behind that hedge I could be free of this because I knew that you would not make love to me there."

He stepped back with a deep sigh.

She found the courage to turn and face him. "Please do not hate me, Dante. I hate myself enough already."

"I do not hate you. If it is how it must be, then I accept it, as I promised I would. You were honest with me."

"Not entirely. This afternoon I lied, without intending to. To both of us. I am very sorry."

He smiled ruefully. "This is probably just as well for your sake, Fleur. I doubt that I would be a good husband in the normal sense. I would only make you unhappy eventually."

Maybe so, but she would have traded that risk for the chance to learn where this friendship might have led.

He walked to the door. It went without saying that they would not share a bed tonight. Or ever again.

He began to leave, but paused. "It would be best to return to London soon. I would like to leave in the morning."

"Of course, Dante."

The door closed behind him. The cursed, triumphant fear released its hold, leaving her empty and spent.

She sank to her knees beside the window and cried out her disappointment in herself.

chapter 7

G regory Farthingstone walked through the streets of a city just wakening to a day without sun. Barely able to see in the fog, he aimed toward his destination with long strides.

He hated rising before the dawn for these appointments, not to mention having to walk so no one would know where he went.

Actually, he hated this whole business. Hated the worry and the subterfuge. He detested the vague foreboding and the sense that he inched along a precipice. Mostly, however, he resented playing a game in which someone else held all the best cards.

He turned down a little lane, then hurried along the alley between two rows of handsome houses. Entering the garden of one, he strode to the stairs leading down to the back kitchen door.

Like a damn servant. That was how he visited this house.

There was no choice. He hardly wanted to be seen. All the same, it raised his irritation. He did not need it to be so obviously demeaning.

The cook was up as she always was when he came. She paid him no mind as he hurried through her fief. A scullery maid sat by the hearth, building up the fire. Presumably they had been ordered to ignore him, but anyone with a few shillings could probably loosen their tongues.

Up above, the butler waited for him. As he followed the butler up the stairs, he noted once again the very fine appointments in the home. Its owner had a taste for luxury that far surpassed Farthingstone's own. He preferred a more sober environment himself, as befitted a bank trustee and man of serious disposition. He would not choose to live among all this color and texture even if he could afford them.

A hot resentment beat in his head all the same. He knew very well how these carpets and chairs and paintings were purchased. He knew all about the legacy that had paid for them.

He found his host in his bedchamber, sipping coffee while perusing a newspaper. The man still wore his robe and had not even bothered to don a morning coat yet. Farthingstone did not miss the reminder of who held the good cards.

The valet poured another cup from the silver server, offered it to Farthingstone, then left.

"Well, this is one hell of a mess, Farthingstone," Hugh Siddel said, smacking the newspaper down on the table that held the coffee service.

Farthingstone did not need to examine the paper to understand the reference. He recognized the notice of Fleur's marriage to Dante Duclairc from ten feet away.

"You said it was dealt with," Siddel added.

"It *was*. Brougham clearly instructed them to wait. I never thought they would be so bold—"

"If you had not hesitated that night, not allowed sentiment to interfere—"

"What you proposed was *illegal*."

"And what you intended was not? At least with my plan she would have been permanently controlled."

Farthingstone paced away. His heart fluttered uncomfortably. The last few months had taken a toll he did not care to assess. An agitation of the spirit caused palpitations in his body that were not healthy.

He forced some calm on both and faced Siddel. "Brougham will be angry that they took this step. He will now be amenable to expediting my petition. Once the court declares her unfit, the Church will put the marriage aside."

Siddel snorted in derision. "Duclairc is certain to fight you. By the time it is all settled, he will have let her sell all the property she owns. He is the kind who prefers money to land. Easier to squander." He scowled and combed his dark hair back with his fingers. "Those damn Duclaircs. Her entanglement with Laclere at least made some sense, but this marriage to Dante truly is madness."

Farthingstone did not have a high opinion of Duclairc, but he had less confidence than Siddel that Dante was a fool. Also, Duclairc might have some affection for Fleur. Siddel's own interest in her had always seemed a little unhealthy.

"You will have to be indiscreet if you want things settled quickly," Siddel said. "Let it be known that she has gone strange. You probably should claim that you saw it in her mother too. You will have to get society's opinion behind you. That will make it easier in Chancery."

Farthingstone's heart thudded again. Fleur was one thing, but Hyacinth was another. While he had hardly married for love, he still had some loyalty there.

He glanced over to the newspaper. He did not welcome doing what Siddel suggested, but there was probably no choice now.

It was Fleur's own fault. If she had just listened to reason . . . but, no, she never would, and now she had gone and married that man.

"If I succeed in having the marriage annulled due to her inability to make sound judgments, she will be unable to marry anyone else, of course." He mentioned it offhandedly, but he wanted to be sure the implications had not been missed.

"Of course. Since you hesitated that night, that plan is now out of the question."

"Then we are agreed. I will try and rectify this unfortunate development. I will find a solution to overcome the complication that this marriage creates."

"I certainly hope so, my friend." Siddel rose and headed for his dressing room. "After all, this problem is yours alone, and always has been. I am merely an interested observer who has been trying to help you out of your dilemma."

A week after his marriage was announced in the London papers, Dante entered Gordon's gaming hall. Sidelong glances and a low buzz followed his progress through the smoky, cavernous room.

He aimed toward a group of young men at tables in the northwest corner. Someone had years ago dubbed the fluid group that congregated there the Younger Sons Company. The name referred to the diminished expectations in fortune and marriage caused by most of their birth orders.

This was the first time that he had seen most of them since his aborted run to France. Some heralded his approach with alerting jabs at their comrades. Each step closer brought more eyes on him.

He took a chair at a *vingt-et-un* table where McLean sat with Colin Burchard, the amiable, blond-haired, second son of the Earl of Dincaster.

Three tables away a young man rose to his feet. With exaggerated ceremony he bowed to Dante. Then he brought his fist down on the table in a slow series of thumps.

Another rose and joined him. Then a dozen more. They all pounded their tables in time. Even Colin and McLean got to their feet. Soon Dante found himself the center of a thundering ovation.

The man who had started it raised his glass. "A toast, gentlemen, to honor greatness in our midst. May we all be punished for our debauchery and sin in the manner he has been."

"As you can see, they are as impressed as I was," McLean said after everyone returned to their drink and gambling. "We exult in admiration that you not only escaped ruin but did so by marrying the wealthy and beautiful Fleur Monley. Only the marriage of Burchard's brother, Adrian, to the Duchess of Everdon surpasses this triumph."

"My brother's marriage is a love match," Colin said defensively.

"Of course it is," McLean said. "As is that of Miss Monley to our friend here, I am sure. More reason to celebrate his good fortune. I am delighted to see you back among us, Duclairc, and so soon after your nuptials."

"My wife is not only beautiful but of sweet temperament. She does not expect me to sit in attendance on her for several weeks, as if we have entered a period of mourning."

He did not add that their one week of togetherness had been an exercise in strained, careful politeness, relieved only by the distraction of settling him into Fleur's house. His wife had not appeared surprised or disappointed to see him leave this evening.

"Very open-minded," Colin said.

"Isn't it," McLean drawled. "Although her mother's husband may not see it that way. I daresay he will fill everyone's ears with a different interpretation."

"Farthingstone? Has he been spreading tales?"

"McLean is just being indiscreet, as usual," Colin said.

"What is my wife's stepfather saying?"

"That you have taken advantage of an addled woman, in whom you have no interest beyond her fortune," McLean said. "Don't give me that severe stare, Burchard. If the whole town is hearing it, he should too, so he can deal with the man."

"Farthingstone has shown a tenacious interest in my wife's affairs. However, I expected cynical gossip from him and others."

"He has been telling 'the true story,' as he calls it. Everyone knows that he went to Lord Chancellor Brougham about her condition and that you were told to wait on Chancery before marrying. Everyone knows that Brougham is angry about the elopement. Everyone knows that she bought your way out of a sponging house with fifteen thousand."

"I'm sure that Duclairc is delighted to learn that his marriage is the tattle of every club and drawing room," Colin said. "You have outdone yourself in tactlessness, McLean."

"That is what friends are for."

Dante gestured to the tables surrounding them. "If everyone has heard Farthingstone's claims, this welcome surprises me."

"The decent men assume that you conveniently found happiness with a rich woman. The scoundrels are reassured to know that, faced with an incredible opportunity, you grabbed it just as they would have done."

"Whatever anyone believes, I want to make it very plain that my wife is not addled."

"Of course not. Anyone who knows you has no trouble understanding why a completely sane Miss Monley would marry you. Women are drawn to you like iron to a magnet, and it seems that even angels are not immune. I wish that I knew your secret. The good ones always run away from me."

"You would not know what to do with one of the good ones," Colin said.

Nor do I, Dante thought.

He tried to force his mind away from thoughts about the good woman to whom he found himself abruptly and permanently tied. She had been all grace and sweetness the last week while she rearranged her home to accommodate his intrusion.

She had turned the study over to him. She had given up the large bedchamber adjoining hers that she had used as a private sitting room, and had refurnished it for the new master of the house. Masculine dark furniture and textures now filled that space. During the days workmen still repainted its wood.

One door had not been refinished. The narrow white door that stood between Fleur's dressing room and his.

She did not lock it. He had discovered that two nights ago, after a quiet evening of reading together in the library. They had barely spoken through those hours, but it had been surprisingly pleasant all the same. Maybe that was because looking at those pages permitted them to be together without looking at each other.

Embarrassment still glimmered in her expression whenever their eyes met. He suspected that everything he tried to hide behind a forced good humor was reflected in his own. Reading those books had let them drop their guard a little. Something of the old, relaxed friendship had returned in the companionable silence.

However, a dropped guard could be dangerous. It had stripped him of the indifference that his frustration and anger had constructed that night in Durham after he left her chamber.

Late at night, raw with desire, he had found himself facing that provocative adjoining door.

The easy turn of the handle implied a level of trust that was hardly warranted, considering his intentions. It had been enough to send him back to his bed alone, however, where he had spent the next few hours making love to her in his head in every way imaginable.

McLean broke into his thoughts with a nudge and a point. "It appears that your arrival has piqued the interest of someone outside our notorious circle."

Dante's gaze followed the gesture to where Hugh Siddel stood by the roulette table in the center of the room. He kept glaring in Dante's direction with dark eyes glazed from too much drink.

"It is probably your recent wedding that has provoked him," Colin said.

"Another man with a peculiar interest in my wife's welfare."

"Peculiar only in the persistence of the interest," Colin said.

"What do you mean by that?"

"He was besotted when she came out as a girl. He and I were friends back then, and I have rarely seen a man so enamored. He even stopped drinking while he courted her. He did not take it well when she settled her affection on your brother."

Dante resisted looking Siddel's way again, but he could feel those bright, liquid eyes on him. Colin's memories explained Siddel's anger at finding Fleur in that cottage, at least.

"Hell, here he comes," McLean muttered.

Siddel's shadow edged over their table like a storm cloud. "Duclairc, good to see you again. My congratulations on your marriage. Fleur Monley, no less. Word was that she had decided never to marry."

"It appears word was wrong."

"Our last meeting at Laclere Park revealed that much more was misunderstood about her than that."

He smiled like a man amused with his own clever wit. Colin leveled a warning gaze at him that he blithely ignored.

"The saintliness, for example. The whole world believed it."

"The evidence of her virtue speaks for itself."

"We both know that recent evidence speaks otherwise. Her alliance with you, for example. Hardly the choice of a saint." He cocked his head in mock consideration. "Unless the rumors are correct, and she is too addled to know her own mind. But surely not. That would make you an insufferable scoundrel."

"Which would make me excellent company for you. However, I assure you that her mind is clearer in its judgments than yours has been for years."

"Then we are left with a misunderstanding of her character. The woman we all thought her to be would hardly agree to marry you if she was in her right mind. Did your brother discover the truth about her? Is that why he threw her over? Since we all know that he was never the paragon he pretended to be, I daresay it was more likely that he initiated her before he dropped—"

"One more word and I will kill you." It was out before he realized it, a reflexive response to the insults being flung at Fleur. The brittle coldness of his voice revealed the icy fury that had gripped him. He meant what he had just said. If Siddel uttered one more word about Fleur, he would kill him.

McLean spoke in a lazy drawl. "Siddel, when you are only half-drunk you are sometimes half-amusing, but you are neither tonight. Show a penny's worth of sense and leave before I hand Duclairc the pistol that I have under my coat and let him make good his promise."

Siddel stood his ground. A snarling smile distorted his face. "Did I hear a challenge?"

"You heard a warning," Dante said.

"Ah. Of course. Not a challenge. You don't issue them, do you? You let your brother fight your duels for you."

Something snapped. Resentments and agonies roared out of time past. White heat flared, burning away the ice and obliterating thought. Dante rose and grabbed Siddel's collar. In the next instant, he slammed his fist into that smirking face.

Siddel flew. His whole body catapulted backward onto a hazard table. Dice jumped, glasses overturned, and players cursed with astonishment as he landed like a dead weight, sprawled unconscious amidst the game.

A curious hush spread from the corner to the whole hall. It held for a few moments while heads angled for better views, then everyone calmly returned to their games. The men whose play had been interrupted merely moved to another table.

McLean went over to examine the damage. He ambled back, sat, and lit a cigar. "Out cold. I haven't seen you do that since we were at Oxford. Here I thought that your marriage might make you dull company."

Dante scowled down at his knuckles. "He was almost out cold when he walked over here."

"The hell he was. That was quite a blow. He certainly deserved it, though," Colin said. He looked over at the body. "I think that I'll get some of Gordon's boys to put him in his carriage." Colin went looking for help.

McLean checked his pocket watch. "I must be gone soon too. I have an appointment with Liza, and her performance is almost finished." He smiled slyly. "Just how generous is your wife? Liza has a new red-haired friend who is breathtaking."

Dante pictured McLean's comfortable chambers with their soft, welcoming furniture. He imagined a few hours taking his pleasure with the breathtaking friend. He thought about the warmth and relief promised if he accompanied McLean, and remembered the bed of nails and the damn white door waiting at home if he did not.

"Not that generous. We *are* newly married."

"Of course," McLean said gravely. A twinkle in his eyes indicated that he had not missed the possibilities left open by the second statement.

Colin returned with three husky men. They proceeded to carry Siddel away.

McLean watched with amusement. "None of my business, but it was just Siddel being Siddel."

"I lost my temper. It happens to all of us."

"Rarely to you." He casually tapped out his cigar. "What did he mean? Right before you hit him? That remark about your brother fighting your duels."

"I have no idea."

McLean rose. "I must be gone. I almost hate to keep my appointment. You will probably start a street brawl and I will miss it. You are sure that you will not come along?"

"I'll join some of the others here."

McLean left, and Dante carried his wine over to the dice. As he passed the spot where Siddel had recently lain, he felt again the man's bones beneath his knuckles.

He would like to say that it was the insinuations about Fleur that had provoked it, but they had only primed him. It was the remark about his brother fighting his duels that made his mind go white and had caused his fist to fly.

He had reacted so strongly because Siddel was right. Years ago his brother Vergil had in fact fought a duel that he should have stood to. Only a few people knew about it, and none of them had ever revealed the details of that cold day on the French coast.

Or so he had always thought.

Fleur gazed at the letter she was writing. The words turned into blotches as her sight blurred. She rubbed her eyes and scratched another sentence. She should be in bed, but she had already tried to sleep, with no success.

She paused and looked around her new, crowded sitting room. A yellow damask settee almost blocked her writing desk, and the apple-green chair near the hearth barely fit. She would have to store some of the furniture. This chamber was only half the size of the one she had given to Dante.

She returned to her letter. It dismayed her that she had not been able to concentrate on this missive regarding her Grand Project. These plans had excited her for two years. She had returned from France to complete them, and had escaped from Gregory to pursue them. Tonight, however, she actually resented the role they played in her life.

She found herself thinking what a sad substitute they were for really living. The Grand Project struck her as just another good deed by the uninteresting, virtuous Fleur Monley.

Worse, they had done nothing to distract her from the speculations about Dante that had interfered with her sleep.

He had not returned yet. She had spent the last few hours trying not to wonder where he was. No, that wasn't honest. She really had been trying not to think about whom he was with.

A woman, probably. Maybe not. Most likely. Almost definitely.

Of course he was.

The only surprising part was that he had waited this long. She had expected him to disappear the first night back in London. It had startled her to find him staying in their home for a week. He had done that for her sake, so that people would not talk.

It had been awkward for them both. The new intimacy of sharing this house had only reminded her, and probably him too, of the other intimacy that she had cut short. The last week had taught her that living with him was going to be very difficult.

Especially on nights like this.

Hopefully, with time she wouldn't even care. Eventually she would barely take note of his leaving. Soon, surely, she would not fill with awe when he came down from his chamber, crisply dressed, as dangerously beautiful as a dark angel, that shimmering quality surrounding him like an invisible halo.

Perhaps next time her heart would not fall like a lead weight when she realized that he was finally going out to find his pleasure elsewhere.

She had not been able to move after he had gone. She had just sat there, fighting the sickly hurt, trying to rationalize the disappointment away, knowing that she was reacting stupidly. It was the bargain. What did she expect? Nothing, really. Nothing at all. Only, that did not stop the horrible sensation.

She could probably sleep now. The hours of battling jealousy had exhausted her. Unwarranted, ridiculous jealousy. She scolded herself again. This was the life that her nature had given her. She had better get hold of herself, or it would be one long hell.

As she closed her *secrétaire*, an unwelcome image flashed through her mind. Dante's face, above her, looking down while he caressed her body in the sunlight behind the hedge, lowering to kiss her in that exploring way.

She began to rise but a sound stopped her. Steps were mounting the stairs. It must be Dante, because the rest of the household was asleep.

Through her closed door she listened to his boots as he approached his chamber. Suddenly they stopped. She held her breath and hoped that he would not notice the light leaking from this room.

The boots sounded again, coming toward her.

She wished that she could fly through the wall to her bed, but the door that she planned to have cut between the two rooms had not been constructed yet.

She hurriedly sat down and opened the *secrétaire* again. She hoped he would not conclude that she had been waiting up to see if and when he returned. That would be too humiliating.

The door opened and he looked in. Seeing her, he entered with the confident ease that always marked his movements.

"I thought someone had left a lamp burning, but you are still awake. It is very late, Fleur. Well past two."

His glance raked her from head to toe. She became acutely conscious of what he saw. The saintly spinster, writing letters in the shadows, wearing an old bed cap and a plain, serviceable, pink cotton robe over her full, high-necked bed gown. A comical, pitiable image. He had probably just left perfume and lace.

"Is it that late? Goodness, I lost sense of the time." She made a display of closing the desk.

She expected him to leave. He didn't. He paced around, taking in the chamber. "It doesn't all fit in here."

"I will be moving some things and rearranging the others."

"I have disrupted your household and habits."

"Change is not the same as disruption."

He examined the porcelain figures set on the mantel. The polite thing would be to ask how he had enjoyed his evening. She could not bring herself to do so. It might sound like the probing query of a jealous woman.

He turned with a thoughtful expression. "I am glad that you do not mind change, because I have decided that you need to change a few other things."

Her heart kept fluttering, as it always did when he was near her. It was one of the discomforting things that she was trying to learn to live with. Tonight, with the silence of the house looming, it was worse than normal. Or maybe it wasn't the silence, but the lights in his eyes and the way the candles emphasized the perfect planes of his face.

"What sort of changes?"

"Farthingstone has been talking. All of it is around town, including his accusations about your judgment. We both knew he might do it, but I hoped he would show some discretion."

"We angered him, I suppose."

"I want you to go out and be seen. Make a presence in society again. Purchase some fashionable clothes and attend some parties. The best argument against him will be you yourself, mingling with the people who matter."

Not "I think that you should" or "it may be best if you did," but "I want you to." Not a suggestion but an instruction. He had left this house a guest, but, by some inexplicable turn, had come back a husband. Even his entrance into this room, *her room*, had happened as if he assumed it was his right to demand her company when he chose.

"I was long ago struck from most social lists."

"Only because you regularly declined engagements. Call on my sister Charlotte and let her know your plan. She will see that the first invitations come. After that it will take care of itself."

"If you think it would help, I suppose I could try." Actually, it might be nice to move in society again. She had only withdrawn in order to avoid the attentions of suitors. Now that she was married, that reason was gone. "If I am going to reestablish myself, I suppose we will need a carriage. A coach for evenings, at least. Maybe a landau—so we would be able to have it open for rides in the park—will be necessary too. Would you see to that part of it?"

"If you like."

"If that is all, Dante, I think that I will retire."

"Not quite all. I saw you returning to the house this morning. Do you often walk out alone?"

"I have become accustomed to it."

"That should end now too. It will appear that you are careless with both your safety and your reputation otherwise and give Farthingstone more fuel for his fire."

She had no intention of obeying this command. Being free of trailing footmen or maids was one of the only benefits of spinsterhood. No one noticed when she walked out, and no one would care.

Dante lifted one of the figures from the mantel. The movement caught her attention.

"Did something happen to your hand? It looks red and sore."

He returned the porcelain to its place and stretched out his fingers. "A small altercation."

"Are you hurt?"

"Not nearly so much as Siddel."

"Siddel?" The news shocked her. She could do without Dante starting brawls with Mr. Siddel, of all men.

He turned his attention fully on her. "Did you know about his affection for you? During your first seasons?"

"He paid addresses to me, like some others."

"Like many others. So you explained in the cottage when I inquired about his interest. But did you know that it was more than that? That the man was in love with you?"

She could not shake the impression that she was being interrogated. Nor could she ignore the signs that the dark ridge had risen to the surface. If they shared a normal marriage she would think him jealous, but that was an absurd notion. Still, there was a definite husband-to-wife quality to this entire conversation.

"If what you say is true, I was not aware of it. I did not welcome the attentions of suitors. If a man was in love with me, I would not have paid enough mind to notice or care."

Something changed in his expression. A sharpening. A darkening. It flickered in his eyes and straightened his mouth.

"I expect that is true. You would not notice or care."

His flat statement made her uncomfortable. "That sounds like blame."

"Not your fault, but it would be hard for a man to take when he realized it. An open dislike is one thing. Indifference is more insulting. I do not think he forgave you that."

"I am very sure that he never thinks about it anymore."

"I wonder." He headed to the door. "I will bid you good night. I will see about the carriages in the next few days for you."

"Thank you."

At the threshold he paused and looked back at her. Again his bright gaze took her in thoroughly, resting a moment on the pink robe. "I think that there are some other changes that I want you to make, Fleur."

More instructions. To her mind, this had not been part of the agreement.

He gestured to her cap and robe. "Do you always dress like my childhood nurse when you retire?"

"My garments are practical, and no one sees me but my maid."

"I may see you now. When we have a late conversation again, for example. When you order the new wardrobe, have some prettier things made."

"I doubt that we will have more late conversations."

"I expect that we will. I am rarely in the mood to sleep as soon as I return at night, and it appears that you keep late hours too."

If he expected her to entertain him when he came home from his rutting, he had better think again. "I cannot countenance such a frivolous expense."

He walked over to her. With warm, rough fingers under her chin, he angled her face up toward his. She looked into eyes distressingly similar in their penetrating warmth to the ones she had just seen in her memory. Her skipping heart took a huge, trembling leap.

"You can accommodate the expense, and you will do so because I require it of you. It displeases me to see you shrouded like a poor, old woman. I am your husband, Fleur, and your beauty is mine to enjoy, even if the rest of you is not."

His hand fell away and he walked back to the door.

Her reaction to his touch dismayed her, but a prickly irritation rose too. What did he care if she dressed for bed like an old nurse? His lovers would surely display enough feminine beauty to satisfy him.

"Is there anything else? Any more changes?" She threw the questions at his back and heard them crackle with resentment.

"One other. I want you to lock the door between our chambers. A saint should know better than to taunt the devil."

chapter 8

Gregory Farthingstone avoided looking at the man soiling the library chair. It wasn't the man's clothing that besmirched the upholstery. The garments were actually of astonishingly good quality, and the man well turned out. Only his hard expression hinted at his character. For all the fine clothes, there was no mistaking the sort of man this was.

Well, what did he expect? He'd gone looking for a criminal, and now he was facing one in his own home. A very successful criminal, from the looks of things.

The ease with which he had found this man was shocking. A vague query to a pawnbroker who traded in some of society's jewels had led to a money-lender who bled some of society's sons. A request for references there had resulted in this dark-haired man who called himself Smith arriving card in hand as if he were a friend. The note scrawled on the back of the card, the secret word Farthingstone had said should be used, assured that he was received.

"You make an odd offer, Mr. Farthingstone, and not what I expected," the man said. "What you require is not my usual occupation, so to speak. There's them that do this all the time for men of your cut. Why not go buy a runner?"

Farthingstone forced his attention on his guest. It was the eyes he did not like. Slit and sly, they displayed a boldness that was disconcerting, as if they saw something familiar in the man they examined.

"I do not require a runner. I merely want her followed and her actions reported to me. Any unusual actions, that is."

"Well, now, what do you mean by unusual? There's some things that are more usual than some men want to believe, when it comes to women." A smirking smile accompanied the observation.

"I am not seeking evidence of—It goes without saying that you will not discover that she has a lover. I speak of odd behavior. Eccentric activities. If her carelessness endangers her, for example. If she appears to wander the streets aimlessly. I don't know what you may discover, damn it. If I did, I would not need you to do this."

"No need to get angry. Like I said, it is an odd thing you ask, so you can't mind me wanting to understand just what you expect."

The hell of it was, he did not know himself what he expected. He only knew that he needed as much evidence of Fleur's peculiar habits as he could get. He had to go into Chancery well armed. All the stories he had let slip about her erratic behavior might not be enough.

Despite his reassurances to Siddel, things were not looking good. He needed fresh evidence for his case. At the minimum, he needed to get the court to prevent her from disposing of property while the matter was examined. Otherwise, she might convince Duclairc to allow her to go through with her intention to sell her aunt's property in Durham and build that damn school.

The very notion had sweat dampening his brow.

"You are not to let her see you or guess that she is being followed," he said very sharply. "Nor are you to in any way interfere with her."

"I'm never seen if I don't want to be."

"There is something else. She has a husband. They are not together much, but if she is with him, make yourself scarce. He is the worst scoundrel and may be more alert to being watched than she would be."

"What does he look like?"

"He has brown hair, dresses fashionably, and has a face that causes women to make idiotic fools of themselves."

"You speak of him with some emotion. You dislike the man?"

"I hate the man. He is the source of all the trouble. If not for him I would not need your services. If not for him, I would not be—" He caught himself, remembering that he spoke to a stranger, and one without honor at that.

Those sly eyes narrowed. "If he is such a trial to you, why not remove him?"

Farthingstone stared aghast at his visitor. To have such a thing so blandly said in one's library . . . But the shock did not come only from astonishment. It also derived from an instant of horrible epiphany as, in a split second, he saw how removing Duclairc would indeed neatly solve the entire problem.

"You are never again to imply that I require such a thing. When I had the word passed that I needed a man, I spoke of someone who could move about quietly and invisibly. I do not seek . . . what you suggested."

The man shrugged. He held out his hand. "I'll be taking the first payment now. My reports will go to that printing establishment, as you want, and you can leave notes for me there too. There's not much cause for a lady to do odd things, is the way I see it. Won't be hard to notice if this one steps out of line. I'll let you know if she does."

Farthingstone ignored the open hand and placed the pounds on a table. He strode to the door, to be away from the whole distasteful situation.

"If you change your mind on how to solve your problem, you just let me know," the man said to his back. "Same money for you and less lurking around for me too. A sure thing as well, and your problem is done with quickly."

Fleur perused a letter that had arrived for her in the prior day's post. It had come in response to a letter of her own, the one she had started two nights ago while she waited up for Dante.

She needed to find a way to accommodate the plans she had arranged through this correspondence. She had been back in London over a week and it was time to take care of a few matters. This was definitely one of them.

Her dressing completed, she went down to the breakfast room. Softly lit through northern windows, it was one of her favorite spaces in the house. The new day always appeared fresh and welcoming through those windows, and the proportions of the room formed a perfect cube that instilled a harmonious mood.

Dante was finishing his meal as she entered. She saw he was dressed for riding.

"I am going out to Hampstead," he explained. "I will also begin looking for the carriages and horses as you requested. Do you have any preferences? Some women are very particular about the colors of both coaches and cattle."

"Since your sister will be taking me to order a new wardrobe, I think I will have enough colors to worry me for a long while. Choose as you prefer, Dante."

"Is that how you will be spending the day? At the shops with Charlotte?"

She wished he had not asked, and mentally slapped herself for inviting the question. "We begin tomorrow. Today I must plan a meeting that I will be holding next week regarding the new school." It was the truth, just not the whole truth.

"We are to be invaded by the Friends? I should probably make myself scarce that day too."

Yes, that would be convenient. Instead of saying that, she laughed lightly, as if he had made a humorous allusion to his sin offending their goodness. Maybe he had.

That was not why she would prefer he not be here, however. She was not at all ashamed of him. She simply did not want anything to provoke questions from him about the school. She had already skirted too close to such curiosity in Durham.

She watched him walk away, with other memories of Durham floating around her, making her sad.

She thought about the letter upstairs. She was glad it had come. Picking up the threads of her life would stop this sighing over what she could not have. Besides, it was past time to do what she had returned from France to see through.

"Are you going out, madame?"

Fleur pursed her lips at her butler's query. Of course she was going out. She was wearing a hooded cloak, wasn't she? "For an hour or so. No more."

"May I send a man to hire a coach?"

"No, I will walk."

"Very good, madame. I will send for your abigail."

"If I wanted my maid with me, I would have told her already. I will not need any escort or carriage, Williams."

"Of course, madame. It is just that Mr. Duclairc saw you returning alone from your walk several days ago, and expressed a preference that you not lack an escort in the future."

Oh, he had, had he?

Williams appeared resolute. The servants did not know the details of the marriage and would assume that Dante was now master of the house. And of her.

"If Mr. Duclairc learns of my disobedience, he may express his displeasure to me. However, I do not see any reason for him to become aware of it, do you, Williams? On this matter, I think that we can continue as we have for the five years you have been with me, don't you?"

Williams had no answer for that. Contented that she had thwarted the butler's inclination to switch loyalties in a heartbeat, she left the house.

A half hour later she entered the church of St. Martin's-in-the-Fields. A few petitioners dotted the nave, lost in their prayers and oblivious to the world. She pulled the hood forward a bit on her head so it obscured her face and walked to a pew along the shadowed northern side.

A man sat there.

He rose and made room for her to sit beside him, next to the aisle. "It has been a long time since I have seen you," he said. "I trust your visit to France was pleasant."

She noticed the discoloration and swelling on the cheek below his left eye. She hoped that his resentment over that blow would not affect his dealings with her.

"My visit was very enjoyable. However, it has not been so long since you saw me, and we both know it." She had decided it would be futile to pretend Hugh Siddel had not seen her in that cottage bed. "I trust you comprehended that the last time you saw me, I was indisposed."

"Of course you were. There was no other explanation to my mind or anyone else's."

"If everyone had been as chivalrous in their discretion as in their interpretations, my reputation would have been well served. Unfortunately, someone spoke of it, because my presence there became known to my stepfather."

"Ten men rode up to that cottage. It is possible that Jameson confided what we saw to one of the others. It was an unfortunate business all around, and I am sorry you were embarrassed by it."

"Since it all turned out well in the end, I cannot say it was all that unfortunate."

She thought she saw annoyance flex over his face at this allusion to her marriage. It reminded her of that tense conversation with Dante when he claimed Siddel had once been in love with her.

Her mind stretched back to her first season. She remembered dancing with Hugh Siddel a number of times and a few conversations when he came to call. Ladies warned her mother that he drank too much, but there had never been evidence of it. Nor had she noticed any indication that he was in love.

She examined his eyes for any signs that he was a resentful, spurned admirer. None was evident. He was always polite and congenial when they met.

"I offer my heartfelt felicitations on your marriage," he said. "Although I must confide that some of the partners have expressed apprehension. Your marriage was not expected at all, and a husband's involvement was not part of the plan."

"My husband will not be involved."

"You cannot sell now without his approval."

"We have an understanding on the matter. Reassure the investors that the property remains under my total control. My husband will not interfere. Nor can my stepfather, now that I am married. No doubt you have heard his outrageous claims about me. I am told it is all over town."

"I was able to bear witness regarding Farthingstone's accusations myself, and the investors are satisfied on that count. After all, no one is in a better position to testify to your good judgment than I am."

"Now you can explain that there will be no interference from Mr. Duclairc either. We are going forward. However, I must now express my own concerns. When we first met and I agreed to have you find the purchasers for my land, you told me it could be settled in a few months. That was half a year ago. I expected to receive word in France that it was all in place. Instead, my letters to you went unanswered."

"I assure you I answered your letters and provided full details of my progress. Perhaps they missed you as you traveled?"

"Perhaps. Did you agree to this meeting so you could tell me it is finished, then?"

"Not quite. I comprehend your impatience, but the need for secrecy means that approaching investors takes time and discretion. I am confident, however, that—"

"Mr. Siddel, where are we exactly? How close are we to our goal?"

"I require two more partners. There are several likely candidates, and I am deliberating the best way to solicit them."

It was as she suspected. He was not applying himself to this with proper determination. He no doubt had many such affairs to tend to, and he had let this one languish.

"I would like the names of the investors you have already found, Mr. Siddel."

"My dear lady, I have promised them all anonymity until the entire matter is arranged. They do not even know one another's names. Only I do."

"Since my role is integral, I think I should know as well."

"I must refuse. Even one word in the wrong ear would have serious consequences. Which returns us to the reason some of the investors are concerned about your marriage."

His lowered lids and serious tone caught her off guard. "I do not understand."

"Your husband is not a man famous for prudence. Furthermore, these men find it hard to believe that a woman can keep a secret from a husband, or would even want to."

"Then they do not know much about women."

"May I give them your promise that you will not breathe one word of this to Mr. Duclairc? That you will resist confiding in him?"

The request startled her. She had returned from France suspicious and discontented. She had demanded this meeting so she could express her displeasure, and now suddenly she found herself on the defensive. Worse, she sensed that if she did not make this promise, the whole Grand Project would unravel.

She had already concluded that she would not inform Dante of these plans until all was in place. It surprised her, then, that giving this promise was harder than she expected. In reality she felt a little uncomfortable keeping things from Dante. Dodging the truth this morning had made her uneasy. It implied a lack of trust. Furthermore, he *was* her husband.

But, not *really* a husband. Not in the normal sense. This was the other half of their arrangement, wasn't it? He had his life and his lovers, and she did not ask about any of it and was not supposed to mind. In turn, she had her life and her plans, and he was not to question them.

That was how it was supposed to work, at least.

Mr. Siddel awaited her response. Considering that he still wore the marks of Dante's fist on his face, she doubted she could convince him that her husband's reputation for recklessness was exaggerated.

"Mr. Siddel, did you agree to see me today so that you can bring my promise back to the investors?"

"I am afraid so. Without it I expect several to remove themselves. We will be set back by months, and going forward may be impossible."

If the concerns were that extreme she really had no choice. "You have my promise. If my husband should learn of this, it will not be because I told him."

Dante rode up to the old manor house in Hampstead. Plaster gleamed between its half timbers, bright white from a recent application of wash. The grasses growing in its clearing had been recently cut. The Chevalier Corbet, whose fencing academy occupied the premises, maintained the property in a way that communicated a tidy, rural, picturesque effect.

Recognizing the three other horses tied to the front posts, Dante cocked his head and listened for evidence of their owners. The sounds of metal biting metal drifted to him.

When Hampton had sent the note suggesting they meet here for some exercise, he had not mentioned that other members of the Dueling Society would join them.

Inside the house, Dante entered the small room used for dressing. Despite the chill in the building, he removed his coats and shirt. The first time he had come here to take lessons he had been his brother's shadow, a boy still in university awed to be admitted to this fraternity of men of the world. No one had questioned Vergil's right to include him. In many ways, Vergil was the hub of this wheel, and all of the spokes had been added because of him.

Naked from the waist up, he walked the few steps to the large hall that served as the practice chamber. Inside, two pairs of men sparred with military sabres. They were all in his state of undress, a requirement of the chevalier, who insisted that learning to use a sword while wearing pads meant not learning to use one at all. The result was that most of the bodies displayed a few scars.

The worst one marked the side of Julian Hampton, the solicitor. He had gotten that wound during a practice much like this one, while he sparred with a friend who was now dead. They had been here alone; not even the chevalier had been present. It was not until months later that anyone had seen that scar or known it existed.

Dante watched Hampton conduct his deadly dance with Daniel St. John, thinking about that scar and the private practice that had caused it. No one had ever asked Hampton for the details, although the scar hinted at mysteries in a story everyone thought was completely known. No one ever spoke of the man who had inflicted that wound or about the events surrounding him that had involved every person now gathered in this Hampstead house.

Dante doubted he would be thanked when he broke that silence today.

He had not brought his own sabre, so he took one from the wall near the entrance. The sound of its removal from its scabbard stopped the clashing metal behind him.

The aging chevalier hailed him. "*Bon*, I am glad you are here. Take my place. Adrian is exhausting me. This old man can no longer meet such skill for long."

"This young man is incapable of meeting such skill for even a minute," Dante said as he took the chevalier's place. "Try not to kill me, Burchard. We both know this is not my weapon."

"From what I hear, your best weapon now is your fist," Adrian said.

Adrian had no doubt gotten a detailed description of the damage that fist had done at Gordon's. He was Colin Burchard's younger brother and the third son of the Earl of Dincaster. Except that everyone knew he really wasn't the earl's son and was only Colin's half brother. His dark, Mediterranean features and hair had branded him as a bastard from the day he was born. Since his marriage last year to the Duchess of Everdon, Adrian had ceased pretending the facts were other than they were.

Not for the first time, Dante thought about the ways in which temperaments forge friendships. Of the two Burchards, he was more likely to spend time with the elder Colin than with Adrian. He was more comfortable with Colin's carefree manner than with Adrian's darkly mysterious one.

Perhaps that was because he knew that for all of his elegance and good humor, Adrian Burchard was a dangerous man. Dante was not flattering Adrian in requesting to be spared from damage. Adrian had actually killed men with his sabre, most recently in a duel eighteen months ago.

"Colin probably exaggerated the skill of my fist. It was a small scuffle."

"Siddel is still wearing the brand on his face and stares daggers at anyone who asks about it."

"Then I had better practice, in case he intends to send pointed weapons in my direction."

"Since I have the advantage here, let us go shoot later, where you have learned to excel. It will even the score."

Dante was in the process of taking his position when that overture came. He proceeded with his salute.

In that moment, however, he realized that the Dueling Society had arranged this. They already knew the questions he would ask and had designated Adrian Burchard as the person to answer them.

Water splashed in basins as the four men washed and dressed. Dante threw aside his towel and reached for his shirt.

Julian Hampton came over to tie his cravat in the mirror tacked to the rustic wall. He appeared oblivious to the rest of the mirror's reflection. For a handsome man, he displayed no vanity, and no awareness of the way women flirted with him. To Dante's knowledge, Hampton strolled past the gauntlets the ladies kept throwing, apparently oblivious to the way they littered his path.

"Our barrister sent an appeal to Chancery, arguing against Farthingstone's right to be involved in the matter of your wife," he said quietly. "He is rightly raising the whole issue of jurisdiction as well."

"There is no need to whisper. I am sure that everyone here knows what is happening. St. John certainly does."

"Not the specifics of my actions. St. John respects my discretion on your behalf, just as he demands it when I act on his."

Dante looked to where St. John buttoned his waistcoat, and then to where Adrian Burchard loitered by the window. "You all think I seduced her, don't you?"

"It is forgivable. She is very lovely and, if I may say, very interesting."

"I prefer hearing that to what you implied during our conversation in the sponging house."

"You have behaved honorably in marrying her, and that is all that matters to any of us." He picked up his hat and riding whip. "I must return to the city. I will keep you informed of developments."

His departure left Adrian and St. John. The latter did not appear ready to follow Hampton out to the horses.

"St. John, Duclairc and I were planning to go shoot before we rode back. Why don't you join us?" Adrian posed the offer as if it hadn't been planned.

"Perhaps I will do that."

"Splendid," Dante said. He had intended to question all of them. Two would be enough, however.

Dante had not always been good with a pistol. As a young man he had been as indifferent to this weapon as to the sabre. Both had been nothing more than sport to his mind.

Which was why, when the time came when skill mattered, his brother had taken his place in the duel he should have fought.

He fired his fourth shot into the target tacked to the tree deep in the woods behind the chevalier's house. As he reloaded, his companions took their turns.

St. John had perfect aim, and Adrian's had improved over the years. Not as much as Dante's own, however. After that episode, he had never treated this or fencing as mere sport again. For two years he had practiced relentlessly at both. No one in the Dueling Society had ever commented on his new commitment.

"What did Colin tell you about that altercation with Siddel?" he asked Adrian.

St. John busied himself reloading his pistol, but turned so he was part of the conversation.

"That he was insulting your wife and your marriage."

"I should have called him out, but he was drunk."

"Colin also indicated that your fist actually flew after Siddel made an allusion to Laclere fighting your duels for you."

"Did Colin understand the allusion?"

Adrian set his pistol down. "He did not, nor did he even realize it was that comment that set you off. However, you are wondering if any of us have spoken about that day, aren't you?"

"Someone did."

"It could have only been a metaphor," St. John said.

"He *knew*. It was in his eyes and his sneer. It was no allusion to my brother's support."

"He did not learn it from either of us," Adrian said. "I have spoken of it to no one, not even my brother. Nor has St. John here. It goes without saying that Laclere would never divulge what happened, and I think it safe to say that Hampton holds greater secrets in his head than this. He barely talks at all, let alone gossips."

Dante knew all of this. He had almost hoped that one of them had been indiscreet, however. It would have provided a simple, if infuriating, explanation.

"There were others there that day," St. John said.

No one spoke for a while. They all knew they were broaching a subject that everyone hoped had been put in the past.

"Wellington would never speak of it," Adrian said.

No, the Iron Duke never would, Dante thought. If that duel became known, it would provoke questions that would be damaging to important men.

"Nor would Bianca," St. John said.

Certainly not. It would be easier to imagine Vergil breaking silence than his wife, Bianca.

"Nigel Kenwood has his own reasons for keeping silent," Dante said.

"Well," St. John said. "That leaves the woman."

The woman.

Dante felt his face tighten at the reference. An ugly anger entered his mind.

The woman who had used his conceit and arrogance to her own ends. The siren who kept stepping back, luring him to follow, until she had him wrecked on the rocks of his own lust. The one woman he had wanted too much, mostly because she did not yield.

He had been young and stupid and vain. The cost of victory when she let him catch her had been devastating.

"Does anyone know what became of her?" he asked.

"She remained in France for a few years. I saw her once, from a distance, when Diane and I were staying in Paris six years ago," St. John said. "I heard that she then went to Russia."

"I am sure that she has not been back to Britain," Adrian said. "Wellington all but threatened to hang her with his own rope if she returned. She is not a fool."

No, not a fool. A bitch from hell, but not a fool.

"It is possible she spoke with someone, who in turn traveled here and spoke to Siddel, but I think it unlikely," St. John said. "Not a word of what she knew ever got out. If she wanted to do harm, describing that duel was the least of it."

"I think she understands that breathing one word of any of it could be dangerous for her," Adrian said.

Dante had a memory suddenly of Adrian going into a cottage on the French coast and emerging with a woman some time later. He recalled the hard look on Adrian's face as he followed the beauty into the yard where her partner in crime had just bargained for her freedom.

"There is one other way that Siddel could have known of it," Dante said. "If he was involved in those crimes, she would have had a very good reason to send a letter directly to him, telling him what happened."

"Possibly," St. John said. "There may be no way to know for certain, unfortunately."

Maybe not, but Dante knew he would have to try now. If Siddel had been involved in the events leading to that day, he wanted to know.

He stepped forward and raised his pistol. Hugh Siddel had suddenly been complicating his life in all sorts of ways. With no planning or intention, their lives had become entwined.

Fleur formed part of that knot too. Siddel's interest in her was troubling. Had he been the one to inform Farthingstone that she was in the cottage at

Laclere Park? If so, Siddel knew Farthingstone was nearby in the county that night.

"Has either of you seen anything to suggest that Siddel has a friendship with Farthingstone?" he asked.

"I cannot recall ever seeing them in conversation," St. John said. Adrian nodded agreement.

"Whom *do* you see in conversation with Siddel?"

St. John thought about that. "He is often at the Union Club when I go there, no doubt plying his schemes among the men of trade and finance who are members. The only association of his that I noted is one with John Cavanaugh, who is a factotum of sorts to the Broughton family of Grand Alliance fame. They are sometimes head to head in quiet talks."

The Grand Alliance was the cohort of families grown wealthy off the coal of the northern counties. The Broughtons were one of the few aristocratic families to have enriched themselves along with the men of lesser birth.

Dante raised his pistol. He knew Cavanaugh from their days together at university. Perhaps he would use his own membership in the Union Club and renew that acquaintance.

He sighted his aim with careful precision.

chapter 10

H ugh Siddel moved through the knot of buyers as a bay gelding stood on display at Tattersall's. Bids bounced off the timber roof of the open-air shelter as the auction began.

Hugh made his way to a man standing on the edge of the little crowd. The man's dress and demeanor marked him as a gentleman. Carefully styled blond hair showed beneath his hat, and a small, womanish mouth pursed in his long, bland face. When he saw Hugh approach he stepped back a few more feet.

"All is in hand," Hugh said, looking at the gelding and not his companion. "I met with her two days ago. Our plans remain private, and she understands the need for secrecy to continue. She has told her husband nothing, nor will she until all is arranged."

Since all would never be arranged, that was no problem.

"An odd promise from a new bride."

"Isn't it." Hugh had been surprised and delighted by how easy it had been to extract that promise. It had opened possibilities about all kinds of other deceptions.

"And the delay?"

"She understands that such things take time." The news of Fleur's marriage had badly displeased this particular partner. It would not do to admit Fleur's impatience.

He thought about the meeting at St. Martin's, and how pretty her eyes had looked as they peered out from under the lowered edge of her hood. The poor thing had married Duclairc to avoid scandal. She obviously held no real affection for him.

If Farthingstone had not been such a coward—well, there was no profit in dwelling on that. In the least, however, Farthingstone should have gone to that cottage at once and taken her back. But no, Farthingstone had sent word to London and then waited for the bailiffs, and now look where Fleur was.

He struggled to block out images of Fleur in Duclairc's bed, but they snuck into his head anyway, inciting the livid anger that they always brought. It was infuriating that she was tied to that wastrel forever.

Or until Duclairc died, at least.

"What about Farthingstone?" his companion asked.

"He remains ignorant and useful. He knows nothing of my relationship with her on this matter, nor of mine with you."

"I do not want them reconciling. If they do and she grows impatient, she may turn to him. He can effect in a month what she wants. Thank God she did not go to him to begin with."

"Rest assured that he does not want that land sold either. Farthingstone represents no challenge or danger. He seeks control of her and that land for his own reasons. If he succeeds at Chancery, we are safe. If he doesn't, we go on as we are. She relies on me on this matter, Cavanaugh. I can keep her dangling indefinitely."

"Assuming that Duclairc doesn't get suspicious."

"He also represents no challenge or danger."

Cavanaugh angled his head and caught Siddel's eye. Hugh turned his attention from the bidding when he saw the subtle smirk on the face examining him.

"I would not dismiss the man, Siddel. He and I were at university together. Duclairc was a lot of fun, always in trouble, good humored and devil-may-care."

"It appears nothing has changed."

"Yes, well, the thing is, when it was all over it turned out he had done very well in his studies. He was the best mathematics scholar while I was there."

"So, he can add. Your point is?"

"My point is that he is far from stupid. Also, it appears that when he sets his mind to do something, he accomplishes it."

"So long as he does not turn his mind to interfering with us, what do you care?"

"As it happens, I wonder if he *has* turned his mind to that."

The suggestion startled Hugh. "What makes you say that?"

"He is a member of the Union Club, but rarely comes. I do not think I have seen him there in years. Imagine my surprise, then, to find him sitting down with me last night."

"He is friends with St. John and some others who frequent the club. No doubt he was meeting them and paused to speak with you because of your old acquaintance."

"Possibly. Mostly we spoke of the usual things, politics and horses and whatever. However, toward the end, he cleverly moved me to another topic."

"What topic was that?"

"You."

Hugh forced a bland, bored expression, although this revelation annoyed him. "He lost a large amount to me some weeks ago, and then he and I had an argument last week. If he is curious about me, it is a personal matter, and not related in any way to my business with you."

"I see that you still wear the remnants of that argument on your face. I hope that you are correct. I am out on a limb with you, and we are both now indebted to powerful men. You will receive no more payments if I think that you have lost control of the matter. Furthermore, I will have to consider other solutions if yours falls apart."

"It will not fall apart. She trusts me."

She did not trust him. Fleur admitted that to herself after several days of ruminating on her meeting with Hugh Siddel.

He had distracted her by raising those concerns about her marriage. She should have pressed him for the names of the investors before they parted. If she knew their identities, she could use their reputations to find the rest of the participants herself. It vexed her that they were so close but that Mr. Siddel expected her to simply wait while he did things in his slow, plodding way.

She could not leave it all to him, that was clear. She needed to learn who had thrown in already and do a little wooing herself. She was not without wealthy associates. Even some of the Friends had invested in such partnerships in the past. . . .

A feminine hand moved in front of her face, turning a colored fashion plate. The gesture jolted her out of a trance of contemplation on the problem.

"Now I know why mothers so enjoy it when their daughters come out," Charlotte said as she pushed an image of a gown in front of Fleur's nose. "Helping someone else buy a whole new wardrobe is almost as wonderful as purchasing it for oneself. This is even better than doing it for a daughter, since I won't have to face the bills of exchange."

Large bills, and getting bigger, Fleur thought. She sat across a table from Charlotte under the expectant eyes of the third modiste whom they had visited, choosing designs for new gowns. The day clothes had been expensive enough, but Madame Tissot had just convinced her to order three evening designs that would prove exorbitant.

She had always loved beautiful clothes, but it had been years since she had indulged in this feminine pastime. She was out of practice in defending her purse against the seduction of the colors and textures.

All of the modistes had smelled her vulnerability. One glance at her simple dress had also informed them of the work to be done. They had shown no mercy.

"That gown is perfect," Charlotte said. She had accepted the mission to relaunch Fleur in society with enthusiasm, and had planned the shopping excursions with meticulous care. "You must choose it."

She studied the plate that Charlotte favored. It showed a lusciously deep-violet ball gown. Madame Tissot cocked her tawny-haired head in question. Fleur held the plate up. Extravagant. Excessive. Gorgeous. "Yes, this one, I think."

"*Bon*, madame. A superb choice. Four ensembles of unsurpassed loveliness you have chosen. Now, perhaps you would like to see the plates for garments more intimate? The most important gowns are the ones worn in privacy with a husband, *n'est pas?*"

The modiste walked to the shelf, holding the plates.

"I think that I am quite done, thank you."

"Oh, you have to see them," Charlotte whispered. "Some are quite shocking, but in the most elegant way. I always ordered one when I had exceeded my allowance. I would wear it the same night I confessed to Mardenford that I had overdone it. It made for a very short scold."

Fleur envied the way Charlotte spoke of her late husband, Lord Mardenford. They had been young when they married, and everyone could tell they were much in love. After three happy years, however, the young baron succumbed to a fever. Charlotte had grieved intensely and then gotten on with her life. She always spoke of him freely as she did now, and one never felt that his memory was painful to her.

Three perfect years. Three years of consummate love and unity. Charlotte acted as if they had been enough to sustain her for a lifetime.

"I am suddenly exhausted and could not face another stack of plates. As it is, I wonder that I will have the presence of mind to choose fabrics."

The modiste regretfully returned the designs to their shelf. "Perhaps another day, when you come for your fittings."

"Perhaps."

Fleur scheduled those fittings, then she and Charlotte walked down to Oxford Street. After an hour at a draper, choosing fabrics, most of the afternoon was spent.

"If you are tired, we should visit that last warehouse another day," Charlotte said. "Let us go to Gunter's for an ice and check our list to see where things stand."

Charlotte's coach took them to Berkeley Square, and her footman went into the confectionery to find a server. Soon two ices arrived at the carriage for their refreshment.

"Diane St. John told me all about the brawl," Charl confided after she had enjoyed a few spoonfuls. "Well, not really a brawl, since Siddel didn't have a chance to land a blow. St. John heard about it at his club and told Diane the next morning. I am proud of my brother for thrashing Siddel after the man cast aspersions on your marriage. Very dashing, I say."

Fleur had not realized that the fight with Mr. Siddel had anything to do with her.

Charlotte handed her empty dish and spoon out to the footman, then pulled out the paper that listed the wardrobe she had decided Fleur needed. Together they ticked off the numerous purchases made the last few days. Gowns and dresses and gloves and wraps and bonnets and petticoats and shoes.

"I think that we overdid it," Fleur said.

"Nonsense. Your restraint was annoying. If self-denial has become ingrained, tell yourself that you do it for my brother. It would reflect on him if you looked unfashionable."

Charlotte stuck her nose to the list again. "Are your feelings hurt because he has been going out every night?" She asked it very casually.

"You know about that too?"

Charl glanced up with chagrin. And sympathy.

Fleur swallowed her embarrassment. She would have to learn to ignore looks like that. She must never let anyone know that her heart broke every night when Dante walked out the door. The familiar hollowness crept through her, ruining her mood.

"It is very normal, Charlotte. I am sure that Mardenford went out in the evening too."

Charl's expression said it all. That of course Mardenford had done so, but that a man's visit to his club or the theater was one thing, and Dante's long hours on the town were another. That Mardenford's company had changed with marriage, but that Dante's had not. That Dante was undoubtedly up to things that a wife might not be expected to suffer stoically.

Unless she had a special understanding with him, that is.

She wondered if Charlotte had heard some specifics, such as whether her brother had already taken another mistress or lover. She may even know the woman's name.

Fleur hoped she would be spared confidences on that. Casual indulgence with anonymous women would be bearable. An ongoing liaison with a particular woman would be torturous to know about. Just admitting the possibility provoked a desolate sadness.

"That is very understanding of you," Charlotte said through pursed lips. "I had rather hoped—"

"Do not distress yourself on my account."

"Well, he had better be discreet or I will give him a good scolding. And when Vergil returns, he will do more than that, I daresay."

Vergil. Fleur had been trying not to think about the Viscount Laclere's inevitable return.

"He is expected soon?"

"They will be delayed a week or so. I received a letter yesterday. Penelope took ill, and they will stay in Naples until she is well. Vergil wrote that we are not to worry. It is not serious, but they did not want to risk her on a sea voyage. When they get back, they are in for a wonderful surprise, because Dante asked that I not write and tell them about your wedding."

"Breaking the news in a letter may be the wiser choice."

"You do not expect him to disapprove, do you? Surely not." Charlotte patted her hand. "That is long in the past, and he and you remained good friends. He will be happy that Dante found someone as good as you."

Approval and happiness were not the emotions that Fleur anticipated seeing in Laclere when the time came to face him. He, and he alone, would suspect immediately just how thoroughly the marriage was a fraud.

"Now," Charl said. "Tell me about your jewels so we can decide if you need to buy or hire some more."

chapter II

The meeting to plan the boys' school ended at two o'clock. Fleur escorted her ten guests to the door in order to have a few private words with some of them.

They took their leave with the same blank-eyed graciousness that had marked their behavior since they arrived. Everyone was pretending not to notice that Fleur's dress today contrasted starkly with her normal ensembles.

No one had commented upon the fact that her blush, wide-skirted muslin set her apart from their own practical dark hues. The women had refrained from asking what had brought about this change in her.

That was because they didn't need to. As they filed down to the street, the reason drove up in a handsome open landau. Their critical eyes took in the elegant carriage and the dashing, beautiful man holding the reins.

Fleur read their minds. The unspoken consensus in this circle of society was obvious. Dante Duclairc, the wastrel and libertine, had turned Fleur Monley's head and was in the process of ruining her completely. The implications for her charitable work had coerced them to develop a schedule for building the school. They wanted it done before Dante spent all the money.

Fleur welcomed the new determination on the school. Unfortunately, it had been over a week since her meeting with Mr. Siddel, and she had received no indication that he had yet found the two additional partners. Her mind considered her options while she sent off her guests.

Dante hopped down and greeted the departing Friends and vicars and reform ladies.

"You move in elevated circles in your charitable work, Fleur," he said when they were gone. "I did not know that you counted the famous Mrs. Fry among your conspirators."

"Her judgment is respected, and I have never had reason to regret supporting her causes. She was kind enough to agree to be a trustee of the school."

"The members of Parliament whom she petitions on her reform projects think that she is an eccentric nuisance."

"No more than I am, Dante."

He laughed, and turned her toward the carriage. "What do you think of it? Old Timothy over in the borough got it, along with the matched pair. Brought it in from Hastings two days ago, and it is as fine as he promised. The horses are better than I expected, and two more are coming. They will do for the coach when it is finished too."

The carriage and its brass fittings had been scrubbed and polished until it looked like new. Two strong young chestnuts glistened in front.

A young man, no more than eighteen, held the horses. He had come in the landau with Dante and now surveyed the house with naked curiosity. He had a half-starved look to him. An old brown livery coat hung on his skinny frame. Wisps of straw hair poked out from beneath a shapeless, low-crowned felt hat.

"That is Luke," Dante explained quietly. "He loiters about Timothy's yard, picking up odd hires. He followed me all around town the last few days once he learned that I was buying a carriage. He offered to serve as coachman and groom for a chamber and meals."

"Are you sure he can manage it? He appears almost frail."

"He is stronger than he looks. He worked in the pits up north as a lad. I have decided to try him for a few weeks, while we decide if we want more servants for the equipage. He will look presentable once I clean him up."

Luke noticed her examining him and looked away. He tried to appear as if he did not care what she decided, but his drawn, pinch-featured face and cautious eyes betrayed his desperation.

It touched her that Dante had taken pity on the young man. "He can live in the room atop the carriage house, of course. However, we should pay wages even if he is young and inexperienced."

"More experienced than you would think. He has been dawdling around stables all his life. He has a natural hand with the animals and has handled a pair before. Get in and we'll see how he does. He can drive us."

He called to Luke and then handed her into the carriage.

"Where are we going?" she asked while Luke moved the horses to a slow walk.

"I thought that we'd take a turn in the park first, then go to the city. Hampton wants a meeting, and I sent word that we would visit him in his chambers."

Luke drove through the narrow streets very cautiously. He took the first corner too broadly and refused to permit the horses more than a funereal pace.

Dante sat beside her, keeping one eye on the new coachman's progress. When they got to the park he instructed Luke to bring the pair to a trot.

The horses took the signal with gusto. An unexpected swerve to the left sent Fleur sliding up against Dante.

He moved his arm around her and calmly gave his new coachman some pointers.

"He has never handled a landau before, has he?" she asked.

"He is doing fairly well. Don't worry. If he loses control, I will take over." He took her hand in reassurance. "I will not let you come to harm. Take the path on the left, Luke, and keep them on it. Watch the right horse. He is the one who tries to break stride."

Getting on the path squashed Fleur closer to Dante. His embrace tightened. It felt very snug and secure in his arm and she did not try to move away. He continued giving Luke instructions.

"Your day has been pleasant?" he asked blandly, as if every curve on the path did not mold them closer together. The proximity, even for safety's sake, had started a silly tingling all through her. He began absently caressing her inner wrist with his thumb, in a slow manner that suggested he was not even aware of his action.

She was. A significant portion of her was aware of nothing else. The slow, velvety strokes mesmerized her.

She struggled to find her voice. "The meeting was most productive. Normally we talk for hours and accomplish little, but today everyone seemed intent on moving forward. If we are going to keep to the schedule that we set for opening the school, I will have to transfer that land to the trustees and also sell some property in the next few months to pay for the building."

"Perhaps you should mention that to Hampton when we see him. He could help."

Up and down, circling, circling—the touch on her wrist sent shivers up her arm, into her body. "I need to decide which land first. I ultimately intend to sell those farms around the school itself, but for now I think the ones in Surrey that my father left me would be easier. What do you think?"

"I am incapable of giving advice, since I was not aware that you hold land in Surrey and know nothing about its quality or income. Unlike most new husbands, I never received an accounting of your property and worth."

"That was an oversight. Things happened so quickly. I apologize. Of course you have a right to know."

"Not really. It is yours to control. One more way in which our union is out of the ordinary, and I assure you that I do not mind." Something in his tone suggested that he did mind, a little.

The wandering caress had her thoroughly flustered now. She was sure her face was flushing. She should extricate her wrist from this tiny assault, but she could barely move. Nor did she really want it to end.

She tried to distract herself. "You will be happy to learn that you were correct about Charlotte's help. Two days ago I accompanied her on a call on Lady Rossmore and she indicated that she would invite us to her ball two weeks hence. Do you think I should accept?"

"Certainly. You will attend looking beautiful and heavenly and completely unaddled. It will show Farthingstone's claims for the nonsense they are."

She thought about entering a ballroom for the first time in ten years and facing those curious eyes. They would have all heard Gregory's stories. Her stepfather might even be there. Her appearance, her manner, even her conversation would be scrutinized.

She instinctively cowered a little nearer to Dante. He had been occupied with giving Luke directions to the streets, but he turned into the subtle movement and looked down at her.

His face, so close that she could feel his breath on her cheek, blotted out her sense of everything else. His sensual vitality slid around her as if he wrapped them both in one cape.

She swallowed hard, very conscious of his arm surrounding her. And the hard body pressed along her side, snug against the side of her breast. And the light, delicious touch on her wrist.

Gentle amusement sparkled in his eyes, as if he recognized her foolish, feminine reaction. Of course he did. He had seen it often enough in his life.

She saw something else in his long gaze, however. A dangerous, calculating light. Like a casual test of his effect, he had deliberately released his masculine power. She could only look at him, as stunned as a deer mesmerized by a bright torch.

He lifted her hand and gently kissed her inner wrist. It sent a shock through her whole body. "You will attend looking beautiful and I will come with you. You will not face it alone. We are in this together, Fleur."

He kissed her lips, and lingered a long moment. His power quivered into her through the connection and spread mercilessly, making her tremble. It was all she could do not to go limp.

She stared at him when he finally released her mouth and retreated.

"You do not have to look so horrified. We agreed that I am permitted the occasional chaste kiss." His smoldering eyes revealed that he knew the kiss had not been very chaste, nor her reaction especially horrified. The latter darkly pleased him, for reasons she could not fathom.

His embrace relaxed slightly, like a signal that she could pull away if she chose.

She shifted so they were not pressed to each other. Although every instinct shouted for her to get away, she refused to scoot to the refuge of the landau's far corner like some frightened goose. She didn't really want to. Her womanhood had relished the closeness, and the touch and kiss, even though he cruelly played with her.

"It is unfolding just as I expected," Mr. Hampton said. "No one has any idea what to do, so a hearing on your wife's ability to make sound judgments is indefinitely delayed."

"And Farthingstone?" Dante asked. He stood behind Fleur's chair in Hampton's inner chamber at Lincoln's Inn. The solicitor sat on the other side of the desk, playing with the feather of a quill.

"Your wife's stepfather had such a violent reaction to Brougham's announcement that we feared he would suffer apoplexy."

"Only he didn't. That would strike him dumb, and he has hardly stopped talking. However, by my question I was asking whether he will give up now."

"I doubt that. I make a handsome living because most men refuse to back down. His intention, I am sure, is to first establish your wife's incapacity to make contracts, and then take that to the Church to request an annulment of the marriage."

"Might he succeed?" Fleur asked.

"Possibly. Eventually. Slowly."

"How slowly?"

"I will explain how things stand. The hearing has been delayed so that the jurisdictional confusion can be untangled. The court needs to decide if Farthingstone has standing at all and whether this should go to the Church at once. Normally, with you married, he wouldn't and it should, but since he is claiming you could not reasonably enter into such a contract—well, you see the wedge he is using. There will be a search for precedents, etcetera, etcetera. Short of your doing something outrageous, something that makes your lack of judgment explicit, I expect everyone will take a good while to deliberate this situation."

"So the argument that the marriage itself is proof of a lack of judgment will not stand?" she asked.

"I doubt that will signify much." Hampton fixed his gaze to her. "It would help if you did nothing to provoke Farthingstone's concerns. We do not want him pestering Chancery to the point that they actually do something just to get rid of the nuisance. You should behave very sensibly."

"Dante thinks that it would help if I reestablish myself in society. Then everyone can see how normal I am."

"That is the very advice I intended to give you today. With Farthingstone spreading tales, you need to be present among those who matter to counter the effect of the rumors. Furthermore, you should curb your gifts to charity. Pull back on the largesse for a while."

"That will not be possible. I am committed to build a school. In fact, I will want your advice regarding the sale of property—"

"Would this be the Durham property that we discussed? Your buyer is ready to move?"

She did not like the sharp look he gave her along with the question. Mr. Hampton had been very suspicious of that sale when they spoke of it while Dante was in gaol. She did not want his curiosity infecting Dante. "I am referring to other property."

"Yet more sales of land? I do not advise it. Not now. If there is another significant disposition of land it will only give Farthingstone dangerous ammunition."

"But the plans for the school are set."

"I cannot stop you, madame, but it is my advice to put it off for a spell." This time the sharp look went past her, to Dante. *She is your wife. You must make sure she listens to reason,* that look said.

"How long a spell?" Dante asked.

"I would think that, barring any surprises, the court will have this thoroughly buried in a year, eighteen months on the outside."

"A year! We hope to have the school almost completed by then."

"The slowness of the courts works in our favor. Of course, there is one way in which matters will be settled at once. If you are blessed with a child, this will end immediately. The issue of your judgment becomes moot then. The Church will never set aside a marriage for such a reason if there are children."

"I expect that is true," Dante said.

"Most definitely."

Dante offered his hand to help her to rise. "Then we must double our prayers for a child, isn't that so, my dear?"

Dante aimed Fleur away from the carriage when they emerged from the building. "Let us take a turn before we ride back. I wish to speak to you and do not want Luke to overhear."

He guided her firmly down Chancery Lane so she could not disagree. She looked as if she would like to.

Her glance darted to where he tucked her arm against his body. Wariness flickered in her eyes as she gave him a sidelong gaze. She was thinking about that kiss. He could just tell.

A mild breeze swam around them. It contained the freshness of spring, and even the smells of the old city could not contaminate it. Its rise and fall fluttered the ribbons on Fleur's bonnet. It was one of her new ones, a pretty little heart-shaped design that sat back on her crown and tied under her chin. The bonnet was part of the new wardrobe that was arriving at the house.

The dress she wore, with its low, broad neckline and full sleeves and skirt, complimented her form in ways her old ensembles never had. Her beauty had bloomed again as she prepared to reenter society. She wore the new garments even in the house, and now wore her hair in a fashionable style. She was enjoying the indulgence more than she would ever admit.

So was he. Sometimes when he returned from his calls he came upon her unexpectedly and she took his breath away. Some detail would mesmerize him—a lock of dark hair skimming her cheek, or the glow of her ivory skin above her bodice. As they chatted he would burn relentlessly, the flame getting larger and hotter until all he wanted to do was pick her up and carry her to bed.

She cast him another sidelong look and his own gaze met hers. During the next five steps of their stroll an entire love affair played out in his head.

In flashing fantasies of startling clarity, he nuzzled and nipped the lovely, flushed ear just visible within the frame of her bonnet. He licked the tight nipples of the breasts pressing against that blush muslin. He lowered the petticoats and skirt and laid her back on a bed so that he could kiss down her naked body and spread her thighs and use his tongue to claim her deepest passion. She resisted none of it in the secret world of his mind. She accepted and joined and begged.

The shout of a passing peddler pulled him out of his reverie. Or perhaps it was the stiffening of Fleur's arm, as if she guessed what he was thinking.

"Hampton's advice is worth heeding. There is nothing else for it, Fleur. You must delay the plans for the school."

"I cannot do that. There is a schedule."

"Explain that the schedule must change because you must not sell any property at this time. The poor will always be with us. Your school will be needed a year later."

"I do not want to change the schedule."

"I must insist that you do."

"You are so confident in Mr. Hampton's judgment?"

"I am confident in my own. His merely agrees with mine."

"Except it is *my* judgment that rules in this matter. You agreed that I would have full control over the management of this part of my inheritance."

He was beginning to hate much of what he had agreed to, and her pointed reference made his mood sharpen. "I am fully aware of the limitations imposed by that settlement, I promise you. However, you sought this marriage for a reason. It is imperative that Farthingstone be given no cause to make a case that will justify an annulment. As to my interfering, I did not bargain away the duty to protect you. Turn your attention to other charities. It is the sale of land that is at issue, not your other contributions."

She pulled her hand free and stepped away from him. Their suddenly stationary bodies formed two obstructing boulders in the flow of the crowd. Passersby jostled and bumped and cursed, but Fleur was oblivious to them.

She faced him with eyes glistening with tears of frustration. "You do not understand at all. This is not like other charities."

"The ultimate goal of them all is the same. So is the satisfaction."

"I never felt *any* satisfaction in the rest of them. I only got involved in such things because I had to do *something* since I wasn't going to have a family. I thought charity work would make me feel my life had some meaning, but it really didn't. Not until I thought of this school."

"Putting food on tables certainly has as much meaning as building a school. There is so much need that you can find many good causes."

"This will be *mine*. It will be something that *I* conceived and saw through. These boys will not be nameless, faceless, deserving souls. I will watch them learn and grow. They will be the only children that I will ever have. Just planning for it makes me feel alive and young instead of old and drab. Can you imagine what it is like to live years with no purpose and then to find one that is exciting and vital?"

"Yes, I can."

"Then you know that the notion of possibly losing it because of a delay— it is unthinkable. I must go forward."

"I must forbid you to do so for now."

Her chin tilted up. "You have no right to forbid."

"I am your husband."

"Not really."

So, there it was, the part of this arrangement that definitely needed clarification. Soon.

"If you send money to radicals, if you use your income to buy an elephant, I will not say a word. However, if your plans threaten the security you sought from me, then I will exercise my rights as your husband. I am doing so now. I say it again. I forbid you to sell any property in the near future, and if that means that the school must be delayed, so be it."

She glared at him. Tears made her rage sparkle.

She turned on her heel and marched back toward the carriage.

As he fell into step alongside, he glanced at her angry, distraught expression. He thought about her long years of being the saintly Fleur Monley who had put herself on the shelf.

The world thought she had answered a special calling. Such a life was supposed to bring enormous contentment. From what Fleur had just said, it barely sustained her.

She would not allow him to help her into the carriage. She refused to look at him when he joined her.

"I understand that you are disappointed, but there is no choice at this time," he said. "I am sorry, but you must obey me on this."

chapter 12

F leur cocked her head and examined Luke. He stood in the middle of her morning room. Instead of the second-hand livery that he had worn since he came, a brand-new brown coat and white trousers encased his thin frame. The brim of a high hat shadowed his gray eyes.

Luke moved his arms and looked down his body. "Seems a bit tight."

"You are accustomed to clothes that are too big for you. That is why this coat feels tight in comparison."

Mixed with Luke's skepticism was a heavy dose of awe. Fleur could tell that he had never had a single garment made new for him before. Like most of the people in his world, he lived in the castoffs of others.

"I'll look fine holding the ribbons, won't I? I'm getting better with four-in-hand too. Mr. Duclairc has been helping me learn and says I'm getting expert at it quickly."

He examined his new clothes, half-awkward boy and half-cocky man, alternating between enthusiasm and caution.

Suddenly he looked up and his gaze met hers. Naked gratitude crossed the space to where she sat.

"There is another shirt in that package, and some other things," she said, pointing to a wrapped bundle on the table.

He felt the bundle, frowning. "One shirt is enough. I'll be needing to send my wages north, you see, and could wash the one shirt and then—"

"The cost of the shirts will not come from your wages. All of this is a gift from Mr. Duclairc. You will still have wages to send home."

He pondered that, flushing and frowning. "They say you are an angel, they do. I think they are right."

"You are here through my husband's generosity, not mine."

"If you had objected, he wouldn't have done it. You knew I wasn't really fit for the work."

"You will be fine for the work."

"I hope so, since I wasn't fit for the pits. Kept coughing when I went in, like the dust sucked right into me. Others don't, but I coughed so bad I couldn't catch a breath." He shook his head. "Not a bad life, even if it was dirty and long. Fine thing when a son of a collier ain't fit for the pits."

"Well, you will be fit for this work. Now, no more about my being an angel. The servants are foolish to speak of me that way, and I do not want to hear it from you."

"Not the servants here who say it. It's them in the north that do. The women, mostly. My mother told me about it last summer when I visited, how the money you sent kept food on the table when the men went out and didn't work. An angel had sent them food, she said." He grinned sheepishly. "Imagine my surprise to learn I was in service to one and the same. Could have knocked me over with a breeze when the cook told me your unmarried name."

Fleur had never met anyone connected to the families who received that money. "It helped, then, a little? It makes me very happy to know that."

"No one was eating meat, but no one in their village starved." He patted down his torso, proudly feeling the new coat. "I'll look the blood when I drive Mr. Duclairc tonight, that's for sure. He said he'll be using the coach."

His reference to the night had her heart sinking. If Dante wanted the coach, he must have some very special plans.

It was taking longer to overcome this silly jealousy than she had expected.

"He will be proud to have you at the ribbons," she said as she left. "His friend will be suitably impressed."

"There she is. The third peasant from the right. Hair like flames," McLean said. "Her name is Helen. Came up from Bath two months ago, where she had done some small roles. Liza has taken her under her wing."

McLean's mistress, Liza, had the leading role, but the red-haired Helen almost upstaged her. Her sloe-eyed, milky-skinned, fine-boned beauty shone amidst the anonymous village folk populating the play's last act.

"Two months and no protector?" Dante asked. He sat beside McLean in a box favored for its good view of the women displayed on stage.

"Liza has encouraged her to set high standards and avoid any casual dalliance that may cheapen her. Good advice. She has the potential to be the mistress to a duke."

"If Liza is grooming her to be mistress to a duke, she will try to be very expensive."

McLean laughed. "She will think that your face is as good as two hundred a month. Nor is she ready for dukes yet. With your change in fortune, you can afford her now."

Probably. He had never arranged such a formal affair before. He wondered what Fleur would say if she discovered he was contemplating such a thing. Nothing. Nothing at all. She assumed that he would take mistresses. She counted on him doing so. If he kissed her again as he had in the carriage three days ago, she might even demand outright that he get on with it.

Not that she hadn't liked that kiss. Which made the whole situation only more hellish.

"What do you think?" McLean asked. "She is well disposed toward meeting you."

"We will see."

"You do not sound very enthusiastic. What more is there to see? She is a jewel."

"I may not care for her character."

"*Character?* You are going to keep her. If she had a good character, she would not let you." He threw up his hands in exasperation. "This must be your wife's influence at work."

"Do not criticize Fleur if you value our friendship."

"What ho! Do I hear anger? Chivalrous protection? An odd reaction regarding a wife whom you spend every night pretending does not exist. It is none of my business, but—"

"You are damn right. It is none of your damn business."

A tense silence throbbed between them. On the stage the play began winding toward its *dénouement*.

"It *is* none of my business," McLean finally said in an oddly gentle tone. "However, if you are here tonight, it is not hard to deduce what the problem is. I can offer no advice, except to say that I have always assumed that decent women, especially maidens of some maturity, require great patience."

"You do not know what you are talking about."

"Of course not. I have never bothered with either decent women or maidens. However, a lady who was both has taken you on as a husband and deserves whatever patience is required."

"I do not need your guidance about women, especially my wife."

"Mere hours ago I would have agreed. Yet you are so sullen and ill-tempered that one might think you are experiencing pangs of guilt. I find myself moved to tell you—and I assure you that the impulse astounds me—to go home to the sweet lady who is waiting for you."

"It is laughable for you to lecture me on marital duty like some bishop."

"Well, this bishop will be sore annoyed if his lover gets angry tonight because his friend insults a certain red-haired beauty. Now, the curtain descends soon. Are you coming? Then shake your insufferable mood. I don't want to have to make excuses for you like you are some raw boy up from the country for the first time."

McLean led the way down the staircase and to the corridor behind the stage. He pushed them through the clutch of men waiting to shower hopeful flattery on the actresses. He entered Liza's dressing room like he owned it, and Dante followed.

They heard the roar when the play ended and then commotion in the corridor. Liza and Helen took their time coming. McLean occupied himself poking around pots of paint.

The door opened and Liza and Helen entered. Both carried several bouquets of flowers bestowed by admirers. Liza dumped hers on a chair and ran to McLean's arms. Helen's slanted eyes examined Dante from behind her colorful blooms.

His own gaze sized her up quickly. Her finely molded face would become either more beautiful or sadly hard as she aged. She exuded an awareness of her beauty, and a cautious reserve about bestowing her charms. She was more refined and inexperienced than Dante had expected.

Liza broke McLean's kiss. "We are being rude, McLean. This is Mr. Duclairc, Helen. The gentleman whom I wanted you to meet."

Dante said the right things and smiled the right smile. Helen looked in his eyes and her caution melted.

That was that. The decisions were all his now.

"We need to dress, gentlemen. Helen's things are here too, McLean, so you cannot stay. Out you both go."

The corridor was emptying of admirers. "You seem more yourself suddenly," McLean said.

Definitely so. However, the Helens of the world were child's play. There was no challenge if you knew that you would not fail. And no illusions about what you won.

He would welcome the clarity of cost and benefit that would mark this arrangement. Some blunt sensuality would be a relief.

"I have a supper waiting in my chambers. Will you join Liza and me?" McLean offered.

"Has Helen ever seen your chambers? I did not think so. Better not, then. She is still capable of being shocked."

"You think so? How like you to perceive the nuances. It is probably why Liza thought you would suit her."

The door opened and Liza emerged. "Helen is still dressing. She will join us shortly."

McLean took her arm. "I think not. Duclairc has other plans. We will dine alone."

They ambled off, and Dante turned to the door. He stared at its panels and pictured the woman behind it. He had rather counted on her being coarse and vulgar. Or at least experienced and calculating.

You should go home to the sweet lady who is waiting for you.

He pictured Fleur in her new sitting room, writing her letters. Not waiting for him at all, but instead relieved that he was not at home. Glad to be free of the hunger that he could barely hide.

If she were completely cold, he could bear it. If she did not tremble when he kissed her, he would cease doing so. But her sensuality was not dead. It was very much alive, just incomplete.

The knowledge of that was slowly driving him mad.

He felt her body beside him in that bed.

He remembered her gasps of pleasure behind the hedge.

He saw her dismay after that last kiss in the carriage.

He pushed the paneled door open.

Liza's maid was just finishing with the fastenings on Helen's pale yellow gown. Helen tossed her flaming hair over a milky shoulder as she turned her head on his entrance.

He gestured the maid aside and finished the fastenings himself. Helen blushed but did not object.

"Liza has left with McLean. I will take you home in my carriage, if that suits you."

She reached for a long blue silk shawl and draped it over her arms. "Thank you."

He escorted her toward the carriage. She had dabbed herself with scent, and its musky, exotic odor wafted toward him like a hot breeze.

Fleur rarely used scent, and when she did it was a light floral one that reminded him of that fresh afternoon in the grass by the hedge.

"You are enjoying London?" he asked.

She responded at length. Her explanation of learning to manage the city's size and complexity filled their walk to where he had told Luke to wait with the new coach.

Luke gaped when he saw the beautiful Helen. He barely hid his discomfort at aiding in his master's infidelity.

Well, the lad had better get used to it. Dante gave Luke directions to Helen's home, then climbed into the closed carriage and sat beside his guest.

"Liza said that your brother is a peer," she said.

"He is a viscount."

"She said that he married an opera singer."

"His wife did not begin performing until after they had been married several years."

She laughed. "But, of course, Mr. Duclairc. It could never happen any other way. It was very generous of him to permit it, however. Very understanding."

"Many think it was insane and scandalous."

"An unusual man, to have permitted it knowing many would think that. Don't you agree?"

"She will be performing in London before Christmas. Perhaps you will be able to hear her."

Helen let the shawl drop down her milky shoulders. "This is a wonderful coach," she said with admiration. "My father had a carriage. No so fine as this, but it could take a pair."

"He does no longer?"

"He and my mother died several years ago."

Hell.

"I shouldn't have said that, should I?" she said.

"I am interested in learning about you."

"Not about things like that. Now you are afraid that I am going to pour out a tale about being left destitute with three little sisters and claim that I really would not have accepted your company except for my dire straits."

"Is that your situation?"

She laughed again. It made her scent fill the carriage. "I was an only child, and left with a modest but livable income. The income gave me the freedom to go on stage, which is what I wanted to do. Rest assured, Mr. Duclairc, you are not taking advantage of me. I know what I am about." Her hand slid up his chest to his neck. She leaned forward until her breasts pressed his arm. "I will show you."

She kissed and caressed him. Not with great art, but it was enough. His arousal quickly traveled a well-worn trail. The pleasure suffused him, as familiar as a boyhood home.

However, like a well-known place that one visits anew after an absence, he saw both its charms and its worst flaws. Empty. No real intimacy. He had never noticed that before, or never minded, at least. The warmth was only physical and the excitement almost . . . lonely.

He sensed that more than thought it. The raw hunger pounding through him permitted little consciousness. He simply possessed a new awareness.

It wasn't because of what she was, or planned to be. It had been the same with all of them. There had been little emotion in any of it, all these years. That had been a choice. A calm, deliberate choice.

He sensed the vacancy for another reason. He knew what it lacked because he had tasted what it could be. With Fleur. Not just behind the hedge, although that had been glorious. Even riding in the coach, holding her hand.

Lying beside her in that bed. Reading a book on the other side of the library. In comparison to those pleasures, this old one seemed almost bleak.

Things were moving quickly and Helen displayed no hesitation. When he instinctively stopped his hands and cooled the kisses, she was surprised.

"We will be on your street soon," he said.

That appeased her. She rested in his embrace, pecking little kisses on his cheek.

"Was Bath your home when you were a girl?"

"A village near it."

"Did you have a lover there?"

"I am not a virgin, if that is what you want to know. You are in for no pleasant surprises."

"Unpleasant surprises, you mean. I do not ravish innocents."

"You don't, do you? That is rather sweet."

"Did your lover offer to marry you?"

"Of course. He thought that he had to."

"Maybe he wanted to get married."

"Well, I didn't."

She kissed him again, aggressively. Her hair feathered his face and her scent saturated his breath, inciting needs too long denied. Her body pressed, offering the oblivion of pleasure.

The carriage stopped in front of an attractive house on a street behind Leicester Square. He guessed that Helen paid a high price to live at this address, but it was money well spent. It let men know that she was a woman to be taken seriously, and a mistress with certain ambitions and expectations.

Luke opened the door and set down the steps. Dante ignored his coachman's stony expression and handed Helen out. He escorted her to the house.

"You do not intend to stay, do you?" she asked, leading him into the reception hall. She had tastefully decorated it with framed engravings and a good table.

"What makes you think that?"

"You gave your coachman no instructions. He can hardly hold the horses out there all night."

She faced him, her beauty enhanced by the glow coming from the brace of candles left lit on the table.

He did not lie to himself. He wanted her. At least part of him did. But the part that didn't truly did not.

"No, I will not be staying."

For an instant she looked very young and vulnerable. Then she drew herself straight and gazed at him boldly. "You think that I am too inexperienced."

"Yes, but that is easily remedied, isn't it? It really has nothing to do with you."

She moved closer and laid a hand on his chest. "I would like to be with you. I will do anything that you want."

"Do you think that my face and my birth make it different? That you can pretend it is other than it is? Ask Liza what it is really about, and what men sometimes want."

"I already know."

He removed her hand from his chest. "You should go back to your village near Bath."

She snatched her hand away. "Has the famous lover become a reformer?"

He turned to the door. "Go back to your village and marry the man to whom you gave your innocence in love, if that was how it was. If you have known that, this can only be sordid."

He was crossing the threshold when he heard her response. "Not with you, I do not think so. If you change your mind, you know where to find me."

Hers was not the door that he wanted left open, but he lacked the strength to slam it shut. His frustration gave him one hell of an argument all the way to the coach.

Luke waited there, wearing a grin of relief. Dante wanted to punch the young coachman in his glistening teeth.

"Home," he snarled, jumping in the coach before his body could have its way and run back.

He closed his eyes and forced his warring reactions into a truce.

He began laughing, at himself.

Damn, but he was becoming a ridiculous figure. Here he was, leaving a woman who offered him anything he wanted, to return to a woman who could give him nothing at all. His freedom had become an unwelcome burden, and his life a marvelous joke.

In marrying his saint, he had made a bargain with the devil. Tasting paradise had thrust him into hell.

And the worst of it, the absolutely worst part, was that he couldn't wait to see her tomorrow.

chapter 13

The window in Fleur's sitting room faced the back garden. She sat in the dark on its deep ledge, letting the cool breeze tickle her skin and hair while she listened to the music.

The house next door, grander than hers by half, had a garden of its own separated from hers by a brick wall. The barrister who lived there with his young wife was entertaining tonight, and the music came from their drawing room. She could see the open doors from up here and the guests who strolled on the terrace and ventured down into the garden. Bits of laughter and conversation drifted on the breeze.

They sounded so gay. She pictured herself among them, lighthearted and carefree.

Despite the low commotion next door, she heard the carriage rumble down the alley. At the far end of the garden, a coach lamp twinkled along the wall and stopped. Then a brighter light shone through the distant window of the carriage house. Soon the hulking form of the coach obscured the window. The light moved away, toward the stable in the mews.

Luke was back. She pictured him removing his new hat and coat and unharnessing the horses. He would take a long time rubbing them down, making sure he did it perfectly. He would want to be certain that Dante would not find fault.

Dante. Her ears sought the sound of him in the house. She listened to the void and comprehended its meaning. Luke was back, but not his passenger. Dante was spending the night elsewhere. Early tomorrow morning Luke would hitch up the horses again and go fetch him from his lover's bed.

The sickly sensation swelled inside her. She gritted her teeth and forced it down. He had probably done this before. She made it a point to retire long before she expected him back so that she wouldn't know. Tonight the music had distracted her, however, so she did know.

The chamber suddenly felt confining and hot. Her own body did too, as if her skin encased a restless and anxious spirit. The breeze promised the refreshment of more than her body.

She went to her bedchamber for her robe. She would go sit in the garden and enjoy the party from behind the wall. Maybe the music and laughter would soothe her.

He noticed her as soon as she emerged from the house. She looked like an apparition floating in the moonlight as she strolled among the plantings. Not a ghost, however, despite her light garments. More like an angel.

It was not a formal garden that framed her slow, aimless walk. No neat beds such as one might expect of the tidy Fleur Monley. Instead, spring flowers peeked out from under shrubs and blazed amidst carpets of ivy. Only by the wall could one find a little patch of nothing but blooms.

He watched her from the shadows beneath a tree where he sat on a stone bench. As she passed nearby he saw that she was wearing the pink robe. Its pale color caught the moonlight almost as much as the billowing white gown beneath it, making her glow. Her flowing hair made dark streaks against the luminous cloth. The long row of buttons, dark blue as he remembered, formed so many dots from her neck to her breasts.

The musicians next door stopped playing. Fleur halted, as if she required the notes to move.

A waltz began. She looked to the wall and listened. Her body began to sway to the music.

Her arms rose and she swung around, dancing a few steps with an invisible partner. She stopped abruptly and her arms fell to her sides, like she feared someone would see her foolishness.

The music would not release her. Her arms rose again and this time she succumbed. Stepping and swirling, she floated among the plantings, dancing an angel's waltz.

He rose and walked toward her. She saw him and froze in mid-turn. The bed gown kept moving, its billows of drapery sliding around her legs.

He opened his arms, offering to take her ghost partner's place. She hesitated, then took the step that brought them together.

They waltzed in the moonlight. The narrow garden paths confined them, giving him an excuse to pull her closer. Only thin cloth separated his palm from her warm back. Their bodies grazed each other as they turned and flowed.

She looked so lovely. Her unbound hair flew out in the turns and the gown fluttered around his legs. Her small smile showed in the moonlight, and her joy in the dance spiraled along with their movements.

It both lasted forever and ended too soon. The waltz's conclusion seemed abrupt, a rude interference in the swirling ecstasy. Dancers frozen in time, they faced each other motionlessly, still poised for more.

No music came. Voices in the other garden increased as guests came outdoors to refresh themselves. He felt Fleur's breaths slow as her body calmed from the waltz's exertion.

Awareness of their formal embrace broke through her fading euphoria. She glanced around, suddenly self-conscious. Her hand fell from his arm and she began turning away.

"Thank you. It has been years. I had forgotten how enjoyable dancing could be."

He did not release her other hand. It stopped her short, body half turned away.

"I think that I will retire now," she said.

"No."

"It is very late. I am tired."

"No," he said more firmly. "It is a beautiful night, and I want your company."

"I don't think—"

He touched her lips with his fingers, gently silencing her. He did not want to hear her denials, because they would not make any difference. He could not let her leave. He had known he would not as soon as he saw her enter the garden.

He let his touch linger and caressed her lips, treasuring the sensation of their delicate warmth. The pools of her eyes stared cautiously.

He drew her to him. He shouldn't, but he was beyond really choosing this.

The embrace made her tremble in that subtle, innocent way of hers. Any shreds of conscience disappeared as those little tremors saturated him. He held her feminine warmth tightly, relishing the soft curves under his hands and against his chest.

She reacted. He heard it in her breath and felt it in her body. She also resisted the reaction. Her hands held his shoulders, neither accepting nor denying.

He began to kiss her. With a little gasp she angled her face away.

"It is just a kiss, darling. We agreed it was permitted."

"Like friends. Friends do not kiss when embracing like this."

"Husbands and wives do, and we are married."

"Not truly."

"Truly enough for this."

He kissed her. Lights burst in his head and blood. Somehow he found the restraint not to consume her. Instead, he lured her with small pleasures before finally demanding more intimacy.

Bliss. Holding her, caressing her, pressing her. Tasting, exploring, entering. Sensation layered on sensation. The warmth deepened and spread and engulfed. His body and soul exulted in the pleasure and intimacy.

He wanted more. It could never just be a kiss. Not tonight. His mind filled with images of everything he wanted, most of which he could never have.

But he could have her at least. For a while. In his arms. He could have whatever passion she could know, and whatever closeness she could give.

He kissed more deeply, pulling her arousal higher. Despite her trembling, her body arched toward him. He caressed the swells of her hips and cupped her bottom with his hands and pressed her closer. She turned her head away with a gasp.

"You do not have to be afraid. You are safe with me. I know what you cannot give."

"Then you should not . . ."

"Probably not. But you are beautiful in this night, and I have no defense against that."

His desire demonstrated how little defense he had. Hunger cracked through him like a clap of thunder. He cradled her head, holding it to a fierce, reckless ravishment.

Her objections melted away. She molded into his embrace with shy compliance and slid her arms around his neck. The fast rhythm of her heart beat against his chest, and the lovely sighs of her breath played in his ear.

He broke the kiss and held her to him, bending to kiss the fluttering pulse in her neck. He glanced around the garden, half blind. He should stop, but he couldn't.

The music began again. He took her hand and led her toward the wall, right into the bed of flowers. He shrugged off his coat and laid it out. Lowering to his knees, he tugged gently on her hand, coaxing her to join him.

She resisted, and glanced over her shoulder to the carriage house.

"Luke is asleep by now, and there is that tree outside his window anyway. He could see nothing," he reassured. "Sit here and enjoy the music and night with me."

She gazed down at him and her confusion was palpable. He pulled her to her knees in front of him, a devil tempting a saint.

"You are as safe as behind the hedge in Durham. More so. At least fifteen people laugh and talk on the other side of this brick wall. But if nary a one did, you would still be safe." He moved so that he sat with his back against the wall. "Sit with me."

His position must have reassured her. She crawled over and sat beside him with her legs cushioned in the flowers. "It is their first large party," she said. "He remarried two months ago. A young girl. She is his third wife. His last one died two years ago."

"Was she your friend?"

She nodded. "I knew it was going badly. You can just sense it, when a woman is lying in and things are taking too long. The house was like a tomb for two days. Catherine had been so happy as her time approached, but I was so afraid for her." She turned her head, as if she could see through the wall. "I am glad he waited this long to remarry. I think it means he held some affection for her, don't you?"

"I think so, yes."

It wasn't much reassurance, but she seemed thankful for it. She rested her head on his shoulder. "Luke was grateful to receive the livery today."

"He looked very smart in it, and very proud."

"It is very nice that you are giving him this chance. You can be very kind sometimes."

He turned his body toward hers and slid his hand into her hair. "Sometimes, Fleur, but not always. Not tonight." He kissed her the way he had wanted to for weeks. Frustration drove him and it turned hungry and hard and then consuming and furious. The passion that was not dead responded until, when he finally released her, she was breathless.

He did not give her time to think or object but lifted her onto his lap so that her back rested against his chest and he could embrace her. "Forgive me, darling, but tonight of all nights I need to hold you."

His arms gave her no choice, but any hesitation she felt melted. He guessed that she found her position safe enough. They were not lying together. He was not on top of her, much as he wanted to be.

The music played behind them. Voices mumbled through the stone. Fleur relaxed. He turned his head so that his mouth rested on her temple and he could inhale her sweetness.

Her palms rested on his arms. They stayed there when his hands moved. He could never just hold her. She had to know that. His subtle caresses did not seem to surprise her. The entrancement of the music and the garden made it a natural thing to do.

He stroked through the cloth of her garments, feeling the soft curves of her sides and hips. "You are beautiful. Even that pink robe appears ethereal and lovely."

She laughed. "It is the moonlight. Even your childhood nurse would look beautiful in it."

"The light is not that generous." He kissed her shoulder and released his crossing embrace so that his hands could move more freely over her body. She could bolt now if she wanted to.

He felt the slight flexing of her hips that revealed she was aroused. Her bottom pushed against his erection until he pressed against her cleft.

He clenched his teeth and accepted the unintended caress. He returned those of his own with his hands, more purposefully glossing her body through the wrap, stroking her stomach until her shortened breaths told him she was past rejecting this pleasure. With kisses and nips on her ear and neck, he lured her in deeper, so he was not the only one going mad.

His contained desire possessed a savage edge. The press of her hips maddened him. Half blind, he peered down at the obstructing dark buttons. Deliberately, ruthlessly, he caressed up her body until his hands cupped her breasts. Before she could object, he gently fondled their fullness and stroked their nipples with his thumbs.

She both accepted the pleasure and fought it. The little battle caused her body to move. She pressed her hips against him harder to relieve the sensations. Her breaths shortened and little sounds of desire floated on them to his nearby ear.

He listened and caressed until he knew pleasure had defeated any resistance. Continuing to arouse her with one hand, he began unfastening the buttons with the other.

She stiffened when she realized what he was doing. Her hand covered his, as if to stop him.

He ignored the gesture. "You will let me, darling. If you truly did not want me to, you would have left by now."

She whispered something, but his hunger did not let him hear it. He parted the robe and made quick work of the bed gown's ribbons. He spread the halves of both garments until her breasts were exposed. He watched his fingers follow the lovely outlines her curves made.

The sight of her body, the warm connection of skin on skin, almost turned his desire cruel and dangerous. He leashed the primitive impulse to possess, but granted it one small liberty. Not waiting for signs of assent, he pulled the garments down her shoulders and arms until she was naked from neck to waist. At least this part of her would be his this night.

The exposure frightened her, but also aroused her more. The cautious notes on her cries barely sounded among those of a woman approaching abandon. Using his hands, he deliberately seduced her closer to that, to prove to them both that it was in his power to do so.

He stroked her breasts slowly, making circular patterns with his fingertips, teasing close to the tips. Their fullness swelled as her passion rose and rose. Her hips squirmed, rubbing him erotically.

When he finally moved his fingers toward her nipples, her body arched, begging for it. Her relief when he finally touched her did not last long. He palmed the tips very lightly, tantalizing her. The intensity of the pleasure soon had her crazed and biting back whimpers of frustration.

Her cries and movements made the urge to take her rise in his blood. Only focusing on her reactions and finding ways to increase her pleasure kept him in control. The impulse grew, however, dark and determined and convinced she wanted it. An emotion deep in his soul checked him. He could never betray her trust that way, nor risk hurting her.

That kept him from laying her down even though his body roared for him to. Even though her cries and movements said she was as ready as any woman he had ever had. Instead, he caressed down her body with one hand, to at least give her release from the mounting insanity.

She did not comprehend his intention at first, but her body knew. As he slid the bed gown up her legs, revealing their slender beauty, her legs parted and her knees bent, as if her womanhood welcomed what her mind did not understand. The movement made the garments' billows slide down to her hips.

He pulled them up more, so he could see the top of her raised thighs and the dark patch of hair and the way she waited for what she insisted she did not want and could not have.

He caressed the soft flesh of her inner thigh and watched her hips subtly rise in invitation. Erotic images flashed in his head, of kissing where his hand lay, then higher. Of teasing the soft flesh hidden amidst those dark curls with his tongue until she moaned with pleas for completion.

The sight of her, the rocking of her hips, the intense fantasy, her cry of pleasure and surprise when he touched her—they all created a chaotic and relentless spike of need. When he slid his finger deep within the cleft obscured by those curls, his hunger peaked and split apart as release flooded him.

While the little cataclysm blinded him, Fleur rolled away and scrambled onto her hands and knees. She faced him during a moment of frozen silence that echoed with spent passion and shattered arousal. He doubted that his climax had shocked her back to her senses, since she was too inexperienced to understand what had happened. Probably the intimate touch had frightened her. She watched him like a cornered animal might eye a hunter.

He reached for her. "Come back, Fleur."

She scooted away and rose up on her knees. Fingers fumbling, she covered herself and fussed with the buttons on the robe. "I do not understand you. You have no need of me for this."

"If I had no need of you, we would not be here tonight." He leaned his head against the wall and watched her fix her garments. Her confusion filled the air and colored her accusatory words. "Also, I think you understand me very well. It is yourself you do not understand."

She got to her feet. "I understand myself, Dante. You are the one who forgets the truth." She turned away. "I should have heeded your warning when
you said you would not be kind tonight."

He jumped up and grabbed her arm and swung her around to face him.
"You found me unkind, Fleur? If I had decided to take you, do you think
those voices in the next garden would have stopped me? I'm not even sure
you would have stopped me."

"I would have had no choice but to try."

"It did not sound that way to me. Do not pretend that you did not enjoy
it."

She pulled her arm free and walked away. "Do not do this again, Dante.
It does neither of us any good, even if at first I enjoy it."

Fleur sat at the window of her chamber again, unable to sleep. The party
next door was ending, and muffled farewells came from the street in front of
the houses.

Down below in the garden, Dante still sat among the flowers. What was
he doing there? Perhaps he had fallen asleep.

Memories of being down there with him would not leave her head. Sweet
memories, of the beauty of the night and music, and the intimacy of his embrace. Heady memories of pleasure owning her for a while, as it had behind
the hedge in Durham.

Dreadful ones, assaulting her when he touched her in that scandalous way.
The shock of the intense sensation had shattered her stupor. She had sensed
the dangerous energy rising in him like an uncontrollable force. Awareness
of her vulnerability had split through the mindless fog he had created in her
head. Opening her eyes, she had seen her legs bent and spread and his hand
reaching around her and . . .

And blood. She had seen red covering her thighs. That image had been in
her head, but it looked so vivid and real. A chill had slid through her. It had
numbed her so much that the pleasure instantly disappeared.

Only when she claimed the sanctuary of this chamber had she begun
warming again. Returning to life. With resurrection had come the same horrible disappointment she had experienced in Durham. Disgust with her in-
adequacy still permeated her.

Dante still had not moved. He just sat there, one leg bent and knee raised,
with his head angled back against the wall, as if he looked to the sky above
her.

It *had* been unkind of him. He did not need her in that way, least of all
tonight when he had surely been with a lover earlier. It had been cruel to remind her of what she could not be, could not have. Was he incapable of

restraining himself when he was with a woman? Even her? Had she been so reckless as to tie herself to a man with boundless, indiscriminate appetites?

If so, they could not even be friends. That saddened her so much she almost could not accept it with composure. For a while tonight it had been much as it had on their wedding journey. Their embrace and pleasure had been as harmless as that behind the hedge.

Until her trust had been destroyed by that touch, and the image of blood, and the dangerous power he exploited.

It is yourself you do not understand. Maybe not completely, but she understood enough. She had known that all her life.

She could not have passion. She could not have a husband or children. She could not have what most women took for granted.

It now appeared that she could not even have the pretense of some kind of a marriage. She could not have a friendship and closeness unthreatened by sensual expectations.

She had been stupid and naive to think it could be different with Dante Duclairc, of all men.

Dante still had not moved, but she did. She forced herself away from the window and tried to shut the sad longing out of her heart.

She looked at her *secrétaire* as she passed it. A letter lay there, written but not posted. It was to Hugh Siddel. She had delayed in sending it for reasons she did not even understand, reasons having to do with Dante.

The letter would go out in the morning.

She would not pretend anymore that her life had changed and that she should accommodate this husband.

After all, they were not really married.

Nor would they ever be.

Dante stepped out of the Union Club on Cockspur Street. A damp fog had rolled into the city. He had seen it coming and had walked, so the horses would not be left standing in the mist.

He debated whether to go home. He wondered if Fleur would still be awake. Probably not. She made very sure that they would not be alone together again while the household slept. She even avoided him during the days now.

She probably realized that it did not take the silence of a sleeping house to tempt him. His desire was not waning, but instead gaining a keen edge. Three nights ago in the garden, he certainly had proven that. Whenever he saw her, whenever they spoke, he contemplated seducing her.

He headed in the direction of Mayfair anyway. He tried to block the fantasy that she waited for him so that the garden's intimacy could be repeated. And expanded and prolonged.

Memories of Fleur's naked body and breathless passion completely distracted him. The image of her at her window later, still connected to him by thoughts if not by flesh, dulled his senses.

The blow caught him totally unprepared.

It smacked into his shoulders with a force that sent him sprawling. A kick to his side made him flip onto his back. He instinctively crossed his arms over his head. Another blow aimed there, but he caught it on his forearms.

The stick crashed against his bone. Snarling, he grabbed for the weapon and held on despite the pain in his arm.

A flurry of kicks punished him. "Think to fight, do ya? Not so fancy now, is he? Give it to 'im good, for making us wait all this time in the cold."

A passing carriage pulled to a stop in the street. The coachman yelled something and another voice joined the alarm. Through the mind-fogging pain, Dante heard boots running toward him and others running away. He fell back on the pavement, still clutching the thick stick.

"Hell, it *is* you," he heard St. John say. "Thank God curiosity got the better of me and I followed you out of the club to learn what transpired in your conversation with Cavanaugh. Say something, Duclairc, so I know you are not dead."

"I am only half dead, and regretting the part that lives," he muttered.

"That will pass." Firm arms braced under his shoulders. Two men lifted him to his feet. "My coach is right here. Easy now."

"That hurts more than the blow." Dante tried to move his arm away from St. John's pressing fingers.

"I need to see if anything is broken."

Dante sat on a chair in St. John's library, stripped to the waist, as St. John conducted his examination. Diane St. John stood behind him, pressing a compress to his shoulders. A riot of pain screamed out from both their ministrations.

St. John ordered him to move his arm and fingers in various ways. He then did some excruciating probing around his ribs. "You will survive, although I do not think that was the intention."

"The intention was theft. Where did you learn to be a leech?"

"It was useful on ships in my younger days."

St. John appeared indifferent to both the damage and the pain he was causing. Diane, however, looked very solemn.

"This blow from the back could have killed you," she said, removing her compress and replacing it with another. She loosely draped a blanket over his shoulders. "A few inches higher and it would have gotten your head."

She stepped around and examined his arm. Their return to the house had pulled her from her bed, and her chestnut hair hung down her undressing gown in lengthy waves.

"I think that we should send for Fleur," she said.

"There is no need. I will bring Duclairc home to her shortly," St. John said.

"I will not need an escort. Also, I would prefer that Fleur is not told about this."

Diane pointed to his side and the swelling on his arm. "Once she sees that, she will expect an explanation."

Except she wouldn't see this, Dante thought. St. John's wife was currently seeing him more naked than Fleur ever had or would.

"I will give a story that does not worry her," he said. "They were just thieves looking for a few pounds."

She raised one eyebrow as she glanced at St. John. "I will leave you to my husband, then. He is far better handling such as this than I am."

She departed.

"Did she mean you are better at handling wounds from a fight, or handling such as me?"

St. John lifted a brown bottle from a nearby table. "The wounds. Although I would never allow my wife to rub this liniment on such as you. Arms up."

Grimacing, Dante lifted his arms. St. John rubbed some liquid from the bottle over his torso. It produced a warmth that burned at first and then penetrated to his muscles.

St. John moved behind him and sloshed some on his shoulders too. "I saw you speaking with Cavanaugh again. Have you learned anything from your inquiries?"

"Absolutely nothing."

"Perhaps there is nothing to learn."

"I think there is. He knows Siddel, you have seen them together. Yet he avoids any mention of the man and changes the subject whenever Siddel's name is raised."

"That is not very artful. If the avoidance had been less absolute, it would not be suspicious, but complete silence makes one curious."

"Exactly."

St. John replaced the stopper in the bottle. "That will help some, but not much. Tomorrow is going to be hell. Now, tell me how this happened tonight."

"They were lying in wait for someone to come by. Whether it was me or just someone who appeared a good mark, I cannot say."

"Let us assume it was you. Let us assume that the goal was not a few pounds but a good beating, and perhaps worse."

"Let us not."

"Duclairc, if you are someone's target you need to take care."

Dante put on his shirt with slow, painful movements.

St. John helped him with his coats. "Could Farthingstone have arranged this? If you are gone, she is again unmarried and vulnerable. With his efforts in Chancery delayed, he may have sought another solution."

"They may have only been thieves, St. John. Or in the employ of someone who wanted revenge for something."

"Or someone who wants you to stop asking questions."

"Or someone from my past who would like to see me thrashed. Husbands can harbor resentments a very long time, I expect."

St. John laughed. "That we can. I will have the coachman take you home now. Since it isn't clear why this happened, and if the goal was your purse, your pain, or your death, I ask that you watch your back in the future."

"I am relieved to see that the bruise on your shoulders is healing nicely, sir." Hornby made the observation as Dante put on a shirt. His valet had taken great interest in the progress of the swelling and discoloration over the last week, mostly because it gave him a chance to keep inviting the explanation that never came.

"Then you will be happy to know that my arm also no longer pains me, Hornby."

While the valet laid out a choice of cravats, Dante took a little box from his dressing-table drawer and slipped it into the pocket of the frock coat hanging in front of his wardrobe. He intended to give the jewelry inside the box to Fleur this morning, so she would have it when she dressed for Lady Rossmore's ball tonight.

"Do you know if my wife has gone downstairs, Hornby?"

His valet's cherubic, pale face remained impassive beneath his thin dark hair. "I believe that she did, sir. Some time ago. She rises quite early."

Hornby was the sort of person who spoke volumes with the most subtle inflection of his voice. His last sentence, uttered as a mere observation, had contained the barest nuance of dismay.

Dante had inherited Hornby eight years ago from a friend whose budding fortune had sunk with a ship in the Sargasso Sea. Hornby was an unusually loyal valet, willing to economize when bad wagers came due, happy to ignore the excesses of his master's life. Time had bred familiarity, and in some ways Dante knew Hornby better than he knew anyone else.

The timbre of Hornby's voice had not been a slip. The valet knew something that he shouldn't repeat. If his employer insisted on dragging it out of him, however, he could be coerced to put discretion aside.

"Since she does not keep late hours, it is not surprising that she rises early. It may be unfashionable, but my wife is not a slave to society's expectations."

"So Williams has explained to me."

"I hope that the two of you have not been discussing her habits. I won't have it."

"Williams was only trying to settle me in. Alert me to the household customs, so I would not be concerned. There was no tattling intended, I am sure."

Tattling? Hornby must be bursting to be indiscreet if he dangled that word.

"She has customs that concern you?"

Hornby feigned discomfort with the pointed question. He handed Dante the hair brushes and tilted the toilet mirror just so. "Since you demand it of me—She walks out alone quite a bit."

"On my instructions, that practice has stopped. I told Williams either to send for the carriage or have an escort accompany her."

"Yes. Well. So he explained." Hornby allowed himself a little sigh.

"And?" Dante obligingly prodded.

"Since you demand it of me—it appears that the lady countermanded your order, and even implied Williams would be released if he interfered or confided in you."

"Are you saying that my wife disobeyed me and blackmailed Williams into cooperating?"

"He is distraught and does not know how to perform when his loyalties are divided in such a way. No servant would, of course."

Hornby conveyed relief that, as a valet, his own loyalties would never be pulled in two directions.

"Since he does not know quite what to do, he has tried to please you both," Hornby continued, while he concentrated on folding towels. "She goes out alone. However, Williams has someone follow her."

Dante's arms froze with the brushes poised over his crown. "The butler is having my wife followed?"

"To see that she comes to no harm, and to have an answer should you ask where she has gone." He busied himself wiping around the washbowl. "Also, to make sure someone knows where she is, so that the episode from last spring is not repeated."

Dante put down the brushes and turned his attention on Hornby's very bland, very innocent face. "To what episode do you refer?"

"Since you demand it of me—last spring she would disappear and not return until after dark. It went on two days. Williams grew concerned and the third day he followed her. It transpired that she had been . . . visiting a brothel."

"That is preposterous, and I will release Williams myself for spreading such tales. Fleur Monley did not go to male brothels. I doubt she even knows they exist."

"Not a *male* brothel. Good heavens, no. One with women. A short while later she contributed substantial funds to a charity dedicated to saving soiled doves. She often conducts a few investigations, to make sure the charity can make a difference."

Dante imagined Fleur paying morning calls on brothels to ascertain if the women wanted saving. There would be hell to pay if Farthingstone ever learned of this.

Hornby held up his coats and Dante slipped them on.

"It was just such an investigation that led to her arrest in the Rookery the previous winter, which is why Williams knew at once why she was at that brothel."

This casual revelation hit Dante as he buttoned his waistcoat. He sighed. The day was not starting well. "When was this?"

"February a year ago. You remember, surely. There was that trouble. She was there, looking into the conditions of several widows and their children, and got swept up by the police along with the rabble. Fortunately, it did not become public, but—"

But several people knew, including everyone in this house.

Except him.

The servants had not spoken of it, not even when St. John had them interrogated. They had only admitted to Fleur's secretiveness and communicated vague concerns.

Dante checked his cravat. "No doubt you are aware of the accusations that her stepfather is making. I am sure you know it is essential that none of the servants ever speaks of these episodes to anyone, lest it all be misunderstood."

"Of course, sir. However, perhaps it is well that you know, since we all do."

Dante left his chamber and entered Fleur's through its door on the corridor. He heard her maid humming in the dressing room, already making preparations for the long ritual of dressing for a ball. Considering the day she faced, this had been a peculiar morning for Fleur to go out.

He had not seen much of Fleur since that night in the garden. He could not decide if she avoided him because she thought he had insulted and misused her that night or because her own reactions had frightened her.

He fingered the little box in his pocket. He had intended to give it to her personally, but now the gesture seemed somewhat pointless.

He could coax passion out of her, but she really desired no such intimacy with him. She did not think of him as a husband and felt free to ignore his most benign instructions.

He removed the box from his pocket, placed it on her bed pillow, and left.

He went down to seek out Williams. He found the butler in his pantry, counting plate. Williams dropped two spoons when he saw the master of the house at the threshold.

"If you had sent for me, sir—"

"I am told that you have been having my wife followed when she walks out alone."

"You had said . . . then she said . . . well, I did not know what else to do."

"Where has she been going?"

"Most times she only walks in the park. Christopher—that is the footman I send—stays out of sight, but he makes sure she is not interfered with."

"Most times, you say. Other times, where does she go?"

"She has paid calls on a house in Piccadilly, and also on Lady Mardenford here in Mayfair. She has on occasion visited St. Martin's. A bit out of the way, but perhaps she wants a good walk first. That is where she went today."

"She has returned?"

"When Christopher sees that she is going there, he comes home. He can hardly lurk in the portico, and we assume she is safe enough in a church."

"Send for the carriage, Williams. And she is not to be followed in the future. I will not have her subjected to such undignified subterfuge."

chapter 15

Allow me to explain things to you, *again*," Mr. Siddel said. "Finding the last investor is the hardest, because the most likely men have already been solicited. I urge patience, madame."

"And I am saying that I know people who would be likely as well."

"This is not a proposal that ladies should be confiding in drawing rooms. I trust you have not been doing so."

"Of course not. I am not stupid, Mr. Siddel."

For all their *sotto voce* efforts, their argument seemed to ring off the church walls. Only one other parishioner had entered since Fleur arrived, however, taking a pew far from them. Up near the altar a canon prepared for the next day's service.

"I must say that I find your behavior since returning from France troubling," Mr. Siddel said. "The frequency of your letters, your insistence on this meeting, your shrill demands to know the investors' names—I find myself regretting my participation in the whole matter."

Fleur gritted her teeth to avoid getting very shrill indeed. "And I find your delays in responding to my letters and your prevarication equally troubling, sir."

"Are you questioning my honesty? Since you have no cause to do so, I must wonder about your judgment in other areas as well."

"You keep using the language of my stepfather's rumors today, Mr. Siddel. Is that supposed to put me off?"

"I merely make an observation. There is no logical reason for my prevaricating in this affair. I gain nothing until it is completed. Considering the long-term benefits once the land is sold, you should find some forbearance in the short term. Is this all Duclairc's doing? Did you confide in him and he is pressing you to in turn press me?"

A loud "ssshh" from the canon riveted her attention to the altar. Their voices had risen loud enough to invite the scold.

"Mr. Siddel, my husband has no knowledge of any of this. If my demands have appeared excessive, it is because I fear we will lose the advantage. I would be grateful if you kept me better informed. For example, do you have any prospects regarding the final investor?"

"Actually, I do. I am so confident that he will agree that I will be meeting with all the others today, to introduce them to one another. I had arranged an earlier appointment, in the interests of maintaining secrecy, but your insistence on seeing me required that I change the time." His tone implied that should the investors be angry, or should the meeting now become known, it would be her fault.

She rose and stepped into the aisle. "Then I should not keep you. I trust that you will let me know the results of your conversation."

Mr. Siddel slid out of the pew. "I will inform you of progress when it occurs. If that does not please you, perhaps you desire to obtain another adviser, who will accommodate you better. If so, you are at liberty to do so."

Of course she had no such liberty. As she sank back onto the bench, she admitted as much. Beginning over would be folly if the goal was so close.

Mr. Siddel knew that and could proceed as he chose. There was nothing she could do about it.

Or so he thought.

She listened to his steps clicking on the floor to the front portal. She waited for the thud of the door closing behind him, and slowly counted out two minutes of time.

She got up and followed.

Dante peered out the closed landau at the facade of St.-Martin's-in-the-Fields.

If Fleur liked to walk alone, this was as good a destination as any, and better than most. At least she wasn't visiting brothels again.

He knew he was reacting more strongly to this continued habit than was warranted, but that did not blunt his annoyance. He had only requested this change for her own safety and reputation, and he did not care for the implications of her disobedience.

When he confronted her about this, she would probably remind him that they were not really married, as she had when he told him to delay the school.

She probably had not obeyed him about that either.

His hand was on the carriage door, to go and get her, when the church portal opened. A man walked through the portico and down the steps and aimed south toward the Strand.

It was Hugh Siddel.

Dante felt his jaw tightening. His memory suddenly saw Fleur's dismay that Siddel had been one of the men who saw her in that cottage bed, and Siddel's own anger at the discovery.

A savage fury roared through him. Of all the men for Fleur to deceive him about, this was the worst.

The least infuriating explanation, and it turned his thoughts hot all the same, was that Siddel was involved in that land sale and possibly trying to defraud her the way Hampton had feared.

Other, far worse explanations had him almost reaching for the pistol hung on the carriage wall.

He forced some rationality. There was no proof they had a friendship, let alone a liaison. Fleur may have left the church long ago.

As if fate was determined to taunt him, the door of the church opened again. Fleur stepped out, encased in a simple hooded cloak. It was the kind of wrap women wore when they did not want to be recognized.

She paused beside one of the portico's columns and peered around it surreptitiously. Then she walked down to the street. Staying close to the buildings and in their deep, morning shadows, she aimed in the same direction as Hugh Siddel.

A furtive quality in her pace and bearing pricked Dante's curiosity.

He jumped out of the carriage, climbed up beside Luke, and took the reins. "I am in the mood to handle the ribbons myself this morning, Luke."

"As you prefer." Luke crossed his arms over his chest and sulked under the insult.

From his perch, Dante could see Fleur up ahead and in the distance Hugh Siddel turning east, on to the Strand. For some reason, Fleur was following the man.

Dante remembered a love affair from long ago. When the excitement dimmed, his lover had sensed his attention waning. She had followed him one day when he took his leave early, and had discovered him visiting another house and another woman. Society dined on the resulting scene for weeks.

He fought to keep speculation about Fleur and Siddel out of his mind, with no success. The heat of rage gave way to a calmer, more perilous ice.

He gave the signal for the horses to move, but held them in.

"Do you think one of the horses is lame, sir?" Luke asked. "We are going very slow."

"I choose to go slowly. If it embarrasses you to have me up here, get inside."

"No reason for *me* to be embarrassed, sir."

Dante followed Fleur to the Strand. Up ahead, Hugh Siddel entered a shop. Fleur abruptly stopped to peruse a flower stall. As Dante reined in the horses more, he noticed something else. A hundred feet ahead of his horses' noses, a well-dressed man also paused.

"Luke, see that man there with the high hat, the one standing idly on the corner up ahead on the left?"

"I see 'im."

"Watch him for me. If he turns down another street, let me know. If he looks back and notices us, let me know that too."

Luke gave him a curious look. "Are we following him? Is that why you are going so slow?"

"Not him, Luke. But I think that he is following someone too, and I want to know if I am correct."

"Too? If you aren't following him, who *are* you following?"

"A pretty lady."

Luke pulled down the rim of his hat and folded his arms again. He exhaled a disapproving sigh.

Dante almost boxed Luke's ears. Considering that the pretty lady whom he followed was his own wife, who had just had a secret assignation with a man he hated, he really wasn't in the mood for that sigh.

Fleur had just convinced herself to take a peek in the tobacco shop when the door opened and Mr. Siddel came out. He paused to check his pocket watch. Tucking the watch away, he strode on with more purpose than previously.

He stayed on the Strand, which meant the passing bodies helped obscure Fleur's presence. Even so, she tried to stay a good distance behind because, should he look back, he would probably recognize her hooded cloak.

After a rigorous walk, he angled toward the buildings and his head disappeared into one of them. It was The Cigar Divan, a popular coffeehouse.

That seemed a very public place to hold a secret meeting, but in some ways ideal. A group of men smoking, drinking coffee, and reading papers would not invite speculation.

She debated what to do. The investors were in there with Mr. Siddel, and she wanted to know if she recognized any of them. Then, should there be more delays, she would have the chance to conclude matters on her own.

Unfortunately, women did not frequent such establishments. She could not merely enter the front door unobtrusively and take a quick look. If she tried that, the reaction of the patrons would announce her arrival.

Turning at the next corner, she sought the alley behind the row of buildings. The front door may be forbidden, but perhaps the back door could be nudged open.

Following the smells of coffee and cigar smoke, she found the back of the establishment. The door stood ajar, to allow the spring breeze in. She peeked around its edge and into the back room of the coffeehouse.

Mostly it held sacks of beans and boxes of tea. A metal washbasin, murky from the dried leaves and coffee remnants of dirty cups, stood in the far corner. Two cauldrons of water boiled on hooks set in the small hearth.

The door to the coffeehouse's public room faced her. Slipping in, she aimed for it. She eased it open and peered out.

A frock coat blocked most of her view. A man stood inches from her nose, his back to her. Just past his right shoulder, however, she could see part of Mr. Siddel's face. He was sitting on a divan near the wall and talking to someone.

The man shifted his weight enough for her to see Mr. Siddel completely. She opened the door more, rose on her toes, and angled her head to try and catch a glimpse of his companions.

One came into view. A young man with blond hair and a long face.

Watching the door's edge carefully, to make sure it did not touch the frock coat, she tried to make enough room to get her head through for a moment so she would be able to—

"See here, what are you doing?"

The voice made her swirl around. Another man had entered through the back door, carrying a sack of sugar.

"Stealing tea, are you?"

"I am not stealing—"

"Some went missing last week, and now you are back for more, I can see."

"You are mistaken." She tried to walk past him but he blocked her path.

The other door opened, and the man whose back she had just been facing came in. "What's this?"

"Found this woman in here, Mr. Reiss, making sure you were busy, getting ready to steal. She probably already has a box of tea under that cloak."

"My good man, I have no tea under my cloak and had no intention of stealing anything."

"Oh? Then what did you intend? No reason for anyone to be here, let alone a woman," Mr. Reiss said.

"I thought that I saw someone enter. Someone I haven't seen in many years. I wanted to know if I was correct."

"Did you, now? Who might this person be?"

Head muddled from the worst kind of excitement, she could not think of a good "who."

"Go for the constable, Henry," Mr. Reiss said.

The constable! "My brother. It was my brother, who has been gone many years. We thought him lost at sea. Imagine my shock when I saw a man who resembles him walk by and then turn into this establishment. Well, I had to know, didn't I?"

Henry was halfway to believing her, but Mr. Reiss would have none of it. "Long-lost brother, eh? Conveniently seen entering this place on a day when you are wearing a cloak that is mighty handy for hiding goods. The constable, Henry. I'll keep an eye on her until you get back."

"Do not be hasty, gentlemen," a new voice said. "I think that you should believe the lady, Reiss."

Fleur knew that voice. Although it inspired incredible relief, it also made her stomach sink. Explaining this adventure to a constable would be easier than doing so to Dante. A constable might even believe her lie.

Taking a deep breath, she faced the back door. Dante stood just inside the threshold.

"Mr. Duclairc, sir. You know this woman?" Mr. Reiss asked.

"I have made her acquaintance. Imagine my surprise to overhear these accusations while I was taking a cut through this alley."

"The evidence is rather strong, sir."

"She has given an explanation, however. Furthermore, it is very obvious that she is not a thief, just from the look of her."

"Thieves come in all sizes and types. The appearance of some quality only makes it easier to escape notice, and there are those who have figured that out."

"I do not think she is one of them. I am sure that the lady has no goods hiding under her cloak. Why don't you satisfy these two men on that count, madame."

Making her prove she was not a thief was hardly a chivalrous act, but then, right now Dante did not look very courteous. She could not ignore that the darkness had not only risen, it dominated his spirit and gave him a dangerous presence.

Feeling her face burn, she parted the edges of her cloak. Mr. Reiss, who had looked ready to give Dante an argument, raised his eyebrows when he saw the quality of the dress hidden by the serviceable wrap.

"Allow me to escort the lady from the premises. Also, permit me to compensate you for trade that you lost during this distraction." Dante placed a guinea on a shelf stacked with tea boxes.

Mr. Reiss eyed the coin and sniffed. "See you do not come back, madame. Even if you think you see your long-dead cousin enter next time."

Fleur strode past him and out into the alley. As she headed back to the street, she heard steps behind her and looked back. Dante was striding to catch up, and another man was entering The Cigar Divan's back room.

The expression in Dante's eyes made her walk faster. He caught up anyway.

"What are you doing here, Dante?"

"Paying off coffee sellers so they do not lay down information that you are a thief."

"For which I am grateful. However, by my question I meant how did you happen to be available to save me."

"I was passing in the carriage and saw you just as you turned down this alley. A fortunate coincidence." He caught her arm and stopped her before she reached the sanctuary of the street. "What are *you* doing here, Fleur? Besides hoping for a reunion with a brother lost at sea."

He had heard her lie. He must have stood outside the door listening before saving her.

"Perhaps you are doing one of your investigations prior to contributing to a charity. What would this one be? The Society to Prevent the Overimbibing of Coffee?"

"Such establishments have always seemed very convivial to me, and I thought that I would take a look."

"So you walked for blocks on end until you came to this one. Do not treat me like a fool, Fleur, nor expect me to assume that you are one either."

Blocks on end? He had not merely chanced to see her. He had been following her through the city.

"What are you up to, Fleur? Not solitary walks for exercise, it appears."

She was grateful he had just helped her out of a difficult spot, but she resented this interrogation. Worse, his masculine energy filled the air. His anger embodied the same tension that his sensuality did. She did not like the way that confused her reactions. It was very discomforting to find a man vexing and exciting at the same time.

"I am living my life, Dante, just as you continue to live yours."

Her reminder of their agreement did not appease him. Quite the opposite. "I asked you to make some small changes in that life, for your protection. Such as not walking alone."

"No, you presumed to demand that I make those changes. I complied on most."

"Not on the ones that you found inconvenient, it seems."

"Or unreasonable."

"My demands have been anything but unreasonable. As married women go, you have extraordinary freedom to continue living your life as it was, by day as well as night."

The insertion of the last reference, and his tone as he said it, made her cautious. "Yes, I have. *As we agreed.* We are not really married in the normal sense. Do not expect me to submit to every whim you have as if we were."

A very different man was suddenly looking at her. She felt like a mouse caught in a big cat's calculating gaze. "There are several parts of this marriage that I will be renegotiating, Fleur. Regarding your submission, however, I remind you of my warning in the cottage. If challenged, the choice of weapons is mine."

He took her arm and firmly guided her back to the street.

He opened the carriage door.

Considering his last words, she did not want to forsake the street for the privacy of that carriage.

"I would rather walk, Dante."

He smiled slowly. It was *not* a reassuring smile at all. "Are you afraid to ride with me?"

"If it means sharing your dismal humor, yes."

"Get in the carriage, Fleur. You face a long day of preparation and a tiring night. I will continue on foot. We will talk about the reasons for my bad humor tomorrow."

Fleur examined her reflection in the long mirror. A stranger peered back at her.

No, not a stranger. An old friend, not seen in ten years. The girl she had once been greeted her.

She stepped closer so the low lighting could not obscure the details that said she was no longer a girl. The eyes were less innocent than they had been then, and the face less soft in its form. Her body showed curves the girl had not possessed, although not a pound had been gained. She was a woman now.

She wanted to believe that the years looked good on her. She needed to think that tonight. For a decade she had been free of all this fretting about her appearance. Suddenly, however, it mattered again, and she was unpracticed in controlling the way it created dissatisfactions with little flaws. Inside her body, wings of nerves beat and fluttered. She had not even been this unsettled the day she attended her first ball.

Tonight would be a second coming out, only more important than the one when she was a girl. Back then it was her future marriage at stake—which meant nothing was at stake, since she planned never to wed.

"The carriage is waiting, madame," her maid said as she held up a cream satin mantle.

Fleur took it around her shoulders. The gesture brought her right hand to the mirror. Light crackled back and forth between the glass and the large sapphire shimmering on her finger.

It was a beautiful ring. It looked perfect with her cerulean gown and the hired diamonds that bedecked her neck.

The ring had been waiting in her chamber when she returned today, sitting on her pillow in a little box. No note had accompanied it.

She had not been able to thank Dante for it yet. He had stayed away until early evening and immediately begun his own preparations upon returning.

He had done that to avoid her. Tomorrow, she did not doubt, he would take up the matter of her blatant disobedience. That pending conversation was one more reason for the nauseous worry that plagued her tonight.

Fleur forced herself to move. She walked down to where Dante waited for her.

The sight of him made her pause on the stairs. He was almost unbearably handsome in his evening clothes, a dark, strong column of impeccable tailoring and grooming. The hint of boyishness that usually softened his countenance was absent tonight. The dark ridge was still bared, giving him a hard maturity that made his face and presence very . . . exciting.

She felt an utter fraud suddenly. She would enter the ball on the arm of this man and everyone present would know the marriage was a farce. The best interpretation she could hope for was that she was an addled fool who had bought a husband she could not hold on to.

In his first glance at her he saw the annoyance about her excursion this morning. However, that anger dimmed as he came toward her. "You are incredibly beautiful, Fleur. I do not think I have ever been this awed."

It was such a kind thing to say that she wanted to weep. She had been lying to him and he knew it, but he still sought to put her at ease.

She held up her hand that wore the ring. "Thank you for this. It is magnificent."

"It was my mother's. I sent to Laclere Park for it. I left it there so that I would not be tempted to sell it when I got in too deep."

"I am honored to wear it tonight."

"It is not a loan. It was given to me to give to my wife, and that is who you are."

Not really.

A hard glint in his eyes almost dared her to say it. She had the good sense not to.

He offered his arm. She slid hers into place. He patted her hand in reassurance. "Once you are there, it will be as if you never missed a season."

It was not as if she had never missed a season, but her fears eased once she was at the ball. It helped that Charlotte took her in hand immediately.

"Go see your friends, Dante, while I take Fleur around," she ordered. "Come back for the third waltz."

Dante bowed in obedience and walked away.

"Now, come with me. I have it all arranged," Charlotte said, guiding her through the shimmering gowns and jewels.

Charlotte brought her to Diane St. John, who epitomized restrained elegance in her dark silver gown. The neckline skimmed her shoulders perfectly; a half inch more or less would have ruined the whole design. The sleeves, while full, did not overwhelm her thin arms. One stunning diamond hung at her throat, and Fleur guessed it was not hired. Her abundant chestnut hair was piled in a style that was not fashionable but very alluring.

Diane stood back and examined Fleur's ensemble. "Perfect. You both did well."

"Diane visits Paris several times a year, so if she says we did well that is a high compliment," Charlotte said. "Where is Sophia? She is part of our troop tonight."

"Coming up behind you," Diane said.

Fleur found herself being introduced to the dark-haired Duchess of Everdon and her somewhat foreign-looking husband, Adrian Burchard. She did not need any prompting from Charlotte on the history of these two. The last decade had removed her from society's balls but it had not removed her from the world's gossip. She knew the story of the duchess in her own right, and of the bastard son of an earl whom she had married.

"My husband has mentioned you," she said to Adrian. "I believe you are friends."

"Good friends, madame. He, St. John, and Hampton form a private circle, along with Laclere, of which I am fortunate to be a part. We have had some unusual experiences together."

"Is Mr. McLean a part of this circle?"

Charlotte and the duchess giggled. Adrian pretended they had not. "Like most men, your husband has several circles. My brother Colin enjoys that of Mr. McLean, not I."

"I certainly hope not," the duchess muttered.

"Mr. Burchard, you must excuse us now," Charlotte said. "We have things to discuss."

He backed away. "If you ladies are plotting strategies, I will wisely make myself scarce."

The duchess took Fleur's hands. "Before there is any plotting, I want to welcome you to our own circle. I would have called on you by now, but I was in Devon until this week. I offer my best wishes for your happiness in your marriage."

Fleur was touched by the quick acceptance. The duchess was a short woman, and about thirty years old. She was not a great beauty, but her clear green eyes conveyed sincerity and frankness far in excess of what one expected in a duchess on first meeting.

"Thank you, your grace. You are too generous to me."

"Finding new friends is a joy, not generosity. And, please, you must call me Sophia."

Now, that *was* generous.

"Did the boys come up with you?" Diane asked.

"Of course. It made for quite an entourage, what with nurses and whatnot. However, Burchard commanded they both come. He has not seen the baby in a month."

"Ladies, we will all assemble in two days to discuss women things, but right now we have work to do," Charlotte interrupted. "You all know the things Fleur's stepfather is saying. Tonight we prove him false. I want Fleur to meet every lady here who can influence opinion. I want her dancing with peers and admirals." She turned to Fleur. "We will position ourselves so that you always have a friend nearby."

"I will go first," the duchess said. "Come, we will start easily. I see Adrian's aunt Dorothy. She probably remembers you from your first season, so will not be a total stranger."

They were as good as their word. Fleur was never alone. When a dance partner brought her to the side of the room, one of them joined her in a snap.

She relaxed as the night wore on. She knew many of the people here, even if she had not spoken to most of them in years. There were precious few allusions to her marriage, and almost none that was unkind.

She rarely saw Dante. Sometimes as she danced she caught a glimpse of him dancing with someone else. When the third waltz began, he was there to lead her into the dancers. The room spun around until they became the center of a whirlwind. The dance evoked memories of the last time they had waltzed, in the garden. His expression did too, but continued to be tinged with the anger of the afternoon.

By the time of the banquet, Fleur was feeling reassured that she had acquitted herself well. Attending a ball and doing nothing outrageous was an easy achievement if you were completely sensible and normal.

Daniel St. John offered his escort to the supper. She guessed that the troop had arranged that.

As she chatted with him, she looked down her table at the other couples. A stunning woman with blond hair and smoky eyes caught her attention. The woman was wearing a gown of dark violet, similar in color to the one Fleur had just had made by Madame Tissot, and it was the gown that first attracted her interest.

The lady moved slightly, turning to her companion. The shift made her more visible. Fleur vaguely noted that this was probably one of the most beautiful women at the ball.

Then her gaze locked on two details of the woman's ensemble.

Small details. Glittering ones. A pair of amethyst earrings dangled from her lobes, catching the light, matching the gown to perfection.

Fleur's breath caught. Her heart thudded while she stared at those earrings. She had seen them before. She had carried them in her reticule to a gaol.

She tore her gaze away and looked down at her plate. The noise of the room turned into a buzz. She ceased to hear what St. John was saying.

She looked at the earrings again. She could not stop herself. "That lovely woman down there, in the violet. Do you know who she is?" Her question interrupted St. John in the middle of a sentence.

He glanced down. Was it her imagination that he hesitated?

"That is the Baroness Dalry. Scottish title."

"She is extremely beautiful."

"Yes."

He knew. She could tell. St. John knew the baroness had been Dante's lover.

She felt chilled suddenly. Cold and warm all at once. A pain lodged in her chest that would not go away. She had to work at breathing to get some air in.

Dante had resumed his affair with the baroness, and had given her the earrings again. St. John knew about that too. Maybe Charlotte and Sophia and Diane did as well. Maybe everyone did.

She breathed deeply. She had known this day would come. Eventually it would be one specific woman, and she would learn who it was. She sought refuge in the indifference and acceptance that she had promised, but both deserted her.

She wanted to die. She felt as though she might.

"You appear unwell," St. John said with concern. "I fear the night has been too much for you."

"Yes, unwell." She barely got the words out. The pain in her chest had turned excruciating. It wanted to burst out of her, and the effort to keep it in had her light-headed.

She pushed to her feet. "Please, excuse me. I will . . ."

St. John's hand was under her arm at once. Half escorting and half supporting, he sped her out of the banquet room.

The pain grew until it filled her throat too. She felt tears flowing even though she was not crying.

Somehow the duchess was beside them. St. John handed her into Sophia's yellow satin sleeves.

Fleur did not hear what the duchess whispered to her. An image had entered her head and she could not make it go away.

She kept seeing Dante holding the face of the baroness and gazing into her eyes, then gently kissing her twice, once on the forehead and then on the lips.

Her heart broke. The duchess pushed her into the withdrawing room just as the flood started.

She laid on the chaise longue sniffling like a fool, feeling so stupid she wanted the building to bury her. She could not stop the tears, no matter how much she scolded herself. Her throat burned from her efforts to keep some composure. Women came and went, pretending to ignore her but getting an eyeful all the same.

The troops had deployed around her, forming a bar-rier with their skirts that offered a modicum of privacy. Charlotte and Sophia stared down any lady who looked too long.

"I cannot believe that none of us carries a vinaigrette," Charlotte said.

"She is not faint," Diane said.

Fleur wished she *were* faint. Better if she had keeled over in the corridor and dropped to the ground. She prayed for oblivion to claim her now. Anything to stop seeing these images of Dante with the baroness.

"We need to know what caused this," Diane said. "If someone insulted her, or spoke of her stepfather's accusations in her presence—"

"St. John said it began right after she asked him about the Baroness Dalry," Sophia said softly.

The three women fell silent. Fleur knew they were pitying her. That made her feel even worse.

"It was the earrings," Charlotte said. "I will *kill* my brother. He should have told her not to wear them. He knows Fleur saw them."

"Well, I will leave you to kill him, while I take Fleur home," Sophia said. "Before you kill him, inform him that she has left. Diane, would you find Adrian and let him know that I wish to depart."

Charlotte made to follow Diane. "Sophia, I hope that you will never receive Lady Dalry again. There was deliberate cruelty on her part tonight."

"Or total ignorance. She may not have known that Fleur would recognize the earrings."

"Possibly. One person did know, however, and when I am done with him—"

"Please do not," Fleur managed to say. "I have made enough of a shambles of the night. Do not accuse Dante of anything, or blame him. It isn't his fault at all."

Charlotte patted her face. "You let Sophia take you home now. I will visit in the morning and speak to Dante then. Tonight he is completely safe from me."

"You black-hearted scoundrel."

Charlotte hissed the insult as soon as she pulled Dante out of the ballroom and backed him into a private, dark corner.

"You thoughtless, conceited, cruel man. How *could* you? You knew what this night meant. How could you be so stupid when—"

"That is enough, Charl." He was in no mood to have insults hurled at him.

His humor had not improved since putting Fleur in the carriage this morning. If anything, the hours had darkened it more. He had barely maintained civility at this ball, because his head swam with hard questions and infuriating answers.

At some point he had recognized this primitive anger for what it was. He was jealous. Of Siddel, and whatever secret relationship the man enjoyed with Fleur. Speculations on what that relationship might be had occupied most of the day.

Fleur's furtive following of Siddel encouraged a conclusion that made his head split—that Colin Burchard had gotten it backward, and *she* was a spurned lover who kept grasping for the man she had lost and who refused other men because of her love. Only his conviction that Siddel would have grabbed Fleur's fortune if offered it kept him even partly sane.

Now, to finish off a day that had started badly and then gotten worse, he was suddenly the object of curiosity and sympathy. From what he could tell from the buzzing gossip, Fleur had just created a disaster. When Charl had found him he had been trying to figure out how to limit the damage.

"It is *not* enough, and there is plenty more," Charl snapped. "Do you know what has happened?"

"I overheard the story, so I have a good idea of how it will be remembered tomorrow. My wife abruptly lost control of her emotions at the banquet, had to be carried away, wept hysterically in the withdrawing room, and eventually had to be spirited from the ball by the Duchess of Everdon before anyone else could hear her ravings. And, to hear of it, there was absolutely no reason for this display except her unstable constitution."

"Oh, heavens, that is all much exaggerated. By tomorrow the gossiping fools will be saying that she tried to drink poison."

"Yes. Farthingstone should be delighted."

Charlotte stepped closer, hands on her hips. "It was not for no reason, you wretched excuse for a husband. She saw the earrings."

"What do you mean?"

"The amethyst earrings that I had her bring you in gaol. She saw them on the baroness."

"Are you saying that Fleur caused a scene because she was jealous?"

"She did not cause a scene. She behaved magnificently, considering that she was devastated. The worst part is that she blames herself and not you."

Of course she didn't blame him. *She didn't dare.* If he had resumed his affair with the baroness, she could not object.

Except that the baroness was not his lover, which made the entire drama ridiculously ironic. Almost as ironic as the fact that *he* had caught *her* secretly meeting with a man this morning.

He would laugh except that a scathing fury filled his head.

Charlotte noticed. "You are angry with her."

"Damn right."

"Perhaps you think that she should be sophisticated about this. She has been out of society for some time, however, and it may take her a while to reaccustom herself to the casual infidelities expected of husbands."

He was tempted to explain the whole impossible predicament to Charl and exonerate himself. She was not the woman he needed to have it out with, however.

"If you want to insult me further, you will have to call tomorrow. I will leave now and attend to my wife."

F leur lay in the dark, as miserable as she ever remembered being. The images of Dante and the baroness had been joined by others. She kept seeing how she had made a fool of herself tonight.

She thought of Charlotte confronting Dante in the morning. She would have to rise very early herself and go to Charlotte and beg her to say nothing to Dante about the reason for tonight's behavior. Better if everyone concluded she was unstable and strange than anyone learned the truth, especially Dante.

Because she was awake, she heard the rapping that began on the door. It was loud and sharp enough, however, that it would have probably woken her even if she were asleep.

She sat up in bed and reached for her pink robe. The sound was not on the corridor door but on the little one that separated her chambers from Dante's.

She tiptoed through the dark to her dressing room. The raps sounded with a staccato demand.

The knocks stopped as she stood there, holding her breath. It appeared he had given up.

"Open the door, Fleur, unless you want me doing this in the corridor where all the servants will learn of it." His voice came low and tight, as if he knew she was standing on the other side of the wall and could hear him.

She turned the little key. The handle moved and the door swung toward her.

Dante stood there, with one arm raised and resting on the jamb. He had removed his coats, collar, and cravat, and his white shirt glowed in the light thrown from a brace of candles on the washstand.

There was absolutely nothing of the carefree, good-humored wastrel in his face or body.

"You are recovered?"

She nodded. "I am very tired, however."

"I am sure you are. However, I need to impose on your time for a while." He stepped into her dressing room. The light from the candles illuminated enough of his expression to show that he was angry.

He reached around the door and extracted the key. "I have grown to hate this door. I erred in insisting you lock it. It was one of several mistakes I have made with you." He threw the key back to his chamber and it clattered into the washbowl. "I do not ever want it locked again."

She did not know what to do or say. They just stood there in the dressing room, facing each other through the shadows.

"That robe does not look at all attractive without the moonlight in a garden. I told you to buy some prettier things."

"It seemed unnecessary, since I am asleep when you return home."

"You have taken great care to make sure of that. However, despite your efforts, here we are." He gestured to the wardrobes. "You wore something else that night in Durham. Where is it?"

"I do not think—"

"Put it on, Fleur."

She went to a wardrobe and removed the nightdress and boudoir robe.

He was beside her suddenly, a dark, male presence in the night. His hands began to unbutton the blue dots on the robe.

She pictured him doing that with the baroness and wanted to weep again. "I do not need your help."

"I choose to help. Do not object, Fleur. This is not the night to remind me of what you think we should not share."

He barely touched her as he peeled the robe away. His fingertips hardly grazed her skin as he untied the bed dress and slid it down. He might have deliberately caressed her naked body, however. Undressing her proclaimed a right just as intimate.

She reached for the bed gown, but his hand closed on her wrist, stopping her. She froze like that, arm outstretched, with him much too close.

She did not look at him, but she felt him looking at her. Very little light entered the dressing room, but enough did for him to see her nakedness.

"Let me put on my bed gown, Dante."

He pulled off her cap so her hair fell.

"Dante—"

"Not yet. It gives me pleasure to look at you."

She closed her eyes and suffered it. Despite her humiliation, a slow excitement beat like a pulse. That rhythm was in the air, coming from him, being carried into her, stimulating her body.

"I should insist you stay like this," he said. "I should make you come into the light and look at you for hours. I have damn few rights in this marriage, but this is one I did not bargain away."

"You are being cruel."

"Are you in pain? Am I hurting you?"

"I am embarrassed."

He released her wrist but cupped her chin instead. "You are not only embarrassed. You are also aroused. Do you think that I cannot tell?"

He released her. "Come to my chamber now."

She trembled as she scrambled to get into the silk ensemble.

She had not been in his chamber since it became his domain. Nothing of her old sitting room remained, and she felt a stranger as she examined the carved bed with its dark-green drapes and the tables littered with his personal things.

He lounged on a chair, as confident in his physical presence as ever. She chose to stand, far away. She crossed her arms and pretended to study the redecorating.

"Charl and her friends took good care of you tonight. They have my gratitude."

"I know I behaved badly. I know it will only give Gregory's lies validation. If you intend to tell me what a mess I made of things, you do not have to. I have been castigating myself for the last hour."

"I did not seek you out to scold. I want to know what made you lose your composure."

"I was overtired."

"Charl said it was something else. She said you were distraught because you concluded I am having an affair with the Baroness Dalry."

She was so humiliated she could only stare at the floor. She wished Charlotte had been good to her word and waited until tomorrow to upbraid Dante.

"Was she correct? Did seeing those earrings distress you this much?"

She could not admit she had been so stupid, so pointlessly jealous.

"Well, Fleur, we have created a little hell for ourselves, haven't we? You promised never to be jealous, but then break down when you suspect you have seen my lover. I promised never to take you, but spend my time thinking about little else."

He was thinking of it now. It was in his eyes and body. It still affected the air. She told herself she was safe with him, but she did not entirely believe it right now.

"I should have guessed that somewhere in that ballroom there would be one of your lovers—from the past, surely, and possibly your current one. I just did not think about it, and so I was surprised. I will know better in the future. You are understandably angry, but this will never happen again."

"I am not angry because you were jealous."

"I have no right. I know that."

"No, you have no right. All the same, you became jealous on very little evidence. I, on the other hand, actually saw you meeting with a man this morning. At least my jealousy is based on something of substance."

Dear Lord, he had followed her longer this morning than she thought. If he knew about that meeting, he had been at the church.

She strolled around the room and debated her response. She tried not to look like she was pacing, but he was making her very nervous. The aura was pouring off him without restraint, filling the chamber, washing over her without mercy. His calm tone did not hide his mood, and his gaze revealed a mind making calculations that she dared not guess.

"I will not lie," she began. "You are correct. I met with Mr. Siddel this morning. Surely you know that it was not—that we are not—that would be impossible."

"So you claim."

"Are you doubting me? Good heavens, are you wondering if I lied about that? You cannot believe that I would so callously play you false when I proposed this marriage."

"I do not know what I believe anymore, since very little of this marriage has met my expectations and since you have not been honest in other ways."

"I am being honest now. Mr. Siddel and I do not have that kind of alliance. We are not even friends. We met on a matter of business."

"What business?"

"I cannot tell you."

"You mean that you will not tell me. Are you going to throw our agreement at me if I insist? As I said, this is not the night for that."

She felt trapped. She desperately sought words that would appease him.

"Is Siddel an adviser to you in the use of your inheritance?"

"Yes, you could say that."

"Then you are to find another one. You are to have nothing more to do with the man. No communication, no meetings. If you require a counselor, retain Hampton. If you want advice on business affairs, St. John will gladly help you, and when Vergil comes back he will be as good an adviser as you can find. Hugh Siddel, however, cannot be trusted. I'll be damned before I tolerate your meetings with him."

He had no idea what he was asking. *Demanding.*

Any thoughts she had of arguing disappeared when Dante rose from the chair and strolled toward her. She eased away to keep some distance.

It did not work. In no time she was standing against the wall and he was in front of her.

"You do not care for my instructions about Siddel, do you?"

"No."

"Do you have affection for this man?"

"It is not that, I have told you. However, these matters are supposed to be mine alone."

"Ah, yes. Because of our settlement."

The way he said it, the sparks in his eyes and the dangerous smile that slowly formed, had her sinking into the wall.

"If you are finished, I will get some sleep now, Dante."

He rested his hand high against the wall, propping his casual stance, but it also seemed a gesture to block her path to the small door. "Not yet. There are several other things I want to say to you tonight, Fleur."

"Then say them." She wished he were not so close. When he sat in the chair and she strolled the room she could avoid looking at him, but she couldn't now with him hovering like this.

"She is not my lover. I returned the jewels because they belong to her, and I had no need of her generous gesture after we married. They are hers to wear when she chooses, however."

She resented the way her heart rose with joy at his announcement. She hated how the night's sadness simply fell away. Her reaction only proved how enslaved her emotions were.

The humiliation did not disappear, however. This reassurance mortified her. "Then I handed Gregory a victory and I don't even have an excuse. This has truly been a disastrous night."

His fingertips feathered some strands of hair back from her face. "I disagree. I learned that you are jealous of all these lovers I am permitted in this marriage. I am glad to know it. That changes everything."

His vague touch had her senses alert and alive. Her body could feel the warmth of his even with twelve inches between them. "I do not see how it changes anything."

"We both gave up rights when we spoke in that sponging-house yard. You gave up the right to jealousy, but you are still jealous. I gave up the right to want you, but I still do. It could have worked anyway, except for one problem. You want me too. If you didn't, my interest would fade. If you didn't, you would not be jealous."

"So it is my fault."

"It is mine, for assuming I could want to protect a woman and not also want to possess her." He watched his finger draw along the line of her jaw. "This arrangement is impossible now that we know the truth of what exists between us, Fleur. It cannot go on. I am not inclined to live my life like this."

Heaviness returned to her heart. He wanted to be free of this false marriage. He wanted to be free of her.

"We can arrange never to see each other. Even sharing this house, we can do that. After Gregory has retreated, you can move elsewhere. Unless . . . unless you want to cooperate with him, and then procure an annulment. If you are truly unhappy, I will not fight that solution."

She dreaded the implications of that annulment, but if Dante wanted one she would not ask him to change his mind. He was right, and this marriage had not been what they expected.

"Those are all solutions, Fleur, but not the one I want. We are married, and I think it is time to act as if we are."

"Not—"

"Not really married. That is what you were going to say, isn't it? Not really a husband. The agreement led you to think of me that way. That locked door did too. I don't much care for this belief you have that we are not really married. It is time to admit that we are."

He rested his fingertips on her cheek. "It is also time to admit how much we want each other."

"That will only lead to unhappiness."

He kissed her, lingering, letting the power of that kiss do its worst, forcing her heart to accept what her body wanted.

"Did that make you unhappy, Fleur? When I held you in the garden, were you unhappy?"

She stared at the gap in his shirt where it lay open at his neck. A jumble of reactions confused her. Pleasure and gratitude clashed with the memory of a fear so visceral it could turn her to stone.

"It will eventually. I cannot give you what you want."

He did not respond. She snuck a glance up. His expression stunned her. A man who had never been refused by a woman was studying her, judging her strengths and assessing her weakness.

He lifted her into his arms. Another kiss, a ravishment, demonstrated his hunger and called her own forth. The heat of his passion almost made the roots of the fear wither and die, but she knew it survived in her. Even as she responded, while her body flushed and her breasts got full and sensitive, she knew that even Dante Duclairc could never conquer what lived in her.

He embraced her, pressing kisses to her shoulder and neck as his hands caressed her through the silk. "The door stays unlocked, Fleur, and we will share a bed."

"No. You promised—"

"I am not going to force you, but I never promised that I would not try to overcome whatever it is that makes you deny me."

"It cannot be overcome."

"I'll be damned before I accept that."

He kissed her furiously, giving expression to the angry determination of his declaration. With one hand sprawled possessively across her bottom, he arched her body against his and caressed up with the other until he cupped her breast.

Wonderful sensations streaked down her body, and the pulsing warmth grew. The excitement he so masterfully created almost overwhelmed her. For a brief while, as he stroked her nipple through the thin silk, she pretended they were behind that Durham hedge and this pleasure would be limited and benign.

He stopped kissing her, but his fingers still made titillating patterns on her breast. She opened her eyes and saw him watching how she reacted.

The sensual severity of his expression frightened her. The realities of the night assaulted her. They were not behind a hedge. They were in his chamber, and he would not stop this time.

The hated fear rose with a relentless wave. He must have seen it, because he kissed her again, as if the force of his passion could stop the tide.

It almost did. A blaze passed from him to her, burning away her sense of everything but intimacy and pleasure.

His embracing arm pulled her closer until she lined his body completely. He moved her toward the bed. "You will sleep here with me tonight. I want you in my arms."

Not only in his arms. She could not lie to herself about that. With each step the fear grew, threatening to deaden her.

She wanted desperately to believe he could win this battle for her. The poignant memory of sleeping with him in Newcastle made her throat thicken with tears. But if she got in this bed, it would not be like that. It would be horrible and humiliating. Even if he stopped it would be dreadful, and if he didn't—a little whirlwind of panic spiraled up her body, into her head. Images of blood and soundless screams flashed through her mind.

Already her nature was having its way, killing the pleasure and the joy, making her so miserable she thought she could never be happy again.

She pressed her hands against his chest. "Please, do not," she whispered, trying to hide how terrified she had become.

"I said I will not force you. There is no reason to be afraid."

There was every reason to be afraid. This was not Dante the kind friend, offering chaste intimacy. It was Dante the man, a prince of sensuality, wanting her more than was safe.

She pushed harder, until he released her. "I do not want this."

"Yes, Fleur, you do."

She turned and ran to the door. "Something in me does not, Dante, and even you cannot defeat it."

chapter 18

Dante was already in the breakfast room the next morning when she went down. She wondered if that meant he had slept as poorly as she had.

For the next half hour she sipped coffee while he read his paper and mail. The room seemed filled with last night's events. The silence became a continuation of them.

She caught him looking at her once. His gaze communicated no contrition. No backing down. He had made a decision about this marriage, and her flight last night had not changed his mind.

He had taken the key, so she could not lock the door now. She expected that some night he would walk through those dressing rooms to try and seduce her.

That was hopeless. She wished it was not, but it was.

Williams announced that Dante's sister had come to call. Charlotte entered the breakfast room, full of apologies for the early hour.

"If you have come to upbraid me further, there is no need," Dante said. "I have explained to Fleur that the baroness is not my current lover."

The bold announcement left Charl chagrined. "Oh."

"Yes. Oh," Dante repeated pointedly. He rose. "Since you ladies will want to discuss the ball in tedious detail, I will retreat." He did so before Charlotte could say another word.

Charlotte took Fleur's hand. "I hope there was no row when he got home. He appeared angry when he left the ball, and I feared there might be one."

"He was understandably displeased, especially since he says she is not his current lover." Fleur had not missed the wording of his statement. It left open the real possibility that some other woman *was* his current lover.

"Your misunderstanding was excusable. Any woman would have reached the same conclusion."

Not any woman. Not one who trusted her husband to be faithful, the way

Charlotte had trusted Mardenford and the way, Fleur suspected, Diane trusted St. John.

Not a woman who joined her husband in passion instead of demanding he find it elsewhere.

Not a woman who accepted the intimacy he wanted instead of running from the room.

"It is good to see you in good spirits, because I think Dante will want to make a short journey with you soon. If he had not left so abruptly, I would have given him the news forthwith."

"A journey to where?"

"Sussex." Charl plucked a letter out of her reticule and waved it. "It came this morning from Laclere Park. Vergil and Bianca have returned from Naples."

Fleur's stomach jumped, then landed with a sickening plop. "How wonderful."

"Penelope decided to stay in Naples. Vergil reassures me that she is back in good health and that he will explain everything when he sees us."

"Does he indicate that he knows about our marriage?" Fleur asked feebly.

"He says nothing specifically, although I expect that the servants have told him. Dante will probably want to go down soon, unless that will inconvenience any plans that you have."

Fleur wished she had a diary full of important plans that could not be inconvenienced by a visit to Sussex. Weeks of them.

The last day had tilted her world in ways she did not understand yet. If she had to face Laclere, that world might turn upside down.

The rambling neo-medieval manor house came into view, then grew in size as the carriage rolled up its approaching lane. Two boys played out front, throwing pebbles up against the house, seeing how high they could make the missiles land.

The sound of the coach distracted them. The younger one, who looked to be about four, jumped up and down, waving his arms.

"Someone is excited by your visit," Fleur said.

"That is Edmund," Dante said. "The elder is Milton. The little one adores me, although I don't understand why."

"Perhaps he knows you are not the type to scold him for throwing stones at the house."

Both boys crowded the coach door as soon as they stopped. Dante had trouble getting out. Edmund tugged on his coat, squealing an endless sentence about big ships and a new pony and his hateful tutor and some secret spot near the lake where he had seen a little snake yesterday.

Dante took the child's face in his hands and bent to calm him. "We will see the pony soon, and this afternoon we will go looking for more snakes. Right now, however, there is a lady who cannot descend from the carriage. Make room, and welcome her like the young gentleman you are."

Milton offered his hand to help her down. Unlike Edmund, who was fair-haired, Milton had the dark hair and blue eyes of his father, the viscount. "Welcome, Auntie. We are not supposed to know that Uncle married yet, but I overheard the butler giving Papa the news."

"*Married?*" Edmund looked up at Dante in horror. "Tell Milton he is wrong."

Dante placed his hand on the child's shoulder and gave a gentle squeeze. "Remember, like a gentleman, Edmund."

Face folding into an expression of heartbreak, Edmund made a little bow. "We are joyed to meet you."

Fleur bent down to the distraught little man. "And I am joyed to meet you, Edmund." She gave him a conspiratorial wink. "Mr. Duclairc made me promise not to interfere with important manly affairs like ponies and snakes, so I doubt you will find me much bother."

His relief bloomed and his smile returned. "Oh, *well*, then, *welcome*."

"Yes, welcome," a very adult voice said.

Fleur looked up into the piercing blue eyes of the Viscount Laclere.

His wife, Bianca, stood beside him, wearing a big smile. As two girls skipped down the steps to join their brothers and the greetings flew, Bianca embraced Fleur. "The news was a wonderful surprise. We are so pleased that Dante has found happiness."

Fleur played her role as best she could. She was grateful for the confusion of children and baggage, however. Laclere and Dante managed a few quiet words together. Since both laughed, it did not appear that the visit would be *too* uncomfortable.

"Come," Bianca said. "I will take you to your chamber. I was going to put you together, but Vergil scolded that you should each have your own."

Fleur glanced over to where Laclere was lifting Edmund down from where he had climbed up next to Luke.

Bianca did not know the truth, it appeared. Laclere, however, had reached his own conclusions.

Two horses cavorted on the field. Milton rode the new pony. Dante rode a gelding, with Edmund on the saddle in front of him.

Fleur watched from the terrace of the house. Even from a distance she could see the fun all three boys were having.

"My wife will permit the child on a horse with no one but Dante, me, or herself. Of the three of us, I worry least when he is with my brother."

Fleur startled and turned. Laclere stood a few feet away, watching the joyful play as well.

She glanced around anxiously, but Bianca was not present. The two of them were alone.

"They appear to love him very much," she said.

"He is the perfect uncle, willing to plot with them against us. Every boy should have an uncle like him." He stepped forward, until he stood beside her. "He loves them too, and can still take pleasure in their games. If ever a man had the temperament to be a father, it is Dante."

She swallowed hard and kept her gaze on the horses. Dante had arranged a little race and was in the process of letting Milton and the pony win.

"He is my brother, Fleur. My *brother.*"

She closed her eyes at his tone. He was not making any allusions to her past with Laclere himself or to any unseemliness in this marriage on that count. He was dismayed that she had not considered their old friendship before luring Dante into the marriage and that she had not spared Dante out of respect for that friendship.

"I am correct, am I not? That you offered him a marriage such as you once offered me?"

"I was very honest. I did not play him false. He knew what the arrangement would be when he made his choice."

"He was up to his nose in debt and you threw him a line. It does not sound like much of a choice to me."

"He had other choices, didn't he? He could have relied on friends. He could have turned to you once more. He preferred not to. He knew what he gained and what he lost in this marriage."

"He has no idea what he lost, because it is something he never had, and therefore he could not comprehend its value." He gestured to his sons and brother. "However, he is of an age when he will begin to think about it soon. No children. No intimacy with a woman he loves and wants to hold forever. He is condemned to live the rest of his life as he has so far, with passing passions and no center to his life. A young blood forever."

She had to look away from those horses. She focused on some blades of grass just below the terrace. She wanted to tell Laclere he was wrong, that Dante did not care about such things. Only she wondered if he did, and if he had already begun to resent that he had given them up.

"I have been dreading your return," she said. "I knew you would disapprove and blame me for using him badly."

Laclere's hand covered hers on the stone railing of the terrace. "I do not blame you. I apologize if it sounds that way. I am only concerned for his happiness, and yours."

She welcomed his touch. Until Dante, it had been the only masculine one she could bear. Chaste and caring, it had always been an expression of deep friendship and trust.

She had thought she could have the same friendship with Dante. Only Dante affected her as Laclere never had. As no man had. Now that was leading them to misery.

"Did you explain it all to him, Fleur? I expect it would help if he understood the reasons."

She finally looked at him. His harshly handsome face showed acceptance and concern, not anger. He was Dante's elder by only two years, but he had always been the big brother of the family, even when the firstborn was alive and held the title. Responsibilities had seasoned him at a very young age, and if Bianca had not entered his life and turned it upside down, he may have grown old before his time.

"Of course I explained. He understands it is my nature to be thus, and that it is not my choice."

"I meant, have you explained why it is your nature?"

"There is no why to it, Laclere. I was born this way."

He cocked his head and studied her as if she had said something curious.

"Yes, I expect it is not something you would want to contemplate much," he said. "Let us go and find Bianca. She is very anxious to get the details of this elopement from you. She finds it very romantic."

"Then she does not know the whole story, I assume."

"No, Fleur. Only three of us will ever know that."

Dante knew that sooner or later he and Vergil would have to have a man-to-man. That was what he called the often furious private conversations that they periodically held. Normally Vergil would be at wits end over Dante's debts and bad behavior. Dante had come to view those meetings as the cost of being the viscount's brother, and the price of the allowance that kept him in acceptable style.

This man-to-man, however, was going to be different.

Therefore, he chose to avoid it.

He had other business in the county, and in the afternoon he took a horse from the stable and set out through the park. His ride brought him to a hill that bordered the estate and looked down on a large neighboring house.

He rode toward it through fields that looked well farmed, and noticed a couple of cottages that had been built since the last time he saw this property.

The butler took his card, then returned to lead him to the library. A blond-haired man in his mid-thirties was buttoning his frock coat as they entered.

"Duclairc," he said. "This is a pleasant surprise."

Dante greeted Nigel Kenwood. Kenwood was Bianca's cousin and the second baronet of Woodleigh, the title that Bianca's grandfather had been granted by the Crown.

"My congratulations on your marriage. My sincere hopes that you overcome Farthingstone's challenge to it," Kenwood said. He sat in a handsome chair near a pianoforte. Kenwood could play the instrument very well. Dante expected that music gave him great comfort while he lived in obscurity, land poor in ways that prevented other luxuries.

"Despite your exile from town, you heard about that," Dante said.

"One hears everything if one wants to."

"It is some people's ability to do so that I hoped to discuss with you today."

Kenwood made a display of checking how the closure of his frock coat lined up on his chest. He had always been an elegant man, much enamored of fashion.

"I should have guessed this was not a social call, Duclairc."

"Hardly that."

"Hell, it was years ago. Laclere receives me. You should let it all be buried too."

"At the moment I cannot. I need to know something."

With a deep sigh of resignation, Kenwood lazily flipped his hand. "Go ahead, then."

"That little blackmailing scheme you had ten years ago. Were there others involved who escaped detection?"

"I had *no* blackmailing scheme. If others, whom I thought were friends, used me—"

"You blackmailed Bianca, so do not plead innocence with me."

Kenwood turned sullen and silent.

"Were there others involved?"

"How the hell would I know? I didn't even realize I was involved. What transpired with Bianca—fine, I accept your condemnation. However, I knew nothing about the others. Laclere understands how it was."

"Did you ever sense that there were others involved besides the ones we learned of, however?"

"I suspected that Nancy had other lovers. It is possible that one of them knew what she was doing."

"Was Hugh Siddel one of those lovers?"

"Siddel? Possibly. I wouldn't know."

Dante felt as if he were chipping away at granite. Kenwood had been in the dark about most of that business. It had been unlikely he could shed much light on it now.

"She did know him, however," Kenwood added. "He drifted around the edges of her circle. He even called at her house. That is how I met him. I arrived early one evening, and he was there."

Well, that was something.

Kenwood's lids lowered and his gaze turned contemplative. He rose and strolled around the library, eventually ending up at the pianoforte. Frowning down at the keys, he casually began poking them, creating the slow opening bars of a Beethoven sonata.

"There is something else. I never thought of it before, never considered a connection."

"What is that?"

"Siddel pointed me on the path I took, in a way. It was the night Bianca first performed. He was in the corridor when Laclere came to bring her home. He insinuated they were lovers. Well, the need to both save her from ruin and save her inheritance for myself became of paramount importance. It was very obvious he was right, once he pointed it out. The potential scandal over that became my wedge, so to speak."

Dante pictured Siddel dangling the bait in front of Kenwood, and then a certain ruthless woman making sure it was swallowed.

"That is all useful to know. I appreciate your willingness to speak of it."

The melody stopped. "Do you have cause to think all of that is going to come to light now? I have tried to make what amends I can to Bianca and Laclere, but—"

"I have no reason to think the past will be unburied. You do not have to flee the realm."

"In the event I should, you will warn me, I hope."

"I will see that you are warned."

Dante took his leave and began the ride back to Laclere Park. He sorted through what he had just learned. It wasn't much, but Kenwood's memories added a few more threads to the knot that tied Siddel to recent events, and to old ones.

"Why don't we have our port in my study, Dante?"

Dante almost laughed as he walked beside his brother down to the viscount's study. A man-to-man almost always started with that suggestion. Vergil vainly hoped that the privacy of the study would prevent the servants and family from hearing their arguments.

Little had changed in the study since his last visit to it. Dante noticed a new watercolor on the wall and an extra little wagon among the toys lining the window's deep sill.

"Did one of your sons make this?" he asked, testing the wheels by giving it a little push.

"Milton," Vergil said as he handed over a glass of port.

"His interests take after yours, then. Machines and such."

"Yes. His temperament, however, is closer to our father's and brother's. The water runs very deeply."

"Perhaps he will become a famous poet." He raised his glass. "To your return. Bianca appears as lovely as ever."

"Performing infuses her with life. I could not refuse her this opportunity, even though it meant neglecting my duties here and in the government. She was magnificent, Dante. The years only clarify her voice. It has been some time since I wept when she sang, but I confess that I did in Naples."

Vergil's love for his wife had always awed Dante. The frank way he admitted it, and his willingness to defy society because of it, had always been astonishing. Dante had never understood the deep emotion Vergil clearly experienced, but seeing his solid, self-possessed brother laid low by any sentiment was impressive in itself.

Today his reaction to Vergil's naked admiration was different than in the past, however. He realized that he better comprehended why Vergil believed his wife was worth any cost.

"Penelope must have enjoyed Naples a great deal, if she has chosen not to come home," he said.

Vergil sat in the chair behind his desk and set his glass on the desk's top. "I do not know the whole story with her. She received three letters from the earl while we were there. She abruptly made her decision after she got the last one."

"The man must know by now that she will not return to him."

"Who knows what he thinks. I suspect that Pen realized that in Naples she does not have to live under his shadow. She made friends there, and no one cares that she separated from her husband before giving him his heir." He watched the port swirl as he turned his glass. "As to her decision to remain there, if it relates to the earl, I expect Hampton will know soon. She sent a letter back with me for him."

"He will never tell us what she wrote."

"No, unfortunately. His professional discretion is welcome in my own affairs, but an irritation when he holds secrets I would like to learn. Your marriage, for example. I received two letters from him written after it transpired, but not once amidst all those business details did he even allude to the surprise waiting for me."

"I decided to wait until your return to inform you of the happy event."

Dante sat in the chair on the other side of the desk. He turned it sideways against the front and let his legs sprawl.

How often over the years had they sat thus, Vergil in the position of family head on one side, while he made it clear by his pose and demeanor that, no matter where he sat, he was not a petitioner?

"Hampton advised me not to marry her," he said, to make it easier. "I told him I would explain to you it was just my being reckless again."

"Why would he advise that?"

"The terms of the settlement are not typical."

"Since she had you in a bad place, I expect she could demand any terms she wanted."

"You could say that."

He looked at Vergil, who looked right back.

"I assume that Hampton does not know all the terms," Vergil said.

"No."

Vergil got up and strolled over to the window with its toys. He looked out into the night. "When Fleur offered me a white marriage, the family finances were in dire condition. I confess that I was tempted to solve the problem with her money."

It was an admission that Vergil could understand a man grabbing such a prize. It was not the reaction that Dante had expected. "It must have disappointed you to learn she demanded it be white. You had courted her a long time."

Vergil turned, surprised. "You misunderstand. I always knew. The whole time. The ruse of our courtship was not only hers. I agreed to it. In fact, I arranged it. So, when she suggested marriage, I knew what kind she meant."

"You knew from the beginning? She told you this before you were close? That is hard to believe."

"I learned almost by accident. One day, when I called on her, she confided in me. So I learned the truth, and the reasons. The episode resulted in a friendship and in the mutually beneficial lie that there was more between us."

"Reasons? What reasons?" He was not sure what angered him more—that there were reasons he had not discovered, or that Fleur had confided it all to Vergil but not to him.

Vergil read his mood with a glance. "She did not tell me the reasons. I surmised them. I wonder now if she is even aware of them herself."

"She told you enough that you had grounds to do your surmising, however. What damn reasons did you damn surmise?" His voice cracked through the room.

Well, hell, it wouldn't be a true man-to-man if one of them didn't yell.

"In my entire life, I have never been as tempted to betray a confidence as

I am now, Dante. I have debated all day whether I should do so. However, this is between the two of you, and I should not be in the middle."

He reached down and with one finger rolled his son's wagon back into place beside a carriage he had made when he was a boy. "You might ask her, however, about the day I found her in her parents' garden, weeping. The day when she told me my courtship was in vain."

chapter 19

The knock on her bedroom door interrupted Fleur's dressing. She sent the girl assigned to assist her to fetch the morning tea, then turned to check her finished hair in the mirror of the dressing table.

No tea arrived. Nor did the girl return. Instead, a frock coat and high boots appeared in the mirror's reflection.

She glanced over her shoulder. Dante leaned casually against the wall behind her, watching her primp.

He appeared handsome as sin, as usual. She wished that he didn't. Living with him might be easier if there were some glaring flaw on which she could concentrate whenever she saw him. Perhaps then her heart would not begin a little jig and her skin would not feel so flushed.

She fussed pointlessly with the hairpins and scent bottles on the table. "You rose early today. Do you have something special planned with the children?"

"I told them I am not available today. I rose early to have some time alone with you."

She glanced quickly at his reflection again. His expression reminded her of how he looked the night of the ball. Too composed. Too serious. Too hard, as if the edges of his mood had affected those of his countenance.

"We will go for a walk," he said.

Not an invitation, but a command. No doubt that was part of his plan to be *really* married.

It was the other parts that worried her. "I will join you as soon as the girl returns and I finish dressing."

"I sent her away. I will help you."

"You are inclined to assert your rights this morning, I can see."

"Demanding your company and watching you dress are the least of them, so you should have no objection. Besides, it will not be the first time I did this."

Not the first time that he had dressed or undressed a woman, that was certain. Not even the first time with her.

She began to untie the ribbons that held her powdering gown together. Suddenly he was behind her. She watched in the mirror as his hands came around and gently pushed hers aside. His masculine fingers drew the ends of the ribbons so that the ties came undone, one by one. His hands were so close to her breasts that she imagined their caress even though he did not touch her.

He slid the robe off her shoulders until it pooled around her hips on the chair, leaving her in her petticoats and stays and chemise.

He did not move. She dared not either. She could not see his face, only his torso and hips behind her. She could feel the warmth of his body, however, and the gentle firmness of his hands on her shoulders, where they came to rest.

Excitement and anticipation lured her. Memories of the numbing dread, however, made the moment threatening too.

He moved away. "Let us get you into your dress, so we can enjoy the day."

In the reflection she saw him lift the garment. Her heart flipped with relief, but she also experienced a visceral disappointment.

They walked side by side, not speaking. Their silence was heavy with words waiting to be said. Fleur did not doubt there was a purpose to this outing.

He brought her to the lake in the park. They ambled along the wooded path that surrounded it until they reached a clearing where the family often held parties and picnics. The site provoked old memories, and Fleur couldn't help smiling.

Dante saw. "What amuses you?"

"I am thinking how this visit should be awkward, but is not," she explained. "After all, your brother once courted me, and I once saw you kissing Bianca not far from here."

He laughed quietly. "I had forgotten that you were one of the witnesses to that. I assure you I did not initiate that kiss. She grabbed me."

"Do you think she was trying to make Laclere jealous?"

"I hope so, since she succeeded magnificently."

He did not follow the path through the clearing but aimed to a little rise with a stand of oak trees.

As he did in Durham, and then in her garden, he removed his frock coat and spread it for her to sit on the ground.

"You will have to excuse me for being cautious, Dante, but every time I sit on your coat, I end up in your arms."

"I only want to talk to you this time. In the house the children will find me and interrupt us, unless we hold this conversation in your bedchamber. Would you prefer that?"

He did not intend it as a threat, but his manner indicated that would not be wise. His sensuality had been rippling all morning, like a power that he barely contained. It had been thus since the night of the ball, and her spirit kept waiting, waiting—the waiting itself would be delicious, if she did not know the hell she would experience if the waiting should ever end.

She settled herself down on the coat and Dante sat beside her. He rested an arm on one bent knee and looked to the lake.

"My brother spoke with me," he said.

"Did he say that you were a fool to make this match?"

"No, not that I would have cared if he had. He spoke of the marriage you offered him."

"I think that Laclere should mind his own affairs. He is your brother and my dear friend, but sometimes his arrogance can be annoying and—"

"He also alluded to the reasons you demand a white marriage."

"I told him there are no reasons, except the simplest one."

"What is that?"

She felt her face burn. She hated Laclere for provoking Dante to ask such cruel questions.

She began to rise. "I do not want this conversation and will not be subjected to it."

He grasped her arm before she could stand. Gently but firmly, he forced her to sit again. "What is this simple reason?"

Her whole face tightened. Her teeth clenched. She wanted to hit him. No, she really wanted to hit his brother, who went around meddling in other lives as if he had the right.

"I was born deficient. Lacking. There, are you happy, Dante? I have said it outright. I am unnatural. Incomplete. Less than a full woman. I am inadequate. *Cold.*"

She was close to tears by the time she finished. Only indignation and resentment held her composure together.

She tried to jerk her arm free.

"Darling, you are not—"

"Release me so I can walk my worthless self back to the house where the totally fulfilled wife of my friend the viscount can show off her children and remind me with every look she gives her husband of what I will never have."

"Fleur—"

"*Let me go.*"

"Fleur, you may have thought all of that about yourself once, but you cannot now. We both know you are not cold. There is no deficiency in your nature. There is a difference between being lacking and being afraid, and you are the latter."

"Whatever I am, it is not what you want."

"That is where you are wrong."

She felt the tears coming, burning their way up her throat. She turned her head away, so he would not see them.

He pulled her to him until she rested in the sanctuary of his arms. His embrace soothed her as nothing else ever had, and very few of the brimming tears actually fell. A million might have, however. The mood between the two of them was as heavy as if she had poured out her heart.

He pressed a kiss to her head. "Tell me about the time my brother found you in your parents' garden. The day when you told him you would never marry."

"Please, Dante, let us be done with this."

"Tell me, Fleur."

She sighed. "I had gone to the garden to read a letter I had received. Laclere called, and my mother left him in the garden while she went to find me. She did not know I was there, of course. I think she wanted to speak with me before I met with him, to give me instructions on how to handle this suitor. She often did that. So he was alone, and while strolling the garden he found me in the arbor and we had a chance for some private words."

"You used the opportunity to confide that you would not marry and that his addresses were in vain?"

"Yes. I admired him and did not want to treat him unfairly."

"Did you tell him why you would not marry?"

"Of course not. I was not in the habit of explaining it to acquaintances."

"Yet he knew it was not a girl's whim. He knew you were very serious. When you later offered marriage, he knew what kind you meant."

Seething resentment scorched through her again. It was furious and dark and very frightened. The sensation of panic in her head was similar to when the dread took hold.

She pulled out of his embrace. "I do not want to talk about this anymore."

"I do."

"Then talk to your brother. He seems to know everything about everyone. Get your explanations from him."

"I want to talk to you, not him. You are my wife."

"Not really."

She said it deliberately. She noted with satisfaction the flash of anger in his eyes. Good. Now maybe he would leave her alone instead of picking away at this scab that never healed.

He looked right in her eyes. Determination glowed in the lucid depths that examined her. "He said you were crying when he found you in the garden."

"Was I? I don't remember. Perhaps my father had scolded me that day for not giving an important suitor enough encouragement. He often did that."

"If he often did so, it would not reduce you to tears."

She shrugged, and turned her attention from him to the lake. She contemplated the little ripples the breeze made on the water and allowed her thoughts to wander away from him.

"What was in the letter you were reading that day? Who was it from?"

Heavens, the man was relentless. *Enough.*

"Perhaps it was a letter from an old love, whom I lost and have never forsaken. Maybe I refuse other men because of him."

She threw out the spiteful lie, trusting it would silence him.

It did. Dante went icily still.

She looked over and saw fury flickering in his eyes. He had considered the possibility of that explanation before, she realized. He was prepared to believe it.

She knew two things in that instant. She knew that she wanted so badly for this conversation to end that it maddened her.

She also knew that if the only way to end it meant losing Dante completely, she could not do it.

"I am sorry. I do not know why I said that. It was a cruel thing to throw at you, and it is not true."

"Tell me what was in the letter, Fleur."

Why did she cringe from speaking of it? Why did her heart become so heavy and her throat so tight? "It was written by the mother of one of my girlhood friends, who had married the year before. The letter informed me that my friend had passed away."

He plucked at some grass, watching his fingers while he wore a thoughtful frown. "You must have told my brother what the letter contained."

"I do not remember telling him."

"If he surmised as much as he did, you must have." His hand moved to cover hers. "Did your friend die in childbirth?"

"Yes. How did you know?"

"You were distraught over that letter, and the next thing you did was tell Vergil you will never marry. He saw a connection."

"Then he saw wrong. This did not start that day with that letter. I have always been like this."

"Maybe only for as long as you remember. I think he was right, Fleur. We both know that you are not cold. Not deficient, as you put it. You are by nature very passionate. It is not intimacy you avoid. It is having children."

She rose to her knees in shock. "Now you are insulting me."

"There is no insult."

"There is, and you are vile to—I love children. I would give anything to have them. It breaks my heart that I never will. How dare—"

"I do not think it is motherhood that you fear or deny. I think it is the danger women face in giving birth, darling. Making love can put you in that danger, as it did your friend, and so you will not accept the intimacy."

It was a startling suggestion. She began to object again, but her fury and its words died on her lips as she considered what he said.

He rose to his knees too. He took her face in both his hands and looked down at her. "Do you remember what you said to me that night in Durham? That out by the hedge you could lie to yourself, because you believed in your heart that I would not make love to you there, while a farmer was nearby."

She *had* believed that. But later, in the house, she had known differently.

"Even if you are correct, it makes no difference, Dante."

"It does if you understand that you are not unnatural."

"It is still unnatural. Other women have a normal life, even knowing of the danger. They do not think of death but of the life they carry. They are joyful. Catherine, my neighbor—I worried for her, but she never did for herself. And then—"

He pulled her into his arms and stroked her hair as he held her. "How many friends have you lost this way?"

"The same as most women, I expect." She nestled in his arms and rested her head on his shoulder. She tried to remember if there had been others. Her mother's friend, Mrs. Benedict, had died lying in, now that she thought about it. Her mother never said so, but Mrs. Benedict was big with child and then gone.

Three then. Not so many.

Too many.

An image came to her suddenly, either from her past or her imagination, she did not know which. A picture of blood and of a woman screaming soundlessly. It was the same horrible thing she saw when the panic gripped her, and now it flickered through her mind and made her shudder. Only this time she was watching it, and there were others around the woman, holding her down as she screamed and screamed.

"I think I saw it once, Dante. When I was a girl." She tried to remember when it had been, and where. "Not at my home. It was in the country. Maybe I passed a cottage and heard something and looked in. I think I saw it through a window. I still see it when—when I get afraid. Not clearly, just pieces."

He kissed her temple. "Do not force yourself to remember."

He sat again, and rested against the tree. When he reached out his hand, she took it, and he pulled her back into his arms.

It was wonderful snuggling there with him. White clouds moved across the sky above the lake. They reminded her of the clouds in Durham and the game she and Dante had played. The breeze was cool, but his warmth saturated her.

She let herself go limp against him, more spent than tired. She felt very close to him, as close as when they were in the cottage.

She was glad that he had made her talk about this if it meant that intimacy could return. He said he could not live in their false marriage, but maybe they could remain friends now.

"Laclere said if you knew the reason it may help," she said. "I cannot see how it would."

"He was right. I am glad that I understand."

"Understanding does not change me."

"Perhaps not, but it makes very clear which intimacies you cannot permit and which you can."

And which you can?

"There are ways to make love that do not result in pregnancy, Fleur." His voice flowed to her ear quietly. "You would need to trust the man in order to avoid the fear, I expect. You would need to believe that he would not take those things that you cannot give."

She stayed very still, listening to his heartbeat, luxuriating in the warmth of their embrace. But she sensed a change in him. He had released that special vitality. It entered her and made the waiting return.

He turned her in his arms, cradling her shoulders so he could see her face.

"How much do you trust *me*, pretty flower?"

"I am not sure it is possible for me to trust any man the way you mean."

He kissed her. Not a kiss between friends. She suspected that whatever else this day wrought, his kisses would never pretend to be chaste again.

The long connection moved her deeply. Her heart wrenched with the awareness of what it could not have, but also filled with the sweetest longing. She almost regretted that he understood and accepted what was wrong with her. That was how confused and aroused his kiss could make her—her body wanted him enough that it betrayed her own defenses.

"It may be that you cannot trust any man enough, Fleur. However, I will have to find out now."

She half-expected him to try and find out then and there. She half-wanted him to. The likelihood that she would fail the test saddened her, however. When that happened, he would never hold her like this again. He would stop kissing her in a way that shook her soul.

Did he sense her hesitation? See her concern in her eyes? Suddenly his embrace was gone and he was helping her to rise.

He dipped his head to kiss her again. "Later."

Taking her hand, he led her back to the house.

"A letter came today from Adrian Burchard," Vergil said as he and Dante sat in the music room that night, politely listening to Vergil's oldest child, Rose, play the pianoforte. "It was the usual welcome back to the country. However, it included a message for you."

Dante had not been paying much attention to Rose, except to notice that with her blond hair, blue eyes, and heart-shaped face, she resembled her mother, who turned the pages for her.

His attention had been on the other females in the room. In a far corner Fleur sat with Vergil's younger daughter, Edith. Fleur patiently plaited the little girl's dark hair, taking her time, prolonging contact with the child.

"What was the message?"

"He asked that you call on him when you return to town. He has some information for you. That was all he wrote."

Fleur finished the plaits and pinned them into a circlet that made Edith look too old. The child grinned impishly at her cohort, as if they had done something naughty.

Edith gave Fleur a big hug and then skipped over to her father to show off her grown-up hair.

Dante watched Fleur's attention follow the girl. He saw her bittersweet expression as Edith climbed onto her father's lap and began beguiling his attention away from her sister's performance.

Fleur's gaze shifted and she caught him watching her. The conversation from the morning suddenly echoed silently in the air between them. Especially the last part.

He went over and sat with her. "Your expression is enigmatic. Both welcoming and cautious. You probably do not know how alluring that can be to a man."

Her face flushed adorably. Her nervousness was palpable, charming, and provocative as hell.

"I will not be coming to your chamber tonight, if that is why you are so unsettled."

"Not unsettled . . . More confused and . . . Well, *somewhat* unsettled, but—"

"I will be borrowing a horse from the stable and riding back to town early tomorrow, to call on Adrian Burchard. You can come home in the carriage later. So you are safe for another day."

She laughed lightly, and looked so beautiful that she almost was not safe tonight after all.

"Are you thinking that you should deny me, Fleur? Is that the debate I see taking place behind those lovely eyes?"

Her lids lowered, and it appeared that she reflected deeply for a moment. She gave the subtlest shake of her head. "I have realized how vulnerable I will be, however. In ways that have nothing to do with trusting your restraint."

"You fear it will be as in the past?"

"Yes, that too."

"Then we will discover for certain what can and can't be. I think it is time to know, don't you?"

"Yes, Dante. I think it is time to know that."

chapter 20

Ⅰt was time to know.

Fleur chanted that to herself the next day as she supervised the packing of her trunk.

"We will be coming up to town next week," Bianca said. She sat on the bed, watching the preparations. "I count on your accompanying me to the theater as soon as possible."

Fleur appreciated the invitation. It had not been the first such overture, and Fleur wished she had used this visit with Bianca better. If she had not been so absorbed in herself, they might have become good friends. Then perhaps Fleur could have asked her about things.

Such as those other ways to make love that Dante mentioned.

She had no idea what he meant. Her imagination utterly failed her when she tried to puzzle it out. Perhaps she should put him off until she found out. . . .

No, it was time.

"Laclere is very pleased with your marriage. He confided to me that he sees a change in Dante and thinks no woman would have suited him better."

"Did he really say that?"

"Just last night. You look surprised."

"I thought that he considered the quickness of it unwise."

"He may have at first, but a letter from Charlotte yesterday gave him a right understanding. She explained the matter with your stepfather. Vergil had no idea, and neither Dante nor you had said anything about that."

"I suppose it seemed a world away." That was not the only reason. She had not explained about Gregory because it would sound calculating and self-ish—that she had married Dante to save her own skin.

"It was very noble of Dante, of course, but also hardly a great sacrifice. Not because of your fortune, but because of his affection for you."

Bianca's frankness only unsettled Fleur more. Somehow she saw to the closing of her trunk and Bianca called for the footmen to carry it down.

Alone in the chamber, Bianca gave her a very direct look. "So, everyone is agreed that this marriage is good for Dante, that it will ensure both his solvency and his happiness. Is it also good for you?"

The bold question took Fleur by surprise. Bianca was not a woman who dissembled much, and that could be disconcerting in a world where most people dissembled all the time. It left Fleur with either responding honestly or not answering at all.

"There have been many surprises in my alliance with him. In many ways, this marriage has not been what I anticipated it would be. As to whether it will prove good for me, I think there is a chance that it will."

"I am happy to hear that, and hope if there is that chance, you will grab it. I believe a woman should decide what she wants and fight for it, not allow herself to be merely buffeted by the winds of life."

As Fleur took her leave of the household and rode through the Sussex countryside, she thought about Bianca's advice. She did not know if the winds about to blow through her life would bring good or ill, but it was time to decide what she wanted.

It was also time to know if she could experience passion with a man without turning to stone.

It would only be possible with Dante. No other man had stirred her at all, let alone enough to contemplate such a risky experiment. If he had not entered her life again, she would have never suspected that she had been wrong about herself all these years.

However, in thinking all night about what was to come "later," she had thought about other things too. As she lay in her bed, so saturated with anticipation that she wished "later" did not mean in London, her thoughts had turned to what being really married to Dante would mean.

Pleasure, to be sure. He had already shown her that.

Friendship, she hoped. Friendship unfettered by the confusion that had interfered with it recently.

But also, maybe, unhappiness. He had warned as much in Durham.

He would not be faithful. She accepted that he could not give her that, just as he accepted what she could not give him. He himself did not believe he had it in him to be constant.

However, if his affairs had wounded her while they were not really married, when his visits to other beds were not betrayals of her, how would she live with them after "later"?

She could not deny Dante because of it. She would not give up the chance to know what they could share. But she did not lie to herself. Knowing the passion would leave her exposed to horrible heartbreak.

As the carriage entered London's environs and aimed to the city, all thoughts of potential unhappiness fell away. Most other thoughts did too. An image invaded her mind and stayed there, banishing all emotions except excitement and longing.

It was the memory of Dante on their wedding day, looking in her eyes as he held her face in his wonderful hands. The rest of the way home she experienced again the perfect, sweet unity she had known that day when he kissed her, once on the forehead, and once on the lips.

A woman should decide what she wants and fight for it.

She experienced an instant of total honesty as she glimpsed her future in all its possibilities. She knew which one she wanted with a security that all the arguments in the world could not have achieved.

It astonished her how easy it was to make her decision. She did not know if she had the courage to fight for it, however.

Especially since the person whom she would be fighting was herself.

An empty house wears its abandon in invisible ways. One senses the silence as one walks past. It exudes loneliness onto the street.

That was what Fleur thought as the carriage stopped in front of her home. For a moment she felt it had been closed forever.

It startled her, therefore, when the door opened and Dante came out to the coach.

"Your meeting with Mr. Burchard was successful?" she asked as he handed her down.

"It was interesting. I will tell you about it later."

Luke removed her trunk, and Dante helped him carry it into the house. "The day is fair, Luke. Take the afternoon for yourself after you have done with the horses. We will not need a carriage today."

Delighted by this unexpected gift, Luke hurried out to get on with his duties.

Fleur stood in the reception hall and listened to . . . nothing. "Are they all gone?"

"Yes."

"I do not think I have ever been alone here before."

Arm along her waist, he strolled with her toward the stairs. "You are not alone now. Think of it as another cottage, where you find yourself with no one but me for company."

"Who will cook for us, and dress us?"

"We will do for ourselves, as we did there."

"I did nothing there. You did it all."

"Then I will here as well." He handed her up the stairs. "I want no one else here today. No sounds, no service, no interruptions. We will read together, or hold conversations, or just sit together, with no duties or demands. There will be no world outside these walls, and the only world inside them will be the two of us together."

He parted from her on the first floor and went into the library. She continued on to her chambers.

Essential comforts had been provided. Water had been left in the dressing room so she could refresh herself. Scones and jam and punch waited in her sitting room. Knowing Dante, he had instructed the cook to leave enough prepared food in the kitchen so they would not starve.

Alone. The lovely silence derived from more than the lack of sound. The absence of people brought an exquisite peace to the house. She could feel Dante's presence distinctly, even far away, because absolutely nothing else intruded.

Conversation and companionship. Confidences and friendship. She had no idea how Dante had seduced other women, but he knew her very well.

She drank a little of the punch and looked at her *secrétaire*. Inside it were all the pieces of her Grand Project. It astonished her to realize that today, right now, she did not care about it at all. Dante occupied her mind, and the most poignant emotion swelled her heart.

She allowed her hope and longing to have its way. She was beyond fighting either. She would not know how to contain what owned her even if she wanted to. The hope gave her strength too. She would need that.

Looking in her mirror, she removed her bonnet. She gazed in her own eyes and admitted the sad truth. She was not a girl, not a child. She was a woman who had allowed an unknown fear to waste the best years of her life.

She was also a woman who was hopelessly in love with a man, and who wanted all of that man that she could have.

Gathering her courage, praying that she had enough, she went down to the library.

She found him sitting on the divan, waiting for her.

She walked over and stood in front of him. "I do not think it was wise to empty the house of servants, Dante."

"Whatever you require, I will see to it. What do you need?"

"I would like to remove this dress, and I have no maid to assist me." She turned her back to him.

She expected him to say something clever and to help her at once. Instead, a stillness formed behind her, and he did not move. She kept her pose long enough that she began to feel foolish.

She glanced over her shoulder.

His gaze met hers. "You are sure, Fleur?"

She loved him so much right then. It had always been like this, however. He had always protected her, even when it went against his own interests and desires.

"I am very sure that I want to remove this dress, Dante."

His hands went to work on its closure, but his gaze did not leave her face. The sensation of the cloth parting and his hands touching caused the restrained anticipation of the last day to deluge her. The look in his eyes captivated her. She had come down determined to be bold and confident, but already she was in his power.

"Will you be requiring assistance in donning another dress, Fleur?"

She could not find her voice. She merely shook her head.

He plucked at the knot where the lacing to her stays ended. "Then I should attend to this as well."

Holding her steady with one hand on her hip, he unlaced with the other. "You surprise me, darling."

"I have been working on my courage all day, and thought I should not risk its deserting me. Am I being too forward?"

"Not at all. I had planned a slow seduction, but only because I expected to need one."

She faced front and closed her eyes to savor the sensations already titillating her. "You have been seducing me for weeks, Dante. We both know it has been slow enough."

The stays gaped. She had to grasp her garments to her breast to keep them from falling to the ground.

He rose behind her. Holding her shoulders, he pressed a kiss to the side of her neck. A sparkling shiver danced through her.

She stepped away, out of his reach. "Thank you. I can manage the rest."

Heart pounding, she hurried back to her chamber.

Somehow, she held on to her resolve. Even though she shook as she peeled off the rest of her garments. Even when she slid the pink silk bed gown over her nakedness. Even when she heard the movements on the other side of the wall that said Dante was in his chambers.

She stood still, listening, deciding what to do. Initiating this so quickly had used up a lot of her bravery.

She summoned more.

She needed him to believe that she knew what she wanted. She also needed to prove it to herself.

She turned the latch and opened the door to his dressing room.

.   .   .

She intruded while Dante was removing his shirt. He turned in surprise.

She entered and closed the door behind her. She rested her back against the door.

"You intend to stay while I undress?"

"Should I not?"

He shrugged. "As you wish." He continued with the shirt.

He shed his upper garments. Naked from the waist up, he sat on a chair to remove his boots.

His body fascinated her. She had seen sculptures and paintings, but never a real male form without clothes. How beautiful he was, leanly framed but tight with muscles. She had thought it would be embarrassing to see him unclothed. Instead, nothing could be more natural, and she was not embarrassed at all. Aroused, but not embarrassed. She recognized the physical purr inside her for what it was now.

He looked at her, and she could tell that he knew what she was thinking and experiencing. He stood and faced her, as comfortable with his physical presence as ever, in control of this disrobing even if he was the one who stripped.

"Do you intend to continue watching?"

"Shouldn't I? Do you want me to leave?"

"I do not want you to leave, although I cannot remember ever being watched so obviously."

"I thought that since you have seen me, it was only fair for me to see you."

"I am not seeing you now."

No, he was not. She had stacked the deck, to buy herself some courage. Nor had she planned to just stand and watch him. She had intended to speak with him when she opened that door. Seeing his body had become a delicious distraction.

He had challenged her, and she was determined not to play the shy virgin today. She stepped away from the door. "Do you want to see me? Will that make it more fair?"

"Yes."

She walked over to him. That brought her very close to his chest and shoulders and skin and hardness and . . .

He did not touch her. He looked down, as if waiting for something.

"Aren't you going to assist me, Dante? I thought it was one of your rights."

"You said that you can manage it yourself, and you are certainly acting as if you can."

"You would prefer I did it myself?"

"Sometimes."

This time.

Removing that gown was more difficult than she expected, because of the way he watched. She wondered if he had found her gaze so disconcerting a few minutes ago. She could not deny, however, that she enjoyed the wicked thrill of sliding the silk down her arms and lowering it to the floor. She liked the way his expression tightened with the subtle signs of how she affected him.

Her initial awkwardness passed, replaced by a sense of power and pride. His gaze made her magnificent and noble and strong. Standing naked in the afternoon light in front of Dante, she became a goddess.

He reached for her hand and drew her toward him, into his arms. The embrace astounded her. The warmth of his body, touching hers skin on skin all over, pressing her breasts, surrounding her completely—the new sensations piled up, threatening to bury her sense of everything else.

Somehow she held on to her mind. She had come through that door with a goal, and he needed to know what it was.

"I need to say something to you, Dante."

He nuzzled her neck. "Tell me later."

"It must be now. You see, I have changed my mind about this."

His embrace loosened until he was only holding her waist. His lids lowered. "You have not been acting like a woman who has changed her mind."

"You do not understand. I am not saying that I want you to stop. In fact, I do not want you to think that you have to stop at all. Ever."

"You are correct. I do not understand."

"If I believe you will not do anything to impregnate me, I am sure that the fear will not come. That is how much I trust you. There is no need to test that. It is always there for us."

His expression turned serious, and perplexed. "Are you saying that you would like to test something else instead?"

"Yes. I think that even if you do not promise restraint, the fear still will not come."

She had assumed he would have more enthusiasm for her decision than he now revealed. He looked deeply in her eyes, as if searching to see if her heart supported her words.

"I do not want this dread to own my life anymore. In naming it, maybe I have defeated it." She laid her cheek on his chest, so that the taut warmth of his skin touched hers. "I want us to be fully married, Dante. I want to have a family. I want these things so much that I believe my desire for them can conquer any fear." She looked up at him. "I want you too. Completely. That alone would be enough for me to make this decision."

He laid his hand on her face. "If you are wrong . . ."

"If I am wrong, we will know very soon."

"I do not want to frighten you or hurt you."

"I will not let you. I will not try to brave it out. I am incapable of controlling this if it takes hold. You must promise me, however, that you will not make the choice for me. I will only know if I am free if I believe your intentions have changed."

A small, charming smile broke. "I think I can promise that if you demand it."

"I do demand it."

"Then know now that I will take you if I can, Fleur. Believe it."

His kiss displayed his resolve. It also revealed the passion of a man who had been listening to too much talk, even if he welcomed what he had heard.

The kiss awoke all of the anticipation her body had buried during the long weeks of wanting him. Her skin was wickedly alert as he caressed parts of her that had never felt his touch directly before. Her back and hips and thighs responded to his warm palms and fingers. New sensations startled her again and again.

He kissed her deeply, in a way he never had before. She could not ignore the subtle difference. It came from his aura more than his action. A primitive part of her could tell that he had not lied. The man who kissed her, who dominated her with his body and embrace, who handled her so possessively that the claim of rights could not be ignored—this man intended to have her if he could.

She understood that without thinking it. Her soul knew.

The fear knew.

It shot out one of its strangling tendrils. She recognized it for what it was. Images of crying faces invaded her head. Her body wanted to recoil defensively, to end the assault.

She would not let it.

She embraced Dante desperately and focused her physical awareness on the delicious feel of his skin and muscles, on the tension in his body and the hardness under her hands. She let her consciousness dwell on his reality.

She summoned more than pleasure to her little battle, however. She let her love for him free. In the warmth and glow of its promise of fulfillment, the fear abruptly withered and shrank and ceased to threaten her.

The victory left her euphoric. Liberated. She had thought she could not control this dread, but she could. With Dante she could. Acknowledging her love gave her a weapon the fear could not face.

Dante knew what had happened. She could tell that he did. He stopped kissing her but his caresses continued, following her curves and feeling her nakedness, tantalizing her. He looked down with eyes that recognized what had just occurred in the last few moments.

A hard challenge entered the lucid depths gazing at her. His caress moved down her body. Daring the fear by making his intentions explicit, his hand smoothed up her bottom, then slowly descended. His fingers skimmed down her cleft and followed the line to where it met moisture and softness and a maddening pulsation.

The touch on that spot shocked her. Wonderfully. Gloriously. Her whole body reacted, but not with fear. She stretched up, seeking his kiss hungrily, needing a way to release the stunning, deep, sensual throb.

The war was won, and they both knew it. She announced her victory by kissing him as intimately as he did her. With her tongue she expressed her pride and excitement.

Heady with liberation, proud of her boldness, she kissed down his neck and his chest, tasting him, enthralled by unfettered pleasure.

The full force of his sensual vitality broke free, encompassing her more completely than his arms. She welcomed the way it dazzled her, controlled her, taught her.

He lifted her in his arms and carried her into his chamber. He laid her on the bed and finished undressing while he looked at her.

"You are very beautiful, Fleur."

She did not doubt him. Right now, lying on this bed in the filtered light, euphoric from fighting for her right to love and feel, she was sure that she was the most beautiful woman who had ever lived.

The most beautiful man in the world now stood by the bed, his full magnificence revealed, so stunning that her heart did not know whether to race or simply stop. He was a fitting consort for the goddess she had become. His body fascinating her so much she could not look at him enough.

He came to her.

"This is a remarkably singular occurrence, Miss Monley. Finding you, of all women, in my bed."

He had said that in the cottage, but his tone was different this time. He was not teasing.

Only she was no longer Fleur Monley, the saint, the angel. She was a queen, a warrioress, a handmaiden of Venus, a—

"You are very proud of yourself, aren't you?" He kissed her nose, which hardly befitted her new power.

"Bursting with pride."

"As you should be." He watched his hand caress down her neck and around her breasts. "All the same, you must let me know if I frighten you."

"I am not going to stop you, Dante."

"You can still let me know your pleasure, Fleur. If I do something you do not want, you can tell me that."

"There is nothing I do not want. I have been denied this too long. I have no intention of missing one thing because of cowardice."

"You do not understand what I am talking about, darling." He kissed her lightly on her cheek. "You will soon, so remember what I said. I do not want any silent sacrifices. You have a whole life to try everything."

She stretched her fingers through the hair on his head. "I would not be cautious if I were you, Dante. I am probably braver now than I will ever be again." She pressed him down so she could kiss him.

He did not allow her to control the kiss long. With a masterful embrace he took over and bestowed dozens of nuanced pleasures on her lips and neck and ear. He made her want him with kisses alone until the waiting possessed her again, and built and built.

Her body craved the return of his caress. He was slow in giving it to her, so that when his hand trailed down her chest she almost begged him to touch her.

He teased as he had in the garden. The same wanton pleasure enslaved her. His circling fingertips had her gritting her teeth. She was helpless to the hunger he demanded.

His head dipped and his tongue began the same slow patterns on her other breast. The desire deepened, went lower. It filled her hips and made her vulva cry. She lost awareness of everything but the sensations and the pleasure and the frantic desire.

His fingers gently touched one nipple. His tongue flicked at the other. An arrow of shivering pleasure shot down her body.

Then another, and another. It felt so good that she wanted it to go on forever. Her body demanded, ached, for relief even as it begged for more.

She could not contain the chaotic need. She heard the sounds of her delirium but did not care.

His head moved and he kissed her again. His hand moved and she rebelled at the pleasure's end with a muffled cry. He broke the furious kiss and looked down her body. His caress slid lower, to her stomach and thighs.

Her desire moved lower too. The waiting became very focused, very intense. Her legs parted to encourage the caress she desperately wanted. The newly freed primitive part of her comprehended this passion in ways her mind did not.

He caressed closely until her hips were rising toward his touch, begging for more. She saw the expression of hard command when he finally responded to her body's demands and her audible cries. He looked back at her face with the first touch and then watched as his slow strokes created a pleasure so intense that she lost all control.

She did not care that she had forsaken sanity and dignity and begged for something she did not understand. She did not care that he controlled her madness with his hands and eyes.

He kissed her lips, then her breast, then her stomach. He kissed lower, leaving her arms bereft as his body moved down.

"I am glad that you are so brave today," he said softly. "Because I have been wanting to do this for weeks."

She watched, confused. Her body understood, however. With each kiss closer, her vulva shivered.

His kisses went lower yet. His body moved more. Her mind finally comprehended. The notion shocked her. His hand lured her. Prepared her. She closed her eyes just as he moved his body between her thighs and gently lifted her hips.

His tongue replaced his fingers, and her brief spike of sanity shattered. She submitted to the excruciating combination of pleasure and devastating desire. It just got better and better and worse and worse as he drove her to the edge of a terrible, wonderful experience.

An unbearable peak beckoned. She reached for it because there was no place else to go. Her passion leapt, touched a glorious spot of pure pleasure, and showered through her essence.

He was with her suddenly, back in her arms, lying between her legs as he had in Durham. No garments interfered this time. She grasped him, intensely aware of his weight and warmth.

Her vulva still pulsed, still possessed that craving need. The sensation of him entering brought incredible relief. He pressed deeper and the fullness astonished her emotions.

Pain wanted to intrude on her daze. Her passion absorbed it, ignored it, conquered it. He thrust and they were fully joined and he filled her completely. The intimacy of holding him, of feeling him a part of her, moved her more than the highest pleasure she had just learned. She closed her eyes and savored the complete bond.

His passion guided the rest. She sensed a restraint on his desire, and knew when it fell away. His power controlled them both then, creating a whirlwind of tumultuous, fevered kisses and thrusts that awed her. She could only accept and absorb and feel. Nothing at all existed for her but love and intimacy and the reality of him in her body and arms.

The end left her dazed and astonished by her own emotions. Holding him in the stillness afterward, it was as if her heart and soul had been left without any protection. She held him to her, so alert to his scent and breaths and skin that it seemed new senses had been born in her. Special ones, which existed only for knowing this man.

She wanted him to stay on her forever, bound like this, but eventually he moved. Even after he withdrew and shifted his weight off her, she still pulsed as if they were connected.

"Did I hurt you?"

"No." She did not know if he had. It did not matter.

"Did I shock you?"

"No . . . well, a little." She turned on her side to face him. "Was that everything?"

"No."

She smiled. "Stupid question. Of course it wasn't. After all, you forgot to show me that sensitive spot behind my knee."

"That I did."

"And the trick with the base of my spine—no doubt you are saving that for another day too."

He laughed quietly. "I promise to do better next time, when I am not so impatient."

She drew a little pattern on his chest. "And the discovery about how a woman's body can be more sensitive after . . ."

"It is not too late for that." His caress moved down her body. "Part your legs wide, then do not move."

She obeyed. His first touch shocked her whole body. His finger stroked low, caressing flesh unbelievably sensitive from their lovemaking. The pleasure was almost unbearable.

Abandon claimed her with a violent break in her control. Almost instantly she tottered on the highest point of arousal, begging for more, shuddering with desperate expectation. It was more intense and dangerous than the last time. The pleasure was unearthly, excruciating, shattering.

Her body released her. She cried as a powerful climax quaked through her. She floated in a bliss of perfect sensation, with the echo of a cry filling her head.

Awareness of the bed and chamber returned to her slowly. It was some time before she rose above the sensual stupor, however.

Dante was waiting for her when she did. She opened her eyes to find him watching her. It seemed that the room still rang with her scream.

"I think it is a good thing that I sent the servants away," he said.

"Oh, yes." She also thought it had been wise to delay "later" until after they left Laclere Park.

chapter 21

It is just as you said it would be, Dante. No world exists outside these walls, and only the two of us exist inside them." Fleur nestled closer. "When will they return?"

Her words pulled him out of the cloud of contentment in which he had been floating while he held her closely.

"I handed out enough coin to keep them busy at theaters and taverns most of the night."

He turned on his side and propped his head on his hand. Her beauty awed him. Her courage did. He had not been able to lure her from the fear with pleasure. It had taken her own will, her own choice, to do that. It humbled him that she had donned such bravery in order to share passion with him.

She had been determined, magnificent, glorious.

I want to have a family.

Her soft, pale skin felt more luxurious than the most precious cloth. He caressed her shoulder and arm slowly and her lids lowered as they shared the touch.

I want you.

He had never in his life heard such flattering words. They had been spoken by others, but not in this way, or for this reason. He wanted her too, also in ways he had never desired before.

That is how much I trust you. There is no need to test that.

He would never forget those astonishing words.

I want us to be fully married.

He glanced over to his writing desk and thought about the letter in its drawer. It was from Farthingstone and had been waiting for him when he returned this morning. The man wanted to negotiate, and Dante suspected the direction those negotiations would take.

He gave his wife a kiss, to put thoughts of Farthingstone and his maneuvers out of his mind.

It was not to be. Fleur turned to him, looking so lovely with her hair half down and her nakedness draped with the sheet.

"What did Mr. Burchard want? You said you would tell me later."

The meeting seemed a lifetime ago, not mere hours. Dante had to force his memory back to it. Anticipation of Fleur's return meant he only partly listened to Adrian's information, and he had not deliberated its meaning at all.

"Burchard undertook some inquiries on my behalf."

"You asked him to do this?"

"No. He has some experience in such things and used his own initiative as my friend."

"Much as St. John and Mr. Hampton used their initiatives and made inquiries about me, you mean. You have very dedicated friends. Although one might also say they are a little presumptuous."

"One might say so."

"What sort of inquiries did Mr. Burchard make? More regarding me?"

"He inquired about Farthingstone. He learned little that could not be discovered by anyone. That Farthingstone received a legacy as a young man, which included that property in Durham that neighbors yours. He lives simply considering his income and is well regarded."

"We already know that."

"The rest was more interesting, however. Farthingstone was not always so sober and upstanding. He had a wilder youth, and as a young man looked to be one who would come to no good. Burchard's aunt remembers him from back then and related how a miraculous transformation occurred rather suddenly when Farthingstone was nearing thirty years old. The change was so complete that his past has been all but forgotten."

"I would prefer he still gambled and drank and ruined himself than that he presented himself as so respectable while he tried to imprison me and then destroy my reputation. The world is too quick to judge for good or ill in these things. I daresay your friend McLean is more honorable than Gregory, but McLean is notorious and Gregory is admired."

There it was, the world as seen through Fleur Monley's eyes. He was glad that she tried to perceive the essentials, even if sometimes she saw more than was there. When she looked at Dante Duclairc, her optimism blinded her.

"If that was all he could tell you, it wasn't very interesting at all. Was there more?"

"That was most of it." Dante was not sure he wanted to broach the rest. Not now, at least. He did not want it intruding on this day and this bed.

"I am curious now, so you must tell me all."

He caressed her shoulder again and turned his gaze away from her face so he would not see her reaction. He was not sure what he avoided witnessing. "He also discovered that there is a connection between Farthingstone and Siddel. A distant one, and it probably means nothing."

She did not respond for a while. He might have said nothing at all.

"Did you ask him to make inquiries regarding Mr. Siddel, Dante?"

"I asked him if he had cause to think they are friends."

"They are not."

"Fleur, your stepfather learned you were in that cottage. Siddel is a man who could have told him. If he did, it meant that Siddel knew he was in the county that night. It may even have been Siddel whom you overheard speaking in the next chamber the night before."

She tilted her head and looked up at him. She did not appear angry, but thoughtful. Very thoughtful. "What connection did Mr. Burchard discover?"

"Farthingstone has no apparent friendship with Siddel. He did, however, have one with Siddel's uncle. They shared bad behavior together."

"Much like you and McLean?"

"Much like that. Siddel's own comfort depends upon a legacy of his own, from this uncle."

"Or from his business affairs. I expect his success in those has enhanced his fortune considerably."

"It is not at all clear that he is so successful in business. Burchard could find little evidence of any grand financial schemes, despite Siddel's reputation for them."

"No doubt he keeps them secret."

"Burchard has the means to discover secrets when he wants to. He undertook inquiries for the government when he was younger, and there are men willing to share information with him that they would not give to others."

He could see her weighing that, although her expression did not change.

The night of the ball, he had demanded that she not use Siddel for an adviser any longer. She had not welcomed that command, and he had not been convinced she would obey it. She may not have.

She looked right in his eyes. "You do not like him at all, do you?"

"As I told you, I do not think he can be trusted."

"It is more than that. You get very hard when you speak of him. Even now, your mood has darkened."

"Perhaps that is because I wonder if your relationship with him continues."

Her fingers touched his face and drifted over his cheek and jaw. "What is this man to you?"

He stopped her hand and took it in his own. He gazed down at the delicate fingers and ran his thumb along the back of her palm.

She waited for him to answer, but she would accept it if he did not. If he kissed her, the question itself would be forgotten.

"Some years ago, there were some people blackmailing prominent men. They were stopped by my brother. I think that Hugh Siddel was one of the blackmailers but escaped detection."

Her expression fell in surprise. "That is a serious accusation to make, Dante."

"I will not make it publicly unless I have proof. It is doubtful I ever will."

"If you don't have proof, how—"

"He knows things he should not, Fleur. Things he could not know unless he was involved." He hesitated, and told himself no good could come from explaining it. Yet the impulse to go on was greater than the one to spare himself the pain of forming the words.

She said nothing. No prodding or insistence. She just watched him. Her expression was so thoughtful. Her eyes held worry and concern, but no expectations.

"I inadvertently helped them, Fleur. A woman among them used my desire for her to gain access to some documents. Those papers were then used to blackmail two men. Both of those men killed themselves."

He had never told anyone this. Never even said it aloud. It sounded even more damnable than he expected. His chest felt heavy, as if the air in his lungs had thickened.

Fleur caressed his face again, more deliberately. "The crime was not yours, but theirs. No man could have foreseen what would happen. You should not blame your—"

"One of the men who killed themselves was my eldest brother."

A flicker of shock flashed in her eyes. Then she looked at him with the warmest sympathy he had ever seen.

She understood. He did not have to say more. Her honest, clear eyes seemed to see into his mind and even his heart and perceive the guilt he carried. He could tell she knew that no excuses or absolution could make a difference.

And yet, somehow, just her gaze changed things. That accepting silence eased the weight of this old memory. Finally sharing it with this friend brought some peace to the corner of his soul where he kept this disgrace hidden.

She shifted closer and embraced him, laying her soft cheek against his chest, holding him more than he held her.

"We have let the outside world intrude, after all," she said quietly. She sounded a little sad.

Not the outside world. Their world. The one in which they lived, full of the people and events that affected their lives and this marriage. He knew what she meant, however.

He gently tugged on the sheet. It slowly slid down her body as the soft folds receded. He caressed her, his hand following the same path as the sheet's edge over softness and curves. He pulled her closer, to his heart.

"I know a way to make the world go away, Fleur. I know a place where it cannot find us."

"Yes," she whispered. "Take me there, Dante."

The next afternoon, Dante waited in the study for a visitor to arrive. He had spent little time in this chamber, and this was the first time he would conduct official business here. Or anywhere.

He had always avoided the serious financial dealings that he associated with studies. As a young man he had found them boring and bothersome, the kinds of matters best left to old men and dutiful sorts like his brother.

He studied the Piranesi engravings lining one wall and the Canaletto painting showing the Grand Canal of Venice on another. If meetings like this became a habit, he would keep the engravings but the Canaletto would have to go. He did not care for the artist's *veduti* of Italy. They were so dully acceptable. No risk at all.

The door opened and Williams brought the expected card. Farthingstone was precisely punctual.

"It was generous of you to receive me," Farthingstone said when he arrived. "May I say at the outset that I hope you and I can settle amiably the entire problem that besets us, and in a way that ensures the welfare of Hyacinth's daughter."

They sat in two chairs. Farthingstone took in the room and smiled when he noticed the painting. "Ah, the Canaletto. I remember when Mr. Monley purchased it. I favor his art. That is an excellent example, if I may say so."

Dante studied this dull man who favored dull Canaletto and tried to picture him chasing naked girls through a summer garden, as Burchard's aunt had described one scandalous rumor of a long-ago bacchanal.

"You had important matters to discuss, you said," Dante prompted.

Farthingstone's expression grew very serious. "I regret to say that I suspect you do not know the full extent of Fleur's condition. What I have to say may come as a shock to you."

"Consider me prepared for the worst."

Farthingstone had the decency to flush and feign hesitation before he gave the bad news. "I have discovered that prior to your alliance with her, her behavior was even more odd than I knew. Among other things, she visited brothels and went about town so unprotected that she even was arrested during a disturbance."

He treated Dante to the details of both events, while Dante speculated on which of the servants had been coaxed to reveal this.

"It sounds as if both episodes were long ago."

"Even a brief lapse does not bode well, sir, not at all. However, there are more recent happenings of a more serious nature." Farthingstone tilted his head and looked up dolefully. "She was caught stealing. Tea, no less. She hardly needs to, which makes it all the worse. For all we know, she goes about the city on those solitary walks of hers, acting the thief for reasons only her sad condition explains."

"I know of the incident. She stole nothing. It was a misunderstanding."

"Indeed? Then her explanation for being in the back room of The Cigar Divan should stand? Better she admit to theft, sir. The alternative is even worse—her belief that she saw her long-lost brother enter. Especially since she never had a brother." Farthingstone shook his head sadly. "I fear that part of the time she lives in a world of her mind's own making. Normal proprieties and judgment do not exist for her because of it."

"Farthingstone, I have no evidence that my wife lives in any world other than ours. I have witnessed nothing that indicates she is anything other than completely rational."

Farthingstone's lidded gaze implied he found his host stupid at best. "I think that you do not fully comprehend her mind, sir. You force me to a matter that I had hoped to avoid."

"If you feel forced, do not blame me. This conversation was not at my request."

"Hear me out. It is in your interests to do so." He managed to appear shocked, stern, and sad all at once. "I regret to say that I have reason to believe that she has formed an alliance with a man besides yourself." He peered over, waiting for the reaction.

Dante let the silence stretch past the point of drama. At least now he knew who had arranged to have that man follow Fleur.

"You appear remarkably indifferent, sir," Farthingstone said disdainfully. "If you do not care about her welfare, I at least expected you to have an interest in your own reputation."

"I care a great deal about both. I am merely wondering what you expect of me and why you have come here to lay out all this information for my consumption."

"As things stand, you are responsible for her. I did not approve of this marriage. I can still go forward on the question of whether she had the presence of mind to make such a contract. I believe that if I do so with what I have just told you, in addition to what I knew before, I will succeed."

"I doubt that."

"With this new evidence, I am very confident. It is Fleur's well-being that concerns me, however. If I were convinced that she was in good hands, that her husband understood the need for her to be controlled and her fortune to be preserved, I might be willing to stand down and avoid the lengthy legal battle that looms. After all, she cannot move in any way without your approval. You must sign any contracts or deeds. The law gives you total authority, no matter what independence she may be under the illusion she still has."

Dante kept his expression bland, but Farthingstone had finally said something interesting.

Farthingstone knew about the private agreement regarding the disposition of Fleur's inheritance.

Which meant Fleur had told someone. Dante guessed who that someone was. Her adviser would need to be assured that she still had control over her fortune; otherwise, any advice would be meaningless.

She had told Siddel, and now Farthingstone knew.

"Sir, surely you understand the implications of what I am saying? I know that you have little interest in financial matters or business, but—"

"I understand the implications for me. I am wondering what you think they are for you."

The door opened, Farthingstone rushed in. "Her frequent sales of property must be stopped. Land is still the best investment. She has spoken for some time about selling the land in Durham. I think that would be unwise."

"Is her welfare your only concern on that matter?"

Farthingstone reacted with insult. Halfway to high dudgeon, he thought better of it. Somewhat sheepishly, he shook his head. "You are sharp, sir. Very sharp. I always said that you were underesteemed. You force a confession from me."

"Do not feel any obligation to explain anything to me."

"No, no, it may be for the best. I must confess that I have an ulterior interest. It is not only the rashness of selling that land that I deplore. I also do not care for the use to which a part of it will be put."

"The school."

"My land adjoins hers. This will not be a school for sons of gentlemen. She is not planning another Eton, is she? It will be full of the rabble of the world, ill-mannered boys who lack discipline or intelligence. Not only is it a fool's errand, but it is one that will significantly affect my enjoyment of my own property."

Dante liked Farthingstone even less than before. He also wanted to laugh. If Farthingstone was being honest, if all of his machinations had been for this reason, it meant that Fleur had gotten married because her neighbor did not want a boys' school ruining his view while he rode his horse through his farms.

"I trust that no sale has occurred yet. That no deeds have been signed," Farthingstone ventured.

"No, not yet."

Farthingstone could not entirely hide his relief. "I am willing to make it worth your while to keep her from selling that land and building that school," he said. "Shall we say, oh, two hundred a year to ensure that the land remains as farms. I calculate that the proceeds of a sale, if put in the funds, would give that amount. Accommodate me on this, and you can have the money and still hold the rents."

It was an outright bribe, but an interesting one. Two hundred pounds a year would not support a school, but if Fleur sold those farms and put the money in trust, it appeared that was all the income would be.

Farthingstone's bulbous nose reddened as he awaited an answer. That rosy glow announced the man's excitement as no physical agitation could.

"I will need some time to consider this," Dante said.

"There is no time for long consideration, sir. She is having the designs for that building drawn even as we speak." He cocked his head curiously and assumed a very smug expression. "Or didn't you know that?"

Dante suddenly knew why he disliked business affairs. It was not the affairs themselves that he found tedious and unpleasant, but the sorts of men so often drawn to them. Men like Gregory Farthingstone.

"Your offer is a handsome one. I will let you know my decision," he said, rising.

"Soon, I hope. As I said, I would rather not present what I know to a court, since that is so public. It would embarrass both her and you. I expect we all want to avoid that."

A bribe, and now a threat.

"I will decide soon, I assure you."

Farthingstone took his leave, and Dante sat at the desk. Someday Fleur would lay out contracts for him to sign regarding the school on this surface. He had thought it would be a year at least before she did so, but it appeared not.

It was time to learn how thoroughly his wife had disobeyed him while they were not really married. He also needed to know what she was really up to with that property.

Fleur sat at her *secrétaire* laboring over a letter. Dante's revelations about Mr. Siddel had weighed on her mind since hearing them. She could not deny that the evidence was mounting against him. That did not speak well of her judgment in allowing Siddel a role in the Grand Project.

It was time to demand an accounting, and if he did not give one it was time to release Mr. Siddel of his obligations to her.

Dante's unexpected arrival startled her. Her head snapped around at the sound of his bootstep.

She set down her pen and, as she turned toward him, closed the *secrétaire*.

She tried to do it casually, so she would not appear furtive. It did not work. She saw his gaze take in the action.

He stood over her, with an expression both serious and alert. With one hand he opened the *secrétaire* again. "You do not need to stop because I am here, my dear."

The lowered lid revealed her recently received mail and sheets of papers. It also displayed the letter she had just been writing. He did not really look at any of it, but she worried that he saw the salutation to Mr. Siddel penned at the new letter's top.

He caressed her face much as he did when they made love, with thoughtful concentration. She sensed something besides desire in him as he looked at her.

"What is it, Dante?"

"I am wondering if you are truly willing to be completely married, Fleur."

"I would think after yesterday it is obvious that I am."

"I am not only talking about sex. Nor did you, in the dressing room. There is more to marriage than sharing a bed."

His gaze made her uncomfortable. Her open *secrétaire* did too. Her heart jumped when he gestured to the papers. "You are very busy with something that you do not want me to know about."

She shifted the papers around, pretending to dismiss them as insignificant. It gave her the chance to slip the letter to Mr. Siddel below some others. "I engage in the usual correspondence of a woman. It would be of no interest to you."

"I would find the usual correspondence very dull. However, there is a part of your life that I would find very interesting, I think. Not only for practical reasons, or those relating to my responsibilities as your husband, but because it is something very important to you. I cannot know you fully unless I know it."

He was accusing her of withholding herself from him. Of giving him her body but not the deeper parts. She could not say he was wrong. The last two days she had felt guilty whenever she considered the Grand Project. Being really married had turned it into the Grand Deception.

His hand moved to the desk's surface. With alarming precision, he slid the letter to Mr. Siddel out until it was visible.

"I told you not to communicate with him further, Fleur."

She closed her eyes, mortified. Disobeying him before had not seemed so terrible, since they were not really married and she had reserved rights to her own life in their arrangement. All that had changed now, and the letter was a betrayal.

She had known it was. It had been impossible to write because of how acutely she felt she denied Dante in doing it. After half an hour, only two lines had been penned because of how guilty she had felt.

"You told me once that you have a purpose in life, Fleur. One that made you feel alive and young and that could not be denied. I would like to learn more about it, as your husband and lover, because it is important to you. If Siddel is involved in it, I want to know how."

"Are you demanding to know?"

"Yes. However, it is my hope that you would like to share this with me. If you were willing to trust me with your fear, I would like to believe that you can trust me with this."

She looked up at him. She had promised not to tell him, but she had made bigger promises since then. With her body and with her heart. She had made promises even Dante did not know of, in choosing the kind of marriage she wanted. That was why it had been so hard to write this letter. She did not want to deceive this husband. She did not want to compromise what this marriage could be.

She rose and walked over to a coffer in the corner. "I intended to tell you, when it was all arranged. I would have had to. There was no way you would have signed the documents without hearing it all."

"Did you fear that I would not keep my promise?"

"I think that you always keep them. It is why I extracted one from you. However, if you learned of it before it was all arranged, I expected you to worry that my plans were unwise and try to stop me." She opened the coffer. "Not only unwise. A little addled. The sort of thing that a woman who was not entirely sound of mind would dream up."

"There is nothing addled about a school, Fleur. I told you to delay it, but I never said it should not be built."

She lifted some long rolls of paper from the coffer. "It is not only about a school, Dante."

He followed her into her bedchamber. She dumped the rolls on the bed. Choosing the largest, she opened it fully.

It showed plans for a large building of four levels. Chambers had been denoted for various uses. The architect's address, on the bottom, was in Piccadilly. That must have been where the footman followed Fleur.

"The school," he said. It was much bigger than he expected.

"It is only preliminary. There are changes to be made, and much work to be done."

"You had this made recently, didn't you? Even though I told you to delay it."

"I wanted to see how the building would look. I also needed to estimate the costs."

"You also had no intention of delaying anything." He was not truly angry, but he was also not in the mood for even mild dissembling.

"No. I had no intention of delaying."

She had intended to go forward and arrange the sale of whatever land she needed to finance this school. She was going to present him with documents to sign that he thought should not be signed for her own protection. In gaol, Hampton had predicted just such a development and laid out the conflict between honor and responsibilities that could result.

"I could not delay," she said. "The rest of the project was going to happen soon or not at all. Once it became known, the school would have been a mere addendum. The school was only my private reason for the rest."

"The rest?"

"It is all here." She unrolled a smaller sheet. It bore a map of County Durham.

He bent over it. "What are these little squares with numbers, along these lines?"

"Parcels of land. The numbers refer to a key I have created that indicates the ownership. See, here is my property, and I am number one. Up there is Gregory's, and he is number two, and so forth."

He noticed the number one in some tiny parcels, in some cases at a distance from her large property. "You have been purchasing some of this land, haven't you?"

"That is how I used the money from the lands I sold."

She had sold land and bought other land. It would not be notable, except that her plan was to sell the Durham lands too. Why bother, unless she thought it would be easier to make one big sale instead of many when the time came?

"The first thing you must know is that I realize my plan is risky," she said. "I expected some resistance from you. That was why I wanted to wait until every piece was in place, which I thought would be very quickly done."

He lifted the map to examine it more closely. Those little parcels flanked lines on the map. Two long, sinuous lines moved from the center, joined, then snaked to the coast to form a long "Y." The point of jointure was right on Fleur's lands.

"What is risky about it? You are selling land to endow a school. It sounds quite simple."

"It is not the proceeds from the land alone that will endow the school. There would not be enough. It costs a lot of money to support all those boys."

He saw another line, much like the "Y," stretching from Darlington to the town of Stockton.

"I will be using the proceeds from the land sale to make another investment. That is the risky part."

He only half-heard her. His concentration on the map sharpened. Suddenly he realized what he was looking at.

Those lines were not there to help Fleur keep track of bits of land she had bought. Nor were those lines roads. The turnpikes had other markings.

"What is this risky investment?" he demanded, already guessing the answer.

She stepped close and ran her finger along the "Y." "That is going to be a railroad, Dante."

A railroad.

His wife, the saintly Fleur Monley who had put herself on the shelf and devoted herself to helping the downtrodden, planned to build a railroad.

He looked at her. Her expression was a combination of pride and worry.

"It is more than risky, Fleur. It is almost untried."

"Not completely so."

"Did Siddel lure you into this?"

"It is all my idea. Look." She peered over his arm and pointed. "There is coal here in central Durham. Everyone has known that for a century. Only it is difficult to transport it to the coast, and the land is not suited for canals. With a railroad, however, it can be moved and those coal fields can be opened."

"You have the coal going to Hartlepool, not to Newcastle."

"The surveyor said it would be easier that way, and also it will not have to cross lands owned by members of the Grand Alliance. I do not think they would allow it."

He let the map fall back on the bed. He stared at it, more stunned than he wanted to admit.

She had devised this on her own. She had seen the possibilities and had paid for surveying the route of this railroad.

Not only so she could endow her school. He guessed that more had driven her than that. Not greed either. *Purpose.* Accomplishment. The satisfaction of doing it first and doing it well. *It is all my idea.*

"I hope that you don't disapprove. Many people do not favor the railroads and think they are blights. They will not go away, however, and—"

"How long have you been at this?"

"Two years. I had thought about it, and when the land came to me after my mother died, I began planning. It was a game at first, just to see if the idea had merit."

"On your own? No help at all?"

"I had some advice at the beginning."

"Siddel?"

"Not Mr. Siddel. Mr. Guerney of the Friends answered some questions for me. He is Mrs. Fry's brother, and—"

"Quaker Guerney? The financier? He is your secret adviser? He is behind this?"

"He gave me some advice, early on. He is not behind it. One railroad is enough for him. He was able to tell me the sorts of profits that could be made, however."

Huge profits, when it worked. Huge losses when it didn't. Dante did not know the details, but he knew that the Stockton-to-Darlington line that Guerney had invested in had cost over a hundred thousand pounds. And Fleur's "Y" was much, much longer.

"You were correct, Fleur. When you brought this to me, I would have demanded a lot of explanation. I will not be able to sign anything unless I get it."

She sat on the bed and gazed forlornly at her map. "I will explain it all,

Dante, but I think it is unlikely now that I will be asking for your signature. I made one very big mistake."

"Siddel."

"Yes."

"How did he become involved?"

"I knew of his reputation in forming investment partnerships. So when he came to me, offering to purchase any land I may want to sell—he had heard of my recent dispositions—I made use of the renewal of our acquaintance to eventually propose the plan. Now I wonder if he already knew of others who had similar plans and wanted to purchase my land for that reason to begin with."

"I think it more likely that he first spoke to you on Farthingstone's behalf. Whether Farthingstone has his own plans for a railroad or just doesn't want a school there, I cannot say."

She began rolling up the drawings. "I have been wondering if he approached me for Gregory too and has been stalling me at Gregory's request. I wish I knew for certain if he and Gregory have an association."

"I am sure that they do, Fleur. I just met with Farthingstone. He knows about our arrangement. He knows that you believe you can make plans like this without my approval and that I have agreed to give my signature."

She did not move. Did not look at him.

"You would have had to let Siddel know that, after we married. Otherwise his efforts on this railroad were a waste of time."

"We had separate lives, Dante. You did not have to end your old one because of our marriage." She looked up at him. "I am sorry anyway. It was hard to keep this from you, even if it was my right to, and even though secrecy was vital. I wanted very much to share it with you, as my friend, because it was so important to me."

He understood, more than he wanted. She wanted to share it with him, but instead she had shared it with Hugh Siddel. Siddel's involvement with this project, and Fleur's involvement with Siddel, dated long before those days in that cottage.

It angered him anyway.

The jealousy was not rational, not fair. He knew that. He controlled it. For now. It gave him one more reason to dislike Siddel, however.

"I want you to remove Siddel from this project, Fleur. Can you do that?"

"He has put me in an impossible dilemma. When I asked him to find the investors, I emphasized the need for secrecy. However, I never expected him to keep secrets from me. He refuses to tell me the investors' names, even though he claims to be close to finding enough. I have begun worrying that he is stalling me while he works with others to pursue an alternate route. If so, I will lose the advantage and there will be nothing I can do about it."

Dante ran his fingers over the northern strip of the map. "It he is stalling, it is possible that he is merely preventing any railroad from being built. For Gregory or someone else. New pits will produce coal that competes with that in the north. If the port of Hartlepool grows because of coal shipments, it will compete with Newcastle. If one connects the western coal fields to the coast, there are powerful men who will not be pleased."

"Do you think Siddel told them?"

"I know that he has a relationship with a man who is employed by a family in the Grand Alliance. However, whatever he has done, it does not matter. Siddel is out of this now. Do you understand that?"

"Yes. I think that one way or another, he betrayed me. Which means I have failed. I do not think that I can go forward on the school. I can afford to build it but not to create the endowment that will ensure its thriving."

Her voice was firm but her expression very sad. She appeared bereft as she announced the death of her dream.

"We will find a way to build the school, Fleur. You will fulfill your great purpose. If a different way must be found, we will find one."

She looked up with a trembling smile. It was not clear that she believed him, but the warmth in her eyes said that she appreciated his resolve.

"I must write my letter to Mr. Siddel."

She walked toward her sitting room, and he aimed for his own chambers. He also had a letter to write.

"Dante," she said, stopping him. "When I told you about the school being my purpose, after we met with Mr. Hampton, you said you understood."

And he did.

"You said that you could comprehend what it meant to live without one and then to find it."

He could.

"Perhaps one day you will tell me about your purpose, Dante. I would like to hear about it, and share it with you."

He watched her disappear into the sitting room.

You, my love. The purpose that I found is you.

chapter 23

Hugh Siddel stared in shock at the letter he held. It contained only one sentence, penned in Fleur's neat hand. With no ceremony or explanation, she released him from their agreement regarding his role in the railroad project.

His fingers closed on the paper until they made a fist. That bastard Duclairc had forced her to write this. The stupid woman had confided in him after all, and he was using this opportunity to exact a little revenge for that game of cards.

Forcing some calm, he calculated what this meant. There was no way for Cavanaugh to learn this letter had come. If Fleur was giving up on her project, Cavanaugh would remain ignorant of that too. Those payments Cavanaugh made to ensure the project was delayed could continue a long while.

He smiled to himself. Actually, Fleur's decision concluded matters very neatly. Stalling had gotten difficult. He had worried how long he could continue putting her off. If Duclairc had discovered their association and forbidden her to continue it, he could not have chosen a better moment to interfere.

Then again, perhaps Duclairc was still ignorant. Another whim had captured her attention, perhaps. Some other project. Maybe her social diary was filling so completely with parties and diversions that charitable endeavors now bored her.

Contented that the letter afforded the opportunity to dangle Cavanaugh indefinitely, Siddel left his chambers to go out. He met his butler on the stairs, coming up with a salver in his hand.

Siddel read the card. "In broad daylight? Astonishing. Where did you put him?"

"He is in the morning room, sir."

Siddel detoured to the morning room, where a very agitated Gregory Farthingstone paced the floor.

"I am surprised to see you here, Farthingstone. Did you just walk in the front door, where the world could see you?"

"This could not wait for the dawn, sir. I face such ruin that it may not matter what the world sees in any case." Farthingstone's face had gone very red. He paused in his pacing and breathed deeply to compose himself.

"Sit, my friend, and calm yourself."

Farthingstone obeyed. Rest only brought an expression of extreme desolation. Overcome, he did not speak, but merely held out a piece of paper.

Siddel took it. It was a letter from Dante Duclairc. Brief like Fleur's, it also contained but one sentence: *My wife will have her school, even if I have to cut and carry the stone myself.*

"He is mad," Farthingstone muttered. "They both lack the sense of newborns. She found a man just as impractical as she is. A fitting match, and I am destroyed because of it."

"Why did he write this?"

"I met with him. I laid out my evidence, and it is very strong, sir, very strong. New facts have come to my attention, you see. I believed I had a right understanding with Duclairc regarding the scandal that would result if we went to court. I offered him a handsome sum to leave that property as farms."

"That was your solution? To bribe the man?"

"I can do without your scorn. It was hell on my pride to approach him as a gentleman."

"With the fortune he has now, I doubt the amount you could offer would sway him."

"You do not need to remind me how little is at my disposal for negotiations. Nor should I have to remind you how those negotiations will benefit you as well. A man in your position may even decide that half a loaf is better than none and aid me out of my predicament."

Siddel let that suggestion pass. The thing about loaves was, if you gave away half, you went hungry.

Farthingstone dully accepted that the overture would have no symphony. "Duclairc would have been better off with two hundred than if she sold. The man is an imbecile if he did not comprehend that. I thought he did, but—" He gestured to the letter and his face reddened again. "It is very vexing to have one's future at the whim of such fools, I tell you."

Siddel looked at Duclairc's letter again. He comprehended its implications more than Farthingstone ever could.

Duclairc knew everything. Even the parts Farthingstone did not. Worse,

Fleur was not giving up. She planned to pursue her Grand Project as well as build that school, and her worthless husband had agreed to permit it.

If she succeeded, not only the payments from Cavanaugh would stop. All of the income that supported him and his pleasures would cease. His uncle's legacy would become worthless.

He handed the letter back to Farthingstone. "You cannot allow this to happen, of course."

"Damnation, I know that. However, I am at a loss as to discern how to stop it. Duclairc's barrister has drowned Chancery in petitions and my own man cannot make headway quickly enough. It could be months before my standing is even accepted, and by then . . ." He shook his head and closed his eyes. "I learned that she is having the school designed already. She intends to move soon."

"Not soon enough, if you move more quickly." Those designs must have been commissioned when she thought most of the investors were collected. Starting over would take some time. Still, it did not look good.

Farthingstone exhaled his misery and his body shrank in on itself. "Duclairc will probably get his brother to buy the rest of the land so she has the funds to build. Or his friend St. John. Or his friend Burchard. Land is always desired. Once the funds are in hand, she will start on the school."

"You must stop them from selling. You definitely must stop them from building. It is that simple."

"Easy for you to demand. There is no damn way to damn stop them, I tell you."

"Of course there is."

Farthingstone went still. He stared at the floorboards.

Siddel strolled over to the window and gazed out. He pictured Fleur in that hooded cloak the first time they met in the church, her blue eyes sparkling with excitement while she explained her insane scheme. She had looked so much like the girl he had loved that—

Well, no good would come from such sentiment now. She was not a girl anymore but a married woman who was determined to take actions that would inconvenience him most severely.

"Tell me, Farthingstone, I am curious. What happens to that Durham property if the current owner passes away without children?"

The answer was slow in coming. "It is bequeathed to a charity devoted to the reform of prisons."

Siddel turned to him. "I have always thought that prison reform is a worthy cause, deserving of support. Haven't you?"

Farthingstone looked away. He said nothing. The flush in his face drained, leaving him very pale.

.   .   .

Fleur collected all the letters and papers relating to the Grand Project. She removed them from her desk and placed them in the coffer along with the drawings for the school.

As she closed the coffer lid, she admitted that she would miss the thrill of planning for her railroad. It had been exciting. Even the secrecy had appealed to her. She had been foolish to think that she could bring it off, however. Such elaborate plans can founder on one wrong step, and she had taken a big one. His name was Hugh Siddel.

Eventually she would build her school. No Grand Project would derive from doing so. No great endowment would ensure its survival. She would find a way to support it, however. Dante would help her.

Dante. She regretted that she did not have the Grand Project to distract her tonight. She had attended the theater with Laclere and Bianca, but Dante had not joined them. He had gone elsewhere, and she was trying hard not to speculate where that elsewhere might be.

A new kind of jealousy wanted to take root in her heart. She fought to prevent that. She suspected how desolating it would be.

She had decided not to think about the life he led when he left this house, but only about the one they shared when he was here. When she had chosen the kind of marriage she wanted, she had known she would probably not have it exactly the way she hoped.

The night was still young, but she prepared for bed. She would continue this habit, she decided. She would not lie to herself, nor would she picture him with other women, but she would make sure she never knew if he did not return of a night.

She got into bed, but sleep did not come peacefully. Her dozing was fitful, full of images of Dante, and her heart heavy with a fear of heartbreak.

Suddenly she was very awake. Instantly alert. She turned her head and saw candles in the room, over near the door to her dressing room.

"Dante?"

He came to her. "I thought you were asleep."

"Not yet."

He put the brace of candles on a table and sat on the bed. "Did you enjoy the theater?"

"Very much. Your brother's box was busy, with everyone visiting to welcome them home. I wish you had come."

She instantly regretted saying that. She scooted around and sat beside him on the bed's edge. "I am sorry. I know that even being really married does not mean that we spend every evening together. I am out of practice being sophisticated, that is all."

He untied his cravat and pulled it off. "Do not be sorry. I do not want you to become sophisticated. I know all too well that it also means becoming indifferent."

He shed his collar and waistcoat in silence. She could sense his mind working.

He paused a good while before turning to his shirt and other garments.

"You have not asked me about my evening, Fleur."

She did not know what to say.

"I know why you did not ask. You have been practicing that part of being sophisticated for some time now, haven't you?"

Yes. And not mastering the skill at all.

"I went to my clubs. It was fairly boring. The cards do not interest me as they used to."

"Did you win?"

"Yes, but it still grew dull after a while. I found myself thinking that your company would be much more interesting."

"I am glad that you did."

"McLean thinks my sobriety is your fault. He says that marriage games have ruined me for all others."

"I would like to believe that, Dante. However, you have been a man on the town for many years and I think that you know more games than I can imagine. I am at a disadvantage."

"There is no competition taking place. You are at no disadvantage."

That was not true. The saintly Fleur Monley had little to offer a man with his worldly experiences. Even the goddess Fleur Duclairc was at a disadvantage.

He turned to her and began unbuttoning the top of her bed gown. "Are you trying to say that you want to learn other games, Fleur?"

"I am so ignorant of what they could be that I do not know if I want to learn them."

"I have already shown you one."

She knew what he meant. "These other ways seem to ensure the woman's pleasure, not the man's."

"I get great pleasure in making you scream for me." He slid her gown off so that she sat naked beside him. "However, to be precise, I only showed you half of one."

He kissed her, embracing her against his skin, still sitting side by side as politely as if the bed were a garden bench.

Her mind worked on what he had just said. A very shocking notion of what the other half could be presented itself.

He sensed her astonishment. As he kissed her, she felt his small smile form.

Turning her in his arms, he laid her on her back across his lap, with her head and shoulders on one side of his thighs and her hips on the other, and her body sprawled, arched and vulnerable. She could not even embrace him like this, and her arms fell limply on either side of her head.

His gaze slowly moved over all of her. His trailing hand followed the same path. Both made her body very sensitive, all over. The most delicious anticipation purred through her.

His light caress titillated mercilessly. Anticipation of more purposeful touches had her half mad. His fingers kept glossing close to her nipples and thighs, but never actually touched the places she really wanted. It aroused her anyway, slowly, relentlessly, incredibly.

"There is no competition, Fleur." His lids lowered and his hand brushed against her nipple, making her gasp and arch. "It is very good with you."

His palm gently circled over her breast, teasing the tight tip. Laying here like this, watching him watch her arousal, unable to embrace him or hide her growing madness, was incredibly erotic.

His phallus pressed against her right breast and she bent her arm so she could touch him. His gaze moved to her face while his hand continued its breathtaking patterns. She touched him lightly, as he touched her, so the erotic torture would be mutual.

He raised her shoulders and she expected him to kiss her. Instead, he gently flipped her, so her face and breasts pressed the sheet and her hips crossed his lap. A long, firm caress from her neck down her back commanded she stay like that. Blind now, she could only feel.

"You are so lovely, Fleur. By day or night." His hand smoothed over her bottom. She could not contain how arousing it was to lay in this submissive position. A wicked, dangerous element colored her climbing desire, even though his caress was gentle.

His hand moved down to the flesh of her inner thighs. Her excitement immediately centered near his hand, and her muddled mind started a silent begging.

"I have never seen anything more beautiful than you in your passion, darling."

The slow caresses on her back, her bottom, her thighs pushed her past control. She heard the notes of wonder and pleading on her own gasping breaths. The waiting became wonderful and unbearable.

His other hand lifted her shoulder. "Kneel."

She did not understand. He showed her. Hands on one side of his thighs and knees on the other, she propped herself. He reached below to caress her breasts, and the sensation was so intense her whole body shuddered. Her hips squirmed impatiently as his other hand ventured closer, closer.

"Part your knees more."

She did, half insane with furious need.

The touch made her cry out. She heard the sound on the edges of her awareness. The way he touched her nipples only intensified the sensation. He kept creating more hunger even as he partly relieved it.

He moved the caress to her back and bottom again. His fingers trailed along her cleft to touch her from the rear. Her body arched into it, hips rising and shoulders lowering, demanding more, anxious for relief and completion.

The movement made her arm press his phallus. In her stupor she turned her head and kissed it.

He instantly went completely still.

A wicked sense of power tinged her abandon. She kissed again, right on the tip. "No?"

His fingers twisted into the hair on her head. "Yes." His voice sounded a little savage.

She rearranged herself a little and kissed again. A different arousal and madness owned her now. She flicked her tongue, very pleased with her own boldness. It was not nearly as scandalous in the doing as in the thinking. She used her mouth more aggressively.

The fingers in her hair tensed and lifted her head up. He claimed her in a furious, ravishing kiss that left her mind and lips numb.

He laid her down and bent her knees high to her chest and entered her deeply, so deeply that she felt him touch her womb. Rising on his arms, he withdrew entirely and entered again, slowly and completely. Her vulva throbbed with the fullness of him and with expectation when he left.

His face remained hard with control and determined passion. The slow, commanding thrusts continued, demanding that her passion rise with his. Her own body was grateful to accept and submit and follow once more.

The end was hardly gentle, but she did not care. Her own passion welcomed his wild intensity and ruthless domination. She loved feeling and seeing his completion. She reveled in the hard, deep thrusts that bound them together in a beautiful madness.

Most of all, however, she loved the way he slept beside her afterward, in an embrace that kept them heart to heart.

"Has my wife gone down yet, Hornby?"

"It is not for me to notice such things, sir."

"Certainly. However, has she?"

"Since you demand it of me, Mrs. Duclairc left her chambers a while ago."

Dante turned to leave his as well.

"However, I do not think that you will find her below, sir, if that is the reason for your question." Hornby walked over to the open window and inhaled deeply. "Such a lovely morning this is. It is mornings such as this that beckon one to a long turn amidst grass and flowers."

Dante could not muster any annoyance at this indication that Fleur still walked out alone in the mornings. After last night, he would be incapable of anger over anything that she wanted to do.

"I think that I will take a turn in the park, Hornby. Is there any spot in particular that is singularly pleasant in the mornings?"

"I have heard the footman Christopher say that strolling around the reservoir is quite lovely this time of day."

Dante left the house and walked the few blocks to Stanhope Gate and entered Hyde Park. At this hour no carriages rolled down the lanes and only a few people strolled. Women dotted the green, accompanied by maids or friends. Several older men walked by briskly, taking deliberate exercise. Most of the noise came from the songs of birds.

He strolled slowly, enjoying the quiet and the odd experience of visiting this park merely to enjoy its beauty. He rarely came here except for the reasons most people did, to see and be seen. The park merely served as a stage for the social dramas of the fashionable hour.

He decided that he liked it just as much now. He understood why Fleur walked here most mornings. He looked forward to sharing it with her today.

He approached the reservoir and surveyed the landscape, looking for Fleur. He could see no woman at all, just a man walking away toward the Grosvenor Gate beyond it. He stopped and looked all around.

He turned and swept his gaze over the rest of the park, looking for a figure in a hooded cloak. All of the women he could see were decked out more fashionably.

He must have missed her. She had probably been leaving through one gate as he entered through another.

Deciding to take a turn around the reservoir anyway, he ambled toward it.

He strolled around, looking more to the ground than the park or water, thinking about last night and the last days. His mind turned to Fleur's school and her Grand Project and the likelihood that either would come to fruition.

He laughed to himself. Farthingstone claimed she was addled. Far from it, although there were many men who would think any woman who dared dream up such a scheme was totally mad.

She was hardly mad. Audacious and smart, but not mad. He was still accommodating himself to just what he had in her.

He passed a section of the reservoir where some reeds had taken root. Out of the corner of his eye he saw their vertical lines and the way the water pooled around them.

Something else caught his eye and pulled him out of his thoughts. He turned and looked at the water. A five count passed before he accepted what he was seeing.

A yell roared through him, both soundless and deafening. Too horrified to think, he laid down on the reservoir wall and reached toward the dark shadows floating just below the surface, fluttering in languid folds.

He grabbed one edge and his heart stopped. He knew what it was. Just knew. Pulling hand over hand, he dragged up the cloth and could feel how a weight held it down in the water. He pulled harder and a body bobbed at the surface.

The roar in his head became a howl. A vicious, savage, terrified yell. He grabbed her body and hauled her up. The sodden cloak fought him. He got her face above water and dragged her to the reservoir's edge and up on the ground.

Half-blind, his gaze shot around. Small dots moved in the distance, too far away to respond to a call for help. He yelled one anyway as he turned Fleur on her side and began forcing the water out of her.

Time slowed. His blood raced. She looked dead. He turned her stomach-down anyway and pressed her back. Water left her mouth in a steady stream.

Then he saw the blood.

It oozed through her hair, mixing with her damp locks, adding to the wetness. He bent closely even as he continued pressing her back and saw the wound on the back of her head.

For an instant, primitive fury cracked through him. The next moment it was gone, replaced by an icy-cold resolve.

He would kill whoever had done this, even if she lived. If she died, he would kill the man *slowly*.

A sound broke through his horror. The smallest cough shook Fleur's body. He turned her on her side again and coaxed another out of her. Water spewed out of her mouth as a convulsion racked her.

He laid his palm against her face and felt some warmth beneath the chill. "Come back, darling. Look at me."

Her lashes fluttered. Her body flexed. Her lids rose. Her eyes appeared sightless for a few dreadful heartbeats, then focused on him.

"Dante."

"Do not speak. Do not move." He released the cloak so it fell away from her body. He stripped off his frock coat and tucked it around her. He wanted to weep with relief. Only caring for her kept him composed. The total realization of what he had almost lost began penetrating his shock, terrifying him.

A curricle approached on the closest path. Kneeling, he lifted Fleur in his arms. As he stood, his body reacted to the weight, but he ignored it. He could have carried her a mile if he had to.

He bore her around the reservoir, shouting for the carriage to stop.

.   .   .

"You should calm yourself before you go to her," Laclere said. They paced together in Fleur's sitting room while a physician attended her in the bedroom.
"She should not see you like this."

"Like what?"

"With murder in your eyes."

Dante strolled over to the mantel and examined the porcelain figures it
held.

His brother was wrong. He did not need to calm himself. He had never
been calmer in his life.

"It will not be murder. Burchard will return soon and tell me where to
find him."

"Calling out a man like Farthingstone is as good as murder. You do not
even know for certain that he—"

"I do not need lectures from you, today of all days. I *know* he arranged
this. If it were your wife lying in there, you would not be so damnably dispassionate. If you are here to dissuade me, get out."

Vergil sat in the chair near Fleur's *secrétaire*. "My apologies. Of course you
must deal with the man as you choose." He paused. "I am not dispassionate,
Dante. I have been where you are, when the woman I loved was endangered.
I may have challenged a man in the name of a different person and a different honor, but my heart was not so pure."

Dante folded his arms and looked at the cold hearth. Vergil was speaking
of that duel, fought to protect the honor of their dead older brother. It was
a topic they had never discussed. Vergil had demanded to stand to that man,
but now admitted more had motivated him than his right of precedence or
fear that Dante would fail.

It was a generous confession, in ways Vergil probably did not know. It
dimmed Dante's anger at his brother's attempts to mollify him.

"Farthingstone had a man following her," he said, to reassure his brother.
"He knew that she walked in the park in the mornings. I saw the man once,
and Farthingstone told me enough of her movements to indicate this man
had trailed her for some time."

"Do you know why he had her followed?"

"To accumulate evidence that her mind was not right and her judgment
impaired." He shook his head. "Better for her if he had succeeded in killing
me instead. When I think how close . . . a few more minutes—"

"Do not think of that. She is safe and that is the important thing." Vergil
got up and came over to the mantel. "However, what is this about succeeding in killing you?"

Before Dante could answer, the door to the corridor opened and Adrian Burchard entered.

"Where is the bastard?" Dante asked.

"Not in London. His manservant said he went down to his house in Essex."

"It appears that you will have to wait to confront him," Vergil said.

"I want to know when he returns to London. I want to make sure he is nowhere near Fleur until I can deal with him."

"I know a good man who will watch the Essex house if you want," Adrian said. "As soon as Farthingstone sets foot off that property, he will let us know."

"Do you know another one who will watch Siddel?"

"It can be arranged."

"Siddel? What has he to do with this?" Vergil demanded. "And what was that business about someone trying to kill you? When did this happen, and why wasn't I told of it?"

"Ask St. John," Dante said. The physician had just opened the door to Fleur's bedroom and beckoned.

Vergil headed for the corridor with an expression that said St. John was in for a severe interrogation.

"I am not ill, Dante."

"You have had a shock and you will rest."

Fleur sank back on the pillows and suffered his attention as he tucked the bedclothes around her.

She did not have the heart to argue with him. He had saved her life, after all. Concern had veiled his expression since he entered the bedchamber and banished Charlotte and the physician and taken over her care himself.

He had also kindly not mentioned that he would not have had to save her if she had taken an escort when she walked in the park.

Mostly, however, she did not argue because the experience had left her docile and frightened. The specter of death kept breathing on her neck, as if refusing to leave unsatisfied.

"I will rest if you say I must, but I do not think I will sleep. Could you ask Charlotte to come back?"

"I will stay with you if you don't want to be alone, Fleur."

"I would rather not be. Not yet."

He pulled a chair near the bed and sat in it, propping his boot on the bed's edge. "I think that we will pass the time in a little game, since you are indisposed and cannot be seduced."

She laughed. Her heart glowed at this evidence that he remembered those hours in the cottage as well as she did.

"What kind of game?"

"Not that kind. That will have to wait until you have recovered. This is a simple one. I will ask you questions, and you will answer them."

"If I play this game, do you promise to play the other kind when I am recovered?"

"Certainly."

"Another new one? I still have a lot of catching up to do."

"Darling, I am trying to be good even though you look adorable in that bed. Even the bandage becomes you. You could help a little and not tempt me by offering anything I want."

"My apologies. Ask your first question."

"Could you recognize the man who passed you as you took a turn around the reservoir?"

"Not with certainty. I was not watching him. I was walking, he approached, we passed, and then . . ." And then she remembered nothing at all until she opened her eyes and saw Dante looking down at her with eyes wild with worry.

She felt the bandage wrapping her head. "I suppose he hit me with something."

The humor had left Dante's eyes. Talk of the attack had turned them into sparking, cold crystals.

"Are there more questions?"

"Is there any reason why Farthingstone would want to keep you from building that school?"

"I doubt he approves of educating boys of lower condition."

"That is not enough reason to try and kill you."

"We do not know Gregory was behind this, Dante."

"I can think of no one else. He wants to stop you from building it, Fleur. Very much. I think that everything he has done, all of it, was to prevent that. He came and offered to pay me to stop you."

"He tried to bribe you? That is very insulting."

His expression showed he had not missed the insult that Gregory assumed he would choose money over loyalty to his own wife. "I think it is not a coincidence that this happened to you right after I refused."

"There is nothing special about that piece of land, Dante. It is just a cottage and a garden and some fields. It isn't even the best land there. The soil has too much clay, which is one reason I was going to use it for the school to begin with."

"Could there be something underground? Coal or minerals? Something that he hopes to own someday?"

"If there had been, he could have profited while he was married to my mother. He controlled the farms then. He could not sell them, but he could exploit them."

Dante thought it all over. "His tenacity regarding you has been odd, Fleur. There is a reason for it. A good reason. This attack on you speaks of a man getting desperate."

"I cannot imagine what the reason is. If you had agreed to accept his payment, the property would not become his. It would have stayed as it is now and as it has been for years."

"Then he must want it to stay as it is. We need to know why, and the answer is in Durham."

chapter 24

Fleur rarely visited her Durham property. Her arrival with Dante, so soon after her last visit, sent the couple who cared for it into high agitation. Mr. Hill set off at once to the village, to hire women to bring back before it got dark. Mrs. Hill bustled around the house, lighting fires and removing covers from furniture.

She interrupted her work to help Fleur settle into her chamber. As she shook out dresses, she gossiped about the tenants and local happenings.

"The Johnson family has left their place, of course," she concluded. "But they are happy with their new cottage, and grateful that the fields are still theirs to work."

The Johnson family had been living in Aunt Peg's cottage while the plans for the school unfolded.

"They were unhappy at first, even with the offer of the other cottage, since it is not so convenient to the fields, but now that they have made the change they are content."

"There was no need for them to be inconvenienced. I do not need that property yet."

"There must have been some confusion, then. Your stepfather wrote on your behalf and said that you did. The Johnsons knew how he still watches matters here for you."

Of course they assumed so. They thought of the land as his to control because for years they had paid the rents to him while her mother owned the property.

"Has he moved any other families?"

"Not that I can think of. He has always kept an eye on things for you, however. The tenants understand how it is."

"Where did the Johnson family move?"

"A new cottage, right on the edge of Mr. Farthingstone's land. Not too far from the fields."

Not so far to cause Mr. Johnson to complain to her because he lost a season's plantings or had to walk miles to reach the fields.

She left Mrs. Hill to complete the unpacking and went outside. Standing in front of the house, she looked west. One could see the old cottage from here. It was a gray speck against the overcast sky, sitting atop a low rise in the land, close enough that Peg could see her sister's home.

She went back upstairs in search of Dante. He was in his chamber, washing. He had taken the ribbons most of the way from London because his skill with four-in-hand far surpassed Luke's and he had no interest in a leisurely journey.

"I believe you were correct, Dante. The answer may be here in Durham. Or at least, the answer to something may be here."

She told him what had transpired with the cottage.

"Since that is where you intend to build the school, it may be connected to our mystery in some way." He had removed his coats and now put them back on. "It will be a while before dusk. Let us visit this cottage. I have grown very curious about that property."

He took her hand as they walked. The day was not breezy and bright as it had been the last time they strolled together along this lane. Gray clouds threatened rain and blocked the setting sun, and the air held the pending dampness. Fleur felt as lighthearted as she had that day, however. Even her brush with death had not dimmed the glow that her love gave the world.

The cottage slowly grew in size with each step.

"How long was this cottage vacant?" Dante asked, looking toward it.

"While Aunt Ophelia was alive. She hoped that her sister would be found at first, but even after the body was discovered, she did not put a tenant there."

Dante paced on another few yards. "When did your aunt Peg disappear?"

"Years ago, Dante. I was just a girl. Aunt Peg and I used to play together back then. I would visit her and we would play with our dolls."

"How old were you when she went missing?"

She had to calculate that by working back through the milestones of her life. "I think that I was eight or nine. My mother and I had come to visit as we did most summers. I remember going to play with Aunt Peg, and then the great confusion when she went missing. It was a very sad time, and I do not remember those days much. However, Aunt Ophelia died eleven years ago, and that was soon after Aunt Peg's body was found and she had been missing at least ten years then."

It made her uncomfortable to speak of this. The damp penetrated her more, and the heavy clouds appeared darker.

So did Dante's expression. A frown marked his brow and he observed the cottage they approached with thoughtful speculation.

"The woman who cared for your aunt. What became of her?"

"She left. She took a position elsewhere. Hill probably knows where. I wish that you would not dwell on this, Dante. It is as unpleasant as our conversation by the lake at Laclere Park."

In some ways it was more unpleasant. His questions evoked memories of those days after Aunt Peg disappeared. Sensations crept into her of loss and shock and walking through a house heavy with dread. Another reaction nibbled at her as well. Guilt. If she had been playing with Aunt Peg that day, she could not have wandered off and gotten lost.

The cottage was close enough now to see its shutters and stones and the little garden that the Johnsons had planted. She remembered running along this lane, carrying her doll, to go play with Aunt Peg in the sitting room while the caretaker read a book in the corner.

She had not realized at the time how odd it was to have such a playmate. Aunt Peg had been gone for years before she understood why this grown woman enjoyed a child's games. At the time she had simply thought that Aunt Peg was kinder than most adults, and much more fun too.

They approached the cottage from the side. Dante went up and peered in the window. "It is too dark inside to see, and this window too dirty in any case."

She held back. That window . . .

"Has the walk been too much for you, Fleur? You are looking pale."

"I am fine." Only she really wasn't. A very unpleasant sensation churned in her stomach. She kept looking at the window. She knew the chamber inside very well. She could see Aunt Peg sitting on the floor, dancing her doll across the rug toward her.

It was a happy memory, but she was not feeling happy at all. She was feeling very sick. The notion of looking in that window with Dante made her cringe.

She searched her memory, trying to make things fit right.

Dante came back to her. "What is it, Fleur? You do not look fine at all."

"I am thinking that perhaps Aunt Ophelia had tenants here after all. I must have forgotten that. We came less often once Aunt Peg was gone. Yes, that would explain it."

"Explain what?"

"The window, Dante. Do you remember how I said that I thought I once saw a woman in agony while giving birth? I see her face and body through a window. That window."

"Then I am sorry that I brought you here."

"Do not be. It explains part of the fear." She shrugged. The uneasy sensation had retreated. "I think that I would like to go in. I loved Aunt Peg in ways I could never love most adults then. She was a playmate every summer. I feel bad that I do not think of her much anymore, and have not for years."

They walked around the house. Dante opened the door and she stepped over the threshold.

And froze.

"Dante, look."

He stepped in behind her.

Little light entered except from the door, but it was obvious that the cottage had no floor. All of the boards had been removed and neatly stacked along one wall. The packed earth underneath had been completely exposed.

Dante kicked the ground with his heel. "Dry, and hard as rock. Difficult to dig with a shovel."

"Do you think that is the intention?"

"I can think of no other reason for removing the floor."

"Dig for what?"

He did not answer at first. He paced around the walls, studying the ground. "Something valuable enough to not want others to find it when they began digging to build a school."

His expression appeared very hard in the dim light. He crossed his arms and stared at the dirt. She sensed anger in him, but not directed at her.

"Then Gregory has arranged for this," she said.

The low rumble of distant thunder rolled in the door. "A storm is coming. I will come back tomorrow and see if I am right."

"Right? What do you think is here, Dante?"

He shrugged. "Who knows. Perhaps Farthingstone learned there is a great treasure hiding." The thunder rumbled again. "Come along. We need to get back before the rain comes."

The storm was moving fast. Lightning sliced the distant sky. It was not the rain that Dante wanted to beat, however. It was the dusk.

In a corner of the cottage, almost hidden by the floorboards and the shadows, he had seen two oil lamps.

He helped Fleur down the threshold to the cottage. As they walked back to the lane, he heard a sound besides thunder float on the heavy air.

He turned. Two horses rode cross country, barely visible in the graying world. At the same time that he saw the riders, they noticed him. One gestured and the horses broke into a gallop.

Fleur's eyes widened when she saw the horses.

He began pulling her back to the cottage. "No doubt they are only travelers aiming for the mail road, trying to outrun the storm," he said. "All the same, let us go back in here and see if they pass."

He did not believe they would. They had actually been aiming toward this cottage. But he and Fleur could not outrun them and he would have a better chance of protecting Fleur if she was not out in the open.

Not much of one, if that shorter rider was who he thought. Very little chance at all if what he suspected about this cottage was correct.

Cursing himself for not anticipating this, blood already coursing with the sickening excitement of the hunted, he threw the bolt over the door as soon as he had Fleur inside. He checked to see that the kitchen was secure as well. He went to all the windows on the first level and closed their shutters, shrouding the cottage in darkness.

Returning to Fleur, he examined their sanctuary. The stone walls and thick door would make it hard to get in, but this was hardly an impregnable fort.

"The rider on the left . . . I could barely see him, but I thought it was Gregory," Fleur said. "I thought he was in Essex."

He heard the tremor in her voice. He pulled her into his arms. "So his servant said. Even if it is Farthingstone, there is no reason to be afraid."

"Do you think he is coming to do the digging?"

"He may have only been riding and not recognized us. He may be coming to see who is trespassing. He still watches these farms for you."

She felt in the dark for his face. "You do not believe that. You would not have bolted the doors if you did."

"I am only being cautious in the way of husbands, Fleur." He kissed her. "Do not worry. I think that I can thrash him if I have to."

She laughed. He held her closer while he listened hard for the sounds of approaching horses.

They arrived with the storm. Fat droplets began pounding the windows as hooves pounded up the lane. The heavens broke as a hand worked the latch and met the resistance of the bolt.

A man cursed. Dante recognized the voice.

So did Fleur. "It appears he did not go to Essex," she whispered.

"See here, open this door and show yourself," Farthingstone ordered. "We know you are in there, by Zeus, since the damn door is bolted."

"There seems little point in pretending we are not here," Fleur said quietly.

Dante did not agree. Farthingstone knew a couple had entered this cottage, but he had not recognized who they were. There was a chance that the rain would discourage him and his companion and they would leave and come back later.

In any event, he was not going to make this easy for them.

Mumbles sounded on the other side of the door, then silence fell. Dante felt Fleur's heart racing and the tension tightening her body. He held her and listened for the sounds of horses leaving.

A crack blasted the silence as a huge weight fell against the door. A metal point poked through a plank, then disappeared.

They had come tonight to dig after all. The had a pickax with them.

The pick fell again. The plank splintered.

Fleur cringed closer. "Dante . . ."

"He will be chagrined when he goes through such trouble only to learn it is the owner of this land inside this cottage."

She tucked her head against his neck. "You do not have to pretend for me. I know that we may be in a very dangerous spot."

The pick landed again. A hole appeared in the door. The shadow of a face peered in. "Cannot see a thing with it all closed up," Farthingstone said.

"Stand aside," another voice replied. A voice that Dante did not recognize.

The pick made short work of the door, enlarging the hole. An arm reached through and lifted the bolt. The door swung in.

Two men ducked in from the pouring rain. "Who is there? Who are you?" Farthingstone demanded, peering into the corner where Dante held Fleur.

"Just me, Farthingstone," Dante said. "What are you doing, destroying property like this? I got caught by the storm and took refuge here to wait it out. I did not expect a trespasser to come by and break down the door."

The other man fetched one of the oil lamps and lit it. A yellow glow spread, showing Farthingstone peering gape-mouthed from beneath a sodden hat.

When he saw Fleur his eyes widened in shock, as if he had seen a ghost. He shot his companion a horrified, furious glance.

"You have an explanation for this intrusion, I trust," Dante said, making the most of Farthingstone's astonishment at seeing Fleur alive.

The other man lit another lamp. That gave enough light for Dante to examine this stranger. He had dark hair and narrow, unpleasant eyes.

Not entirely a stranger. He had seen him before, following Fleur from St. Martin's down the Strand. If he was surprised by Fleur's living body, he at least did not show it.

"I thought *you* were the trespassers," Farthingstone said, fumbling through the words as he tried to collect himself. "Closing the shutters, bolting the door—why did you do that?"

"I was thinking that the rainstorm and this cottage afforded a splendid opportunity to make love to my wife, and the shutters and bolt would assure her of privacy. I see that I erred."

Farthingstone's face reddened. He appeared just as chagrined and confused as Dante had hoped.

"I would invite you gentlemen to stay and keep dry, but I am sure that you want to be on your way."

"Yes, well, perhaps we will be off—"

"He knows." The statement came from the other side of the chamber, where the other man stood near the stacked floorboards. "No reason to barricade himself and his lady in here otherwise. Not to dally for pleasure, I don't think."

Farthingstone pivoted in alarm. His gaze darted to his companion, then back to Dante. No longer chagrined, he examined the embracing couple suspiciously.

"Who might you be?" Dante asked.

"This is Mr. Smith, an acquaintance of mine," Farthingstone said.

"He knows," Smith repeated. "This one is not stupid, and he is playing you for a fool with his talk and manner. He saw these boards here, and the lamps. I think he knows what is happening here, and maybe why."

Farthingstone almost burst from agitation at these allusions to the cottage. "I would prefer if you did not speak of—"

"I think he knows about matters in London too. If so, I don't like that I've been seen with you." He had been holding the pick, but now he let it drop. Reaching under his coat, he withdrew a pistol.

Farthingstone almost jumped out of his skin. "Good God, man, what—"

Smith quieted him with a scowl. He paced over and looked out the door. "Getting dark, and no one will be about in this rain anyway. We best be taking them back with us, while we consider how to deal with this complication."

Dante eyed that pistol, trying to judge whether he could lunge for the man before it fired. As if expecting such a move, Smith had pointed it more at Fleur than him.

"We are no complication, so there is no need to deal with us. We do not even know what you are talking about, nor do we care," Dante said.

Smith chuckled and gestured to Farthingstone. "He may not know how to judge a man, but you could say my life depends on it. I want to think a bit before I let you out of my sight. You ride with him. The lady comes with me. That way I know you will behave."

Let us get you out of those wet clothes so you can wrap yourself in this and get warm." Dante stripped a blanket off the narrow bed and handed it to her.

The ride to Farthingstone's house in the pouring rain had drenched everyone to the bone. Fleur's ensemble hung in sodden folds and water still dripped off the brim of her bonnet.

The fire Dante had started in the tiny attic chamber helped some, but getting the wet garments off would help more.

Fleur looked at the blanket skeptically. "What if one of them comes up here?"

Dante bolted the door. "Now we are locked in, but they are also locked out."

"They could use an ax again."

"It was left at the cottage. Get dry, Fleur. I don't want you catching a chill."

She removed her bonnet and threw it in a corner. She turned her back so he could help unfasten her dress.

"Not quite like the last time," she said sadly as his fingers worked at the closure. "That man. He was the one who hurt me, isn't he? He did it for Gregory. The look on Gregory's face when he saw me . . ."

"We do not know that for certain." He tried his best to lie, because he did not want her frightened. He wanted to spare her as much of that as he could.

He should have seen Farthingstone's tenacity for what it was, the desperate stubbornness of a cornered man. He should have comprehended weeks ago what that spot of land meant to him.

If he was right, he and Fleur were in danger for their lives. Right now, down in a lower chamber, Smith was probably explaining that to Farthingstone. How long would it take to convince him how it had to be? How much longer to devise a plan that might escape detection? Dante calculated that they had the night for certain, and maybe a day at best.

The dress fell. Fleur stripped off the rest of her clothes and wrapped herself in the blanket. While Dante undressed, she laid her garments over furniture, then did the same with his as he discarded them.

Finally the chairs, washstand, chest, and wall hooks were covered with their clothing. Wrapped in their blankets, they sat in front of the hearth.

"This would be very cozy," Fleur said. "If not for—"

"We will not be disturbed tonight."

"You sound very confident."

"I am."

She seemed to accept that. The fear dimmed from her eyes. "You do not really think that Gregory intended to dig for buried treasure in that cottage, do you?"

"Who knows what he may be seeking."

"Dante, I said that you do not have to pretend for me. I know that there is only one thing to explain what he has done. His attempt to imprison me or put me away. His legal maneuvers to have my independence revoked. Finally, the attempt on my life. There is something in that cottage he does not want found, because it will endanger him if it is. He fears exposure of a crime."

"Yes, that is likely."

"It would have to be a serious one, for him to go this far. I think there is a body in that cottage."

"It could be something else."

"I think it is that, or something just as dangerous."

Dante was not sure that he wanted her knowing this much. He was very sure that he did not want her knowing the rest.

"Why there, Dante? He could have buried a body anywhere on his land."

"If something happened at or near that cottage, it would be easier to deal with it there than to carry a body somewhere else. The floorboards would hide the grave, and the place was vacant."

A tiny shiver shook through her. She pulled the blanket closer. "Are you very sure that we have the night?"

"I think we have far more than the night. Hill will wonder what has become of us once the rain stops. He will start a search when we do not return."

"The rain does not look to ever stop."

"We will wake up to find the sun, darling."

She clasped her knees with her arms and pressed her chin to them. She looked very young, huddled in that blanket and gazing at the fire. "I do not think Gregory could hurt us on his own. Even if he once did such a thing, I do not think he could now. It is one thing to pay someone to do it when you are not even in town, and another . . ."

Dante wanted to believe Farthingstone no longer had it in him. The problem was that once a man took that step, he probably found it easy to step again. Especially if he saw himself hanging if he did not.

And if he could not do it himself, Smith could.

"They are probably smart enough to know that their best chance is to run, Fleur. They will realize that too many people know we are here and will be looking for us."

It appeared to help. The arms circling her knees relaxed and fell away. She resettled herself and allowed the blanket to fall loosely, as if she no longer needed its comfort.

He got up and went to the small window. "We will close out the rain and share this fire and tomorrow I will deal with Gregory and Smith. You are not to worry, Fleur."

As he opened the window to pull the shutters, he noticed a dark shadow moving below, heading to the stables. From the size, he guessed it was Smith, going for a horse.

Going to dig, Dante guessed. He doubted Smith intended to unearth old bones either. More likely he intended to make two more graves.

He turned and watched Fleur, with her hair a tangle and nothing but a blanket wrapping her nakedness. The fire cast a gentle glow on her. She looked so beautiful. An emotion swelled in him that was so poignant, so exquisite, he could not move.

She was more precious to him than anything he had ever had or known. The very thought of life without her was so blank, so frightening, that his mind shrank from such contemplation. He had been nothing before she stumbled into his life. Taking care of her had become his first welcomed responsibility. She was his purpose for living.

He had not done his duty by her very well. He had not fathomed how dishonorable Farthingstone could be. She had, however. She had known in her heart all along that Farthingstone was constructing a lie for his own ends. They should have been looking for his reason all along, not merely working to thwart the man.

He pushed a heavy chest to the door, not caring that its scrapes on the floor would be heard below. He positioned it to block entry even if an ax cut through the door itself. It would not stop someone, but it would delay them.

He went over to Fleur and sat facing her, so he could see her face and her eyes and all the parts of her that would be beautiful forever.

The fear left her gaze as she looked at him, and the most generous warmth took its place.

He took her face in his hands, painfully alert to the softness of her skin.

He kissed her forehead and her lips, and each instant contained a lifetime of perfection.

Not caring where they were, indifferent to time and place, he pulled the blanket away and lifted her. He moved her legs until they circled his hips and she sat on his thighs. His own blanket fell away with their embrace.

She glanced down at her position. "The new game that you promised me?"

"A new closeness, so that I can see you in this lovely light. There have never been games with you. Not since the first time I touched you."

She looked down and gently caressed his arousal, making his teeth clench. "I do not know whether to be jealous or happy, Dante. The latter, I suppose. I do not like to think of your sharing things with other women that you do not with me, but I like that it is different with me in some way."

He watched his own fingers gloss over the curve of her breast. "It is very different, in all ways. Even the pleasure is different. Nor do I share anything at all with other women, Fleur. Not even games. Not since those days in the cottage at Laclere Park. Even when we both believed we could never have this, I have wanted no one else. I have loved you too much."

Her caress stopped. The way she looked at him stunned his soul.

"I do not think I could have been loved by a better man, Dante. Nor could I love one better than I love you."

He wrapped her in a caressing embrace, tasting her skin, feeling her heartbeat. It was very different this time. He could not control how it affected all of him—his senses, his pleasure, his body, and his heart. He felt her awareness of him just as he was filling himself with her.

He lifted her hips and joined. The most profound contentment slid through him, warm and serene. He wanted to hold her like this forever, connected and expectant, seeing her face as the tremors of pleasure enlivened her.

They touched slowly, watching each other, letting the passion build gradually so it would last. Her kisses, warm and velvety, slowly covered his neck and chest. Her soft fingers stroked his arms and back, his shoulders and torso, while his own circled her nipples.

He felt her arousal rise with his in perfect union. Abandon claimed her at the same moment that need maddened him. Their kisses turned fevered and their caresses grasping as they pulled each other toward a ferocious peak of carnality.

They jumped together, clinging to each other. He did not lose her, even in that physical climax. She was completely there, totally his, shuddering with him as the intensity split the world with its power. Her pulse and her love and her essence filled him, and replaced his own.

.   .   .

The morning did not bring the sun.

When Fleur awoke in the bundle of blankets in which she and Dante slept on the floor, the patter of rain could still be heard on the roof.

His arm circled her, and even in his sleep his strong fingers held her. She closed her mind to the rain and the chamber and drank in his embrace and warmth.

As long as they stayed here, just like this, he was safe. If he never woke, he would never do something noble and brave and dangerous. If they remained in this blissful cocoon, the world would go away.

He stirred. She stayed very still, hoping that he would sleep on. Then she could hold on to the beauty of lying in the arms of a man she totally loved.

Who loved her too. Hearing that had been wonderful. Seeing it in his eyes had been breathtaking. Feeling it in their lovemaking again, knowing it for what it was, giving it a name, had left her completely at its mercy.

It would echo forever, speaking to her heart. Even after they were both gone, she did not doubt that the love would be a part of her.

Dante shifted. He rose up on his arm and gently kissed her shoulder.

"It is still raining," she said. "Let us keep the shutters closed and pretend it is still night."

He laid her on her back and kissed her on the lips. It was a long, sweet, regretful kiss. "I must dress, and so should you. When this is over we will find a bed and stay in it for a week."

He rose and went to the window. He opened the shutters to reveal a sky still heavy with rain. Gray light streamed in.

So did the sound of a horse galloping away.

Dante leaned out the window. He stayed like that, his naked torso half out the small opening. As she dressed, Fleur could see him taking in the surroundings.

"No way down, and too far to jump," he said. He looked at the blankets thoughtfully. "We are too high up to let you climb down those. It would still be a dangerous drop."

"Whose horse was that?"

"An express post rider, I think."

"Gregory has received an express post?"

"Or he has sent one."

He pulled on his clothes and fished for his pocket watch. "It is ten o'clock. Later than I expected."

Later than he expected them to be left alone, was what he meant.

"Perhaps no one is here but us."

"I doubt that, darling. Someone is below."

"If we yelled, perhaps a servant would come and we could explain we are being held—"

"I saw no servants when we arrived, and have heard none in these attic chambers. Farthingstone must have sent them away when he knew Smith would be coming. He would not want it known he associates with the man."

She looked out the window. It faced the back of the house and looked toward the stables. If only there was a way for Dante to climb out—

A movement below in some bushes caught her attention. She squinted through the rain.

The bushes moved again. A bit of brown and a glimpse of straw showed, then disappeared.

"There is someone here besides Gregory and Mr. Smith, Dante. In the bushes by the path to the stables." She waited, and the thatch of straw rose and dipped again. "I think . . . I think it may be Luke."

Dante stuck his head besides hers. The straw crown rose and eyes appeared, sneaking a peek at the house. "Get me something to throw, so I can get his attention when he looks this way."

She glanced around the chamber while she tried to contain the excited hope that began shrieking through her. Her gaze lit on an old wooden candlestick wearing years of crusted wax.

"Will this do?" She handed it to him.

Dante angled his shoulder and arm and head out the window and hurled.

He stayed like that, waiting. Fleur saw his finger go to his lips and then a broad gesture.

Angling to peer out and down, she saw Luke slip from the bushes and come to stand beneath their window.

Dante made gestures that Luke understood better than Fleur did. His soaked straw hair moved along the back of the house surreptitiously as he peeked into windows.

He came back more quickly. "None in these chambers back here that I can see." He spoke just loudly enough to be barely heard. "What are you doing up there, sir? When you did not return I thought it odd, but Hill said you most likely got caught by the storm and found shelter, but I—"

"Whatever you thought, we are grateful you are here. Mrs. Duclairc is with me, and Farthingstone is up to no good. Go and get help, Luke. It has to be someone who can stand up to Farthingstone and who listens to what you say with interest."

"I don't know people in these parts, and they don't know me. Who will—"

"Find the justice of the peace or another man of position. Use my brother's name. Go now."

Luke did not wait for another command. He dashed through the rain to his bushes, then aimed away from the house.

Fleur threw her arms around Dante as soon as all of him was back in the chamber. "Thank God for Luke. If we had waited for Hill to sit out the storm . . ."

He held her, grateful that she had found reason not to be fearful. He wanted her to stay that way and not be too conscious of time passing. He led her over to the bed and pulled her down to sit beside him on it. "We have some time until Luke returns. Tell me all about your school and your railroad, from the day you first conceived the mad scheme."

She nestled against him and told her story. He asked for details to lengthen the tale, so that hours passed before it was done.

"It is an impressive plan that you conceived and followed, Fleur. I do not think any man could have done better."

"Do you really think so? Do you think it could have worked if I had not been betrayed by Mr. Siddel?"

"I think so, yes."

"It makes me very proud that you say that, Dante. Your good opinion is worth more than actually succeeding with the plan itself."

He thought that a very flattering thing for her to say, but also a little odd. Since he was hardly famous for financial judgment, his opinion on such things wasn't worth much at all. Her conviction touched him, like all of her trust had. It was one more example of the unwarranted optimism she had about him.

He pulled her closer and kissed her, to let her know he was grateful that she had been addled enough to think Dante Duclairc was worthy of her trust and love.

A sound interrupted their embrace. Boot steps sounded outside their chamber. They both looked toward the door.

A key turned in the lock.

chapter 26

The voice demanding entry between wheezes and coughs was Farthingstone's.

"I've some food here, Duclairc. Don't you want it?"

"If I can convince him to take me down below, do not object," Dante whispered to Fleur. "Once we leave, block the door with whatever you can move."

She did not like the plan, but she helped move the chest away from the door, then scurried to the farthest corner.

Dante threw the bolt. He opened the door on a very flushed and breathless Gregory Farthingstone.

Who carried a pistol.

His other hand, which had been holding his chest, pointed down to a tray of ham and bread on the floor. "Pick it up and bring it in. Only a bit of ham. None to do for me right now."

Dante lifted the tray and placed it on the bed. "Of course not. You could not host a man such as Smith with servants about. Nor would he want you to. Of course, I doubt his name is Smith, don't you?"

Farthingstone got redder. He continued catching his breath and pretended to examine the chamber to hide his physical discomfort.

"He is not coming back," Dante said. "If he has not returned by now, he will not."

Farthingstone scowled. "He will be here soon."

"He rightly concluded that his odds were better if he ran. He will disappear into the world from which he emerged." Dante stepped toward Farthingstone. "I am sure that there is a way out for you as well. Let us go below and think it through."

Farthingstone backed up and pointed the pistol more directly. "Stand back, sir. I am not without allies even if he has run."

"Since you are the one with a pistol, you are safe from me. Allow me to come down so my wife can have some privacy without my disturbance. She is weak from this ordeal as well as an accident she suffered last week, and these close quarters have become a burden to her delicate sensibilities."

Fleur managed to appear faint on cue.

"A few minutes, Farthingstone, at least," Dante whispered. "So she can have privacy for personal matters."

Farthingstone flushed a deep red, from embarrassment this time. He eyed Dante skeptically. "You stay a good distance from me or I will shoot. I am well versed in firearms, and I will not miss."

"Certainly. I am not a man famous for courage, nor do I welcome a demise that is any earlier than necessary."

Descending the stairs left Farthingstone as breathless as mounting them had. He sank into a chair in the drawing room and gestured Dante into another some twenty feet away.

"You appear most unwell, Farthingstone. Perhaps you should have a physician see to you."

"It will pass. It always does."

Dante let the time tick by. Despite his distress, Farthingstone kept a surprisingly steady hand on that pistol.

"A man who brings food to the condemned is not a man likely to play the executioner," Dante finally said. "If I am correct, and Smith has run, what are you going to do?"

"He will be here soon."

"He was willing to attack me and Fleur in return for money, but the outcome of this is not secure and your silence if you are caught not guaranteed."

"He never caused *you* harm. I have been cursing myself that I did not deal with matters that way, I assure you."

Dante was inclined to believe him. That meant someone else had set those men on him outside the Union Club. Or it had just been an attempt at theft after all.

"What do you intend to do with us?"

"You will learn soon enough."

"Are you expecting one of your allies? Is that why you told Smith to send you an express rider? I saw the rider from the window above. It was generous of Smith to accommodate you before he disappeared. A criminal's loyalty does not amount to much, but that was something."

Farthingstone's expression fell.

Dante leaned forward and rested his forearms on his knees. "If you sent for Siddel, I do not think he will come either. That is your ally, is it not? He is the man whom you think can do what you lack the stomach or heart to complete."

"I do not know what you refer to. I barely know Sid—"

"He owes you nothing in this and would not risk his neck for you. Unless what you have been paying him is so high that he cannot live without it."

Farthingstone's eyes widened. "You do not know—"

"I know that he may be a blackmailer. I think that he has been black-mailing you."

"What do you mean, you know he is a blackmailer? If anyone knew such a thing, he could not do it. Unless—" His eyes bulged in astonishment. "Has he bled you too?"

"Not me. Others whom I knew. It was a clever scheme, unearthed ten years ago. The people responsible were stopped, or so it was thought. Siddel knows what they did. I think he was one of them. As for you, I think that he kept you for himself and did not share with them. When he escaped de-tection, you kept paying."

Farthingstone's disquiet was visible, and it now had nothing to do with climbing stairs. His eyes misted. He appeared on the edge of his composure.

"It has been hell, sir. Hell, I tell you. To be at another's mercy . . ."

"What did he have on you? The secret buried in that cottage?"

Farthingstone glanced over sharply and suspiciously. "It was *not my fault.*"

"How did he learn of it?"

"His uncle. My *friend.* He told him while on his deathbed. That is the legacy he left for his nephew, and the only one of value. The means to bleed *me* of *my* legacy."

"How much did you pay?"

"All of it." He gestured furiously around the drawing room. "The rents from this estate. Every pound, for thirteen years now."

That was not good news. If Siddel was receiving that much while the se-cret remained buried, he had good cause to want it to remain undetected.

He might come after all. And he could do what Farthingstone needed done. Dante did not doubt that Siddel had it in him to kill in cold blood.

"It is a hell of a thing," Farthingstone said dolefully. "If I do not solve this dilemma, I will swing. If I do, I will go on bleeding."

And the man bleeding him was his only hope of not swinging.

The day still was gray, and the drawing room grayer. Farthingstone's body slumped and his fleshy face sagged too. His eyes glazed in contemplation of his situation.

Dante watched the barrel of the pistol, waiting for it to move so he could lunge.

The time passed. Farthingstone appeared quite dazed. Still the pistol did not waver.

"If he does not come, I have seen that he will go down with me," Far-thingstone said into the silence. "He will be very sorry that he left me on this precipice." He patted his chest again, but not because of any exertions this time.

Dante let Farthingstone drift back into his daze. With any luck, the man might fall asleep or drop his guard. He had probably been up the whole night, and the hours were taking their toll.

A half hour later, a sound intruded on their mournful silence, half-drowned by the relentless patter of rain. Distant and vague, it reminded Dante of nothing he had ever heard before.

It grew louder bit by bit, sounding off the hills and ground outside, finally defeating the rhythm of the rain. It began sounding like the noise of a festival.

Farthingstone finally noticed. It pulled him out of his thoughts. He cocked his head and his brow creased in perplexity.

Keeping one eye on Dante, he went to a window and opened it to the rain. The noise poured in, not far away at all now.

Farthingstone squinted. His body straightened in alarm. He slammed the window shut. "Gypsies! What in the name of Zeus—"

Dante went over to the window. The scene outside amazed him as much as it did Farthingstone.

"Not gypsies, Farthingstone. Gypsies do not arrive on a coach and four."

The coach rolled up the lane at a good speed. Luke held the reins. Beside him sat a substantial woman of middle years with a pinched face and straw hair, wrapped in a simple woolen shawl that also shielded her head. Her resemblance to the young man beside her was unmistakable.

Other women peered out the coach windows. Four more sat on its roof, clinging to the wood. Two more took the place of footmen.

They all carried pots that they pounded and beat with spoons and ladles, making a noise that rang through the countryside.

Luke's mother climbed down as soon as the coach stopped. She spoke to a young matron, who ran to the back of the house.

Farthingstone just stared out the window, speechless and confused.

The young woman came back and nodded. From his place where he still held the horses, Luke called for Dante.

Alarmed, Farthingstone backed away from the window and aimed the pistol right at Dante's chest. "Do not respond. They will go and—"

"They know I am still here, Farthingstone. That woman just called for Fleur at our chamber window and knows she is above."

Farthingstone's face flushed again. The red just kept coming. He looked frantically to the window.

A woman's voice called from the drive. "My son says you've Miss Monley in there. We don't leave until she comes out and them that knows what to do with the likes of you arrive." Pots clanged in cacophony to punctuate the announcement.

"Good God," Farthingstone mumbled. "It is not to be borne! To have such rabble trespassing—"

"I sent Luke for help. He must have gone to his collier village up north."

"Colliers! What have they to do with me?"

"Fleur's charity kept the children of those women from starving when their men withheld labor last year. I expect they would kill for her." Dante gazed out the window. "They certainly look prepared to if necessary."

Luke's mother called again. "All the farmers we passed saw us coming. No way to hide we were here. There's them back at the village that know we came, and why. Our men will learn of it once they leave the pits."

The other women began calling for Miss Monley too. The pots and pans sounded louder.

"Tell them to stop that hideous noise," Farthingstone groaned, moving farther back into the room.

"It sounds like the harps of angels to me."

"I will shoot them all. I will—"

"You will have to shoot me first, and by the time you reload they will have you on the ground."

"Good God. This is an outrage! To be besieged in my own home by a horde of mad women! I will—I will—!"

Dante surveyed the little troop. Luke's mother had placed herself front and center of a phalanx of colliers' wives. Proud and brave, she faced the house with her hands on her wide hips, full of the determined strength that hard living bred in such women. She did not look like someone a sane man would want to cross.

"Good God." The mumble came lower this time, and with a much different tone. A heavy thud punctuated the last word.

Dante turned. The pistol had fallen to the floor. Farthingstone's face had turned unnaturally pale. Holding his chest, he stared at the rug with unseeing eyes.

He looked up at Dante with an expression of horrible comprehension. His legs folded.

His body fell.

"Get them all warm. Find them food," Fleur instructed Hill as the women climbed off the coach and filed into the house. "Build up the fire in the drawing room and—"

"Don't need such a fine fire," Luke's mother said as she passed. "The kitchen will do for us."

"Make yourselves comfortable, wherever that is," Dante said. He stood beside Fleur at the door, welcoming their unusual party.

The ride from Gregory's house had been quite an event. Fleur imagined how odd it would have appeared to anyone who saw them, with women hanging off the coach and those pans clanging, now with excitement and heady victory.

Jubilation when Dante freed her from the attic chamber had crashed into shock when she saw Gregory's body. It still lay in that house, covered with a blanket, awaiting removal.

Luke sat at the reins as the women disembarked their ship. Fleur squeezed past them and went over to him. He was bent down and angled, peering back at the coach with a deep frown.

"You have my gratitude, Luke," she said.

"Please don't blame my mother and the others that the coach is badly scratched. I had a few scrapes with cottages in the village. The lanes are narrow and not fit for a coach like this, and my handling of the horses—"

"Luke, you may have saved our lives. I do not think that a few scratches on the coach signify much, do you?"

He blushed. "I didn't know where to go here. Then I figured if I took the mail road north, even in the rain I would get there in an hour or so. I knew there would be those who would believe me and know what to do."

"Your plan was unusual, but effective. You brought an army back."

"Was my mum's idea. She said it would be a sin to allow ill to befall you after you had helped them."

"She has my gratitude as well. All of these women do."

Dante came out to join them as the last cotton skirt entered the house. "Luke, tomorrow morning hitch two of the horses to Hill's wagon and he and I will go get Mr. Farthingstone."

Luke flicked the reins and headed the coach back to the stables. Fleur used the moment of privacy to embrace Dante.

"I almost fainted from worry up in that chamber. I kept listening for sounds, of Mr. Smith returning or Gregory hurting you or your doing something reckless. I could not move, I was listening and praying so hard. I kept hoping I would hear a coach coming, bringing help—"

His kiss quieted her outpouring. "One did come, and all is well now."

She laughed. "The county will be talking about it for weeks."

"We will give out a story to satisfy curiosity. There is no reason for the true one to be known. He is gone and nothing will be served by letting the truth be told."

The image of Gregory sprawled on the drawing-room floor flashed in front of her. She had only caught a glimpse before Dante spread the blanket, but there had been an expression of utter astonishment on Gregory's face.

She snuggled deeper against his body and within his circling embrace. She closed her eyes and savored everything about him, even the scent of his damp wool coat. She allowed his warmth to conquer every chill and fear and saturate her mind until all sad images left it.

"Did he explain it to you? Did he say who it was?" she asked.

"He said it was not his fault, that was all. You were correct, I think. He did not have it in him to kill. Whatever happened at that cottage, it was not at his initiative."

"Except that he had it in him to pay Mr. Smith to try and kill me."

"Yes. For that alone, I am glad he is dead." He lifted her chin and kissed her lips again. Slowly. Sweetly. "When I go back to that house in the morning, I may not return with the wagon. There is something I must tend to there first."

"What?"

"A small matter." He turned with her surrounded by his arm. "Now, let us find a chamber where we can be alone. I want to hold you in my arms and forget about Farthingstone until morning."

chapter 27

Loving a good woman provokes change in even the least angelic of men.

Dante was contemplating that astonishing truth the next day when he heard the horse outside Farthingstone's house. He closed the steward's account book, which he had been perusing in the library, and placed Farthingstone's pistol on top of it on the table beside the divan where he sat. Next to the pistol he laid the letter that he had found in Farthingstone's coat.

The silent house echoed with boot steps, first hurried, then very slow. Pauses indicated that the chambers were being checked.

The library door opened. A dark head stuck in.

"Farthingstone?"

"He is not here, Siddel."

The head snapped around. The door swung wide. Siddel's glance darted around to ensure they were alone.

"Where is he?"

"He expired. Fate was kind to him."

Siddel exhaled with great relief. "Kind to you as well, I am happy to see."

"You worried for my safety?"

Siddel took a chair and made a display of calming himself. "He sent me an express post of the most alarming nature, rambling about your threat to him. I feared he would do something very rash."

"I did not think you had enough acquaintance with each other to inspire such a letter."

"I advised him on occasion. I do not know why he would write to me, but having perceived his state of mind I could hardly—"

"You did not ride all this way to save me and my wife, Siddel. Quite the opposite."

Siddel straightened with indignation. "That is a damnable thing to say. Of course I—"

"You could not risk his going in the dock if that body in the cottage was discovered. He would speak of you, and of the money he has been paying you all these years for your silence. You would hang right after he did."

Siddel's face went very blank. He revealed no consternation at learning the story was out. His gaze slid from Dante to the account book and the pistol and the folded paper.

"He left an explanation," Dante said, pointing to the paper. "I think it was just written, probably yesterday morning. I suspect that if you had not come, he would have taken his own life and seen that you followed him to hell."

Siddel's gaze locked on the paper. "There is no proof."

"The confession of a dying man is considered very strong evidence. He also admitted most of it to me. Not the part about your encouraging him to kill my wife, of course. That is only in the letter."

Siddel laughed. "Your swearing evidence is the least of my concerns."

"For all my sins, I am not known as a liar. The court will believe me, since I gain nothing either way."

Siddel thought that over, then lowered his lids. "I assume that if you do gain something, it will make a difference."

Dante did not reply.

"What do you want?"

"I want to know what happened ten years ago."

Siddel settled deeper into his chair, the image of a man back in control of matters. "Actually, it was thirteen. My uncle was dying. I was his heir, and I was eager to see his illness conclude. Imagine my annoyance when he called me to his deathbed and told me there was almost nothing left. The man had inherited a handsome fortune but had squandered it."

"That must have been disappointing."

"Hellish. However, he made a deathbed confession to me. He told me a story of an event from years ago. From when he and Farthingstone were partners in sin."

"He told you about the cottage. Who is buried there?"

"Since you know that someone is—my uncle often visited Farthingstone when they were much younger. There would be scandalous debauches in this house. In addition, they formed a casual liaison with a woman in the area who would enter their games. She lived in that cottage, where she cared for the simpleton sister of the woman who owned the neighboring estate.

"They would go over to enjoy the favors of this woman late at night when the idiot was asleep. Only one day they got very drunk earlier than normal and they decided to pay a visit in the evening. The woman put her charge upstairs, and things were well under way when this half-wit comes down, looking for her doll."

"Hardly worth killing for. No one would have comprehended if she told, assuming she even understood what she saw."

"Oh, it wasn't that. My uncle was very drunk. The simpleton struck him as rather pretty. He had his way with her."

Dante found Siddel's telling of this story sickening. The man was completely dispassionate as he described the sordid crime.

"How did she die?"

Siddel shrugged. "She was confused and docile with Uncle, but when he was done and Farthingstone was about to take his turn, she went mad. Screaming, fighting. My uncle sought to silence her. He succeeded rather too well."

That was what Fleur had seen through that window when she ran to play with her friend that evening. The blood had not been that of childbirth, but a virgin's blood on a woman's thighs, and maybe other blood too. Her aunt Peg had then disappeared.

Shock had confused the episodes in her mind quickly and obscured the meaning of it all. If she had spoken of it immediately, things may have been different. But her child's guilt would not allow that, and the shock had done its work to protect her.

"Years later bones were found and everyone accepted that they were that woman's remains. No doubt Farthingstone had encouraged that assumption," Dante said.

"He was relieved to. And that is what happened thirteen years ago," Siddel said. "I inherited a legacy."

"Your means to blackmail, you mean."

"It was in the caretaker's and Farthingstone's interest to keep silent, of course. The crime was theirs too. Farthingstone knew that. When I told him what my uncle had revealed, he actually offered the money."

"When it appeared that Fleur was going to have that cottage torn down and foundations dug for a school, it was in your interest to make sure it did not happen. The payments from Farthingstone would stop if he was exposed. As would those from Cavanaugh, if that railroad partnership ever succeeded."

Siddel's face fell. "Cavanaugh? I have no idea what—"

"I know all about my wife's Grand Project. Cavanaugh's patrons would not want it to be successful," Dante said. "Your situation is not good, Siddel. I hope that you have been laying aside some money, because both of your incomes have abruptly ceased. Once this letter is given to the magistrate, your position becomes dire."

Siddel smiled. It gave his face an unpleasant countenance, because the smile itself was half a sneer. "I do not think so. As I was riding here, it occurred to me that you will probably want to continue Farthingstone's pay-ments. You will definitely not want that letter to land me in the dock."

"There is nothing you have that I would pay for."

"I think there is. Your dead brother's good name, for example. Your own honor, for another."

Dante studied the man's slyly contented expression. Blotches of white heat began breaking in him. He fought to control it.

For Fleur's sake, he had decided not to broach this part of it, much as he wanted to. His responsibility for her outweighed any to the dead.

"You do not appear surprised," Siddel said, with admiration.

"No."

"You are smarter than I thought."

"You should get on your horse and run. I hear that Russia is pleasant in the summer, even if the winters are hell."

"Russia? My, you are clever. You have seen it all. It was my indiscreet slip about the duel that alerted you, wasn't it? I thought that I saw something in your eyes besides insult."

"Yes."

"I do not favor living abroad. Nor, I suspect, is Nancy half as lovely as she was when you and I and so many others queued up for her. I do not think she will be very useful at all in getting young men to do things that unearth their family secrets."

This reference to the woman who waited in Russia made the heat spread. Siddel's taunt about young men had been direct and vicious.

The fury wanted to consume him. The icy cold that would freeze out good sense already loomed on its edges.

"If I choose not to run, what can you do? Give Farthingstone's letter in evidence against me? See me on trial? Who knows what I will confess to then. Or perhaps you will tell Laclere about my other doings and get him to call me out." Siddel began laughing. "I can see it. Laclere and I meeting, and the world assuming that he did so to protect *your* honor. I will let it be known how your wife has secretly met with me."

The heat burned away all rationality, furiously demanding that he deal with this man once and for all.

"Or maybe I will give out the story of that attack on you and say Laclere concluded I was responsible."

"If you know about it, you were."

"Your questions to Cavanaugh were making him concerned. You were be-coming a nuisance. However, the world will only know that your brother is fighting a duel because you are too much a coward to do so." He grinned. "Nothing new there."

Cold blasted over the fire, killing it and its fury, replacing it with a dangerous calm.

He would enjoy killing this man. He had been preparing to do so for a decade.

Siddel's expectant expression was one of a man who assumed he would survive. "Farthingstone's letter must be mine if I win," he said.

Dante tucked the letter inside his coat. He picked up the pistol. "Of course. Let us find you a weapon."

Siddel reached under his coat. "As it happens, I have one right here."

"Then let us go outside."

Side by side, pistols in hand, they walked out to the reception hall. Ice crystallized inside Dante as they moved. The satisfaction he would soon know made him euphoric. Not only Siddel would die. Memories and resentments would too. An old guilt would be expiated.

Siddel opened the door.

The sun was streaking through the clouds and the rain had turned the earth redolent with lovely smells. As if carried by the fresh breeze, an image came to Dante, breaking through the ice with its warmth.

It was a picture of Fleur proposing at the sponging house, trusting against all evidence that he would protect her and honor his word to her. It was Fleur in his arms, opening with a love that made life worth living, that gave it purpose. It was Fleur carrying their child, needing his strength as her worst fears loomed.

Siddel had paused, and Dante realized he had as well.

"We have visitors," Siddel said.

That pulled Dante back from his thoughts. He discovered that both fire and ice had left him. So had the justice of this duel. If he did this, it would be for all the wrong reasons.

He looked down the lane. Two riders, a quarter mile away, approached at a good pace.

"Witnesses would be useful," Siddel said. "Whoever they are, they will do."

Dante stepped outside the house. He gestured to Siddel's horse. "Take it and run. I will see that you are not followed."

"I am not riding anywhere."

"Then you will hang. I will not play your executioner, much as I want to."

"It will all come out. Do not think it won't."

"Then let it come out. I am not going to kill you. It will change nothing if I do."

"You are a coward."

"If we meet you are a dead man. Now, go."

Siddel's swagger left him. He looked frantically at the riders, then at his horse. "I must demand that letter first."

Dante watched the riders get nearer. "Leave while you can or—"

The crack silenced him. An impact on his left shoulder made him stagger. Fiery pain sliced through his chest.

Astonished, he swerved to see Siddel toss aside his smoking pistol and stride toward him with murder in his eyes. Siddel's gaze was fixed on Dante's own pistol.

Dante raised his gun and fired.

Dante stared at Siddel's body. His own legs held him up, but he had no sense of why, since he could barely feel them there. On the edge of his consciousness he vaguely heard horses approaching at a hard gallop.

"Damnation," a familiar voice roared.

A horse stopped nearby and suddenly Vergil was beside him, taking his weight in his arms.

"Morning, Verg."

"Hell. Don't talk." Vergil lowered him to sit on the ground. "When Burchard's man reported Siddel had left London on the northern road, St. John and I decided to follow, but I never thought Siddel had murder on his mind."

Dante did not much care what had brought Vergil here. He did not care about anything at all, actually. The pain was getting worse, and fog had entered his head.

St. John joined them, stepping over Siddel's body to kneel down and examine the wound. "It was so close the ball went through, but we need to stanch the bleeding." He began pulling Dante's coat off. "I asked you to watch your back, Duclairc."

Before St. John succeeded in stripping off the coat, Dante pulled out Farthingstone's letter and handed it to his brother.

The fog closed in and turned black.

chapter 28

D ante appears in good health," Diane St. John said. "Your care of him made for a quick recovery."

"I do not think my care made a great difference, but I enjoyed the duty," Fleur said.

She had relished every minute of caring for him. Sitting with him, changing his bandages, sharing his relief when it became clear that the wound would not leave his shoulder or arm infirm—a mellow intimacy had developed between them the last two weeks. It astonished her how the love just kept getting richer. Deeper.

She had resented the frequent intrusions of his friends and family, because they robbed her of a few moments of bliss. Laclere in particular had been a trial because he visited for at least an hour every day, and she was banished from the sick room while the brothers talked.

She suspected that today's unexpected onslaught of visitors indicated that the idyll of privacy was over for good.

Diane sat with Fleur in the drawing room, enjoying the sweet breezes of the early June afternoon. Diane had called with her husband, who now conversed with Dante in the library.

Not only the St. Johns had visited today. Three other women completed their circle in the drawing room. Charlotte had arrived first, then Bianca and Laclere, and finally the Duchess of Everdon and her husband. The men had gone off together, and other men, whom Fleur did not know, had been brought directly to the library upon arrival.

Fleur was trying not to worry about the business being conducted in that other chamber.

"I expect that they are settling matters," she said to her friends. "Clarifying what happened up north, and explaining how Dante was shot."

"Why do you think that?" Bianca asked.

"Mr. Hampton wore his solicitor's face, for one thing. Then that last man who came appeared very official and sober. Dante told me that he would have to explain how it was and even stand trial. The deaths of two men cannot be ignored."

"You should not worry," Charlotte said. "There were witnesses, and the wound in my brother's shoulder is evidence that he defended himself. The trial will only be a formality."

"It is taking a long time for all of them to settle that. They have been in there an hour."

"I am certain that whatever is transpiring in that library is only good news for you," the duchess said.

Williams appeared at the door of the drawing room. He came over and bent low to Fleur's ear. "Madame, your presence is requested in the library."

Fleur swallowed hard. She did not doubt that Dante would be completely exonerated. The question was whether they could manage that without telling the whole story of Gregory and that cottage and Mr. Siddel's blackmail and the Grand Project and—

She rose. To her surprise, the duchess and Bianca did as well.

"We will accompany you," the duchess said. "I once faced a whole phalanx of men in a library, and it is not something a woman should have to endure without a few troops of her own by her side."

"I hardly go to meet the enemy," Fleur said as they walked to the library. All the same, she was grateful for the troops.

"All of those frock coats can be intimidating if there are no dresses present. When men are together alone, they have a tendency to start acting as if women are children, even if as individuals they know better. Don't you agree, Bianca?"

"It is an ongoing battle that we fight, Sophia. Fortunately, it can be a pleasurable one."

The two ladies giggled. Fleur let herself enjoy a few precious memories of the various engagements and pleasures her own marriage had produced.

The library doors swung and they entered. Adrian Burchard did not appear surprised to see his wife, but Laclere raised an eyebrow at Bianca.

Which she blithely ignored.

The duchess had been right. Facing a library full of frock coats was daunting. They all turned their attention on her. All except Dante. He sat in a chair off to one side, reading some document.

Mr. Hampton addressed her. "Madame, we need you to read these paperss and give your signature if you agree they are in order."

She glanced to Dante. He had taken care of all of it. She would not have to answer questions and dissemble on the details. She had only to sign a statement accepting the events as laid out on paper.

Relieved, she walked to the desk. "Of course."

She dipped a pen and began to sign.

"I advise you to read it very carefully, to make sure you accept its contents," Mr. Hampton interrupted.

Swallowing a little sigh, she put the pen down. She was very sure that Dante had produced a story that she would find acceptable. All the same, she scanned the top sheet of paper.

The first paragraph stunned her.

It was not a statement regarding those events in Durham.

It was a partnership agreement regarding a proposed railroad in Durham.

Ten of the men in the library, including Laclere, Burchard, and St. John, were named as primary partners. So was she, with most of her shares to create a trust to endow her school. Additional shares would be sold to others later.

She looked at Dante, sitting off to the side, flipping through the pages of his copy.

He had done this. He had made it happen.

"Burchard and I will present the bill to Parliament that gains approval for it to go forward," Laclere said.

She sat down in a chair and read the whole wonderful text. It laid out the risks as well as the benefits. When she got to that part, where the partners pledged their fortunes to debts incurred, she looked up at Bianca and the duchess.

It was their fortunes as well that their husbands pledged. They had accompanied her in here to announce that they approved.

"Mr. Tenet will be managing partner as the project goes forward," Mr. Hampton explained, gesturing to an official, sober-looking man. "He has experience in such affairs."

Mr. Tenet bowed. "I am honored to meet you, madame. May I say that the preparations that you put in place regarding the land and the surveying will enhance our success and our speed of construction."

"Yes, well done," St. John said.

They knew. Dante had told them it had been her idea. She accepted the nods and smiles of approval. Only the ones of the Duchess of Everdon and the Viscountess Laclere lacked a tinge of amazement.

"Speaking of land, these deeds will also have to be signed by both you and Mr. Duclairc," Mr. Hampton said, tapping another stack of papers. "Please now state before these witnesses that your husband in no way coerces you to sell these properties deeded in your name."

She gladly stated it. With a shaking hand, she signed everything.

Dante remained on the periphery, his expression very bland, allowing her to complete the ritual on her own.

When the last signature was completed, he rose and came over to sign as well.

She stood beside him, so excited that she could barely contain herself. She wanted to be rid of all these people so that she could embrace him the way she desperately wanted to do.

The duchess came to her rescue. "Gentlemen, let us join the ladies in the drawing room. Mr. Duclairc instructed that some appropriate refreshments be brought up for a little celebration."

The frock coats filed out, congratulating one another. At the door Laclere looked back. He gave her a smile full of the familiarity of their years of friendship.

The look he then gave Dante was of a different sort. Not one of approval, but of admiration.

She threw her arms around Dante as soon as the door closed on them. "Thank you." She did not know whether to laugh or cry, so she just held him tightly and pressed herself against his strong chest and let the heady joy overwhelm her.

He encompassed her with his arms. "I said you would have your school, Fleur. It wouldn't do for it to lack the endowment you had planned."

"They believe in the Grand Project, don't they? Laclere and the others did not only do it to be kind, did they? I would not want—"

"None of the men in this chamber was ruled by sentiment. I explained your plan to my brother and showed him your map. He was sufficiently impressed that he brought it to St. John, who made some inquiries to confirm your judgments. After that, finding the others was easy. They count themselves fortunate to be a part of it."

"So planning this is what was occupying you while you lay abed."

"This, and counting the days until I could make love to you again."

She looked up into his eyes. They contained the most exciting warmth. She could gaze in them forever and be a contented woman. There had always been honesty and truth in those lucid depths, ever since those first days in the cottage. Her heart had understood from the first that this was a man whom it would be an honor to love.

"I am so grateful that you accepted my proposal in the sponging house, Dante. I lied to myself and said it was a fair trade, my money for your protection. I really knew it was not."

"It sounded very fair to me."

She shook her head. "I do not think that I really did it to escape Gregory either. I did not want to lose you. I already loved you, only I could not call it that, not even in my heart, because I could not have that kind of love."

"It is just as well you did not call it love. Admitting you married me for that would have landed you in Bedlam for certain."

"If this is madness, let me never be sane." She slid her hand behind his neck and pressed him down so she could kiss him. "I am so glad that we are completely married and I can completely love you."

They shared a long kiss, full of the excitement of the day's surprise and the anticipation of the private pleasures waiting when their guests left. Dante's aura saturated her, but there was no danger in it any longer, because love flooded with it.

Her eyes dampened with the best kind of tears. She wished there were no guests in the drawing room and they could stay like this for hours, holding each other, enjoying the triumph of the day and their love, not separate in any way at all.

Dante took her face in his two hands. "I want you to know something. I was always glad that we married, Fleur. If you had never been able to give yourself to me, I would have still cherished you and the love I have for you. I would have never regretted becoming your husband."

Cherished. Yes, that was the word for how she loved him. That was the word for the sweet unity she experienced in his affection and friendship and passion.

He gazed down with those mesmerizing, wonderful eyes. No one else in the world existed but the two of them.

Holding her face gently in his two palms, be kissed her twice, once on the forehead and then on the lips.